About the Author

Zachary Maxwell has degrees in nothing in particular but did achieve his PhD in the Lethargic Sciences from the renowned and accredited University of Futility. He happily resides in the attic of his mother's dilapidated home and frequently contemplates solutions to the dense insanity surrounding this Universe.

WampyJaw

Zachary Maxwell

WampyJaw

Olympia Publishers
London

www.olympiapublishers.com
OLYMPIA PAPERBACK EDITION

A CIP catalogue record for this title is
available from the British Library.

ISBN: 978-1-78830-929-5

First Published in 2021

Olympia Publishers
Tallis House
2 Tallis Street
London
EC4Y 0AB

Printed in Great Britain

Dedication

For all the nobodies, going nowhere for no reason.

WampyJaw
Stories compiled by Zackary Maxwell
Translated by Zackary Maxwell

WampyJaw Segments
The Spastic Parade
Salutations to Turmoil
The Moribund Lethargy of Dante's First Circle

The Spastic Parade
Stories Compiled by Zackary Maxwell
Translated by Zackary Maxwell

The Spastic Parade Segments
Opeia
By Topo Kevok (Armenian)
Eni
By Navdar Goran (Kurdish)
Zade
By Shato Perwer (Kurdish)

Opeia
By Topo Kevok
Translated from Armenian by Zackary Maxwell

The Pony Express

"It is amazing in life what one cares about. Material trinkets. A carriage. A house. A loved one. And then when the bowel relaxes, it is tantamount how the toilet becomes the focus overall."
— The Ogre.

It was 1723 between Folkestone and Dover that it began. The cliffs high. Chaucer knew this ground well. He let his bowels go through the many sheds on the overhang three hundred and fifty feet to the crashing shores below. The channel fish loved the offering.

Sisters, Hazel and Zazel Zonk, were there. They had one job. One simple job. They were to gather the fecal matter from the cliff face and put it into huge canvas sacks. The Zonks then sold it later to tanners. It was, relatively, profitable. It was all they had.

The sheds were just tiny wooden outhouses that stood out over the edge of the cliff. The outhouse hole for defecation went straight down the cliff into the ocean below. Turbulent winds through the channel slung the matter onto the pearly white cliff face. This was riches that needed a harvest and the Zonks were there for the job.

A small oak plank served as a seat and hemp rope through both sides provided the swing that was necessary to dangle over the edge below. The rope was attached to a basic pulley system. Two sisters, two swings, two pullies, two large canvas bags and a great deal of courage made this family industry possible. The mortality for cliff fecal gathering was extremely high and the money was not all that good but the Zonk sisters loved the employment for the mere fact that no one, and that would be absolutely no one, wanted this task.

The Ogre was not really an Ogre. Some say he was twelve feet high and weighed over five hundred pounds. But the Zonks knew him to be exactly five foot six inches tall and approximately two hundred and eighty pounds. Short, robust and ugly. The latter both in appearance and temper. He had leprosy. The Ogre owned this particular cliff face and delicate people that needed relief from lower intestinal pressure and privacy from the busy near-by roadway would pay dearly for this outlet. The Ogre would take twenty-five percent of the Zonks' monthly earnings and the Zonks were free to do as they pleased.

The innkeepers in both Folkestone and Dover for the road in-between were paid quite well by the Ogre to induce bovine laxatives in their travel food for patrons exiting their cities. It was Capitalism at its best.

The Ogre lived an opulent lifestyle for an Ogre in a mud, straw and twig-built mound of earth complete with door and window. A small stove provided the heat for both home and cooking. This hovel was nestled neatly into the dense forest on the other side of the roadway cliff. If any patron to the outhouse God, attempted to poo the loo and shoo without payment, the stout robust leper would quickly pounce on the perpetrators and beat the funds, literally, out of them.

The Sisters Zonk also lived in the forest in a mound of earth by the same design as the Ogre. They did not have to concern themselves with any rogue passers-by and nightly slept soundly on a large mound of straw. They ate frequently of their own mushroom harvest and daily had two strong cups of Chinese green tea. The latter bought at great cost from a London import store nearly one hundred miles away.

The sisters' season was between late spring and late fall—depending on the weather. They worked in all climates but wore only the same outfit for each seasonal occasion. Tight fitting ankle bound leather shoes, a leather dress and a flop hat made from, what else, leather. Excrement and urine falling from above was not pleasant but the Zonk sisters stated, "Ah, the smell of money!" And it was.

They became very brazen in their abilities to acquire mass amounts of excreted matter. Unbeknownst to them, they were the best. Ever. Their swings would gander and waffle in a poetic phrase that through a beat of mental prose would glide and skid over the cliff face to fortune. Two sisters. Two pendulums of self-employment skipping and slithering through the muck to produce mounds of canvas bags of wealth. They would optimize their strides through the cliff face to maximize their potential gatherings. Once, when Lord Cuthburt, the obese and flatulent girth of a human, visited it took the twain thirty-six ballet-like passes to gather his foaming retched filth. All were satisfied. The Lord's tip to the leper was his own leprosy-infested top of the glans of his penis. The Ogre made well use of this item to barter with the Lord's family for more than appropriate funds. All was well.

The Ogre was dying. He knew his time was limited. But this Ogre was not going to die a mediocre Ogre. Before his certain demise, he was going to own and eat a pineapple.

Pineapples in Britain, and even Europe, in the 1800s were extremely rare and very expensive. Even kings and nobles, who could afford the golden fruit, would set it out on a banquet table only to be viewed as a token of wealth. Most were not eaten but left to rot in all their glorious bounty.

Lo and behold, in that year, a pineapple was to be auctioned at the Chelsea Physic Garden in London and the Ogre was going to get it.

The Ogre had no family or friends and his only acquaintances, were the two sisters Zonk. He had a plan and he wanted to pitch his idea to Hazel and Zazel. They met under the light of a candle in the mound of earth belonging to the leper. The Zonks didn't mind the leper since they knew him to be a good person who just wore an armor of calluses derived from years of verbal, physical and mental abuse. His plan was stated plainly, his voice cadence firm and methodical, and the Sisters Zonk realized the leper had thought about this decision with some care and planning. The Ogre was dying but he was going to die with pineapple on his lips. For this fate to occur, he would give his land and all the cliff privy business to the sisters, in exchange for their monthly tanning earnings until the Chelsea auction. The Zonks were amazed. No Zonk in history ever had the means to be a landowner even one painted partially in human excrement. They sealed the deal with cups of tea. Chinese tea. But the Ogre chose a strong cup of Earl Grey with a spot of cream. The Zonk sisters told the Ogre that adding a dairy product to the British swill would ruin the antioxidant properties of the liquid. The leper thought the sisters mad and he told them so. Hazel and Zazel carefully looked at each other and shook their heads in disappointment. The deal was made but there was one small caveat. The Ogre had to die by their hands.

Hazel and Zazel were used to death. It was the eighteenth century and death came in many forms. Their father was an itinerant farmer from the south of England and the girls both knew how to kill rabbits, pigs, goats and most anything raised on this land. But they never killed a human, even one with such a terminal need as the Ogre. He stated he could not take his own life and that to die of leprosy, even though painless, was usually caused by an accident generally just because lepers could feel no pain. It was too horrible for him to imagine. Hazel and Zazel knew that in the future a group called Republicans would also feel no pain (nor empathy or sympathy), not from leprosy, but from being extreme right-wing conservatives. The sisters looked each other in the eye and stated that this would be done. The Ogre stated he wanted first to consume his pineapple and he did not want to see his end coming. The Zonks agreed. The Ogre, for the first time in his life, cried. The tears were happy tears.

Obviously, a leper could not show up at an auction and win. The small Chelsea Garden held a huge crowd but only a rare few had money to bid. Then came the Sisters Zonk clad in their leather finery covered in human excrement; the crowd parted—their stench was not bearable. King George called this auction for funds for the city orphanage but he was not present. This was really a 'gift' to the people of England to own a piece of fruit that only Gods could obtain. But this came at a price. The largest bid came from one Lord Cuthburt; he too was dying of leprosy and wanted to taste the exotic noble fruit before his last painless breath. The Zonk sisters bested his bid by a factor of two. The crowd roared with applause to know that fecal gatherers bested a Lord for the golden sweet flesh. There was justice after all.

The Ogre sat alone in his mud hut with three candles lit. One for himself and the others for the Zonks. Alone in the silence he wondered at the stars through the window. They were very bright. It was a moonless sky. His gaze returned to the table. It didn't look like much, this prickly fruit. In the low light it could have been confused as a breed of cactus. But once cut deep, the juice poured forth upon the table and its taste was sweet and tart like the urine of Heaven. Zeus, thought the Ogre, must piss this nectar daily. The last small chuck of gold flesh the leper laid down on the floor next to his constant rodent companion, a field mouse. The mouse came out of his den, sniffed the morsel and nodded its head. The Ogre was confused but suddenly realized that the mouse, not unlike

Royalty, recognized God's harvest and preferred to gaze upon the bounty as wealth and leave the flesh to rot instead, right outside his hole. And so he did.

The next morning, the leper's stomach grumbled. A deep sound like wet boulders falling down a ledge onto granite slabs covered with moist moss. The strong acid from the rare exotic pulp irritated the colon lining of the Ogre. An explosive event was quickly to occur.

Running out to the roadway onto the cliff, he threw himself into the nearest privy. His posterior blinding white alongside the brilliance of the mud-laced cliff face, protruded from the wooden orifice. The sisters swinging like pixies daintily looked up and saw their opportunity. After his first expulsion of sheer light brown liquid, the sisters swung up and quickly and deftly inserted into his exit orifice a small iron tube containing gunpowder and a lit fuse. The Ogre's eyes bulged wide with this intrusion and then there was a flash and a huge blast and a mournful groan.

Just before this ignition, a carriage stopped on the roadway and out pranced a dandy titled Prince Edward the Gross. King George being from Hanover called the gluttonous blob of flesh 'gross' since in German that meant big. And he was. His girth was notorious. He was also gross. And while this large mass skipped quickly to a cliff-hanging outhouse he was busy dislodging a firmly planted large nasal moist crumpet from his right nostril when the flash occurred.

The impact was swift and the skull of the Ogre disemboweled the Prince and all his remaining intestinal contents. Skilled physicians could never remove the nasal offering and left it as it was during the funeral procession. Hence, gross, in English, had a new meaning.

The Royal investigation determined that the explosion was caused by a spark during the massive quick expulsion of flatus from the Ogre. The incident was therefore an act of God. Hazel and Zazel embraced themselves that night on their new land and business expansion.

Zade Zonk woke up. Roger, her fifth dimensional muse, vaporized in the closet of her bedroom. The taste of pineapple was in her mouth.

Opeia, Zade's daughter, was busy burning a breakfast consisting of local Nevada insects. She surmised correctly that anything basted in olive oil, finely chopped garlic, butter and onions would taste fantastic. And she was correct. High in protein, abundant and quite crunchy.

What is with the mornings? Starting new. A day and a night ending. The refuse of shit washed away in memories of dreams. And then the sun's nose to peak around the horizon and illuminate the surroundings in a pink-purple hue. The smell was wonderful. Sage and pine sap wafted.

The Pony Express was just that. It was, historically, a stop for the mail route from east to west and back again—mail brought on the back of a pony. It now was a stucco, straw and plaster gas station on Highway 50 just east from Ruth, Nevada. Painted white, the red letters of Pony Express weathered the eye to the passers-by. Eighty-two to eighty-five octanes were the flavors in the front. Diesel in the back. Zade and Opeia shared a small room and Ms. Legrand inhabited the other. The bathroom was for all patrons. Just one. And one is all they needed. Emergency excretions were handled in the tumbleweeds out back.

Ms. Legrand, Eni, was a child on a farm from Pau, France. She had a vision. A God's vision, a Roger vision, that ate at her bone marrow for her to find a coop for her pigeon to rest. That resting place was with the family Zonk.

Eni arrived at the Zonk family Truck Stop in Pagosa Springs, Colorado, two years earlier. She was beautiful, bright and inquisitive about all things. With just a pair of pants, boots and a sweater, the sixteen-year-old entered The Truck Stop as though she had been there all her life. Gretchen had been sending letters to her to join the Zonk family and assist in their mission to save humans from themselves. Finally, at last, she arrived.

Ms. Legrand just graduated from Université Bordeaux in biochemistry. She spoke five languages fluently. But it took her exactly two years to speak Zonk. And when she mastered that language, Eni moved with Zade and Opeia Zonk to a dilapidated gas station just west of Ely, Nevada. The gas station was called The Pony Express.

The Gunthers

"Don't you see how pure it is. The whiteness. Like freshly fallen snow.
It is in our blood. Our pure blood." — Garth Gunther

The Gunthers had a ranch just south of Ruth, Nevada. It was a large ranch with two major flaws. One, it wasn't a ranch and, two, it was a haven for white supremacists. The Gunthers called it The Compound and the main house was patterned on the German castle of Wachenburg. The castle in the center was surrounded by several smaller cottages dotting the landscape, and seen from a great height they formed a swastika in the semi-arid sage covered plain.

Garth Gunther owned the ranch but his reach extended well into local politics, school boards and industries. His money flowed to specific parts of the land and a community was formed, bound by a pact of whiteness. No individual came into this part of the country and stayed unless they were white and Christian. The Zonks were here to amend their intentions.

A call came into The Compound at two a.m. It was disturbing and the staff and servants hustled to determine just what was to be done. Communication was primary in this family. Never have the leader blindsided by an event through local media if it could be contained with local entities. A lesbian couple with a child moved into the local gas station called The Pony Express.

Zade and Eni were not a couple. They were both scientists and Zade's child, Opeia, was not genetically aware of her sexuality at this time. But the region near Ely did not see it that way. They were queer interlopers to breed the seed of discontent and plant a fruitage of loathsome munchers of the rug. They had to be eliminated.

Cornelius and Gretchen Zonk, Zade's grandfather and mother respectively, had planned this event years prior. The Gunthers' expanse was devouring the latest political climate of nationalism. American races were to suffer. Some radical necessary action had to take place. It was now and it was Zonk.

The Pearl Before Toad

By Opeia Zonk

"You are what you are and you ain't no more." — Opeia.

On a large patch of bog that, coincidentally, Scientist Gretchen Zonk would much later have filled in to limit its methane output, a toad sat saliently on a festering lily pad while decaying organic matter burped gas up to the dark liquid surface.

Bog stench was generally terrible to begin with, but this particular bog was extremely anaerobic and this led the molecules to grasp any other element but oxygen and in this case that was sulfur. The Kingdom called this area on the Royal grounds The Pit of Republican Successes.

Princess Anastassia, daughter of the King, visited this bog every morning. She was a clever princess and realized that anything as malodorous as was this swamp had to contain something really good. Her mother, a de Sade relative, painfully bent the Princess' ear and stated, "You can't heal if you haven't suffered. There is no light without dark. How could you know delight if you haven't been wretched? What good is bliss if you haven't impaled your heart with sorrow?" So, Anastassia correctly concluded that something in this swamp was to bring her ultimate love. And that something was a toad.

This toad was unique to this bog. It was the only life in this filthy muck except for very large flies. This toad was Bufo alvarius or namely, the Colorado River toad. The toad was lonely and wanted companionship and intellectual conversations. He desperately wanted to discuss Milankovitch cycles on this planet and how they systematically align to create huge global climate fluctuations. But aside from numerous delicious flies and one really ugly small human female, there was no other being to communicate with. The toad didn't speak human and the small human didn't speak toad but the toad was fairly sure that if he did speak human, this pathetic looking pale blob with rose tinted chubby cheeks that were laced with a patchouli vomit of an aura, could not fathom the concept of earth's rotation, much less why her own anal emissions were tainted with the same molecules that drew her to conclude her love was in this bog. Her love could easily, based on this same deduction, be down the side of the cliff between Folkestone and Dover! And it was.

The Princess visited the toad early every morning. Before the toad she placed a soft white pearl. She assumed if the toad ate the pearl then indeed, he had appreciation for riches and he was then her true love in disguise. The toad stared at the pearl and understood that it was not a cricket or beetle but a calcified grain of sand that became an irritant in an unlucky bivalve. Why the hell would he put that in his mouth? Obviously, this pale urchin was severely retarded. But, daily, this human female would show up and place that ridiculous stone in front of his face expecting something that would never arrive. And for the toad that was her sanity.

After months of this torturous routine, the Princess showed up one morning but without the pearl. She quietly sat down next to the toad and with a quick and deliberate movement grabbed the toad with her hand behind his ears, squeezed really hard, and kissed his head in what was for the horrified toad an elongated minute. Unbeknownst to Anastassia, the Bufo alvarius species secretes a toxic hallucinogen called bufotenine when pressure is applied to the toad's parotid glands. She suddenly saw the toad for what he really was and that was a Prince. He was handsome and brave. Because of her small size and the large dose of toad venom secreted, she soon fell asleep in his arms and died.

The Princess was discovered three days later by a ground servant. The servant would later describe the scene as a small white clad decaying body near the bog's edge with a happy leaping frog eating the numerous flies blanketing her corpse.

Authors note: My grandmother and great uncle used to write stories so I thought I would give this a try. It was for a special project event for my fifth-grade class. The local PTA members were disgusted by the essay and I received an F from my teacher. I demanded that I at least get an E for effort. And I did. Mom and Eni loved the effort.

The Unlikely Tornado

"It was a small whirling mass of sheer foaming death." — Garth Gunther

It was Friday night in the Zonk house and that meant everyone would go out to eat at Tocolito's and then they would go straight to the library for books. Opeia loved this tradition and she would later carry this on into her tribe's habits. Tocolito's was a very Mexican place with real Mexican food. Eni always got the taco salad with chicken, Zade the chili relleno with chicken, and Opeia would splurge with nopalitos and a side of tomatoes, onions and a tomatillo chili. It was a wonderful evening and they ate out on the restaurant patio underneath a rainbow-colored umbrella. The sky was a clear night and Eni spotted an orbiting satellite that moved methodically across the horizon. Later, at the White Pine County Library, Opeia was drowning her brain in Zola, Bulgakov, Borges and Markham. They returned home at eight-thirty p.m. and that is when shit hit the fan.

It started off with a dull monotone chant like logs of heavy lumber rolling down a slow descent. A multitude of lamps and flashlights eventually appeared and a wave of people pulsated rhythmically toward The Pony Express. Zade and Eni were armed with Benelli M4s complete with 000 buck loads. Opeia saw faces. Numerous rage-filled faces and some from her grade school class. She saw the Mayor, her principal and her favorite librarian, Ms. Hobbs. Some had guns but most had clubs, rakes and one with an enormous silicon replica of a male copulation organ. The entire horde was clad in brown shirts and black shorts. Their right arms were held out at a 45-degree angle to the horizontal with palms up. Eni and Zade figured they could take out fatally, at most, five or seven of their numbers and possibly more wounded, but the wave would inevitably lead to their being shot or bludgeoned to death. Slowly the wave came. It appeared to Opeia like a slow-moving deadly fog.

The chant was clear now. "No queers in our town!" Over and over again it rolled through the dense night air. The shot from a gun followed by two more was heard in the distance. Eni and Zade placed themselves with Opeia behind a small stucco and plaster-covered wall out front near the entrance door. Zade and Eni cocked their shotguns. They looked at each other. No fear glazed their eyes. Just confidence in being a Zonk. Zade whispered to Eni and Opeia, "See you on the other side!" And then the screams.

Opeia stated the tornado came from the left but Zade was sure it came from the right. A small tornado ripped through the horde with faint metallic sparks reflecting the bright lights. There was foam and a strange fecal matter with golden urine liquid spewing out of this small whirling thing. The sound was like that of a hamster being pureed ass first in a Cuisinart Ultra Velocity blender. In thirty seconds, it was all over. Fourteen people were dead or dying and thirty-two were seriously wounded. Among the dying were Ms. Hobbs and the Mayor. Opeia held the hand of Ms. Hobbs as she slowly left this futile dimension. Ms. Hobbs shuddered two times and looked at Opeia, and blurted out from her lips with smatterings of blood and a heavy sigh, "I hate you rug munchers!" And then she left this Orb. Roger reconstituted her on Teegarden C in a brothel. She spent eternality being very gracious in her price point for any of her patron's desires.

The Return of the Klon

"Local violent micro-bursts are not uncommon during this season in East Nevada." — Greg NWS Station Meteorologist.

Opeia woke up and felt refreshed. Some energy welled up within her and she knew all was at peace. Someone let the chickens out of the coop in the back. They were everywhere, balking, pecking and shitting. Eni and Zade were sweeping the front parking area. Opeia noted the propensity of the chickens to peck at blood splatter. She thought they must be innately drawn to this color spectrum. A large monkey was in the kitchen and bathing in the sink. This monkey was also brushing its teeth.

Opeia squealed in delight and hugged the loving Zonk macaque. Queen Klondike had arrived. Monk Shin, the family priest, entered from the back. He too was welcomed by a hug and a slimy smooch to the head. Shin had just removed the duct tape from the hands of the Queen that held the finely-honed blades made by Tsukiji Masamoto. They were now buried under a dry patch of cactus under the tumbleweeds in the back of the station.

Federal government meteorologists investigated this incident and stated it was a rare but not uncommon micro-burst that must have picked up significate metal debris to lacerate this unfortunate gathering of people. Garth Gunther, smoldering in a hate-filled rage, stated loudly in his large secured basement hall to all his legions that it was the lust of the She-Devils that now plagued this town and they had to be eradicated. Master Gunther summoned his followers and they were to have a banquet of all banquets, and all his officers and all his soldiers were to be there to proclaim their allegiance to him and fight the war with the Zonks.

Isn't it strange that an alteration in an appearance, as slight as a pair of glasses, contact lenses and wigs can make a person disappear into the soul of another? The Klondike Catering Company, a recent nubile industry to this area, underbid all applicants for the pseudo-Wachenburg castle extravaganza.

The Wachenburg basement was actually a very secure bunker. There was only one entrance and that too was the only exit. A person had to go through two locked iron doors and several guards to have access to the main hall. Restrooms were to the side of the main hall and the kitchen was staffed now with caterers from the Klondike Clan. The Hall was enormous, like some Viking subterranean trough cave in the desert hills of arid Nevada. The Swastika cottage's inhabitants converged for the magnanimous white soiree. The Klondike Caterers were prepared.

Losing the Loos

"Believe me or not but tomorrow the earth will quake and you will lose your business." — Roger to Hazel and Zazel.

Hazel and Zazel were restlessly sleeping on their large mound of straw. They woke into a dream and there, in the corner of their mound of earth near a dying candle flame, was Roger. His blue robe fell aside to expose his torso and suddenly, noting Zazel's intense gaze, he tied up his garment with some embarrassment. Zazel was despondent and asked him to please open up his robe to reveal his manhood. Proudly, Roger stated, it was indeed his manhood and it was only for men. Hazel and Zazel looked at each other and expired a heavy sigh in disappointment.

Roger stopped in to visit the sisters from time to time to see how the Zonks were doing. Being from the fifth dimension he could easily slide down and up the axis of time. It was October 24 and tomorrow there would be a fairly good-sized earthquake on this coastline in England. The sisters were doing well and they saved a large amount of money from the privy and excrement business. But here was Roger telling them it was all going to be destroyed. They didn't particularly believe Roger, even though, in the past, he was never wrong. But they both decided they would keep the privies open the next day but they, themselves, would keep well away from the cliff. And they did.

Because of secrecy, the Royal entourage did not want their passage known. They stayed the night of the 24th in Folkestone at the Rocksalt Inn and early that morning ate a hearty feast, and they all left slowly to Dover. The local innkeepers, keeping their long promise to the Ogre and now the Zonks, and not liking the Royals at all, fed them at the break of fast an extra helping of the bovine laxative.

A local farmer noted that the Royal entourage's cadence started slowly but mile by mile the rhythmic hooves upon the ground gathered great speed. A hermit crawling out of a bed of dry dark leaves noted that by the time the Royals reached the Zonk privies their carriages were traveling 'at a blistering pace as though they were on fire!'. It all suddenly stopped and the doors were flung open and the Royals all raced to their own individual loo overhanging the face of the cliff. And as if the Gods empathized with their grumbling bowels, the earth began to shake.

Because of their greater mass and the friction of the upswelling wind, all soon to be deceased splashed through their previously expelled slosh onto the welcoming crashing waves on the rocky shore below. The Dukes of Devonshire, Marlborough, Rutland and Rothesay, along with their corresponding Duchesses and two porters, all were sent surfing into another dimension. Roger found them all work at the Church of the None Caring Souls on Teegarden C. Even today, those Royals care nothing for the events that occurred on that earth quaking day.

The Zonk sisters, however, were furious since they were not paid for the privy time. The Royals stated that in lieu of the loo circumstances that they were not responsible for any fee since it was an Act of God. Months would pass, but using Roger as their lawyer, since he could slip through time, he was able to build up a strong case of adulterous behavior by the Royals who easily coughed up funds to staunch the entire matter. Hazel and Zazel became rich.

Since they owned the cliff side property they were going to build and own their own inn, the Inn of Zonk. And with the bovine laxative pulsating on either side of this welcoming palace, they were to manage quite well into the future.

Roger, in retrospect, discovered if those Dukes, Duchesses and even the two porters were to survive on earth that day then they would have eventually produced a mass of extreme conservative right-wing Republicans in the twenty-first century. The Zonk job was complete.

And Night Becomes Day

"Now I am become Death, the destroyer of worlds." — *Bhagavad Gita.*

The festivities began after much schnapps and German wine. The banquet goers, all fully inebriated, toasted to the great new White Wave that was going to purge this new nation of all humans that were a pestilence to this new order. Zade, Eni and Opeia all dressed in typical lederhosen, tight corsets and ponytails, exothermically milked the crowd with pastries, buns and breads all smothered in frostings, butter and cream. The entrees of sausage, cabbage with grilled pork and goat were also loaded into their upper gastro-tract. All of it, all, was laced with a strong bovine laxative.

It was planned systematically. The guards on iron door #1 went first and then the guards on iron door #2 followed. All flushed into the dining hall and went directly to the lavatories. Within twenty minutes, everyone was scrabbling from outlet to outlet. The Zonks quietly sealed iron door #2. Between #1 and #2 was a curiously damaged gas main that quietly spewed forth the flammable rich vapor. The timer was set. Door number #1 was sealed. Monk Shin and the Queen patiently waited for the Zonk crew in a derelict maintenance van and when all arrived the van shuffled across the barren landscape toward The Pony Express.

Detonation occurred at roughly 11.28 p.m. Alice Wheeler and Doug Baskenbalm were on their back porch in Ruth, Nevada, drinking a strong sangria when the lovely cool clear night turned into day. The orange ball of the sun appeared to the south which was quickly followed by the boom of the shock wave and then a strong warm breeze. The sun went out but produced a very large orange growing mushroom that both Alice and Doug exclaimed later looked exactly like an Amanita phalloides. In the distance, the odd sound of a scream could be heard. A happy scream. A scream of final satisfaction. Not coyote, wolf or human. It was a scream of an elated monkey.

The next morning, high up above in a chartered plane was Zade, Eni and Opeia. Looking down at what appeared was a large white, blue and red tinseled covered dimple swallowing up huge amounts of hazmat, county, federal, state and local search teams. The Wachenberg swastika disappeared—to a cottage—dissolved into a vast opening of Hell.

The Cat That Was Caught by a Conundrum

By Opeia Zonk

"It was dead and in a shoe box. I opened it up again and it was alive. Now, I just opened it up and it was dead again." — Opeia, pleading with her mother.

The shoe box arrived just seven days after the enormous explosion south of Ruth, Nevada. It was right there on the backdoor step of The Pony Express. Monk Shin and the Queen had just left for the pearly peaks of Colorado when the package arrived.

It was a normal shoe box that appeared battered through time. An off-white box with a faded red brimmed lid. Inside the box, as I opened it up, lay a grey and white striped tabby cat. The cat was dead. Initially I thought the townspeople, fed by the delusion of Wachenburg, placed this creature at our doorstep to curse the Zonks. But when I went out to a nearby cactus patch to bury the creature, the lid popped off and out sprang the cat.

Just as I am sure it was alive now, it was dead, then. I know. How can an entity entwined be both dead and alive? It couldn't but it did. In the quantum world that was indeed a possibility, but in the classical world of physics this was an impossibility. What was going on?

The cat went into the sage and brush. But the next morning I mourned at the sight of a shoe box that contained the same dead tabby the day before. It was right on my backdoor step. I picked up its cold lifeless body and was assured of death by the rigor it produced. I placed it back into the box, carefully covered it up with the lid, and went into the kitchen to show my mother and Auntie Eni. As I placed the box on the countertop, the lid popped open and out sprang a very alive cat. It scurried out the door and into the tumble weeds.

Mom and Eni did not get this issue. They never saw the cat dead. They only saw an alive cat exit and a shoe box. Granted, I had just gotten my period and I was livid with both my mother and Auntie for not granting me an absolutely necessary hysterectomy. But my hormonal imbalances could not justify the true vision of the death and life of this cat. It was not possible.

The next morning there was the shoebox again. I took my mother's 12-gauge shotgun with 000 buck and at point blank range shot the box containing the cat. As I opened up the lid, the grizzly image of a completely blasted feline emerged. The cat was not alive or dead; it was blasted apart and it stayed that way. I cut out the cat's anus and sent it to my Grandfather Cornelius so it could be host to a burgeoning bounty of the Zonks Family Business creating Christ's blessed foreskins.

Author's Note: This incident actually occurred and I blame Roger for screwing with my mind but he would never admit to any of it. I am sure it was a hoot and a holler on one of his serious green tea binges but I will never know. Again, my English teacher gave me an E for effort. Fuck her.

The Blessing of Constipation

"No single person knows better than we how to plug a leaking hole."
— Zazel to Hazel.

Lomotil was not yet invented in the eighteenth century but the solid opium trade between England and China was just beginning to roar. The Zonks hired chemists and they separated from opium the constituent that constipates its users without the opium side effects. And the foundation of diarrhea control began. Now granted, in large amounts, this chemical too was addictive. But in the 1800s who really gave a crap as long as the liquid crap would stay inside your torso in the form of a solid.

Hazel and Zazel would get this constituent powder and apply it, for a price, to the Inn of Zonk's culinary desires, and this would plug up any bovine laxative induced misery that the Inns at Folkestone or Dover could possibly produce. It was a win-win situation. And it became clear over a period of just a few weeks that if you had a hydrant that was exploding uncontrollably then those individuals needed to visit the Zonk sisters in the Inn of Zonk and they would beg for mercy. And they did. And they arrived in hordes. The Zonk coffers expanded greatly.

Hazel and Zazel expanded the Inn in the 1760s from twenty rooms to fifty, and each contained its own private cistern, basically a brick-lined ball in the ground, to hold the sewage and through a pipe at the bottom transported the personal excrement out to the side of the sheer cliff face. No more outhouses and now just 'inhouses' that became quite convenient. The 'inhouse' idea was Roger's just because he could, and he could cheat with a small bend in the branch of time.

The Inn's wonderful views of the Channel and, weather permitting, even of France were exacerbated by floor to ceiling windows, and the kitchen was staffed exceptionally well with a new French chef, Pierre Yanis Escoffier (Yanni) —who was the great great-grandfather to Georges Auguste Escoffier, who became famous many years later. Yanni's seasonal signature dish was escargot with either cod, mackerel or gurnard doused with plum lentils and everything basted in garlic and butter with more butter. And more butter after that.

Yanni, as an aside, was one of Roger's longest termed lovers. Roger, to this day, states that, "He was not a great lover, but he was a Great Fuck!" And if you'd ask Roger to explain that, he would huff and be mum since it was obvious that the question came from a person that didn't know the meaning of true love.

Yanni died just right before the Napoleonic Wars when he was expelled from England, hence the Inn of Zonk, by the British Empire back to France. By Napoleonic decree, his ship was refused a port in France since the leader of the French empire deemed him a traitor. He eventually died in Roger's arms as the ship made numerous attempts at landing on either side and was left crisscrossing the Channel but to no avail. This is exactly why Roger hasn't eaten escargot since.

The sisters Zonk eventually patented the opium constituent and received a large yearly royalty for the rest of their lives. The patrons to the Inn of Zonk never realized that the two small women who teetered around the establishment were actually some of the wealthiest women in England. Indeed, they wore the same leather tight shoes, leather dresses and flop leather hats. Of course, now, sans excrement. They never made a to do about airs and always treated the janitor at the Inn just as royally as visiting Royalty. Everyone was just the same as anyone else. Which seriously upset the Royals, but the sisters really didn't give a shit since in their lives they had to put up with so much of it.

The Pony Express Again

"No single person knows better than we how to plug a leaking hole."
— *Eni and Zade to Opeia.*

Menstruation was just this thing females did. Some would say endure and others, with endometriosis, would state eradicate. It was necessary for the procreation of the species but what if you didn't want to procreate at all? Of course, this brought back vivid discussions (aka arguments) with Zade years ago but one so young as Opeia could not possibly make that decision. Pads were like sitting in a saddle and very uncomfortable so Zade quickly graduated her up to pons. She was temporarily pleased.

The lab was almost complete. Eni and Zade had the larger space in the garage and Opeia had her space, also in the garage, in the corner, separated by a shower screen. At least she had the window. Complete with desk and an elongated table this was to become her haven.

Opeia was studying human mental rumination. This is a static psychological condition where specific human brains act as ruminants— animals like cows, sheep and goats that regurgitated their cuds. In this case with humans, the mental cud is an obsessive thought. Thoughts like anger, irrational hate, fundamentalism and the putrid stench of radical conservative mental expectoration. Like some cuds, these thoughts refused to flush and always bloated up like some decaying subsurface vomited mass of a carcass. Opeia wanted to flush these mental turds. She was going to create a mental cud flushing toilet. And she did.

In her great corner of the garage, unlike her mother and grandmother, she housed in a huge aquarium a nest full of pre-programmed genetic rats. These rats were fathomed by cutting edge genetic technology to be bred as mentally similar to right-wing conservative Christian human bigots. They all, to a rat, had a penchant for foul rat language and violent behavior to any rat that didn't have the same color coat of fur. And when bred out, all that was left was an aquarium full of pure white fur rats with deep blue eyes. Any rat that didn't have these characteristics was devoured immediately. Their society had to be whole and holy pure. Their little right arms jutted out at exactly 45 degrees up from the horizonal with their little right palms up.

Opeia, with a tad help from Eni and Zade, isolated a hormone in the cerebellum that produced these ruminate thoughts. With diligence she found a serum through the pulverized teeth of corn snakes that would prohibit these thoughts from being regurgitated. At least in theory. On that next Saturday, she injected the formula into all of her Nazi fundamentalist right-wing conservative rats.

Initially, they all froze dumbfounded. Their eyes bulged a little and they began to squeal. But Opeia could not hear their sounds. Their tiny mouths would open in a horrific way and they forced air out of their lungs but no sound was audible. At least not to human ears. In the ultrasonic register, however, it was excruciating. While the white mob of genetically engineered Nazi rats were writhing in their pain, Opeia took the aquarium out back to the tumbleweeds and dumped their scurrying bodies into the desert.

The next morning, the daughter of Zade Zonk awoke with a nervous disposition. She found her mother and her Auntie Eni in the back of The Pony Express standing silently over a multitude of dead snakes. Opeia's rats ran to only fall down and quiver. The snakes, being snakes, ate the throbbing rodents. The rodents, instead of having their rudiment memories suppressed, actually had them amplified. Each and every rat's head eventually exploded and all within a poor hungry snake. Opeia cried. Gretchen called her later that evening and simply said, "Welcome to the Family Zonk."

The Requiem for a King

by Opeia Zonk

"Nature is only as beautiful as society leads you to believe it is." —
Opeia.

There once was a bog in the Kingdom of Republicans and all their 'successes' festered there to produce a toxic greenhouse gas called methane. So did their bowels, indeed, everyone's bowels but who was to go there for remediation?

The King of this Kingdom just lost his daughter mysteriously near the bog and all he had to account for that loss was a very happy toad. The Republican committee on bog-related deaths converged to find witches to blame. And strictly because of their wealth, fame and weirdness, the right-wing committee proclaimed clearly that the Zonk sisters, both Hazel and Zazel, were to blame. They had to be witches since they were female and incredibly wealthy, and landowners to boot. No two women could be so bold. The Zonk sisters had to be evil and they all had to burn.

It didn't matter that this bog was 96.8 miles from the Inn of Zonk or that the sisters had absolutely nothing to do with the death of the Princess kissing a toad. The Zonks were female, rich, successful and rude to the Royals. This made them notorious and they had to be flushed from the ruminant cud of English flesh that failed to dislodge from the orifice that, at present, was in the form of a hole in a water pressured hydrant.

Stating obviously that they didn't do it meant they did and stating they did do it meant they did so they did what needed to be done and they pleaded for pure retribution for their souls. And this came in the form of Roger. Roger farted.

This gas discharge was considered throughout history as the Laki Haze. A volcanic fissure in southern Iceland would erupt and spew forth billions of tons of hydrofluoric acid and sulfur dioxide compounds. This cloud of gas would slowly move south to England and suffocate thousands of residents and farm animals. The Zonk sisters, safely in their basement cellar chained to a post at the Inn of Zonk, survived. Everyone else perished around the inn including the guards, clergy and local residents building a witch burning pyre. Even the escargot succumbed. The chef was spared since he was in a circle jerk with Roger in the root cellar. Miracles never cease.

Hazel and Zazel Zonk were exonerated by the King since obviously their power to create toxic gas was far too great for any one nation to purge. The Zonks were left alone to do as they pleased and they went right back to expand their Den of Oddness: The Inn of Zonk.

The King, disparaged, went down to his bog and like the organic matter below, he began to fester. Something had to pay for his daughter's untimely death. And just then, like an answered prayer, a large happy toad jumped into the King's lap. The infuriated King grabbed the toad behind the ears and attempted to strangle the life from the amphibian, and he almost succeeded, but the King, being a King, noticed the white skin secretions from the parotid glands of the toad tarnishing his Royal hand and he flung the beast across the bog where he safely landed on a rotting stump. The King, being in haste, licked his hand clean.

Now the King had a snake in his garden. He wanted the largest snake in all his kingdom and his Royal adventurers brought back an anaconda. This particular reptile weighed in at five hundred and fifty pounds. The King had his Royal garden and he called it Eden. It had an apple tree and, of course, the snake. But because of some serious foul up with his rabbit hutch servants, the snake had not been fed in a number of months. Looking for sustenance, it easily escaped the garden and went down to the bog looking for basically anything to eat.

Lo and behold, there was the King writhing in a bufotenine hallucinatory haze as he was literally swimming in mounds of gold coins, rubies and diamonds. Naked woman pummeled him with soft kisses. One particular woman slithered up to him and gave him a very grand hug. This hug was so grand it broke the King's back and ribs and he was unable to breath. His eyes bulged out and in his loud Kingly voice gargled out, "Thank goodness, Madam, for your blessed warm embrace!" And then the King died.

The Kingdom never found the King. Rumors spread that the witches, Hazel and Zazel, vanquished him to a faraway barren island. In general, the inhabitants of England cheered with joy. Long live, ah, whomever.

The King's garden servants eventually found the snake happily in complete bliss in the midst of a conversation with a toad about the Earth's magnetic pole fluctuations and why the North Pole's drift is accelerating. The servants also warned the stable master to check to see if any of their ponies were missing. The King's snake appeared to have had a large meal. The snake did proclaim to the toad years later that nothing, and he meant nothing, tasted better than an hallucinating Republican. The snake then stopped short and chortled in clarification that all Republicans are indeed in some state of hallucination since their grasp on reality is so little.

Author's note: After the unfortunate Wachenberg affair, the town, including the schools and all the businesses, seriously mellowed. My sixth-grade teacher, Ms. Hoffman, thought my essay was crass but gave me a C for creativity. Things just might be looking up.

Quenching the Thirst of Ruth

"The Zonks did more to inoculate the citizens of Ruth from their dependency from delusion than any individuals ever." — Mayor Hobbs.

The Pony Express was still a gas station with two gas pumps in the front and one diesel pump near the back. Two bathrooms were now on the side of the facility and apart from the lone soda machine in front the only thing sold in the store were books. The garage was turned into a Zonk Science Lab so no mechanical operations occurred. It was simple and simple was how Eni, Zade and Opeia liked it.

The Zonk women, and this included Eni as adopted, usually wore bib overalls with Gretchen Zonk signature tee shirts, Gretchen's signature bandanas that they wore in their hair, and simple rugged work boots. The locals noted that they always stuck close to themselves, never socialized and when they were not pumping fuel or selling books, they were in the garage making something that stunk awful. This awfulness was Gretchen's alpine flower anti-right-wing conservative juice.

Basically, even after the Wachenburg purge, radical conservative elements still lay hidden like some desiccated virus that cysts up and waits decades for rain, and then rises again to scourge the countryside with its appalling ignorance and hate. The Zonks were going to immunize humans in Ruth against this virus once and for all.

The only water supply in town was Ruth Springs. Granted, the town had to 'share' the water with the neighboring mine but to the Zonks the inoculation didn't necessarily have to be just for the city's population.

Early Saturday morning when the town gently slept off their last night debauchery, the Zonks meandered shortly out of the city to drill a deep well in the Great Basin aquafer. The Basin was really just several basins combined and the only one the Zonks were after was the one that fed the people of Ruth—and the adjacent mine. At some depth, they hit fresh water and began to reverse the operation into pumping in generous amounts of the alpine flower anti-conservative fluid. The job was completed right before sunrise and the happy women went home to 'wake up' to coffee, fresh laid eggs and imported kale salad.

On Monday next, Mayor Hobbs, husband to the late teacher Ms. Hobbs, barged into The Pony Express to plead with the only scientists in town. Apparently, the water supply had a tint of grey coloring and the inhabitants were concerned it could possibly be metal poisoning from the neighboring mine. Alas, upon inspection, the Zonks proclaimed the water absolutely clean and good to drink. And the city did.

Not surprised, Eni, Zade and Opeia noted that during the next year the town of Ruth tested particularly high on the Program for International Student Assessment (PISA) scores relative to the rest of the US. Statistically, compared to other nations, Ruth was in near alignment with Finland and Estonia. This was amazing! Politically, and overnight, the county became stark blue. Oh, there were still arguments that became debates and discrepancies that were resolved through reason and pertinent insight. But gone was 'my way or the highway' and 'we'll agree to disagree'. It wasn't Heaven but it was Earth. The neighboring mine even had weekly Thursday night LGBTQ parties and the local school board actually had a dense inculcation of minorities. East Nevada called this city the 'Brownest town around' and they were not referring to sun tans.

The inhabitants of Ruth, finally, with Mayor Hobbs leading the masses, arrived at the steps of The Pony Express. They were all holding rainbow flags. Eni, Zade and Opeia opened up the front door and were amazed at the cheering crowd. Mayor Hobbs, then Mister Hobbs, remembering his wife's last words, didn't know what to get the Zonks so he had Larry's Fine Carpets unload an unusually large shag avocado green rug at their feet. For once, the Zonks were speechless. It was time for them to go.

Eni

By Navdar Goran

Translated from Kurdish by Zackary Maxwell

The Gathering Storm

"I am not exactly sure what marbles were made for. I realize it was at one time a game of sorts. But at no time should one put the marbles in your mouth and pretend to speak." — Eni on the Kentucky accent

Chester was a pig. He spoke three languages fluently but none of them human. He was sharp and young and he knew enough to know he did not want to become bacon. He lived in a small farm just north of Curdsville, Kentucky, on the Green River.

The Zonk women, specifically, Opeia, Eni and Zade, moved into Curdsville, Kentucky, to ferret out radical conservatism and plant the seed for the Lord Jesus Zonk (aka Opeia). And Opeia was up for the task.

Curdsville was named Curdsville by an inebriated settler who just happened to like H.T. Curd, the steamboat captain on the Green River north of town. As fate often allows, names can sometimes define prominence and the town of Curdsville became the dairy product industry of the southeast US. Milk was viable and wholesome and the neighboring countryside was embracing the vital stimulation of probiotic yogurt and numerous sundry dairy products—including curds. Thank God the steamboat Captain was not called H.T. Turd. Otherwise, the Zonk family would have a major stronghold on the nation's fertilizer industry.

Chester showed up promptly at five thirty a.m. on a Tuesday. He wasn't hired or invited but he showed up anyway to help himself to the rich and ripening tulip bulbs buried deep in the garden. Eni would have gutted the swine but something stopped Zonk to decide he could possibly stay and assist with the family matters. And he did.

The probiotic curd business took time to ripen to fruition. The Zonks had three flavors of curds: yogurt, cottage cheese and cheese – plain, plain and plain. Though most people didn't like plain, the culinary industry around the nation loved plain. They could, of course, add their own flavors and all they really wanted was a solid healthy base of dairy.

And the products were well below price point. The Zonks were beginning to dominate the national curd market.

Eni was out strolling during the afternoon with a strong harness on Chester. He didn't need a harness but he couldn't speak human and Eni could not speak swine so there it was. He gracefully led her through a dense forest and to a world filled with amazing dense undergrowth. Snorting around Chester found love. Love came in the structure of rare mushrooms in the form of black truffles and black morels. The latter, unfortunately, caused Chester to be sexually aroused but this obviously gave Eni a nonverbal clue as to where the morels could be found. And the bounty began. Eni thought it strange that a bifurcated country as in the south that abhorred the color black would embrace that same color in a mushroom. But they didn't. They didn't have the palate to discern the difference. And this made the Zonks even more pleased with Chester's find.

The land that the Zonk women owned was not just a dairy farm. It turned out that their recovery from investments in dairy products, though very good, would be minimal in comparison to the returns on the fungi that Chester found on the land. They all became very wealthy.

The ground beneath them became very dark. Not with fungus Chester discovered, but with the dark clouds that pilfered the horizon. A storm was coming and it was going to be loud.

The Minute Marbles in An Exhausted English Bag of Wind

"It is only intelligence that floats to the surface for the future. All other matter sinks to the bottom to become fodder for the past. Life needs both. Both need each other and both ripen and overripen like fresh fruit to rotten pulp in the expanse of time. It is that harmony we live in." —
Zazel to Hazel.
"Fuck you!" — Hazel to Zazel.

The Inn of Zonk literally became the Den of Extraordinary Oddness. It was early in the Napoleonic wars and the Inn had a new chef. Alton Weaver was from East London and he was good at British basics. Meaning, in English, his food was terrible. He was replaced quickly by Reyansh Kapoor (Rey), a teenager, the great great-grandfather to Sanjeev Kapoor, who was the best chef ever, many years later.

The kitchen at the Inn poured forth masala chai, tandoori chicken, samosa, kofta, rogan josh, aloo gobi and much more. Rey's signature dish was dhaba chicken curry—everyone loved it.

But what was necessary was intellectual expansion. The Zonk sisters, being at that time quite wealthy, were able to persuade the best writers and poets to do readings on their glass bound stage interior to the Inn near the edge of the Cliff. The views were transcendent and so were the readings. One particular Royal, female, was so enthralled that she didn't have the courtesy to sweep away her smegma detritus that cheesed up on the floor beneath her chair. This was later sold by the Zonks as Royal curiosities and their coffers did benefit.

Samuel Johnson was the first to arrive at the Inn. Early. He was not well received and spent a great deal of his occasions bitching (aka critiquing) about existing works that were popular at the time. He was a very precise bitcher and possibly the best ever. Later it was Blake, Goldsmith and Cowper and the crowds evolved. Then the timber rattled the golden frame of God when Clare, Keats, Hunt and Shelley arrived.

Most all died young but they had their time on the stage at the Inn of Zonk. Their initials etched into the root cellar oak basement pillars that Roger presided over are all still there. If only the DNA could be filtered out from the stains left from such illustrious numerous excretions on the wood so that all corresponding stories would resound in exuberance.

On the doorstep of this wonderful Den was found a tightly woven basket of reeds that cradled a cotton swathed tiny female maggot. She was a castaway. There was a blizzard that week that blanketed the eastern shore of England. This creature survived just by being a creature that wanted to live. The Sisters Zonk would call her Badger—for her tenacity. Badger Zonk was to be honored.

Roger attempted to keep Hazel and Zazel alive well into their centenarian age but rumors would fly and the witch bell would bong eventually and inevitably. And it did. Hazel and Zazel took up managing an Inn, just called Zonk, in Teegarden B. Keats, Goldsmith, Cowper, Clare and Shelley were all there. So was randy Roger. All was well. Badger Zonk took over the thriving stead.

Chester the Amazingly Reverential Porcine

"Yes, it was obvious I should have left a note. But Ben wouldn't have been able to read it anyway. I wasn't planning on staying. I just showed up here and never left." — Chester to the Goose.

Ben Curd, the great great-grandson to H.T. Curd, owned a farm just north of the Zonk Dairy Farm on the Green River. Ben also owned a large motorized barge on this river that he used to haul products up and down the connecting Ohio River. Mr. Curd also owned a pig named Chester but Chester had not been noticed for over three entire weeks. Farmer Curd was very upset. He had just renovated an old outhouse on his property to be a splendid meat smoker and he wanted to try out his invention on the tender flesh of his prized porcine. Chester, being Chester, realized that his flesh was on the line and decided to stroll out south into the garden of the Zonks. And there he was. Ms. Goose, overhearing Mr. Curd's curdling blood, ventured out to gander around for Chester. Chester, found, was not going back. Ever.

Small towns do talk and it became apparent that Chester now lived with a lesbian couple who had a child. This couple owned a productive dairy farm just south of Curd's Farm and Barge estate.

A confrontation was imminent and the Zonks dearly loved Chester and offered to the farmer over thirty times the dollar amount for a pig of his age. Although he did need the funds, it was his pride that was on sale and these women were dictating to him and his community what was on the menu, and he was not having any of it. The Zonks stated clearly that whatever was on the menu it wasn't Chester and the duel was on.

Like all duels this one was short. No one won. No one was shot. The billboards funded by the Curds dictating family values had to be only between man and woman, were eventually replaced by a photo of Chester suffocating in a smoky outhouse—the latter funded by the Zonks. This went on for several months until a final truce was given but the Zonks did not offer it.

The Zonk Dairy Farm received a cryptic card stating that the Zonk family members were invited to a gala on board the Curd Barge on the Green River on the night three days hence.

Farmer Curd, Ben to Chester, had his motorized barge outfitted beneath for numerous cylinders of propane. This was scheduled for delivery to Henderson Kentucky in a few weeks. On the deck of the barge, colorful canvas tents and lights illuminated by generators made the barge festive. Fresh gardenias lined the edge of the craft's full perimeter. Curd's plan was to warmly embrace the Zonks for a festival on the floating craft, intoxicate them with alcohol and finally anesthetize them with small tanks containing Xenon gas, cut the barge loose down the river and ignite the pressurized loveliness into a ball of flame. Well insured, Farmer Curd would be able to keep Chester for smoking and purchase the entire booming dairy and mushroom farm of the Zonks. Priceless.

The Zonks showed up promptly at seven p.m. The Fulte band, inbred, were playing a jaunty tune of happiness for the death of a fertile cow that they all lost, to a soul, their virginity. It was odd but the Zonks were used to odd. Pervis was on the Jew's harp; Melvin on a one-stringed broom handle connected to a reverberating overturned porcelain toilet bowl; Clovis was on vocals and washboard, and Ted was on percussion with a No. 2 tin washtub (overturned) and a trash lid on a plunger handle. The handle was well worn and dark brown in color. Eni, Zade and Opeia were clad with their finest, all wearing bib overalls, Gretchen signature tee-shirts and head bandanas, and well-waxed leather boots. What offended Curdsville residents the most was not just that they were lesbians, which they were not, but that they were successful, intelligent, hardworking businesswomen who could all accurately shoot a gun and live off the land without the assistance of a male. Baffling everyone, they just had to go. They did not fit in to the paradigm of their norm.

Eni knew a Norm once from her university days in Bordeaux. Norminski Dudek was Polish and anything but the norm. He was a cherub youth with a penchant to live in the library and be socially unacceptable. Eni liked him. But he could not, and would not, interact with humans, since he was convinced he was a pig. A very intelligent swine but a swine nonetheless. He spoke fluent swine and all his friends, whom he occasioned on various trips to farms in rural France, were in the habit to discuss the climate change variabilities discovered around the globe. Norm was the first to write a paper on non-norm fluctuations with current local weather issues in comparison with the global paleoclimatology of Southern France. Most students thought he was Jewish, and he was, but not Orthodox, and he would eat pig if he wasn't one himself.

Eni found him in the campus kitchen in a meat grinder. Upon investigation, his saturated affection with Marqaux, a young plump strumpet swine of note, was castigated into the bowels of a processing unit. She was once a human many years ago on the western Alsace plains but Martha made her a swine. She gave Norm the best orgasm he had ever had. Did you know swine orgasms, at the least, last between thirty to sixty minutes of amazing pleasure? Norm, being human and pig, obtained that license. He was free. He followed her into the grinder and hence oblivion. Somewhere in sausage land a German belched and a human consumed what was a human with a smattering of sauerkraut and freshly ground mustard.

Eni had slumbered and was being offered a strong aperitif from a serf on the deck of the barge. She declined. A strong visual between Eni, Zade, Chester and Opeia indicated that future plans were on the dial of time.

The wheezing lungs of Clovis 'harmonized' with Melvin and Pervis, and the washboard cracked a tune of solace that was buried in the grave of one H.T. Curd. Not an eye was left tearless. Clyde VanDerBuck passed a jug, as was his clan's way, and they all knelt down in remembrance of this loss.

Quickly, Eni eyed Zade, who eyed Chester, who eyed Opeia and while the mournful prayer pondered, Opeia scampered off to switch out the Xenon cylinders with the remaining Zonk tubes of sympathetic nerve gas. The gas values were opened. Chester jumped ship (aka barge) and waited patiently by the dock.

Kitty, the town's cosmetologist, upped her skirt and parted her panties to urinate off of the bow. The Zonks vanished, Chester gnawed through the hemp rope tethering the shore with the barge. The barge drifted down the undulating flow and the inhabitants of Curdsville, KY, overwhelmed by the gas, embraced each other in a pact of pure love. The barge exploded around the first bend. The remaining inhabitants of Curdsville, including the Zonks, standing placidly on the shoreline, stated that the barge just suddenly appeared like a large growing orange and black Amanita phallodies. All was quiet. It was time to move.

The Thread That Binds Us

By Opeiá Zonk

*"My, my, my said the Mole, there is a maggot in my soul so that must
mean we all have something in common." — Mr. Mole*

Mr. Mole was like all other moles, and there were so many, but why did
he feel different? Certainly, there were other moles that felt like he did.
He knew he was a subterranean mammal and knew the earth better than
most since the earth was his habitat. Mr. Mole actually felt the movement
of the tectonic plates. Slowly and surely and they would get locked up
only to burst out into earthquakes. We all just floated along on massive
floating shelfs under a turbulent ocean of melted rock. Float, float, float
and then there was the subduction zones where the floating plates fell,
one beneath the other, to re-heat and melt, only to float much later on.

Mr. Mole loved floating. He saw himself a sailor on an incredibly
slow-moving rock plated sea. Over the millennia, the North Pole and
South Pole had traded places, etching their polarity into the very rocks
that floated in this sea. The earth was overdue for a polarity swap. It was
coming soon.

Mr. Mole hailed his fellow sailors to have a discussion on the five
extinction cycles that have occurred throughout time in his home called
earth. The other moles were not interested in such things and preferred
to discuss exploiting the environment to enhance their chances of
survival. But Mr. Mole would surmise, that by exploitation of this
environment's riches would lead to a catastrophic imbalance in greed
versus basic living. This would inevitably lead to class structure
degradation and social unrest as to who had access to the large larders of
narcotized earthworms that some possessed. Obviously, the larders
would be protected by the wealthy and the poor would have to survive
off the drippings from that stored flesh. Trickled down drippings of
stored flesh did not work and Captain Mole would not accept this future.

Captain Mole would call these hoarding moles, mindless to the environment that they swam in, Republicans.

Drunks are forever wobbly and most assume it is the inebriant that stumbles their flow, but no, the intoxicant merely makes the animal hypersensitive to the Earth's Coriolis effect. And that is all. We are all just on a very large wobbling, circling ball and some of us are hypersensitive to that rotation. Moles feel this to the extreme and they always appear four sheets to the wind, but they are not and are just one with the planet. Around and around, we go.

Captain Mole was tired of the ignorance and greed. Hoarding stores to let others starve? The wealthy stated it was pure blood that let them obtain this status but Mr. Mole looked into this and their blood was exactly like any others. They stated their brains were better at thinking but if thinking meant greed then yes, they were greedier upon analysis but their brains were no more intelligent than any other mole brain.

All that Mr. Mole could figure was that the divided nature of the mole population was basically social and tribal in nature. And what for? Why couldn't the moles just zoom out to see that they were just tiny specks on a rotating orb in a solar system that was engulfed in a galaxy that was engulfed in a universe? Why don't they get it? All moles are the same.

Captain Mole would ride the waves of this tectonic shift to the Laki vents in Iceland. On June 8, 1783, forty-two billion tons of basalt lava and clouds of hydrofluoric acid with sulfur dioxide compounds, vaporized Mr. Mole and it all went out to suffocate tens of thousands of human souls. Mr. Mole's atoms were there. They were there thriving in the lungs and body of the Sisters Zonk. Hazel and Zazel were now gone, leaving Badger, at the age of nine, running the most prosperous inn on the East coast of England.

Author's note: I was being home schooled at this time in Kentucky so I gave myself an A for Architecture for building this essay. My mom and Auntie Eni approved. Chester, later that night, ate it all. Ah, fleeting is the sanity of the apt focused moron.

The Silk Road

"All roads lead to the House of Silk." — Eni Zonk

Actually, from a great height above, it did appear that all roads did lead to this 'house'. The nearest town was Silk Hope, North Carolina, and the 'house' was, in fact, an ostentatious macabre plantation that was once owned by the notorious Colonel Mortimer Vance. The Zonks bought the place along with one hundred and fifty-four surrounding acres. It had stables, a very large barn, a large pond, five cottages, several sheds and, of course, the main mansion. Even though this entire estate was upgraded to modern amenities, it did need a great deal of maintenance and the Zonks began right away.

Colonel Vance obtained his rank during the Civil War, and even though he lost his war, he did not lose his plantation and land. The only thing that changed was that now he had no slaves and had to pay humans to work on his land. Which was all so much for the better since he was known as the most vicious slave owner ever, and literally slaughtered hundreds of his slaves just because they were his property. There is no deeper circle of Hell for such a person's soul and Roger made sure of that. Roger nestled Mortimer and his entire clan on the planet of KELT-9b—the hottest known exoplanet yet discovered—even hotter than most stars. There they will stay for eternity, painfully weaving and unweaving baskets made from their own seared entrails.

The Vance family cemetery was on a small knoll west of the main estate under a dense grove of oak trees. Eni wanted to burn the knoll to a cinder but Zade had another idea.

The main mansion had thirty-four bedrooms, twenty-eight bathrooms, two massive kitchens, one extremely large dining room with a long mahogany table, and all heated by wood stoves and electric baseboards. Although it took months, Eni wired the entire plantation and surrounding buildings with a huge computerized solar grid with twenty

Tesla batteries mounted in the barn. The Zonks, as they say, were off the grid.

The Zonks obtained a license for this estate to be not only a school but also a home for disenfranchised orphans. Children five to fifteen years of age were allowed consideration, with the only requirement being they had to be human. The cottages were turned into classrooms and the southern boundary was made into a very large garden. Fish were stocked in the pond, and hunting boar and deer seasonally kept the stead in viable protein. Opeia built an infirmary in the heavily timbered cellar. The Zonk Estate was found.

The holder of the title to this entire menagerie was Chesterfield T. Dangleberry, Esquire. He apparently received his law degree at Oxford. He was never to be seen and only held private council with Zonks and staff. The coat of arms etched on the main door was that of a smiling swine with bulging eyes and two large mushrooms: a truffle and a morel. Chester didn't particularly like the bulging eyes but the insignia maker was without sight and he had an odd sort of humor—so it stayed. The grand façade of pompousness was for the pretentious Christian white populace that surrounded this area since they would abhor the reality of what was going on within the bounds of the solid cast iron gate and tall iron surrounding fence line.

Once one entered the Gates of Dangleberry, religions, political affiliations, racism, sexism and any other 'ism' that any other outside tribe would use to define that tribe, were left behind. Those that entered were under the Rule of Zonk—where everyone had a voice and a vote, and were encouraged to use that power.

The first thirty orphans (aka class members) were a stoic and resilient lot and they didn't especially trust or even want this stewardship. Five were Asian, nine were Hispanic and the rest were African American. The Zonks loved a challenge. But how to pay for this monstrosity? Eni had two ideas.

The first was a recent find in Curdsville with great assistance from Chester. Eni discovered that over one hundred acres of this Estate had oak woodlands and the roots were loaded with black truffles. She also discovered vast amounts of morels. This wonderful find should keep the Zonks into the black at least through the present.

The second was an idea she had as a child. Her parents in Pau, France, thought that a two-year venture into the south of India would do her good. And it did. They placed her in an international school in Tamil Nadu. The school was also part of an industrialized silk factory that generated tons of Ahimsa silk, the latter being the only silk made that did not require the death of the silkworm inside the cocoon to obtain the product. The yields were low and the price point twice as much as the inhumane silk, but death of an animal and positive marketing often go hand-in-hand. The price was paid.

The rest of the barn, not housing the Estate's batteries, was converted into a moth (Bombyx mori) asylum and several rows of white mulberry trees were planted to feed the squirming silk producing varmints. Looms were made and spindles spun and the rest was history.

When not in school, the students worked on the Estate. They were paid three times the hourly minimum State wage, and those funds were invested into each of their college or trade school savings accounts. Everyone worked as a team. Indeed, it was surprising that Chester, Eni, Zade and Opeia did not stay in the main mansion but in a small insulated shed on the west side of the property. With just a wood stove, an oven and a rustic outhouse they were fine. No questions were asked. How much room did a person actually need?

There was one mandatory rule, the Rule of Zade, for all Dangleberry students. Daily, they all had to urinate on the graves in the old Vance Cemetery out by the knoll that was covered in dense oak trees. Somewhere in space, on the planet KELT-9b, painful screams could be heard.

Eni taught biochemistry (genetics and epigenetics), chemistry, and western and eastern philosophy. Zade taught biology, zoology, applied physics and quantum mechanics. Opeia taught applied mathematics from algebra, liner algebra, calculus to ordinary and partial differential equations. She also dabbled in thermodynamics and engineering. Chester, even on weekends, taught a course on scrounging for mushrooms and even had an advanced course in psilocybin.

Between teaching, managing, farming, fishing and hunting, the schedule was full. Dinner was at seven p.m. in the dining hall and Chester was not on the menu. The Zonk machine was not perfect, since perfect, hence infinity, did not belong to mass-based particles in the third dimension, but it was very close.

What was amazing about this intellectual experiment was the vast library. Offset from the dining hall was an expansive three-story in height and two hundred feet in diameter cylinder of bricks, all with circling shelfs, spiraling staircases and rotating ladders, housing all the great written works of fiction and non-fiction. The room was called Chester's Trove and there was probably no finer library collection, either private or public. The school children had to read approximately seventy-five percent of the total to initiate the stamp of graduation. Zade, the librarian, kept count. As Zade was fair to say, "It isn't the quantity of the literature read but the quality of the prose within that will stir the mind and blend the soul." Read Beryl Markham.

Fungal spores of the necessary terrestrial fruits in a small sea of oak roots produced a plethora of dainty, expensive morels and truffles. The humane silk fibers flourished to form rare fabric that was second to none. The students, all wearing the insignia of the bulging eyed swine, reveled in their exuberance at being cogs in such an illustrious machine. No one person was better than the other and all were equal.

Chester had just gathered two pounds of liberty cap mushrooms from the nearby cattle ranch. Loaded with psilocybin he was attempting to converse about the pathetic dislodging of the human brain in respect to a colossal impact on a reinforced cement barrier built by conservatives, when his head collapsed into a baked onion. The baked onion was desperately attempting to speak to a brazened carrot and that carrot was Eni. Eni, also ingesting the liberty cap mushrooms, was attempting to rationalize with the octopus with the face of a pig that the Earth was in dire need of assistance and can this Octopig-like thing please help humanity to save ourselves? The Octopig stated absolutely not and that humans were the cause of their own demise. Eni understood but then she met the Rodent of God, in the gold blistering blinding light from some unseen shimmering orb, it told her all was going to be just fine. Hope was going to save the day. Before she left this earthy mental realm into a haze of slumber, she said, "Who is this cunt called Hope?" And all was quiet.

To a child, the initial graduating body of Dangleberry Estates, all were accepted into the best colleges or trade schools in the world. Transportation costs were funded by the Zonks and their saved college funds were more than enough to feed, house them and fund their educational needs. These children would grow to become ambassadors, teachers, librarians and diplomats throughout the global. All spreading the word of Zonk. Chester, mentally writhing in a pit of warm mud that didn't exist, inebriated by a mushroom, expelled his lower intestines on a humane silk tailored rug. He was sorry.

The Master of Remorse

"The Preponderance of Statutory Exuberance." — Badger Zonk

Badger, Ms. B, did not know her origins. Her early memories were of two kindly old women that loved her but only doted on her in terms of non-tangible things—like loads of affection. And she loved it. She was outfitted in a simple leather dress, tight ankle bound leather shoes and a small leather flop hat. This was simple signature Zonk attire and she would wear versions of this garb throughout her entire life. She, like all female Zonks, adopted or otherwise, could see Roger. Roger became her best friend. Hazel and Zazel instilled into Ms. B the importance of humility, frugality, ambition and integrity. That all humans were alike and there was no difference in any person regardless of origin. All religions were bunk, and a person merely needed to heed morally and ethically to a sound philosophy. And the definition of the latter was defined by Zonks.

Ms. B was deep in thoughtful conversation with Roger during breakfast. Rey had fixed her, from Ms. B's own garden, a turnip and potato curried stew. Roger pulled from the pocket of his blue robe a steaming hot cup of pearl jasmine tea. Roger assured Ms. B that Hazel and Zazel were fine and doing well on Teegarden B, and they missed her much and that they would be together soon. How soon? Very soon, relative to the fifth dimension; time in three-dimensions moves incredibly fast. "How soon?" she persisted.

"Oh, about eighty of your years," stated Roger. Ms. B cried.

Their conversation went into the early afternoon. She wanted Roger to assist her in the garden but Roger, being Roger, loathed the English weather with the heavy mist and fog, mud and muck, and the stench of decaying fish matter upwelling from down below the cliff. They sat within the glass dome enclosure where weekend poets nightly fed out their mental flurry for a ravaging feast. Roger told her about her parents, Mikel and Amaia Viskarret. They were Basque. Mikel was a great fisherman of cod and mackerel in the Bay of Biscay, and Amaia sold the fish in a small market in the town of Santander. Amaia, pregnant, told Mikel that she wanted her child to start a new life in America. They sold their business and left from Bilbao to Brest to Calais and then to Dover, England—where their money ran out. Mikel was not able to find employment. He did not speak the language in England. Amaia eventually had the baby. Mikel and Amaia, hearing about the eccentric but wealthy Zonks, decided to leave the baby, during a winter storm, on the porch of the Inn of Zonk. They caught a boat back to Bilbao only to succumb to an infestation of yellow fever. Both died within hours of each other. They are currently on Teegarden B working for Hazel and Zazel. Mikel fishes for the Zonk Chef in the large ocean on Teegarden B and Amaia helps out in the kitchen. All was fine and well.

Ms. B thought Roger was full of shit and she told him so. "Ah, no matter," said Roger. "End the end, I am always correct." And he was. He turned to vapor and Ms. B suddenly felt lonely.

She sauntered through the empty hall to an 'inhouse' and gazed into the mirror. She was pretty, she thought. Though it was pretty in the Zonkish way. No frills or fancy things. Just plain beauty and she liked it. Basque. Well, that explains the pale skin and pitch-black hair. But where did the brilliant light blue eyes come from? Probably Basque, too. She wondered if she could be a great fisher person and captain of her own vessel. While she was pondering, the door chime clanged. It was Daniel.

Daniel Nye was the Zonk family accountant. Generally, he spent his life fidgeting about his East London office but today he made a special trip down to see Ms. B personally. Mr. Nye was a nervous person. Some would say he was neurotic. Ms. B plainly stated he was psychopathically nervous and his mind was agitated by numbers. She was right. Why, she thought, would a person choose a career that was so detrimental to one's health? Because Daniel was extremely good with numbers.

Stuttering—Ms. B hated it when he stuttered—Daniel described the current situation. The Napoleonic Wars were finished but the British debt was two hundred percent of the GDP. From what she could decipher from his babbling was that the Zonk family coffers were fine, but that the British economy would have to tighten its belt and this would mean keeping Inn staff at current wages with no raises and producing vastly discounted room rates to the majority of the patrons. The poet payments would also have to decreased, but since they were generally a manically depressed bunch as they were, it would only add to their depression and hence make them more creative. Great poetry came about from this time in history and the Inn of Zonk unfolded the sultry phrases from the mouth of the writer to a new attentive audience.

Reading a Soul in a Slurry of Leaves

by Opeia Zonk

"Once you discover that the heart of a demon only has a heart full of golden turds, then you get past the allure of gold and it is revealed that a turd is just a turd." — Buyu Li

Frugality and a conscious attempt at perfection in work was the Li family way. Buyu held this spirit. She worked the fields just west of Lincang City, in Yunnan, and picked the finest tea in China. Pu-erh. It was savored, not just for its flavor, but for the inherent healing properties in the leaves. The Li family had strict rules and imagination was just fantasy, and fantasy could not be afforded. Imagination was not based on grounded reality—there was no worth in it. But Buyu had imagination and much of it.

There was a time when China was the King of imagination. They were the first to introduce paper money, their science was at one time the best on this globe, and they invented a printing press and silk production, the latter the finest quality ever. They invented the solid fuel rocket, and hence gun powder, long before Marco Polo crossed the Silk Highway. Their celestial mechanics were fantastic. Toilet paper, porcelain, waterwheels, lanterns and a compass all belonged to the minds of China. But like the ebb and flood of the tide, all things pulse and cycle and now China, like most of Asia, produces efficient robots called humans and the spark of imagination is suffocated by rules and regulations. To break these rules and regulations would mean you were not Chinese and to be not Chinese would mean you were not from China. A dry ridged reed in the wind will break more easily than that of the green flowing stem. But all nations lose their way eventually. Particularly now, there are numerous dry ridged reeds in the US and the weather is very windy.

Buyu didn't care about the US. It was some faraway place that was decadent and slovenly, and the people did not concern themselves with tangible perfection in work. Ms. Li only wanted a place to be free to let her mind wander. To think and create or invent anything her mind could conceive. That, to her, was freedom.

Ms. Li found her solace around the streams that fed the great Lancang River. In her town, she would occasionally 'escape' the confines of humanity and wriggle down to the secret silent area of her own habitat. It had a large tree and several leaning bushes. It created her haven away from her home. There was a stream of pure clear water that laced its way through her haven and she would gently sit on a moss-covered large stone and look into the flowing liquid. This was hers. This area belonged to her.

She camped some nights in her haven protected by the might of a minor split of jade. This green rock was attached to her neck by a clumsy leather string. But it was hers. And it had magic to protect her. She was safe. She curled up into a pile of dead leaves and thought her own thoughts and let her mind run wild. Ms. Li thought of other worlds and other possible dimensions. Of people confined and restricted by the entropy of this universe. Like the inverse of cancer, entropy bathed in the rule of constant degradation. It all averaged out to a life of this.

A bright bluish light awoke her from a slumber into a dream. There was a tall man, not Caucasian or Asian, but with dark skin and dark hair. He was urinating into her stream. He wore only a blue robe. He said his name was Roger and he was actually from Lebanon. A place far away in the Middle East. Buyu did not understand but she granted him presence and they sat down on moss covered stones. He offered her a steaming cup of pearl jasmine tea but she quipped that she would not suffer to have such on her lips and that it would be Pu-erh or nothing at all. Roger appeared flummoxed but realized that was why he was here in the first place. He wanted this tea. The palates of both Teegarden B and C became wont of Chinese leaves, and that left him to further his divine nature into digging deep into the Chinese countryside. He found Buyu.

Roger wanted tea and she wanted a place for her imagination to flourish. The tea was easy in the bargain but Roger really had a difficult time to ascertain an area of pure imagination without rules and regulations. Finally, with a flash, Ms. Li was halfway between Strahan and Queenstown, Tasmania. She was in a simple cabin at the foot of

Mount Jukes. She was free and Roger had his tea. All was well with the Universe.

Author's Note: Once again, being home schooled and now with me being a Professor of Maths at Dangleberry, I gave myself an A for Abstract Academic Achievement. No one contested my deduction save Chester, who once again ate the damn paper.

The Sloths at Alvamore

"I have forded through the Rivers of Pain, Trust and Emotion, and I have found that Pain, by far, gave you the purest answer." — Richard T. Alvamore III

Richard Alvamore III, Dick, was a dick. He came from a long line of Dicks, hence Richards, and he was convinced he was a God. And only Gods could, should, and would be, white Christians. And he was all of that and much more.

The Alvamores were in possession of the large plantation next to the Dangleberry Estates. They raised cattle. Many cattle. This is the area that Chester absconded with the liberty caps that created such great hallucinations. It was also the focus of his advanced graduating class on scrounging for mushrooms. Many great creative ideas would come from this class. Buyu would be jealous.

Dick was not a racist. To be a racist you'd have to believe there was a race of humans beneath you. But Dick and his Alvamore Clan believed anything beneath them was NOT human and what was there, was just animals and they were to be treated as the cattle that they owned. They were not human but fodder for slaughter, meat or trade.

The Alvamore Estate was vast, but not quite one hundred and forty-five acres of lush bottom land. Cow patties aside it was fresh bathing grounds for the psilocybin mushroom to grow and proliferate. The 'Dicks' were megalomaniacs and narcissistic Republicans that pontificated false family values that they could not possible obtain. They were liars, cheats and charlatans yet their wealth pointed to a false success that the poor uneducated class wanted to obtain. It was all a farce. It was inevitable that something had to be done and Eni had a plan.

The Alvamore Estate had a serious weakness. It was built on a bridge of extremely thick limestone and had no easy access to the underground aquafer. They relied primarily on large brick cisterns. Obviously, they eventually resorted to bottled water but this was just for drinking.

Cooking food, bathing and shaving were based on the quantity of the rainwater saved. And saved it was. The cisterns were large brick vessels sunk into the land and fed through tubes and vents from the roofs of the nearby buildings. It was quite a complex operation.

Eni surmised correctly that a granulated form of the liberty cap mushroom genetically altered to adhere to its mind-bending variabilities, could be introduced into their cisterns of water. This inoculation would reveal their true personality and it would be forever etched into their psyche. They would be rendered mad.

Chester and his team of advanced mushroom fanatics dumped the genetically modified (GM) mushroom dust into the cisterns at Alvamore.

Within two days, the regional mental hospital personnel arrived and declared the entire estate insane. After a few tiring months, the Zonks purchased the Alvamore Estate for well under bid and built an asylum for the humane incarceration for the delusional. This asylum would be called the Zonk Farm for the Warped Noodle. Ward Three was for Republicans only. The Zonks were busy and the money was flowing.

The Shards of Tinkling Ice

"The fall of ice has a random arrhythmic sonic appeal." — Badger Zonk

It was cold. It was an English winter cold. The cold went through your clothes and directly into your bones. Ms. B was shivering under a decorative woolen blanket in front of a roaring fire. She sat on a carpet woven from brightly colored Chinese silk. The silk was derived from an inhumane process. Ms. B didn't know about that process. She was thinking of her future. The year was 1831. There was a war on, but at this time in English history, there was always some war somewhere in the British Empire.

The Inn was doing very well. The Zonk funds were full. Badger Zonk was listed as one of the wealthiest females in the entire British Empire. Although to look at her, you would never know it. She never went to any regal galas, she didn't dance nor wanted to, and she didn't welcome any suitors for courting. She managed the Inn, tilled her garden, and when time allowed, she had her nose in a book.

Ms. B read extensively but recently she had The Times delivered to the Inn of Zonk. The Portuguese Civil War was going on. The Baptist War, a slave revolt in Jamaica, was just heating up. Ms. B knew where Portugal and Jamaica were. In her Inn office, she had a large globe of the Earth tilted on a podium with all the known continents, nations and large cities mapped on the sphere. The oceans, seas and main rivers were, of course, included. Ms. B had this globe memorized by the age of nine.

The front door blew open and a mound of powdered snow rushed in to blanket the entry way. Icicles fell from the top door frame and broke on the floor to make the sound of tiny, dull-ringing bells. Rey had just come in with a load of wood. He secured the door and went into the kitchen. Some wealthy elderly patrons enjoyed the Inn so much that they stayed year-round. Ms. Clark, Ms. Fonk and Mr. Burr were in rooms 21, 28 and 35 respectively. Each room had a small cast iron stove to heat the abode. Elderly people particularly liked this Inn, not just because of the great food and weekend intellectual poetry readings, but simply because it did not have any stairs. Everything was accessible on the ground floor. And if you know any older folks, you'd get what that means.

Tobacco was the rage and Ms. B wanted a piece of it. She had a small house constructed with a large shed at the rear. This would become the Zonk House of Smoke. It was built out past the stables near the main road and, weather permitting, would be open around the year. She obtained a tobacco trader in America and ordered her first load of various cuts and flavors of East Virginia tobacco. The ship's wealth would arrive in two weeks at the docks of Folkestone Harbor. Ms. B would be there.

HMS Trincomalee was a decommissioned sailing frigate. She initially was used to run coal from port to port but was now owned by Mr. Wheatly and was hauling any cargo that anyone would pay for. And this round it was tobacco. The ship was late, it was the winter, and Ms. B got a notice that it would eventually arrive within a day. Ms. B took her carriage to the harbor and that is when she fell in love.

The Trincomalee was black with a white frosting on top. Like a spiked version of a very delicious chocolate muffin with pure white vanilla cream dripping from the upper deck. The ship was made of teak in India where the oak lumber was lean. She had fine lines, was quick and nimble, and she was fast. Ms. B bought the ship right there and suddenly didn't much care about the load of tobacco. She paid far more than it was worth but she did not care. She purchased the crew too at twice their going wage. The ship was hers and she was going to have some adventures. And she did.

Between the fading storms of winter and the early blossoms of spring, Ms. B spent her time between the Inn and her frigate. She never knew she could feel ecstatic. But that had to be the feeling that ran lightning up and down her body.

She took up fencing, dagger and scepter, from a retired French master who studied under Jean-Louis Michel. She bought a Hawkins percussion rifle direct from St. Louis and she became an excellent marksperson. She carried two cap lock pistols that were in the same caliber as her rifle. Using turnips and potatoes from her garden as targets, she could hit any tuber or root food within thirty to fifty yards.

The Zonk House of Smoke became a success and the physicians of the day lauded the health enhancements of the inhaled product. Ms. B turned the Inn of Zonk into the Zonk Retirement Villa and, at last, wealthy seniors could relax with the ocean cliff views and the Kapoor healthy eating, and the relaxing nicotine healing haze of the Smoke House's finest products. Within a month, the Retirement Villa was booked solid. Warm hydro baths were installed, a room for chess and checkers, and Rey brought in his brother to handle aromatic herbal colonics.

Between the Inn and her practicing, she weekly led her boat on calm seas into the English Channel. It was very difficult at first. The crew knew what they were doing but she did not. She had to learn to be a captain. She had to shed her doubt and build a solid wall of confidence— and she studied. Ms. B immersed herself in the navel theory of Blake, Nelson, Rodney and Cromwell.

The crew learned to respect her and her abilities grew, and she even managed a few modern moves of her own. The crew did not love her since that was not appropriate for a captain of a ship but they did admire her for her tenacity. She was a Badger after all.

The Trincomalee was decked out with thirty-eight guns, a full belly of salted pork, lemons, rum, wine and tack, and the merry lot set sail for the Atlantic region to stop slavery. All slavery.

The Underground Magnetic Railway

by Opeia Zonk

"I am going into space and I am leaving this planet. I want to exit this messed up nationalistic world. I WILL find a way." — Buyu Li
"Andale Andale!" — Buyu (last words recorded)

Ms. Li, in time, founded the Chinese Tea Import Company in Hobart, Tasmania. With her contacts in Yunnan and other regions in China, and with her remarkable skill set at negotiations, she became very profitable in her new southern hemisphere home. She did not like America. The fuel for the conservative Capitalist was destroying the uneducated into an imagined frenzy of irrational hate that any reason could not eradicate. She loathed Chinese Capitalism. The money was making the wealthy Chinese drunk on materialism and the rich government would not readily produce the imagination required for future new developments—so they stole it. Russia was mired in its own fossil fuel demise, and was frantically grasping out to utilize software for world terrorism as a deflection from its impending death. Where did that leave Buyu? She lived in the old English colonies that were attempting to reign in reason and rationality to a world gone crazy. It wasn't enough.

She hired Wang Chen, an old harbor master, to manage her property. She lived on a steep hillside of Mount Jukes and over time purchased all the land around her cabin. Mr. Chen hired Chinese laborers throughout Tasmania to come to the west coast and work for Ms. Li. And they did. She paid well. They were to dig a very deep and steep tunnel into Mount Jukes. Years went by, but Buyu was patient. The time in between she learned metals, magnetics, friction and scram engines. With a little assistance from Roger, she developed a craft of secure refined metal, and in the mountain hole she put down two parallel magnetic rails and created her space gun. It was a large magnetic rail gun and her craft was the bullet. The 'bullet' had inbuilt scram jets to ignite at maximum rail velocity. Ms. Li was going to be that passenger on the bullet. Buyu thought once she got to an orbit velocity she would continue out into the solar system to another planet in the galaxy. She was only partially correct. She would make a very low Earth orbit.

The 'bullet' was just that. There was no rocket. No terrestrial rocket. Just a seriously strong magnet that applied to two rails would expel the projectile out of this atmosphere, and fuel would ignite for the scram jets to secure that orbit. Ms. Li paid to tap into the Electoworks of Tasmania for her rail devices. Briefly, the island would have a temporary brown out and she would be gone. All was prepared and all was ready.

The bullet housing was made of complex magnetic metal alloys that were light but strong. It was magnetic metal since it had to levitate and skate down the magnetic rail. Inside was a simple chair and harness with computers that would track all pertinent activities and review all operations to the nanosecond. There were no windows since they increased drag but there were optical nodes on the surface that gave digital images in the main cabin.

Buyu had an intense last message in a Yunnan Chinese dialect that was not transcribed, but she reiterated it in another message that was standard English that merely stated, 'Fuck You All!'. She had the latter phrase etched on a plaque that was riveted to the ceiling inside her small flight cabin. And aloft she went.

The g-force from the acceleration made her initially pass out. But she regained cognition when the liquid hydrogen scram jets kicked in. This sailed her craft well into low Earth orbit. She saw the huge curve of the rotating Earth. She was free.

The hydrogen fuel leak occurred due to a poor metallic weld from one Gaspar Crump, but that was never to be revealed. The bullet exploded just shy of the main low orbit and the fire ball rotated around the entire planet twice and was viewed by all nations during night or day. The Etrida tribe near Manus, Brazil stated it was a call from God. All the fish in a nearby stream died as the comet completed its navigation. The fish died because of a low oxygen yield that year due to a low subsurface organic degradation, not because of Buyu's bullet—but the tribe didn't care. Much later, this entire tribe had thriving careers on Teegarden C.

The remaining massive metallic ball fell back to Earth and, at just after midnight, explosively landed right in the west side of the

Republican National Committee building in Washington, DC. No one on the ground was injured and just half of the building was destroyed. But emergency responders did discover a charred metallic plaque lodged in the wall just inside the office of the Chairperson that had Buyu's poignant farewell phrase. The Republicans took this personally.

Author's Note: It was what it was. I was balancing jobs between the Dangleberry Estates and the Zonk Farm for The Warped Noodle. We were very busy.

The Weasels Popped A Cork

"There are no sane people. There are just those that can afford the luxury of temporarily owning a false facade." — Zade Zonk

The Zonks wasted no time in taking over the Alvamore Ranch. Eni once again utilized a grid of computerized solar panels and Tesla batteries to get this entire estate off of public utilities. A well was drilled deep into the Dangleberry's southern area and a pump pushed fresh water into the mansion. The cattle were kept since they turned out to be very lucrative. The cisterns were filled with fine dark organic soil and several vegetable gardens were grown. Doctors and nurses were brought in, some staying permanently in the main mansion, and the Zonk Farm for The Warped Noodle was open for business.

The Warped Noodle took every initiate no matter what their wealth and background. They just had to be human. This facility, however, could not receive the criminally, homicidally insane. At least not yet at this juncture. Orderly, Wilfred Mannheim, designed the facility's logo.

Peace and calm were the orders of all days. Young psychiatrists were brought in, using their best updated methods and medicines. Because of a healthy Zonk family stipend, everything was free. The cattle brought in a moderate income and the vegetable gardens the fresh produce for the kitchens. An artist and craftsperson were brought in to teach indoor and outdoor painting sessions. Opeia thought it odd that no outside security was necessary. Indeed, the entire Noodle grounds were just fenced in by a five-foot-high stone barrier. The real security was in the mansion itself. There were a few guards but mostly trustees and volunteers. The guards had the only keys to all the locked doors. Each of the three floors held patients with varying degrees of mental acuity. Floor one was for near functioning individuals; floor two was not so much functioning, and floor three housed all those that were vacant of any notion of tangible reality. Floor three was for Republicans.

This asylum, like Dangleberry, had a large fishpond stocked with all sorts of native fish. Between late Spring and Fall, the patients, fully medicated, were allowed to roam the grass fields and small patches of trees. Painting, fishing, butterfly catching and croquet were all encouraged. Many were seen dancing in the sun in their pastel-colored robes.

One patient in particular, a Ned Bickle, was especially ornery. Not only did he suffer from a barely functioning mental state, but he also had alopecia areata (no body hair) and to top things off he didn't like clothes on his body. Opeia would often play checkers with Ms. Filbert, who thought she was a hedgehog, on the back porch of The Warped Noodle. How a hedgehog could manipulate checker pieces Opeia would never know. But when Ned was out on the grounds, it was hard to focus on her game, when a white, short, chubby, hairless naked man would run around in quick circles attempting to evade the strong hands of the orderlies. The fact of the matter was Mr. Bickle loved the attention and the orderlies really didn't mind. But rules were rules and patients had to wear clothes.

The Zonk Farm for The Warped Noodle became a national prize. In three years, the facility was awarded the finest mental hospital in all of America. The Zonks were baffled since all it really took was much money and hiring the best and brightest individuals to run and oversee this massive enterprise. It was simple and the Zonks said so. The States and Federal agencies were embarrassed and speechless when the Zonks so curtly pointed out that their agencies could easily obtain these goals if they cared enough. Frankly, it was obvious, the States and the Feds didn't care. None of their funds would be allocated for this type of endeavor.

The Federal government took this as a slight but it made national news and when you can't dazzle them with brilliance, then you have to baffle them with bullshit. And this particular administration only had bullshit to offer.

With much fanfare and media coverage, the US Surgeon General and his entourage showed up on a pleasant sunny afternoon. The Zonks and the facility doctors went floor to floor with this massive pulsing wave of human handshaking flesh, flashing cameras and digital motion montages. It was exhausting, but the Zonks persevered and it all culminated on the back grass-covered grounds with tables of cookies and a huge samovar of pearl jasmine tea—the latter courtesy of Roger.

The afternoon concluded when the US Surgeon General took to the podium and spoke for all Americans how the Federal government cares for the mentally ill. And then it happened. No one knew how Mr. Bickle got into the kitchen's lard supply. That door was locked and all keys were accounted for. Opeia thought it was Chester. And it was.

Ned, stark naked, lubricated his entire body from head to torso to toe with the tallowed ooze and he ran. And ran. And ran. The world became his game of Crisco Twister. The orderlies were not on watch since they were dutifully listening to the pontifications of a ranking Federal employee. Halfway through his belching cure for insomnia, the Surgeon General was tackled by what appeared to be a white lubricated marshmallow. Ned previously attacked a CNN reporter and stole the poor soul's cordless microphone. Mr. Bickle, when he collided with the ranking Federal employee, had this mic dangling out of his ass. It was all caught on dazzling digital media with the soundtrack, a garbled rumble from the lower bowels of Ned's gastro-intestinal tract, piercing the internet. The orderlies were unable to catch Mr. Bickle since he was very difficult to hold, and they continued running and rolling around until Ned ran, full force, into the surrounding rock wall and knocked himself out. This video went viral and most news agencies covered this event live. The US Surgeon General, covered in lard, slipped on the brick steps going up and out to his car. He broke his hip and, on a hospital gurney, was eventually airlifted to the nearest hospital.

The Zonks publicly were quite solemn in demeanor about this incident but privately they could not contain their laughter. Chester was given the Zonk Family Golden Truffle Cup medal, which he honorably wore on his collar for the rest of his life.

The Gynic Voyage of Captain Badger Zonk

"The main issue I had with being a captain was that I was the only female on-board. I also longed for intellectual conversation but there was none to be had." — Captain Zonk.

The Trincomalee (Comalee by the crew) went out in the Spring into fair seas. Captain B was just amazed at how the crew worked in unison and like some macabre dance moved and flowed over the decks to beautiful silent music. With salt spray in her long hair, Badger felt she was finally free and living. They stopped in Ponta Delgada for supplies and headed due south in a slow zig-zag pattern, attempting to snare ships full of slaves coming from the west coast of Africa to America. They caught their first prize just south of Cape Verde. An old whaling vessel outfitted for human African flesh trafficking unfortunately called Commerce was boarded without a shot fired. The American crew was baffled as to why an English frigate would stop their vessel. But Captain B knew they knew. The abolishment of slavery in the British Empire was just being ratified. They had to have known. The American captain thought that, at worst, he would lose his cargo but Captain Zonk put the entire crew into long boats and set them adrift, took the slaves aboard her ship, and she spent the last remaining hours of the light pummeling the Commerce with her cannons into a sinking, pulpy wet mass. She dropped the Africans off on the west coast of Africa giving each enough money to find their way home. Several Africans wanted to stay with her and she agreed, and like the rest of her crew, she paid them very well. Captain B grabbed the helm and headed the craft across the Atlantic to a slave uprising she heard about in a town called Salvador de Bahia in Brazil.

Inspired by a recent successful slave revolt in Haiti, the Muslim African teachers inspired the Muslim slaves to revolt. The Comalee arrived just after the start of the revolt, but the ship was able to get in several broadsides against the slave holders' rebuke. The Muslim slaves lost the battle but because of this brave effort, the Portuguese abolished slavery in Brazil.

Over the years, Captain B and the Comalee crew boarded and sunk seven slave ships heading to America. In all the confrontations, they suffered just twelve casualties. All slaves were returned to Africa or hired by the Captain. Many Africans on the slave ships died from starvation or infections. Zonk and crew mourned and gave them all a proper burial at sea.

During the 1848 Danish West Indies revolt, the Comalee was there giving cannon support to the slaves. This battle was won and led to the emancipation of all slaves in these islands.

Captain Badger Zonk was tired and wanted to go home. But she wanted something from the crew she fought with, sailed with and loved. She wanted a baby. On a sunny afternoon during ovulation, she passed around an empty carafe and the crew, all, donated to her future kin. With the help of a cooking baster, the product was delivered and the seed was sown. Fully six months pregnant, she captained the vessel for her final voyage back to Folkestone Harbor. Badger Zonk was warmly greeted at the Zonk Retirement Villa. Charles Kingsley was giving a lecture in the glass hall on social reform. The fire was roaring. All was well.

Zade

by Shato Perwer

Translated from Kurdish by Zackary Maxwell

The Predicament of Ms. Filbert

"The cages are not to keep us in, but to keep you out. You have to earn
your cage and to do that you have to obtain some semblance of sanity."
— *Ms. Filbert to Zade*

Zade actually loved those with mental issues. Most, in a poetic way, made sense and what a world it would be if they managed the planet. She was convinced that there would be no wars or hostilities. Granted, very little would be accomplished and net productivity would practicably be nil—but there would be peace. A crazy peace but peace nonetheless.

Opeia ran in to inform her mother that Mr. Filbert was gone again. For one that loved her cage, she sure liked to leave the facilities' grounds. But then, how do you attempt to cage a hedgehog?

The groundskeeper found her two nights later in an earthen mound of dirt near Hwy. 64 southeast of the facility. Zade thought the blazing flashlight beams into her hole illuminated a very cute old woman devouring a handful of earthworms. One dangled from her chin in an S shape attempting to escape her oral aperture. It did not succeed.

In her room (aka cage) she was cocooned into numerous cotton blankets that prohibited any violent motion. But Ms. Filbert was never violent. Ever. She easily succumbed to the whims of the insane and let them roll her body over and over. How could you possibly fight insanity? You must quietly lay still and smoothly tolerate the madness. Zade cradled her head on a pillow. Ms. Filbert turned to Zade and whispered, "It must be painful to be so clever in a world drowning in madness." Zade was looking down into her eyes and realized that she was crying. Ms. Filbert was shedding tears of pity for her and her intellect.

The Birth of the Market Grey

"The Zonk chrysalis does not so much produce beauty as it does resilience, confidence and a furious want to survive." — Badger Zonk

The uterus obstruction that birthed itself as a slimy vertebrate blob breached forth and gasped its first breath of salty sea English air. She was slightly bluish but quickly became pink, and typically Zonk, she crapped a dark green mangled turd. Her name was to be Cornelia Zonk and so it was. The seed that made it to Ms. B's ovum during her stay in Coral Bay, Virgin Islands, injected through a tube that contained the semen of all male crew members during her last voyage, was not from the bravest, or the most diligent or hardest-working man. Roger knew. It was spilt by Dudley Frump, a resident from a slum in Manchester's west side. He was the ship's carpenter's assistant. He drooled much of the time and many thought him psychotic but Dudley was extraordinary. He had a photographic memory and he loved wood.

The transcendence of her morphology led Ms. B to breastfeed and work. It was the only way. The Khartoum of her soul would not let her head be on a spike but on the edifice of the Zonk Villas for the Retired. She spread her wealth throughout the coastal regions of southern England. Building inn after inn of homes for the aged. She managed them all and they were to become the best ever. This was the beginning of a new market. This market was gray. Compassion, sympathy, patience, no stairs, hydrotherapy, healthy food, smoking and, above all, herbal enemas were the keys to success. All elderly were accepted and no one was turned away.

Nineteenth century England was notoriously class structured, and still is, and Ms. B wanted to break this down so that all 'classes' were to be as one and treated the same under a common roof. But unfortunately, this was not to be. Traditions ran deep in the British blood, and even though the Zonk Retirement Villas care and lodging were free to anyone, the poor and middle class chose to keep their aged faithfully in the bosom of family and around their families until the eventuality of their deaths. There were a few exceptions, but in general, the wealthy and the very wealthy were the only families wanting to part with a dribbling, incontinent, babbling, deaf, demented elderly person who easily embraced being mired eternally into a rotating echo chamber. What? What? What? And so on…

Also, why spend your wealth on the elderly when you can get someone pathetic and under-classed to do this task for free? Their noses went up and they happily booted out the aged, leaving them to enquire and echo, "What?" And so on…

The Zonk Retirement Villas were a huge success and they were geographically spread out from Dover, Reading, Swindon, Bristol to Exeter. This was costing Badger Zonk a great deal of money, but she felt it absolutely necessary for the health and longevity of England. Because most of the Villas' residents were from wealth this did not go unnoticed.

Queen Victoria was on the throne at this time. On a sunny late spring morning, Ms. B received a Royal carriage with a porter who had a note. The writ stated plainly 'The Queen would like your presence immediately'. Like all loyal patrons to the Crown, she agreed. And off she went.

The Queen, through her security, was informed that Ms. Zonk was very eccentric and to please receive her cautiously. The Queen had heard about Ms. Zonk and addictively read about her exploits in all that was printed. The Queen was a very big fan.

Ms. Zonk did not disappoint. She sprang out of the Royal carriage, gave the driver a sizable tip, and then she waltzed into Buckingham Palace. The Queen was not to be found. The butlers were very embarrassed and Ms. Zonk began to think this entire ordeal was a hoax.

Much to the vast rivers of time and fate, the day before, Queen Victoria heard about a new Chinese restaurant in the West of London. It was simply titled Shin's and was noted for its Xiang five-star spicy cuisine. The Queen ordered the steamed fish head with chopped chili. She never had Chinese food before but she was Queen after all and she wanted all five stars. Chi Wo Shin, a great great-grandfather to a future Zonk family Buddhist Monk, was honored to serve and concurred.

Due to security, the food was served with grace in the Palace's dining hall. The food tasters, after the initial gulp, could not feel their faces or their tongues so no pain, or poison, was registered. The Queen, famished, dove in. In hindsight, diving into this fare was on the verge of basic combustion, but since she was unable to literally feel her upper regions, from her torso to the top of her head, she continued ingestion. Which was a mistake.

Eventually, the next day, the Queen's chamber maids whispered to the Royal guards and they proclaimed that the Queen was indisposed and could not be bothered, and stated that the guest must be patient. Genetically, throughout time, and Roger would agree, the Zonks' main serious issue was that they did not have any patience. None. This led to numerous adventures and stories for telling but in reality, it was a mess.

The Queen's numbness, overnight, graduated and evolved into horrendous pain. It was upon her Majesty's third cumbersome rectal expulsion of shear molten lava that the Royal Loo's door was bashed in and a small but mighty sword-wielding female, dressed in leather tight booties, a leather dress and a leather flop hat, curtsied to the Queen while battling the shortcomings of the palace guards. The Queen roared, "Halt!" and ordered her guards, maids and all the Royal precession to leave. "NOW!" And they did.

The Queen, uncharacteristically, sitting stately on another type of throne, one of porcelain, had Ms. Zonk kneel and upon her proclamation declared Ms. Badger Zonk, now and forever forth, be Lady Zonk. The immense steam derived from the Royal lava to the water below and the honking and hooting of the Royal bowel, this moment, this one moment, taken in by Lady Zonk, became surreal. The Queen, wincing in great pain, kissed the Lady on the cheek, and bade adieu. "Please, quickly, adieu!" her forced voice projecting from clenched teeth. And oft the Lady went.

The Repentance of Gaspar Crump

by Opeia Zonk

"No good deed goes unpunished, but why don't so many bad ones? Wealth and connections? Obviously. But I will make good on my failure." — *Gaspar Crump*

Gasper was now chronically and clinically depressed. In his entire fifty-five years he did not achieve any minor status, welcome any trivial accolades, or merit even a solitary pat on the back for any effort. Gasper, his entire life, was a failure. But he tried. He was exactly like a male Pacific salmon with a severe neurological disorder and no matter how hard he swam up the river to let loose his paltry semen, he always just failed. Oh, this salmon bred: three times in the same vegan maladjusted argumentative twitching orifice. With three hate-filled children and one polemic spouse, who refused a divorce because of some fictional guy named Christ. This Christ was directly responsible for his imprisonment. His mother was going to name him Thaddeus, from the great botanist, Thad Haenke, but no, his father stated he was going to grace the child with the name of Gaspar, from the famous cellist and composer, Gaspar Cassado. Also, in Persian, the name meant treasure master, but in his known life, Gaspar never saved one lonely fucking cent. He could only seem to master poverty. It was amazing, thought Roger, that through the myriad of streams of time and fate, this Gaspar was nearly identical in nature, indeed, to a Thaddeus. And so it was.

Mr. Crump arose from his park bench in Cascade Garden, Tasmania. It was in fact his park bench since he slept on it over two hundred and eighty days out of a three hundred- and sixty-five-day year. The years of sweat, and wear and tear on this bench were immortalized by a well-worn indentation into the stone exactly the size of his frail carcass. He sighed heavily and curiously wanted to die. His swollen, protuberant red eyes watered what liquid he had left in his body. He looked like a desiccated ginger root left out on a granite rock in the sweltering heat of the outback.

He stumbled into consciousness as the piercing rays of the sun penetrated his dry pupils. He realized he could not physically close the lids on his eyes no matter how hard he tried.

Gaspar had a job recently. He could weld. He was not great at this occupation but he needed the work and he desperately needed the money. The dainty silk right shoe of his wife, covered in humane Ahimsa silk from some hippy farm in some hick state in the southern US, was carefully wedged between his buttock cheeks to remind him of his family focus. Ah, a job. He was delirious with pleasure but they almost fired him for his wobbling behavior and slurred speech. He was not intoxicated. Not on a job. But he hadn't slept for thirty-six days and that really jolted his being into carelessness. Gaspar knew he messed up the weld on the scram jet. It did not become apparent until after he awoke on the park bench. But he knew. He was tired. He heard the news. He could not rationalize another failure. He was done. Strangely enough, even if Buyu was to succeed in her orbital effort she would have just traveled around the globe and slowly starved to death. She did not plan very well and had no provisions and that was inexcusable, but even if her acceleration was enough to leave the solar system she would have slowly starved and frozen solid weeks later, covered in her own floating frosted excrement. Mr. Crump actually did her a favor. Buyu died quickly. She now lives on Kepler-442 b, thanks to Roger, and she teaches a course at the university on the massive health benefits of Chinese teas.

Now, frantically conscious and not wanting to lose momentum, Gaspar stole a bicycle and went out down the road to hail a cab at a busy intersection. With what little money he had left, he told the cab driver to quickly go to the Gordon Dam. And he did.

Mr. Crump, staring down into the abyss of four hundred and sixty feet, did not falter in his efforts. Passers-by stated clearly that he did not even close the cab door. He just pitched himself off the ledge, and without a horsehair worm in his noodle, sailed away. Some onlookers thought they heard yodeling coming from his open, rapidly descending oral hole. Through the machinations of time and space, the variables of chance and luck, the improbabilities of fate and the assistance of Roger, Gasper survived. Without a sole scratch or bruise.

Undeterred, stoically, Mr. Crump marched up the slope and tried three more times. Each a colossal failure. Gaspar Crump, for once, felt happy. He smiled. He was finally a success as a failure to suicide!

Roger set the battered soul up in Hobart to manage the Li Family Market. He bought a farm west outside of town and grew the hottest pepper known to humans. The Dragon's Breath. Gaspar sold it exclusively to a monk in Poncha Springs, Colorado at a bizarre Truck Stop in the mountains. His name was Monk Shin and he was notorious throughout the world for serving the most tasty, delicate and volcanically explosive Xiang River region five-star food ever.

Mr. Crump finally became rich. Even though his personal life was still incredibly miserable, he now could afford a virtual computer platform where, in his expansive office, he would daily, with the aid of a headset, virtually strangle the shit out of his wife. Over and over again. Life, like Ravel, loves banal repetition.

Author's note: This just became a habit. I kept a journal of this writing and backed up my digital versions so that the pig of a Chester could and would not ingest my entire work. I began to feel calm writing these works.

Mr. Tungsten Failed to Floss

"Despite your best intentions, when constantly juggling issues, crazy shit slips between your fingers." — Zade
"A pile of manure is just that. A pile of shit. But if you take the time to spread out the dung, gardens grow and harvests will be full. Don't hold on to your shit!" — Monk Shin

The students at the Dangleberry Estate continued to amaze national state college and trade school boards. This small lone facility produced some of the greatest future minds of this failing nation. And all to assist into turning the tide of a divisive failure.

Next door, the Zonk Farm of the Warped Noodle, while exacting in its core principles, still managed to juggle inconsequential trying matters. Turbulent were the eddies against the solid edifices of the troubled soul and once in a great while these walls, held together by a feeble mental adhesive, eventually broke down. And Mr. Tungsten's did.

Senator Tungsten, Republican, known as the Wolf, was used to heat and he often gave off a decisive false nature to his volatile behavior. He was a child molester. His prominence and wealth gave him access to young malleable girls that were in the throes of their blooming. And if they hadn't 'bloomed' it didn't really matter. They were there for his doting pleasure. Butter and not margarine was his main source of lubricant, and he used it copiously. No one human could touch his eminence. He was a God. Especially in the south.

The Senator was chewing pure grade, fermented and cured, East Virginia tobacco in long cut. The same tobacco once sold years ago on an English cliffside store near Dover—oddly owned by a past Zonk. He was a Fundamentalist Christian and he was a child molester. He was an addict on all issues—since he was five years of age. Tungsten was absolved of all indiscretions. He could take the heat. Forever. He was absolved. He was a US Senator.

Tinkling translucent egos of tangible littered minds birthed deviant plagued thoughts of expired intellect. They wanted pure virginal lust.

And it was all programmed early into the soft, waiting wet molded clay craniums of a small network of fooled nubile deluded minds. It all was 'consensual' since that meant, and the girl would receive, a crisp twenty-dollar bill, that could purchase a fine new outfit or toy. That was all that was necessary. These young 'princesses' were farmed to any man willing to pay the price. And the men eagerly paid for something so fresh. It was all there. The local police got their cut. They ushered off, violently, any person delving into their private neighborhood business. It was all thug controlled and it was all fine, and it was all seriously illegal.

As Zade's mother would easily concur, tickling the anus of a hibernating bear could only go unnoticed for just so long, and the resulting burst of awoken energy most probably would be volatile. And it was.

Krissy Ballentine was a small youth, a junior in Girl Scouts, a team leader at her Christian summer camp, a master twirler in her marching band, and was the parade lead two years in a row for the motorcade for the magnificent Senator from the heartland of the south, US Senator Tungsten. It was the Senator himself that hand-picked Krissy to be the lead since he wanted to gaze with pride at her lithe deft dancing, sable-soft fresh buttermilk colored torso. In the back of his limousine, his aides had to constantly mop up the spittle dribbling from his lip-licking mouth that fell copiously on his rather large double chin. Krissy was also member of the Senator's elite club of nubile youths. Krissy also had a serious ADHD condition.

The Ballentine family tried numerous pediatricians, but since this southern town was so small, numerous just meant two. The doctors were old and not exactly on top of their game so school counseling was provided. Ruth Zelotski, a recent Polish immigrant, spoke fluent English and had no previous experience in psychology, psychiatry or even child counseling. She got the job because she showed up and she honestly cared about children since she was unable to have any of her own.

When the US Senator came to stay in his home town for his recess, Dr. Beaverton finally took the time to read an old article on ADHD and told the Ballentines that their daughter needed to be on massive doses of Ritalin. And this occurred. The effects were curious, welcomed and troubling. The normal spastic, quirky, jaunty jumping, hypervelocity child was now as placid and pliable as a small blob of kneaded white wet toilet paper. It was in this state during a counseling session with Ms. Zelotski that Krissy unleashed a long soliloquy of events that mapped out the misdeeds of Tungsten, numerous city officials, policemen, barbers, garage mechanics and so many others. Mostly men but some women too. Ms. Zelotski was particularly troubled by the latter, since she was a very devout Catholic and knew that women on girl lust was exclusively owned by only the most pious of nuns. Knowing most of the small town was 'in' on this matter, she called the FBI and federal agents took over from there.

Thirty-two men and twelve women were charged with child molestation, and nine of those were also charged with the trafficking of minors for purposes of sex. And the big fish in charge that was snagged that day was US Senator Tungsten. Mad with rage he did not go quietly into the night but he went violently into the future, insane as an old English hat maker. Mercury, not Tungsten, will do that you know. All girls on the 'farm' went through extensive therapy, but sadly many would have obvious long-term issues with any solid future relationships.

Mr. Tungsten, Mr. Warble and Mr. Hives, all prominent past Republican southern senators, were all in a heated argument. Mr. Tungsten, incarcerated on the third floor of the Zonk Farm for the Warped Noodle, failed to floss.

Since Ward 3 was a group of highly unstable patients, they were given medication doses with concentrations well above standard issue. This rendered the patient docile, and thankfully in this case, chemically castrated. But what Mr. Tungsten discovered was that if you asked nicely to the nurse for some dental floss, and received it, you could later use it to tie a tight knot around the gonads and attached flaccid organ to trap blood into the schlong to form some sort of rigidity. And then, at your leisure, play with your swollen member. The nurse quickly got a reel of dental floss to calm down Tungsten and his fellow conservatives.

Two weeks later, orderlies discovered three black shriveled masses that were later determined to be penises with attached gonads. The conservative Senators tied the floss too tight, and in the frail lucidity of their medicated minds, forgot all about it. Their organs, without a supply of blood, turned black and eventually fell off the body. Chemical castration treatments were no longer necessary for these three inmates.

Princess Yula and Her Cheese

"Unfortunately, there have been minor incidents where the collateral damage was inevitable." — Cornelia

Lady Zonk employed most all her shipmates off the Comalee and gave them employment, training and education in the burgeoning trade of gerontology. This included all her African employees. Initially, there were some issues with the wealthy patrons and their new dutiful dark-skinned servants but when the Africans made it very clear that these rich pompous turds were only living because of them, their wrinkled doe-eyed faces bolted upright, smiled and were voraciously courteous to the 'caring' gentlemen.

Since becoming a Lady of the British Empire, the Queen pressured the wealthy to assume half of all funding for Lady Zonk's Villas for the Retired. Ms. B just rolled those monies over to the employees' salaries, and some individuals working for Lady Zonk became quite well to do.

Ms. Yula inhabited room 37 at the newly installed Exeter facility. She was from Kazan, Russia, and her family migrated to England during the early nineteenth century. She hated French people, French wine and, basically, French anything. Her family was very wealthy. Everyone in the family eventually died except her younger brother, who graciously installed her into the Exeter complex. She was very old and she was a Princess. She was not really a Princess but she claimed a blood line directly to the Romanoffs. Why not? Her brother's name was Rasputin!

Yula's neighbor in room 38 was Pipi Gagne, a French madam who at one time ran the finest bordello in Toulouse. Pipi once won the Bordeaux Kegel prize in 1815. She could easily take the pressured cork off any bottle of champagne with either her anal sphincter or vaginal Kegel. Easily. Years later this feat was duplicated by a woman in Nuremberg, Germany, who eventually became the wife of a farmer in the mountains of southern Colorado. A State that was not yet a State in America at that time.

Pipi hated anything Russian. The over boiled food, the vodka and the caviar were regurgitated. She was once given a Russian Matryoshka doll as a gift and she politely inserted the nesting wooden contribution into her vaginal canal, and with a swift muscle blast crushed the item into splinters. The war was on.

Cornelia (Nell), seven at the time, was transferred to the Exeter facility from the villa near Dover by her mother's request, to quell the impending confrontation.

Yula was General Mikhail Kutuzov and Pipi was Napoleon I. Unfortunately for Pipi, it was winter and a heavy snowstorm was forecast in southern England.

Nell was going to be too late. The snowstorm stopped her sharply in Swindon and she hunkered down at that Zonk Villa for the duration.

Like two aged jousting knights, both being in bath wheelchairs and armed with stout pine wood canes, they confronted each other in a small field of heavily fallen snow. The employees and the patients watched, riveted to the scene through floor to ceiling windows, out upon the frozen wasteland. The wheelchairs approached at a ridiculously slow speed as they slipped and slimed their way to an eventual and inevitable pathetic impact. Hours later, and much to the relief of the audience, they finally initiated contact.

Both wearing heavy garments of wool and thick scarves impeded their lusty desires to kill each other quickly. It was painful to watch two frozen, aged tortoises focused on violence yet doing so little. The audience—riveted was not the word, and many viewing patrons merely yawned and nodded off to the sounds of the string quartet playing Mikhail Glinka's 'A Life of the Tsar' in the dining hall stage. Unfortunately, Tchaikovsky's 1812 Overture was not yet written.

Yula was initially lucky with a direct pointed blow to Pipi's throat. She was unable to recover her breath for a moment which allowed Yula to blow to her left ear. Pipi, remembering her childhood fencing classes, retorted with a parry and a lunge, and strongly thrusted her cane into Yula's left breast with a following crack to the right-side of her neck. Dazed, Pipi took advantage of the pause to deftly place a charge directly in the middle of Yula's forehead. Yula appeared unconscious and all thought the ordeal was finally over. But Pipi knew the sly tendencies of the Russians and she was going to finish the matter with a strong cane impact to her Romanoff skull.

When Pipi's cane came crashing down, Yula instantaneously erupted with a lower jab and her violent penetration went deep between the legs of her opponent. All was frozen in time. They both looked at each other in amazement. And then, like a laboriously long melt of snow, the muscles on Pipi's lips pursed upward and with a cackling, a grunt and Kegel she split Yula's cane in two. Yula, with her feline movements and the speed of a striking snake, pulled the splintered remains of her cane out of her opponent's nether area and shoved the sharp stick deep into Pipi's right eye socket. And then it was all over. The old adage was proven correct. Never fight a Russian during the winter.

Aarav Kapoor—all the Kapoor family came to staff the Zonk Villa's kitchens during the expansion—produced a morsel of exquisite Camembert cheese. Yula in her lust devoured it and the cheese became a staple, sans medicin, to calm her down throughout the rest of her life. Pipi, though dead, relished the thought that even though she lost the battle, the cheese in Yula's stomach was very much French.

Warren's Gay Revenge

by Opeia Zonk

"A hole by any other name still smells as sweet." — *Warren*

Warren Hammer, genetically and inexplicably linked to the actual inventor of the tool called a hammer, was homosexual. This occurred throughout all animal genomes to some percentage and Warren, a human, was one.

Over the river and through the woods Warren ran, escaping the pecan farmer and his field hands. Warren, in the farmer's work sheds, was caught in the motions of flagrant sodomy with numerous extremely productive laborers. The farmer incorrectly assumed this penetration was responsible for his loss in productivity but much later on, reviewing the data, Warren's interventions actually increased crop harvesting by thirty percent. This fact was vigilantly ignored in 1972 and Warren Hammer became a ward in the State Mental Hospital of Summit Ridge. He was sixteen years of age. Even though homosexuality was removed from the list of mental illnesses in 1973, Mr. Hammer was incarcerated for life in this solid southern state. He was graciously discovered by the Zonks and transferred to the Zonk Farm of the Warped Noodle in 2018.

His frail ravaged body, all orifices vigilantly pilfered by Christian right-wing retribution, lay solemnly quiet on his bed in his own room, pampered by the staff. The Zonks were going to exonerate this poor soul. But what the Zonks didn't understand was that Warren was going to exonerate himself. The mental cocoon that wove around his brain isolated him from any irrational or rational blather and protected Warren from harm. Years of layered humane silk fiber produced a mental impenetrable barrier that even the Zonks could not puncture.

Warren was insane with rage. Not insanity based on an ill mind, but an explosively focused thought like a raped youth deprived of their life. This was beyond hate; it was retribution filled with vengeance. It was love. And love conquers all. So did Warren's passion.

Tungsten, Warble and Hives all swirled around a fathom of condensation that formed, to them, a rational reason to purge this 'grate' nation of LGBTQ individuals. Their legislation was exact and punishing; even though both Warble and Hives particularly liked the penetration of young boys, they voted to eradicate this method by pain of death. Their known proclivity for boy lust was silent and forgiven. God loves all— especially those who represent the vote of the uneducated conservative populace. Early Saturday morning, after the medicinal placation of the third-floor patrons, the Hammer pounced.

He hammered and hammered and hammered with his head and his body, and once with an actual hammer. But he failed to penetrate the dense fog of the conservative mind. He tried and tried but he failed. And then he thought of something new. Weak with weakness he tired and passed out.

Warren came back into this world not knowing where he was or where he had been. A nurse and two orderlies were dragging him by his arms on the floor and his mouth was screaming a noise that sounded like maniacal laughter. He bent his neck up and between his bare feet, and he saw his beautiful creation. Tungsten, Warble and Hives were all impaled on mop handles from their anuses through to their gaping mouths. They all three looked toward heaven in an effort to appeal to a God that was obviously deaf to their pleas. The three handles converged at the top and it all looked like a morbid tepee, which was fitting, since unbeknownst to Warren, the three conservative Senators all passed legislation against the Native American Nations to exploit their lands and allow industries to purge their soil for fossil fuels.

Author's note: I actually knew Warren from my class school in Ruth, NV. He was gay and terribly hidden in a closet. I suppose in hindsight he was doing this for his safety in such a screwed-up world. I heard that he had a very rough life but eventually ended up in Portland, OR, and won a seat as a State Representative.

Tantric Forgiveness

"We loved to dance. I think dancing was the only real way for Edna and me to communicate. Now, of course, we can't dance. We just silently have our memories." — *Lubenel Pike*

Lubenel and Edna Pike were inhabitants of the Zonk Farm of the Warped Noodle. They both stayed in Room 11 even though the rules stated that cohabitation was not allowed. Fair to say, their separation would probably have been better for their treatment, but Zade just could not separate a couple that had been married for over sixty-seven years.

Lubenel and Edna were engineers. They were not your basic engineers. They did not build housing or construct bridges, or design anything necessary for the planet or its inhabitants to survive or positively utilize. They did not blueprint out combine machines or fruit picking devices. They did not even construct robots to eliminate standard repetitive movements that put so many unfortunate people out of employment. No focus was spent on expediting washing, drying, freezing or embalming. No, their brains were harnessed to complete one simple task: to make a better mouse trap. The mouse was a human and the trap was weaponizing anything to hasten the eradication of various and sundry tribes of humanity, the latter deemed 'bad' by the US government.

Lubenel and Edna worked at the Treblenko 'Cleaning' Facility in a small narrow valley in the middle of Utah. The only thing they had in common, besides being engineers, was they were both not Mormon. They together worked alone meticulously fixated on their one true task and that was the instantaneous death of one to numerous US adversaries. Management loved their results. They left them alone. And alone in a basement lab for several years they worked without once uttering a single word to each other.

Somewhere along this pathological timeline the two got married. No vows. The Reverend assumed they were mute. It was a moot point, since they did not love each other and they were inextricably bound by being competitive.

No one knew when it all began. It probably began from their first physical encounter. He stole from her and she stole from him, and their work and their methods overlapped to form a binding result of pure clarity in a machine whose sole purpose was to achieve plain unadulterated imminent death. It was all a success of his, but no, it was hers, ah, no it was his. And it went on and on. The two were not successful without the other but they never saw the unique embrace of two vibrant melding minds: just the wrath of the final true creator's outcome.

Then, one day, Tallulah Stiff, no relation to the ultra-famous and wealthy CEO of the same name from the Stiff Family Mortuaries, discovered this confrontation and understood this needed to be amended for the sake of this wonderful killing industry. She, herself, built with a toilet paper tube, copper wire, transistors, a battery and a speaker, developed a simple AM radio. She carefully brought it down to the Pikes' lab and dialed in, at two a.m., to the rock 'n funk beat of Bubba Jackson.

The thumping cadence was solid. The beat was felt in the heart. The bass was loosening the corpuscles of the liver and the vibe went straight to the reproductive organs. Mine included. The toes started first, then the heels, then calves and thighs, and hips and body and it was all over. The Pikes were jamm'n and for the first time in both their lives they smiled.

Unfortunately, these two were Caucasian and could not find rhythm if you stuck a mono-flow pulsing dildo up each of their asses, but it didn't matter. They were jamm'n like salmon who suffered from serious neurological diseases pathetically swimming up a river to never deliver their paltry semen and eggs to a pool that would never hatch their offspring.

Even though they could not stand each other, they worked and danced and worked and danced and eventually just danced, and their productivity stopped completely. Ms. Stiff was fired since she introduced the music device to the Pikes and she now worked in a meat packing plant on row three behind a large meat grinder that had arrived from France. Norm's soul was in this grinder but Ms. Stiff knew nothing of that.

The Pikes were put on leave and asked to reconcile their issues before returning, but they never returned. They left the facility early before daybreak and entered their Opel Kadatt sedan but instead of driving home directly, they took the mountain pass road to an overlook site to enjoy the snoot of the sun as it peaked out over the desert ridge. It was stunningly beautiful.

Edna and Lubenel suddenly realized that forgiveness was in order. She saw it in his eyes and he too saw it in hers. They knew in their hearts they could not stand each other, and they were at their best when they were the most competitive, but that did not mean they could not forgive each other for the years of unspoken, but valid, hateful glaring body language that regurgitated its visual spikes through both of their souls. At least now they had dancing.

She leaned into him and he into her. They hugged. Unfortunately, Lubenel's knee went up and knocked the manual transmission into neutral, and since the brake was not on, the sedan rolled silently off the edge of the overlook and down into the dry desert valley below.

The Pikes broke their embrace just as the car collided with a large boulder which broke both their spines between L2 and L4. The couple spent the next day crawling back to the top of the overlook with just their arms. Their legs were all dangling useless behind them.

On the top of the overlook were Dottie MacKey and Daniel Vasquez. They too were in an embrace, and in a car, but one of young carnal lust and Dottie was not going to stop her focused ambitions. She being short and rotund was not to find a mate that would take her denotation of hormones, and she was sick of fornicating with her father's Great Dane, so nothing, and she meant nothing, was going to stop her now. Daniel, the son of a migrant worker, was perplexed at this altercation since his mind was seriously stuck in a theoretical physics conundrum. While Dottie was ripping off both of their clothes, Daniel was blathering about black holes and how they could consume entire worlds and solar systems, and that these black holes could be many times larger than our sun and some only the size of possibly an apple. But how could that be? Both now naked, Dottie leaned back abruptly, spread open her thick bulging thighs, parted her labia and yelled, "Let this black hole suck you in, you FUCK!" And it did.

Dottie and Daniel's hollering drowned out the pale pleas from the Pikes, who were helplessly scrounging outside the rumbling car attempting to open up a door. When the pleasant spring storm blew through the Naugahyde, and the two sweat covered carcasses slithered free, Daniel was convinced that black holes could conceivably be smaller than an apple. "Help!" was faintly heard above their pounding hearts.

Dottie and Daniel packed the ragged creatures called Pike into the back of their car and took them quickly to the hospital.

After months of physical therapy, it was concluded that the Pikes were to both be bound to wheelchairs since they were now paraplegics. Because of their one pathetic attempt at forgiveness, they now not only did not have that, they both could not indulge in their newfound love. They could not dance. Lubenel would become matter and Edna would become antimatter. They didn't hate each other, they just wanted to destroy each other. They were shipped off to the Warped Noodle for further analysis.

Zade and Eni had no compunction in letting the Pikes use their laboratory. In fact, they enjoyed looking over their work and reviewing the methods of their madness. And madness it became.

Silently, Edna and Lubenel worked in the lab. They rarely stopped for rest or food. If they heard music, they both became melancholy and made the orderlies turn it off. Finally, after months, their combined efforts of labor were complete. No one, Zade, Eni, Opeia or Chester, had a clue as to what this device was.

In the back of the Warped Noodle's grassy green lawn, orderlies followed the Pikes' instructions to the letter and placed it all out. The design was odd. It was two rails that were laid parallel to each other separated by just three feet. Each of the rails was approximately one hundred yards in length. What no one knew was that these were magnetic rails in which the polarities were switched exactly at the fifty-yard mark. The rubber tires were removed from the Pikes' wheelchairs and Edna, to the left, and Lubenal, to the right, were magnetically locked into the rails, facing each other. Edna wanted to have the starting toggle switch. A small crowd appeared on the back porch and to Zade it looked like two gunfighters ready for an afternoon duel. To power the rails required all the electricity from the Noodle and that too of the Dangleberry Farm.

It was quiet. Not a breeze stirred the leaves. Facing each other, Edna nodded to Lubenel and she pressed the toggle switch. Zade and others said it just became a blur and in less than the time it took to blink just half an eye, there was a series of loud sonic explosions and a massive impact. It was all over. The Tesla batteries on both Estates had to be replaced—they were all burnt out. A scorched blast dimple was at the fifty-yard mark indicating the final impact. Nothing was left and the Pikes, along with their wheelchairs, all were vaporized. Eni later discovered that by the Pikes' notes they were to achieve approximately Mach eight. And they did. All this for a pathetic feint at forgiveness. Buyu Li, hearing the results from Roger, was pleased at the effort.

Nell's Prodigious Placement

"What can I say? Adventure is in us Zonks. Let it be said, we lived while we were alive." — Lady Zonk

The year was 1877. Cornelia (Nell) Zonk was applying to colleges. Her exam scores were well above her male peers but she had one antiquated issue. She had a vagina. Historically, that never stopped the Zonks before and it would not stop her now. Cambridge emphatically stated no. Oxford waffled and could possibly let her attend lectures if only she did so behind a screen and not to interact with the male school populace. And Oxford would not let her matriculate as a graduate no matter how well she scored. Screw that shit.

After numerous declines and rebukes, a small college in Pennsylvania accepted her. The college was founded by the Quakers. It was Bryn Mawr College. Although this was a liberal arts college, and Nell was into the sciences, it was a start. Sometimes all it takes is a small crack to start an avalanche and Nell was going to surf this impending avalanche as far as it would go.

There were no goodbyes. Lady Zonk and most of the Kapoor family assisted her to Liverpool and to the docks. There were just hugs and no tears. The Zonks would survive. It was inevitable. The ship would sail to Boston and a carriage would take Nell to Bryn Mawr. The adventure was on.

America was a foul fowl and really only owned up to the name of freedom in terms of a dissolution of some class structures and an enhancement of personal social norms that were eagerly exacerbated by the rising youth culture. But Zonks throughout history had this ability already. It was in their bones. So this was nothing new, just irritating in how unbridled their so-called freedom would go. The Americans were more interested in the distraction it fed rather than using it toward a greater goal of public assistance. Nellie Zonk ignored them all and buried herself into study and her solitary room. For whatever reason, the northeast US gravitated to English standard etiquettes but Nell, being English, did not know an oyster fork from a salad fork, or a soup spoon from a dessert utensil. It did not matter. It was all crap. One ate and that was it. Tea? One drank and that was it. The steaming beverage could conceivably be served out of a jar. What did it matter how it got into your mouth? That was a waste of time. And Nell's time was precious.

Her dress caused some concern. Her garb of a leather dress, leather flop hat and tight-fitting leather booties made her appear like a mad Indian. But the only Indians she was familiar with were the Kapoor family that served in the Zonk Retirement Villas and she did not look like any of them. And they were not mad; they were her friends and family. The board called her to presence and she simply stated that her family had worn this material for many generations and it was to be tolerated. Lady Zonk, and even the Queen herself, interjected and Bryn Mawr acquiesced, and Nell Zonk could wear her outfit.

Nell did not do sports. Sports was such a social organization in America and she chose not to participate. Thanks to the Lady Zonk's tutelage, Nell could fence, use a dagger and a sword, like few others. She also could shoot both a rifle and pistol with great accuracy. One May afternoon she took on five male fencing masters from a nearby school and she bested them all quickly. A shooting match followed and she outshot all male and female participants. When asked how she managed this feat, she just stated, "Don't fuck with a Zonk!" And they all, to a person, left her alone.

The school board also did not like the fact that Nell Zonk was an atheist. This school—obviously, she knew—was founded by the Quakers and when she was brought to a school committee and confronted with this evidence, she looked them all in the eye and clearly enunciated that the only time she 'quaked' was when the spirit of HER lord, which was she, was in her loins and she was masturbating toward the conclusion of an amazing climax! The committee never requested her presence on this issue ever again.

Nell graduated with honors and was top of her class, but she was absolved of her duties for addressing the petulant crowd since she was translucent to cordial demeanor. Tilda Twat took to the lectern and gave a most pungent droll speech on the growth of the maturation of the female mind. Nell was absent. She was moving to Boston University since she was accepted into a PhD program in biology.

Dr. Zonk graduated again with honors. Upon her name she, again, was vacant from the podium. She didn't attend the ceremonies and even though her Lady mother and the Queen herself stated that she could come back to England to lead the best laboratory in existence in London, Nell went absent and showed up months later in a bar in Cheyanne, Wyoming. Dr. Nell was free.

The prostitutes thought she was an upstart. Looking like a slim potato turd all wrapped up in tanned leather and viewed as a cast-off squaw, she took the latter as a compliment then ignored them all. But she had money. All were amazed at how it all appeared. She may have been a pale Indian but she had poise and she had savvy. She was quicker than a viper in her movements and her wit. Soon she had respect.

Nell moved from Cheyanne, WY, to Hayden, CO, and then to Glenwood Springs. There she funded a health hospital for the feeble minded. She then went to Durango and retired in the southern Colorado town of Alamosa. The lights went out but not until she birthed a young girl via a turkey baster full of rowdy cow poke seeds who were on liberty in the back room of a bar in Powderhorn. Margot Zonk was eventually born in a small cabin outside of the San Juan Forest. She was a healthy spunky slimy squid. And she was a Zonk.

The Haberdasher's Cocks

by Opeia Zonk

*"From rumor I heard that they were the best. I have never seen such
magnificent head and loin wear. Their own designs you know.
Fashioned after classic bowlers and homburgs and such."* —
Karishma Kapoor

Karishma was a friend to Nell and to the Zonk family. Her parents, uncles
and aunts became the kernel of chef salvation for this entire Zonk
retirement industry. Karishma became a confidante to Nell. That bond
would never be broken.

Over the many years, Karishma became ward over the Exeter's Villa
main library. Over time, she matured into the main librarian for all Zonk
manuscripts and publications. All. She was the Librarian of Zonk. She
read everything in this vast library. She had to know this knowledge. She
was the master bookkeeper. Karishma was potentially the most soluble
librarian for research at this time. Karishma had the mind of a master and
she used it liberally. Many notable minds used her expertise to plumb the
depths of known literacy and they were all successful.

The Zonk Family Library was founded by Lady Zonk on a large
patch of land in Cumnor, England, just southwest of Oxford. This
proximity would grant scholars access to rare first additions and some
virtually unknown texts. Lady Zonk was passionate about her collection
and it contained some of the finest scientific knowledge known to
humankind.

Karishma ran a tight ship. There were no books checked out. All
books to be reviewed were requested weeks in advance, and the patron
was able to keep the text in a closed room on the premises for review for
only eight hours. The Zonk Library was generally booked solid for
months in advance. Science researchers, advanced degree university
scholars and two really bizarre haberdashers frequented this
establishment.

Culley and Culley Haberdashery had been in existence since 1786. Their gentlemen's hats, women's bonnets, chastity belts and royal codpieces were the finest in England, if not the world. The Zonk Library was built right next door.

Culley and Culley, who took over from Culley and Culley, were not even remotely related and were even raised on separate coasts of England. Strange, they looked identical. But much later, DNA analysis discovered that they were twin brothers separated at birth and raised in two distinct English lower middle-class families both named Culley that were not related. The two met at Hoxton at the Haberdashers' Company and fell in love. They exhibited the most extreme form of narcissistic behavior known and, being gay, they fell in love with their exact image. There was only one true love and that was the physical love with one's self. Literally. And they did that regularly—even during working hours. Roger was having his fun.

Karishma would often see Jim and James Culley in the Zonk Library. They often would reserve a room and look at past publications to resurrect old archaic fashions, and reintroduce themselves into the now classic English period. And they both were very successful.

Karishma wanted to write a book on the Culleys and their amazing hats, and rich but tawdry accessories. Their wealth of history was just across the street. But how does a non-fictional author writing a fictional story about a fictional librarian that composes a non-fictional book about two gay haberdasher brothers that frequently fornicate during the making of fictional hats, make any sense? Somewhere along the line there must have been truth. And there was. It was all true. No sane person could make shit like that up. But who was actually sane?

The Culley brothers opened up their secret sauce of a factory in the basement of their haberdashery. A locked rusty iron door dripped with condensation from the steam heat necessary for the formulation for their cranial and loin adornments. Creaking open, Karishma fell face forward into their land of wonder.

A golden light splintered the dense fog and it was through this she skated upon soft clouds of mechanical pulsing splendor. The tuck and clomp, and the zig and zag of mechanized well-oiled iron animals flattered the egos of the brothers as they sullied their own hands with felts of wool, beaver, rabbit, horse and camel hair. There were also leather, inhumane silk and velvet tassels. A choir erupted into Schubert and Mendelssohn—later Brahms and Liszt—the bodies of boy assistants, naked from the heat, undulated with the beat of the rhythm of the machines, and they all produced magnificent art to be worn on the top of a human skull or the protuberance of a loin. The choir boys, borrowed from the grasps of Satan's claws, from the parishes of Cumnor Hill, Deans Court and Chawley, were in the embrace of love incarnate. And they were loved.

Karishma, being with vagina, had to leave. It was inevitable, but she had enough inspiration for a first draft and she got to work.

What was amazing to Karishma, and to Opeia and to the actual author of this book was that Jim and James Culley had enormous copulation organs. One gawker, and that would be me, stated that it was as if nature designed three legs instead of two. Obviously genetic but also biologically useless, the brothers suffered. But not really, as Karishma discovered there are so many animals on earth to consummate such an obtuse organ and the Culleys frequently purged.

The 'magic' of their designs was later, and only, revealed to Karishma. In the sweltering basement hollows, felts of various animal hairs were laid down on tables that were systematically tethered to lace leather chains. The Culleys would reveal their flaccidness and pinch close their eyes. Each would envision a hat design and with a wham with their organs on the exposed fabrics, the hats would just appear. Karishma did not believe it at first, but it happened again and again, each with a chorus of male children's voices swelling through the mist of dense haze. It wasn't until much later that the entire town went sane with insanity and the Culleys' magical source of mercurous nitrate became the melded fabric of lore.

Author's note: This was just on my hormonal whim. Being home schooled basically most of my life and only seeing male genitalia through science books, I had to imagine. It was apparently never an issue with Eni or my mother but I had an itch that needed to be scratched.

Tallulah's Incarceration

"Basically, humans, particularly Americans, are messed up with the concept of death. They want to ritualize it and cloak it all with religious ceremonies but the fuckers are just dead anyway and they will just clot up the veins of Mother Nature if the living were to complete their putrid tasks." — Ms. Stiff

Tallulah Stiff—not the poor one in the Utah meat packing plant on row three behind the grinder that contained Norm's soul, but the wealthy one that ran the most successful human dead recycling agency on the planet. The only issue was that she did it with only the Earth in mind and not the living humans that attempted to lay sole claim to the hold of the paltry remaining shell of what was once living.

Chemicals and plugs, makeup and draining, surgical sutures caked in with skin colored paint all to make real the vision of the dead as they were in life. This wasn't natural. This was not what Mother Earth had in mind for her flock of inhabitants. Life fed on life. It always did and it always will. Ms. Stiff, daughter of the Jewish family Steinberg that invented the pumpable penile prosthesis, created the first ever green model of carcass planning. She was very successful. She just didn't tell anybody about the green part.

Tallulah started with five mortuaries throughout the South. Why the South? They were the most fervently religious and they tended to spend extravagantly on their dead. Quoting the business model: location, location and location.

All the Stiff Mortuaries had the same floor plan, engineered with rooms for sullen reflection, a quagmire of self-pity, the searing love of massive guilt and, finally, the cooling bath of retribution through stark opulence to house the dead as a golden chariot waits for their departure to the gates of Heaven. Ms. Stiff had subcontracted a couple of solemnly depressed engineers call the Pikes to lay out this labyrinth of a blueprint. For this feat alone, the Pikes were to receive no money but the platinum plan for the 'final exit'. Much to Tallulah's chagrin, the Pikes did not even leave an atom that would require embalming. The Pikes did it the right way.

The plan was simple. Have all those that entered go through slowly to the cadence of some somber depressing music through each room in order on the only path. The only exit was forward and one merely had to promulgate ploddingly to view the excruciating debt that surmounted by each room's memories of a person that obviously paid more than just a measly $10K-30K for a righteous burial. They paid with their lives. And how much was that worth? A pamphlet, on recycled paper, in large print sternly reminded the relatives that price, not piety, expedited the souls from the living to the open arms of God. They paid. Oh, they paid. Their own souls were cleansed with each dollar provided.

Tallulah believed fervently in recycling. If the body was recently demised, her staff would harvest all the pertinent organs, put them on ice, and ship them off to a list of needing patients who would pay dearly for an extension to their short mortal coil. The remaining carcass would be pitched into a holding pond containing rich organic matter that was anaerobically contained and designed to produce methane that was later piped back into the mortuary for heat and cremation combustion. The service was simply a ruse. The deceased, a mannequin with a 3D-printed latex-covered replica of the dead, was artfully colored into a life-like hue and suited with clothing that would show up on numerous other such 'individuals'. Recycling was key. It was the way Mother Nature operated her foundation of the end of life. Open caskets were the most expensive since the most work. Closed caskets were considerably less, due to the mourning clause, but still outrageous. The more you physically mourned, the more was slightly taken off of the combined total cost. Self-flagellation was encouraged, but if even a hint of painful enjoyment was discerned, then no reduction in cost was provided. And there was always some hint of enjoyment. Always. Cremations were the same cost as an open casket. The urns were expensive, elaborate and magnificent, though, honestly, made in a sweatshop in Bangladesh very cheaply, but who would know the difference? The buyers were in a state of mourning. It was the methane to barbecue the body to ashes that was actually free from the oxygen-free holding pond that was labeled most costly on the final bill to complete the entire toasting process. Well, it took physical labor to haul the carcass to the festering bog to begin with. Work was work and work had to be paid for. Even if that work were mental. And Ms. Stiff and her staff thought much—especially how to cut corners.

Burials were perfunctory and an elaborately adorned casket of oak, teak, humane ivory, gold, platinum or any combination of quite possibly anything that was expensive, was laid to rest, handfuls of dirt were poetically dropped into the hole and all mourners left. Only for Ms. Stiff and staff to remove the casket, extract the mannequin, refurbish the velvet or Zonk-made humane silk padded upholstery, and quickly replace the casket back into the main entrance room with the other caskets for another round of solemn reflection. It was a boon and it was environmentally just.

As is always with the human unit, greed eventually dominated and someone came up with the great idea of removing those slated for cremation to be pitched with the others to the methane-producing holding pond. This would increase methane production and the methane could then be piped into the nearby town to the gas utility grid and more money would be made. It was clear cut. But what actually was burnt in the cremation cylinder? Nothing! Small dead animals from road-kills to 'missing' farm fodder were put on a large wood pyre, and with bellows, turned to ash. Who would know ash from ash? No one. And that was the brilliance of Ms. Stiff.

Five mortuaries turned to twenty, and twenty became thirty and the Stiff Mortuaries flourished throughout the nation. They never got the green star of environmental approval until many years later. The green part of Tallulah's process was still very much a secret.

As with all successful operations, dissension occurred from within. Someone didn't get their promotion because that someone dropped a carcass during a procedure, or something rude was implied about the dead that was not appropriate for the ears of the already demised. The pathetic became apoplectic and employees started to bundle in hateful bunches. Then came the Union for Carcass Handlers and it all exploded from there.

The FBI rounded up Tallulah Stiff and some of her staff. The others plead out their terms of guilt and went free. Some went on to write really bad prose on the subject of the dead that became bestsellers. No accounting for taste in anyone. Most of the nation loathed Ms. Stiff and her efforts, but a small brave group of environmental activists came to her aid and proclaimed her a hero of nature. That said, she was deemed insane and put cautiously into the Zonk Farm of The Warped Noodle.

The Zonks knew Tallulah was guilty only of fraud, but honestly, despite her rampant Capitalistic behavior, she really did a favor for the planet. Tallulah introduced green cemeteries at both the Noodle and the Dangleberry Estates. She invented the mushroom shroud that was a bag of fungi, placed entirely over the body, and the spores would harvest and would literally eat the dead, and produce a wonderful organic mushroom covering. Chester loved it the most.

After eight long years of rejuvenation therapy, Ms. Stiff was released. She became the lead economist for a corporation representing Big Oil and she was responsible for cutting many corners. And she did.

The Temptation of Margot

"Nature is only beautiful when looking from the outside. In nature it is a brutal elegant parade of eat or be eaten. It always has been. You should never romanticize that which you don't understand. There is nothing more feared than when one gets between a baby cub and her mother." — Mr. Casull

Dr. Nell set herself up in her own apothecary. Using her knowledge of traditional medicine and that of her newfound Native American shamans, she delved into the science of herbal health remedies. The Indians called her 'Smoking Moon' since her tiny cabin always appeared to steam with fog from her numerous experiments and mostly during a full moon. She was paid on a sliding scale. If you were rich, you paid handsomely; if you were poor, you paid with what you had; if you lied, you paid with your life. It was simple and easy to understand. Humans needed simple.

Mr. Casull was once a young fur trapper in the Colorado Rockies. The furs grew lean and he became a guide, a mountain man, and then he just settled down in Alamosa as the Sheriff. He was tired. The fact that he even survived that rugged life was a testament to his bravery but he would say mostly luck. He rented out his old cabin and acreage to Dr. Nell. The doctor part was difficult for people to enunciate, she being a female, but if they just thought it was her first name it was easier on the palate.

The snows came and went but Nell felt at home here and grew two large gardens: one for herbs and one for vegetables. She and Margot, in a papoose, would take off each fall on their mule to hunt bear, elk, deer and prong horn. The good doctor was very successful. She canned what she could not consume and jerked what she could not ingest. Nell was self-sustaining and off of the grid. She was one with nature.

Margot's father was unknown and most, to the irritation of Nell, thought he must have been a drunk drifter. DNA analysis later discovered he was not only that but much more. Margot's father's lucky seed in a turkey baster tube in the back of a bar in Powderhorn, Colorado, was none other than the notorious French fur trapper and trader, Coureur des Bois. Finally, the Zonks had some genes to assist in their independence.

It was at the turn of the century and the Boer wars were flaming on in South Africa. The tune the British played was for the Queen and Empire but literally it was for a greedy businessman named Rhodes and his lust for gold and diamonds. His conquest of all those mines cost the lives, in feint of loyalty, hundreds of thousands of souls. All gone. But he got his gold and diamonds and his wealth. He even has an honorable scholarship to his name. Basically, if past names were on anything from a doorknob to a street to a county, those persons were most probably pricks. And they were.

The name of Zonk was not on anything. The name eventually became known historically for perseverance and progressive thought.

Alamosa, Colorado, grew in the west. As a hub in the pathway from Taos or Durango up to Salida to Denver it became a stop for weary travelers. Churches followed with schools. The most affluent were skinners and taxidermy folk that sold pelts and rejuvenated stuffed raging animals to wealthy eastern pansies that could not even shoot a gun. But they tried. And those mountain treks Dr. Nell commanded were all perilous trips and they never returned empty handed. All were pleased.

Nell, still breastfeeding, carried her love load on a board of pine on her back that included laces with deer leather and wool. It was Margot's cocoon during hunting season.

An anomaly is just that. It isn't conducive to a standard set of ideas or rules, and in most religious societies, those differences are viewed as a sickness. Nell and her family were not sick. But the people of Alamosa thought they were.

As in all realms of progression, change was deemed abhorrent. The static nature of just trivial placidness could not, and would not, deviate from the sound monotonous beat of the pathetically mundane. And Nell Zonk and child represented change.

The town was polite and patient. Male suitors, many very affluent, were all turned away. But when more showed up at her door, she presented them with the double barrel of her buckshot loaded rabbit-eared gun. Civility melted as quickly as ice from a late June storm.

The child was innocent and it had to be saved. The town knew it was not baptized by this independent atheistic female. The baby would go to Hell. It was written on whatever the prophets wrote it on, to be read by literate people and the only literate person in Alamosa at that time was the mother of the child who needed to be saved. They formed a committee and advanced on her doorstep. Proclaiming the rights of the religious over the wrongs of the infidel, they chanted, they sang and then cried, beaconing to Heaven for a sign. And, lo and behold, the sign came in the form of a very full porcelain-plated chamber pot that flurried through the air from Nell's open window onto the head of the faith belching Reverend.

The town hibernated in its righteousness and there it festered, and a boil of hate expanded until the pressure was too much for the boundaries of such a small town. Nell and child had to go for the health and safety of this populace. Reverend Cole, in a gut-wrenching slurred rant, brought down the wrath of God himself into the tiny church over packed with a mob of seething mindless energy. To Nell, from her abode, the night's warm blanket of dark attempted to suffocate a glowing boiling cauldron of overcooked potatoes. And the potatoes were spewing forth their spittle of religious venom to form a shield of indomitable tribal hunger. Zonks were on the menu.

Sheriff Casull stood as a pillar between the writhing rancor of religious rabble and Nell's small cabin. He quoted the State and city laws that might soon be broken. Young Abel Ledbetter, who literally understood nothing, was solely in the mob for the mere reason of adulation and comradery by his peers. He would later make a very great Republican. Abel threw a large metamorphic rock that he would never ever comprehend as Gneiss, and as he fell on his knees, the rock hit the Sheriff right between the eyes and Casull careened backwards, then lurched forwards only to fall face first in the snow. He was dead. It was absurdly quiet and then the cauldron boiled back to life and the spewing potatoes ignited into a surge that soon would overwhelm Nell's porch.

The apparition that appeared from the door wore a tight-fitting leather dress. It had two holsters on a belt around its waist with right and left shoulder holsters under its arms. In each holster rode a nickel-plated

Colt. On the vision's back was a papoose that cocooned a giggling giddy child.

Five days later, the carnage was still fresh in the frozen snow. The US Marshall reviewed the situation and declared it was due to some wild unfortunate gangland violence. The town needed a new reverend, butcher, weaver, skinner and, well, many others. The Marshall put into his report that twenty-four shots were fired in total and twenty-four bullets found their way into the heads of twenty-four people of Alamosa. 'Amazing shots all!' was his closing statement. A youth called Abel was found crouched behind a cord of wood in a puddle of his own frozen urine. He would later use this memory as to why women should never ever have the right to vote.

A woman on her mule was heading south for the winter. They said the picking was good down in Texas. A baby in her papoose said her first full sentence. "Good shoot'n, Mom."

Stiff Love

by Opeia Zonk

"You don't need to touch or embrace to love. It is ethereal. Remove all the sensations and there is still love." — Tallulah Stiff

Norm was swimming in a sea of souls but he got tired. Souls get tired since mass in the fourth dimension is really just energy, and a soul has to expend energy in order to swim. Norm chose his resting place in the machine of his death. A very fine German Krupp steel grinder that harshly gnashed the gnarled flesh of French meats—including the tender dull pinkness of the pig. Norm followed his love into the grinder, as so many painfully poetically mangled hearts do, and they did bleed. But now there was Ms. Stiff.

Tallulah Stiff, no not the wealthy head economist that toils for Big Oil, but the poor fired pseudo-engineer that worked on aisle three of a meat processing plant in a valley in the middle of Utah. She was working late during the weekend. The managers realized that Tallulah was attached to her grinder in ways that not all employees tended to fathom, so they let her stay late to dismantle, clean, oil and reassemble the mechanism so that it was far more optimal at serration than before. But, in the cogs of the beautifully designed network of crushing steel binders, she found a globular fog of a mist that spoke fluent English but with a French accent. The silently clicking cogs in the clock on the wall slowed to a stop.

The small ball of fog engulfed Tallulah's eyes and she found herself floating aloft on the hands of many gentle children. Norm was amorphous yet somehow tangible to her mind. They were there together in a field of mud that contained the wiggling pink bodies of freshly born pigs. It appeared from above like a rich chocolate pool dotted with moist pink bubblegum squirming candies. It did not smell sweet but smelled of shit, but it was not repulsive to the nostrils of Ms. Stiff. Norm was there. Norm had been waiting for her. The aroma of Armani's Acqua di Gio crept into her organs and he slipped into her open arms and touched her effervescence. She thought she heard an oink. And then again. It was there in the vibrations of the air. She followed the sound through the walls of reverberance back, back to the source of her own throat. Tallulah looked into the shiny Krupp stainless steel blades and saw an image of a pig. She was a beautiful pig.

Tallulah the pig, with her cloven hoof, manipulated the lever to turn the well-oiled machine on. It instantaneously buzzed like a lubricated chainsaw. In the maul of the device the night air infiltrated the facility, and all was stagnant with the paste and smell of meat and blood. Sometime later a German belched a roasted bratwurst scent with a pilsner aftertaste and human ate human once again.

Author's note: Okay. I was basically riffing off the visit of Ms. Stiff and the Pikes. I thought it had merit. The actual poor Tallulah Stiff eventually ran a pharmacy in Whipup, Utah, and was a serious addict on Adderall and Oxycontin. She was caught stealing for her habit and is now housed in a cell with no windows in a women's prison in a ward in Canon City, Colorado. She goes by the name of 'Grinder'. She is currently the bitch to Vaca Del Mar.

Salutations to Turmoil
Stories Compiled by Zackary Maxwell
Translated by Zackary Maxwell

Salutations to Turmoil Segments
Opeia
by Navdar Goran (Kurdish)
Bootes
by Kohar Hakobyan (Armenian)
Eni and Zade
by Janis Oxolins (Latvian)

Opeia
by Navdar Goran
Translated from Kurdish by Zackary Maxwell

The Clandestine Tart

"The oil and vinegar phases just need a stable emulsion. We can all get along if the balance is just right. It just takes a tremendous amount of energy to shake the shit out of the jar to keep this balance." — Tilda Twat

Tilda Twat was not a twat, but she was the great great-granddaughter of the lame Twat by the same name that was the commencement speaker during the graduation ceremonies of Bryn Mawr, when Nell Zonk was lauded but forgotten quickly. Tilda came from great wealth, but because of her family's proclivities to procreate loosely and randomly, the line of blood got hazy and she ended up an orphan at the Dangleberry Estates. Rich people do that sometimes. The poor do not have the wealth to invent such wonderful travesties.

The door was unlocked and it was time. The clock stated the moment. And Tilda was awakened to unleash her passion for the fresh pastries that trounced the palates of all patrons on The Estate. Twat was the chef of all sweet dainties. She was the chef of the tarts.

No student failed. It was a failure to the Zonks not to find the spark of life in each individual gracing the grounds of Dangleberry. And the Zonks strived not to fail. But then there was Tilda.

Tilda was a transient waif of five feet in height and just a few pounds. She was a skeleton with skin but her eyes were wanting and her chin protruded just enough to form a solid jaw. Her diminutive rose lips encircled a minor mouth filled with nervously chattering teeth.

She was used to the home of her mediocre uncle, who persuaded her to live with him after her parents died. His house was nothing extraordinary but it was plain and warm and necessary at this point in her life. Tilda was seven. Seen from outside, she was unkempt and malnourished. She liked frolicking in the hillsides, streams and neighbor's barns. But the uncle would not tolerate this for his line of blood and she was introduced to a staunch family etiquette.

She fervently was festooned with sultry articles of blessed cloth. All displayed in some gallant array of extravagant undulatory behavior. At seven she was groomed. At nine, her parsimonious placation dominated her pale knowledge of truth and she succumbed to vile molestation. I tried to save her, I the author of this book, but I could not. I would apologize to Roger but he already knows.

To the youth, love became a murky pool tainted with the sour feet of lustful gentlemen. Tilda never forgot that early programming. Her skull hummed with anticipation of wanting to be needed. Always in the company of mature men, she longed to be treated as Royalty like the princess she was told she was.

But her mind was dull since it was never fed and through those few initial years, the pale fruit was forced to ripen before its time and it began to rot to form a bruised sullen girl. And that is when the Zonks took her into Dangleberry's.

To paint the portrait of a life, one needs a stout canvas, but here all laid bare was a soiled rag of tattered cloth. Tilda spent a number of months in the children's ward of the Warped Noodle. Doctors attempted many methods to undo the rancid programming that warped her views of life, but only medication left a small child rocking back and forth curled into a ball silently whispering for any man to be her 'Daddy'. Curious critters crawled. They crawled for knowledge and they crawled for understanding, but what they plodded most for was basic comprehension. All they wanted was the path to take the form of a formattable stone road to reason. They just wanted clarity.

Chester was the one to put her into the kitchen at Dangleberry's. Tilda did not read much at all, but she understood amounts and volumes. She was given access to the Zonk Library's recipe section—and this was substantial. Chester started her off on just the elementary basics of simple soups and salads. And the Zonks were amazed that once she obtained authorization to be needed for anything other than her ability at lust, she grew. They all left her alone to produce any dish she so desired and, eventually, she became the prime chef of the entire Estate at the ripe age of seventeen.

The crusts of the bread need not be removed to obtain bliss and it just becomes a fantasy of purity of ingestion that relinquishes the body to ameliorate the tantalizing flavors of whole wheat. All drowned in this fiber. All. Tilda became a master baker. But what really separated the hairs from the nostril were her fresh lascivious tarts.

Tarte aux pommes, tarte tatin, tarte aux myrtilles, tarte aux mirabelles and the list goes on. These elegant pastries did not require one muscle from the jaws to masticate. They naturally just melted into the mouth in a delicious sweet melodious swirl of salivation. Chester burped.

Tilda did not read seventy-five percent of the Zonk Family Library. In fact, she did not pass the majority of her classes. But she did graduate with special honors in the culinary arts. With the Zonk influence, the Paris school of French gastronomy and cooking, Le Cordon Bleu, took Tilda Twat into their ranks. With some difficulty, she learned French but the hard part was already over. She finally understood that her meaning of love was not lust but a real love of cooking. And in her future, she was much needed for this talent.

The Tutelage of Texas

"A rainbow is the vision of God seen through the prism lens of our majestic tears." — Nell to Margot.
"Mom, screw that! A rainbow is caused by reflection, refraction and the dispersion of light in water droplets!" — Margot to Nell
"Well, at least we know you'll never be a poet. But you are a Zonk." — Nell to Margot

Amarillo was a burgeoning town. Cattle were the market but new-found natural gas and oil started to bring in investors to the panhandle, and the town grew.

Dr. Nell set up shop as the 'new' cutting edge medicine physician for livestock. Even though she was not a veterinarian, her education was far superior to any known animal doctor and she became one. Dr. Nell built up her reputation on successes alone. She did not fail in her vision to do the best that was possible. She was a methodical and vibrant scientist that thrived on life. She fought bovine, porcine and sheep diseases. Some she conquered and others she did not. But she was honest about her trade and honest about her losses. Dr. Nell became well known in North Texas.

Nell and Margot lived simply in a rented-out cottage with a wood stove and an outhouse. Visitors were aghast at the lack of furniture and the crude number of stacked books on the floor, looking like various temples in some Arabic tale. The gates of literacy broke down at their doorstep and with mottled guffaws and sweet dainty nods, all visitors expired back to their dusty rich refuse of ignorance and transitory bliss. A traveling photographer took a picture of Dr. Nell and Margot at their cottage during this time. They both looked ridged in their leather dresses, tight shoes and flop hats. But it was typical Zonk. And the photo was later cherished in a Denver Museum of Antiquities for Western Characters.

Dr. Nell and Margot moved south. They found this part of Texas to be inhabited with males that were condescending, overconfident and turgid. The females were vacuous. Most remain this way even today. Why south? It was rumored that the Germans and Czechs dug a niche in limestone in the southern Texas hill country. They, as a people, were staunchly working conservative but also politically blatantly liberal. Perhaps they could find a home there.

The Zonks set up shop in Fredericksburg, and Dr. Nell wasted no time in expanding a business in herbal medicine to humans and modern medicine to local livestock. This place appeared like paradise. The rivers and springs were amazing. The land was not exactly lush for farming but longhorns were prevalent. With some tilling, gardens would grow. The main central issue was the Zonks were not of German heritage. They were English. And if you were not German you were not them.

Business was not just slow it was stagnant. She was female and English and over-educated for a woman. Nell and Margot sat down for a cup of expensive Chinese tea, and decided to sell all they had and take a train to Seattle. Why not? Chinese tea was cheaper there.

The Copulation of George Stook

by Opeia Zonk

"It is like cribbage, you know. A basic peg into a hole. Isn't that it?
Simple." — Dr. Stook

Dr. George Stook was a gynecologist, an ardent, narcissistic pontificating Republican, and a towering leader of The Boy's Club in the third ward of the Zonk Farm of The Warped Noodle. The main issue with Dr. Stook was that he was alive. A massive re-education of this marbled blunder was a failure since his mind was so hardened by hate. In retrospect, a world without him would obviously notice but relief would easily supplant grief upon his departure. And those that did grieve his omission would eventually follow suit and tag along on his next dimensional journey. But Dr. Stook was not dead. His hate led to madness and madness fed his hate and this cycle, like a heart's piston, fueled his desire to live. His ego was nourished by his mock leadership of a band of conservative minds call The Boy's Club. They ruled Ward Three—or so they thought—but the great minds of medicine were so glad they were still alive so that they could push and prod their minds to reveal the tantalizing secrets of their insanity.

Persuasive facts were revealed by the re-emergence of electroshock therapy sessions. Small amounts of clarity divulged a lead crystalline truth that Dr. Stook was not a doctor at all, unless your just passable degree came with a receipt. Stook's grandfather, Albert Snook, made his fortune in beef running the largest ranch and slaughterhouse at the time just north of Amarillo, Texas. Albert was quick to notice George's passion for vaginas. George was young but was often purchasing time in the latrines for just a gaze at a girl's loins. So, upon his Texas graduation, Albert sent George to Yale for several years. George did not study; he did not have to; his degree was not earned but bought. With a C average, he was now Dr. Stook and he was legally allowed to view as many vaginas as would come into his services. And they paid him for the viewing! What a life.

He was handsome and charming only by his own admission but it was his inherited money that was always the key to the numerous chastity belts drifting through his short radius of dull vision.

What literally saved him from an earlier incarceration were his vast contributions to the Republican Party. Once he joined the upper echelons of extreme right-wing conservatism, he was 'protected' from any truth that was forever deposited at his feet. And like so many piles of real manure that walled his future, the truth and the piles were swept away with just funds, a steadfast rebuttal and a warm embrace by his pseudo-intellectual conservatives. Dr. Stook realized that reality could be purchased and manipulated. That there was no 'real' anything, just optical illusions for a price.

His illusions became delusions when, at a gala, he proclaimed himself a King. They all laughed until they realized he was not kidding and then they laughed again thinking that is what this great nation needed. A King. Dr. Stook received this pleasure in anointing his body in the plethora of accolades, and this gave him energy to state his honest political platform. He would be running for the Republican Senate seat in the great state of Texas. And he won.

The seam in his sanity started to fray and slowly it became apparent that this monster of a man was just a delusional child idiot. During a closed-door fund-raising dinner his speech made it clearly evident that Dr. Stook was not well.

"Isn't it obvious!? Isn't it! Why gay, lesbian and trans people are great actors. They have been acting all their lives. They have been acting to be straight so that when they get in front of a camera, they just act like they have been all of their lives. Isn't in curious?! Isn't it! That Blacks and Jews make the best comedians! Why? Because they have been oppressed! Oppression is the key to squeeze the artistic merits from these abominable minorities. Do you want to have poor lame actors? Do you want a cornucopia of crappy comedians? If you want great writers and great artists and poets, you must keep them OPPRESSED! Pain is a great motivator for the imagination! And who is chosen by God to do this oppression? White Christians!!!"

There were screams and hollering but not of dissent or denunciation just of searing admiration and exultations. These people, and especially Stook, were all crazy. How did this come to be?

Travis Poot was part of a catering team that night. He was not supposed to be there but his friend needed some alone time with his girlfriend since she consistently cheated on him because he had a diminutive organ. Not his copulation organ but his liver. He could not indulge in any ethanol product but it was her necessity and when she was 'lit' she fornicated. And she needed to fornicate since nature's nurturing necessitated this need, of course, to procreate. She just had to do this action under the influence. Travis, being a good friend, replaced him at the last moment and joined this team of food providers. For whatever reason, he turned on his cell phone camera and filmed the entire event—including this speech.

This video went viral, and even though the Republicans pushed back with fake deep state digital manipulation, the product stuck in the minds of the populace.

Dr. Snoot, using a Masamoto stainless steel high carbon steak knife, went raging into a New York synagogue, and this was filmed too, him stating unequivocally that he needed to provide this pain so that comedy would not suffer. He was bludgeoned into unconsciousness by a brass bound Talmud wielded by a very serious, but calm, rabbi. He awoke at the Zonk Farm of The Warped Noodle. Ward Three warmly embraced him.

The Zonks continued his electroshock therapy even though the doctors stated that it was of no use. His brain was baked solid with hate and there was nothing to be done. Dr. Stook was delusional and fading into dementia. The Zonks kept up the massive voltage so that those minute moments of clarity would remind him of his pathetic nature. How can one suffer if you don't remember what you are suffering for?

The Warped Noodle ranch was diminishing in cattle. Cows were purchased but the Zonks, Zade and Eni wanted to start their own stud farm operation. A very old pure Iberian bull was purchased at below cost but he was still tethered by his testosterone mire. Zade's mother bought the bull when it was up for slaughter—it killed two elderly people that attempted to extract methane from his lower bowels. The Warped Noodle gave him a home.

The bull was quite prolific in procreating progeny and this helped the ranch to grow. He was often set free to roam the grounds with the patients. The Iberian became tame and understood the nature of his surroundings.

On a calm autumn morning, a bedraggled form exited the west ground manhole sewer cover. He was coated with a gloss of excrement and hobbled to the center of the back-area grounds. The red maple, oak and hickory were losing their leaves due to the crisp cut of fall air and it appeared in the early morning light like large shadows of slowly falling rain. Dr. Stook struggled to stay afloat in his ocean of medication but he managed to get to a mound of dew-covered trees that the wind made their branches beckon his welcome.

Under the dense foliage was the bull. He slumbered softly remembering his conquests toward genetic posterity. The bull did leave a linage that was very robust and no animal would fault him for gloating.

But Dr. Stook was awash with vile thoughts. He lost a fortune in a viable bull market based on pure stupid advice. The bull was floating there and needed to be reminded of his failure to Stook. He quietly knelt down, pulled down his pajama bottoms, spread wide his buttock cheeks, and through the golden eye of a King, he farted. The bull, deep in slumber, abruptly surfaced in his ocean wave and seeing the bulbous posterior, forced his arousal hormones in intensity and instantly mounted the quivering mass.

No sound would ever be repeated from that of the security cameras. It was too real and raw. Dr. Stook was found lifeless that morning by Juan Mendez, a patient. He stated that the good doctor was face down in cow dung with his ass spliced open. The medics report stated that death was due to massive blood loss from an internal hemorrhage. How that hemorrhage was received was anyone's guess. The security films were curiously erased. Roger set Stook up on a very smoldering planet. Planet KELT-9. He was last seen with the Vance family weaving burnt entrails.

Author's note: This was actually non-fiction. Most of my stories waffled from real to fiction. His name wasn't Stook but I had to protect my family from being sued by his family. But in this day and age, what is fiction and what is reality?

Marvin's Torture

"Technology is the King and it will reign supreme. Technology is a gallant serf that robs the populace by distraction. Which is true? Only the latter." — *Marvin*

Marvin Bartleby was from the wrong side of the wrong tracks in a really wrong neighborhood in Baltimore. He was African American, slight of figure and the only thing big on his body was his enormous thick-lensed heavy black-framed glasses. To a viewer, they made his eyes appear three sizes too big. In some other place, he would be considered legally blind. Marvin did not grow up on the streets. He did not go out. He did not particularly like humans and Father Flanagan left him to his own devices. Marvin literally lived in the library of the Catholic orphanage. This library did not have much but Emma Watson donated her entire classic literature collection to the church, and much to Marvin's need, she gave the library her old Apple Macintosh computer. Marvin was in love.

By the age of five, he completely rebuilt the computer to have three times the CPU speed and nearly a terabyte of internal memory. At six, he developed his own computer language and his own software complier for his own applications. He discovered Dangleberry Estates and contacted the Zonks through email. Marvin Bartleby, just turning seven, entered the iron gates of The Estates.

Of the Zonks, Eni was probably the most proficient at computers and programming. She knew five coding languages fluently, and she completed most of the hardware and software changes for both The Estate and the Warped Noodle. Marvin was going to kick this all up a notch.

Marvin immediately liked the Zonks. Their nature was solidified with some untold singular secret that melded themselves to one another. They did not overtly socialize with the student body, but he realized that they cared immensely for their well-being and for each of their futures.

And he directly enjoyed that God was not at all a part of the school's numerous equations.

Within two weeks, he solely rewired the campus and the neighboring Noodle with T5 lines. Using his own coding structure, he optimized all computers to a single network, with a remote mirrored site, and he set up an impenetrable security perimeter around the Zonks' properties so that no one from the outside could possibly hack into their private communications.

On his eighth birthday, he received his own office with an adjoining laboratory for research design and development. He also realized, at this tender age, that he was black. All his worldly ideas about reality suddenly jolted from a deep subsurface area to the present. All black heroes on this planet generally were professional sports players or rappers, but Marvin didn't play sports nor rap. Not even checkers or a basic beat. Marvin Bartleby made up his mind, then and there, that he was going to change all those ideals.

Zade, Eni, Opeia and Chester all agreed that Mr. Bartleby needed to teach a computer programming course. The Zonks realized that their curriculum focus at this Estate was indeed lacking in computer science and technology. Mr. Bartleby could fill that void.

Marvin set up a bold class portfolio that included the latest fourth generation programming languages. He received his own budget. He also acquired his own classroom with fifteen desks and fifteen up-to-date computers that he himself rewired to be more efficient. And on an early day in October, the students poured into their seats and Marvin, well, Marvin froze.

He stood there with his lecture in hand, his magnified eyes unblinking and his mouth hanging open like a busted screen door without a hinge. Marvin began to salivate and his drool copiously dripped forth like a small cascading waterfall. His spittle glistened in the morning sunlight. Ada Place, always in the front row, realized incorrectly, that he was having a stroke, ran and hit the red panic button on the panel near the entry door.

Marvin awoke on a gurney when the fetid stench of Chester's moist nostrils plunged into his reality. A mildly gnashed morel slipped from the swine's mucus lined snoot and fell on Marvin's chin. It must have been a stroke since everything the diminutive child looked at was melting. Opeia, sensing his discomfort, grabbed his glasses, wiped off the malodorous porcine snot and placed the magnifying lenses back on to the bridge of his nose. All was clear. He was in the Child's Ward at the Warped Noodle.

The Zonks were hovering with their maternal instincts around the small sick child, except for Chester, who had an erection. Morels do that to him—it acts like his divining rod for morel mushrooms—and what a rod it was.

The youth was not sick. The Noodle doctors gave him a clean bill of health. What Marvin suffered from was a simple case of 'stage fright'. This elemental malady, magnified through his convex lenses, detonated after he viewed a classroom of fresh minds to be molded. But up to this point he had never spoken more than a sentence, and only a broken one at that, to any human. This eight-year-old youth was tossed into maturity to deal with humans that he could not stand nor comprehend. The Zonks completely understood. They, as a group, did not like humans. But if they could find a way to communicate to most people, in their own special way, then Marvin could too.

Eni, Opeia and Zade came up with a solution. The 'Boys' needed a night out on the town. They needed to cut the rug, not the same rug in Ruth, NV, that the 'Girls' were accused of munching, but the rug that needed cutting and their primary goal was to have Marvin socialize with humans. On a cold night in November, Chester and Marvin went into town to learn to be social. With the necessary use of prosthetics, Chester drove.

Ripley's Bar and Grill was the only close social point that their non-social compass pointed toward. This place played nightly local live music in the prospering town of Pittsboro—population approximately four thousand three hundred, not including household pets. Q.T. Williams was at the bar and aside from her deep tanned brown swaying tattooed breasts and long blonde dreadlocks, she was a very gifted mixologist and a stalwart Baptist. On the stage that night was Judy Juggs and her Lactation Crew—locally famous not so much for their focused perfection at playing their instruments, but for their unusual dynamic stage performance.

Marvin felt sick. He was not well. He was not used to being around so many humans. They all appeared friendly but he feared, behind this veneer, was a loathsome core of wretchedness. And he was correct. And that debauchery was reliance on manipulated technology.

The band was grinding but Marvin could not hear since his brain turned off that sense. All he could fathom was a room full of humans, all in a dancing social setting, looking down at their cellphones. Their partners, dancing or eating or drinking, oblivious to the slight, were doing the same thing to them. It was if no one needed to be there at all since they were not cognizant of their present surroundings. It was all nauseating.

Chester just munched several liberty cap mushrooms hidden in his vest, and was currently enjoying the whirlpool surroundings of a very poor circus being slowly devoured by a repetitively short circulating blender on puree. Grrrr. Grrrr. Grrrr. The sound of the motor cut off and on.

Marvin, sweating profusely from his technological nausea, asked the bar for an iced tea. Q.T., mistaking maturity for age, thought the eight-year-old dwarf at least old enough and filled his glass with an extremely potent Long Island Iced Tea. Through the syphoning of his straw into the elixir, the wizened youth's perception started to clear.

He realized that no one was actually present. Not mentally. That the physical bodies of the patrons and the staff were looking down into a cellphone that took them to some other place that was not representative of this current reality. Yet they throbbed to the music and danced, ate and drank with partners that were not in visual grasp of their current surroundings. It was madness.

Judy Juggs and her Lactation Crew, all females, took massive injections of oxytocin before each performance. All their breasts were visible under cup-less tight-fitting corsets. Hooped and accentuated, their mammary glands, no matter what cup, A to EEE, were pounding out the solid rhythm of the pulsing sound. Granny Grunt 'Crusty' was eighty-eight years of age and no person could play the bass guitar with such gusto and charisma. She did not use her hands but to hold the guitar. She took her sagging melons that draped over the fret board and slammed them repeatedly on the one string that was there. Glandular secretions were produced with each impact and formed a crust on her nipples. Hence the name 'Crusty'. Her toothless cackling and lit corn cob pipe filled to the brim with sativa, forced the others to follow suit in this awesome flurry of wonderment. Stella 'StarTits' Greeb, on the drums, was actually the only person in the band that could play an instrument. She wanted a legitimate band but realized that raw performance paid better than actual legitimacy, so she pounded the skins and lactated her way to a college education in social idiocy. The country needed direly to have this education since they were plagued by all its facets. The entire cacophony was concluded with a resounding drum solo where all the band members, save the drummer, went through the pumping crowd and distributed their cream to the crop for our future salvation. Everyone but Chester and Marvin were Republican. They now realized this, and Chester, forgetting his prosthetics, drove anyway and they both vacated this glandular mess.

Somewhere westbound on Highway 64, the Dangleberry maintenance van drove off into a ditch and then made it approximately thirty yards into some overgrown brush. Orderlies from the Noodle found Chester and Marvin early that morning both floundering in a large mud puddle. Chester had an erection, which meant that morels were nearby, but no one seemed to care. When they smiled, Al Jolson came to mind, but no soul thankfully remembered Al Jolson. Chester's title remained and Marvin Bartleby now understood the Zonk family formula. He requested, and his request was granted, for Marvin to become a Zonk.

It took time, but Marvin found his voice and confidence, much thanks to Chester, who told him, "No one, not one single human, knows a computer the way you do!" And he did. Marvin never sauntered off the Zonk properties ever again. He had found his home.

The Tall Tales on The Train

"Mother." — Margot
"Don't call me Mother!" — Nell
"Mom!" — Margot
"Yes!" — Nell
"Can I kill somebody now?" — Margot

They, the Zonks, being frugal of nature, traveled coach with minimal luggage. How much does one need? Really? The mother and her child preordained their future by ordering a strong batch of Earl Grey. And, unfortunately for Roger, it was delivered with cream.

Rail travel was a welcome embrace by the Zonks. It never got you where you wanted to go quickly or on time but lumbered on just long enough for a person to enjoy the view. And they loved it all. The train meandered through vast desert lands with no vegetation but cactus. The sunsets were amazing, but the world changed when the train turned north from Phoenix and went slowly up an incline into a world of snow-covered peaks.

Nell knew Colorado and Wyoming but tad Margot only had memories of Texas. And this far west country was amazing in color and inhabitants, and the child fell in love with the mountains.

A blizzard stopped them for several days in Flagstaff. Nell took this time to purchase warmer clothes and boots. Like a velvet whisper Margot heard a hiss from the back of the store. An old man rocking in a chair was wheezing on a pipe while gazing out at the slowly falling large snowflakes. Margot was fascinated by this person. She hadn't seen that many old people before, especially not so up close. With her newly booted soles, she awkwardly clamored through some bamboo fishing poles to get a better look. She ascertained that his appearance was most like St. Nick if St. Nick chewed tobacco, wheezed on a pipe and drunk much alcohol. He stunk of all those things. He methodically removed the pipe from his mouth but the wheezing didn't stop. The wheezing sound,

Margot now understood, was coming from his lungs. In his raw raspy baritone, he gently said, "It is not polite to stare."

Margot promptly replied, "If I stared at a piece of crap, would the crap be offended?"

The old man smiled broadly and said, "Absolutely not since that is what I am!" and he laughed and bounded out of his chair.

His name was Emmitt Casull, whom it was soon revealed was the brother of the late Sheriff Casull of Alamosa, Colorado. Emmitt was under the impression his brother died as a result of some random gang violence, but Nell sat down and told him the real entire story of his brother's death. Emmitt was honored by Nell's honesty and invited the two out for dinner. What a small world it all was. Mr. Casull was a wonderful storyteller, and even if half of it was true, he definitely led a very full life. Margot made a mental note to herself to live a very full life.

At first light, the porter at the hotel told Nell that the train, because of foul weather, was re-routed to Salt Lake City, Utah, and it was scheduled to leave by noon. Emmitt materialized at the door, and did indeed look like St. Nick, covered in snow with a full white beard and bursting red cheeks. He insisted on buying breakfast.

After another full round of tall tales, he bid farewell, but only after a quick visit to Handy's Hardware store. There he bought Margot her first .22 rifle, a Stevens Favorite. It was a single shot trapdoor gun that was admired for being very accurate. Mr. Casull knelt on one knee and whispered into her ear, "You only need one shot. Just one." Then, ignoring Nell's demands, he purchased her a .32 caliber snub nosed Smith and Wesson revolver complete with a leather rig, that he tied snuggly around her small mid-section. Margot was amazed how the gun handle fit just right in her small hand. Back at the hotel, she gazed in the full-length mirror and smiled. She looked almost to a detail exactly like her mother. The train's horn sounded. It was time to go.

The train trudged up through Zion and Bryce Canyon. Nell thought if she were ever to retire, she would retire there. Only a poet could give these vistas justice in any clumsy language.

Nell took this time on this slow-moving rail barge to teach Margot how to shoot. There were two flat cars in the rear of this train that were loaded with cargo. It was here that Margot learned to shoot and shoot very well.

From the first light of morning to the last light before night, the Zonks were on the flat cars shooting. Whether stopped at a siding or lumbering through the snow, the Zonks were shooting. The train chef appreciated the fresh grouse, pheasant, rabbit and young deer that the Zonks brought in. So did the passengers and crew. Even though this winter journey was a slow one, everyone was, at least, very well fed.

They stopped for a few days in Salt Lake City. Margot's zeal for shooting could not be contained and Nell bought cases of cartridges for herself and the young Zonk. It was here in a neighborhood park that the Zonks met with the Claunch family from a valley faraway in California. They were in a wagon heading east, wanting a new life in the Colorado Rockies. They were invited into their wagon and Nell told them all she knew of the land and the people. They were grateful. Mr. Claunch went to the back of the wagon and opened up a wooden barrel that appeared to contain very cold, slightly frozen water. He put in his hand and out came a many-berried vine with dangling succulent fruit. He popped off one morsel and placed it into the mouth of Margot. The explosion of flavor inflamed her jaws. It was amazing. Margot ate her first grape. Young Mr. Claunch and his wife wished them both safe travels and said, "May God look after you."

To which Margot replied, "Oh, Roger does. But he is not really a God, he is a fifth dimensional being."

Claunch smiled and said, "You Zonks are quite different people."

And Nell, with a lifted left eyebrow said, "You have no idea."

The train was to cut across Nevada to Sacramento and then they would board a new train north to Seattle. The salt flats were a vast bed of nothing but white salt. As far as one could see. Young Zonk thought humans would never run out of salt with this massive dry crystalline desert.

Back on the flat cars, Margot could hit anything, either while in motion or still, with her rifle on any target the size of a half dollar and up to one hundred yards. But her pistol was another matter. How could her mother instantly chew up twigs from passing trees with a flurry of her revolver and she could not. "Patience, Ms. M. Patience. It will come," said her mother. Margot, like all Zonks, had no patience. But by the time she got to Winnemucca, Margot could hit any target the size of an apple, moving or stationary, with her Smith and Wesson at thirty yards. It wasn't great, but it was very good.

The mountains parted and the ground became a fertile valley as they pulled into Sacramento. The Zonks were amazed at how cosmopolitan it all was. It wasn't the east coast, thought Nell, but it was very close. They were to be boarded for two days in a good hotel until the northbound train arrived to take them to Seattle. And the cars. Everywhere cars. Nell and Margot took this time to be the first Zonks to drive a car. And they did.

The rented Model T was a burly beast and on a farmer's field they endeavored to master this mechanical monstrosity. It was a comical blend of the blind leading the blind but it did more than teach them to drive, it bonded their hearts together with a lasting memory of completion. They, in total, took out five fence posts and two mailboxes but, by sunset, they could both maneuver a car anywhere and on any surface. From the hotel the next morning, the horn sounded, and they were off for Seattle.

Before the incline at Redding, a newspaper was dropped into Nell's lap. On page three was the blaring headline in tall capital letters, 'Colorado Republican Senator, Abel Ledbetter, Assassinated!' Emmitt, fueled by Nell's truth, found Abel. A witness stated that Mr. Casull yelled before pulling the trigger, "Zonk might have missed but I don't!" In the writ it stated that Abel's eyes bulged, possibly on the memory of Nell, before the gun went off. While in custody, Mr. Casull succumbed to tuberculosis (TB). The characteristic wheezing of his lungs. Margot was sad. Nell didn't shoot Abel back then since he was too young to know the difference. But Emmitt did well. It was Abel's time at this point. And now women were allowed to vote in America. Strange how that works. Roger was laughing on Kepler-62F. He was having a cold one. But at -85-degree F, everything was a cold one.

Heavy snow began to fall. The locomotive pumped and gagged at the ascent. Nell took this time to read and Margot, who would've rather been shooting, reluctantly did the same. Nell had her on a delicious course of Hume and Locke.

The train stopped many times. Sometimes for several hours on end. The passengers were getting curious as to the continual delays and the conductor gave no solid clues as to the cause. The restaurant car was opened and the bar was giving out free juice and coffee. But this deflection would only last so long. The Zonks calmly read and an elderly woman in a fine blue dress with satin tassels walked by and said to Margot in a haughty air, "So, you finally are taking the time to read the Good Book?" This was possibly in a potential reference to a mother and daughter that spent most of their time blasting away with their guns at anything from the rear flat cars on the train.

Margot lifted her dark eyebrows, along with her gaze, from the middle of her book and smiled, saying, "All my books are GOOD books and if you'd ever take the time to read anything at all other than that book which you call GOOD, you might just be able to comprehend the phrase, cantankerous asinine bitch!" Margot was careful to enunciate each word with a delicate but biting flair. The woman puckered up her well wrinkled lips as though something very sour pierced her tongue, and glared at Nell in a deliberate unspoken attempt for the mother to possibly reprimand the child.

Nell calmly looked up into the old woman's eyes and said, "Margot, I would have added skanky before the word bitch, but otherwise, well said." No other conversation between any passenger and the Zonks occurred during the remainder of the trip.

The engineer knew this pass well. He had been on this route numerous times in all types of weather. But he also knew that this heavy fresh snow was piling on top of a hard pack of snow beneath and this was a possible issue going through the Ashland Mountain half bowl. The half bowl was just that. It appeared like a very large funnel cut in half and the train track went directly through the middle. With the heavy snow up above, the throbbing locomotive could possibly start and avalanche at this point. The engineer wanted to wait until the cold of night, which possibly could solidify the fresh snow and secure this train ride through the half bowl without incident.

Well after dusk, Margot woke up with the harsh lurch from the engine. She woke up her mother. They both looked at each other. Nell, too, had an odd feeling. Around the next bend they went into the bowl.

The engineer sped up the train to reduce the temptation of providence's accidental outcomes. Halfway through, the train chugged along and the engineer's shoulders fell slant as though a weight of nerves were lifted from his back. And then the rumbling began.

Initially, it was difficult to discern the difference between the pounding of the engine in the cold night air and that of the collapse of the overhanging snow ridge high above. But the train began to bounce in an unfamiliar rhythm. The engineer, realizing the impeding impact, sped up the train to its maximum velocity.

The first wave, as described by Margot, tore through the middle section of the train. At least five cars went down the bowl off of the tracks. The second wave covered the last rear part of the train but they remained on the rails. The end caboose was only partially covered. Remarkably, the engine and coal car were not impacted. Margot and Nell, through windows with the flickering internal train lights, saw many passengers explode out of the middle cars down into the roaring abyss. Ms. Blue Dress's horror-stricken face blazed in Margot's memory as her petticoat unfolded to reveal her right hand grasping onto her book of faith. Boulders of frozen snow the size of cars engulfed her slight satin-blue covered frame and disappeared into the dark below.

The next morning the sky was clear, but inside the train car with Nell and Margot in it was pitch black with patterns of somber gray unfolding from above. Nell ascertained that the snow depths above them ranged from just a few feet to well over twenty in some sections. Rampant masculinity dominated the next few hours as the males gathered to proclaim natural intelligence to lead the living towards a future salvation from this dilemma. Nell and Margot knew better; they left the rabble and grabbed their materials to bore their way through dense snowpack like moles in a compressed mound of dirt. They surfaced just shy of the caboose.

The caboose was crushed up front from the heavy bombardment of compressed snow but the rear of the car still had a viable bed, a desk and a small pot belly stove. The Zonks realized this was going to be home for some time. This was confirmed when the engineer released the coal car from the rest of the train, got the engine up to steam, and left the massive wreck in an attempt to expedite help. Margot thought the sight of that leaving black locomotive on the background of the pale white of the snow on the other end of the bowl, was the loneliest vision she had ever had.

The Zonk blood kicked in. Nell had Margot designed a maze of mole tunnels throughout a radius of fifty yards from the rear end of the caboose. Uncovered trees and branches would be their fuel for heat. Another snowstorm came rushing in and the thought of leaving this humble realm was not an intelligent possibility. Nell dug forward into the snow of the collapsed caboose to retrieve the dead rear-conductor of his frozen shell. Margot gazed at his open mouth attempting to inhale oxygen that just was not there. Nell quickly gutted him to extradite his intestines that she hung on tiny wires over the warm stove. Margot was speechless at her mother's convictions and her swift methodical demeanor. Young Zonk remained quiet and helpful. Mr. Rear-Conductor would be their sustenance for the next few days. The Zonks did not grieve. What was the point of grieving over a shell of meat and organs? They were absolutely sure that Roger had this gentleman performing some moribund menial task on some exoplanet that suited the conductor's morals, that through time, he exhibited on this planet. Margot stated that humans tasted much like that of a pig. She told Nell she was giving up on pig meat. Why not? Pigs were more intelligent than most humans and since they tasted the same, she could get her 'bacon' elsewhere. Nell laughed. Zonks could find humor in a hurricane from Hell. And they did.

The next morning, Margot arose in a bundle of rags that Nell had dried above the stove. A pot of boiling water was on top of the stove. Margot's milking morning eyes were blinking away at the thick optical mucus to focus on her mother huddled in the corner lacing the conductor's intestines through two lithe but burly bent wooden branches. Soon, Margot was to receive her first pair of snowshoes.

They grouped their supplies and noticed with half a case of ammunition, two rifles and three pistols, the Zonks, if frugal, could maintain this existence well into the near future.

The frozen conductor quickly turned into rock grouse and hare. Nothing was wasted. But the meat was too few and far between. Nell uncovered a carbide lamp from a pile of snow and fitted it into a harness on top of Margot's head. Margot was going to spelunk for a new source of frozen meat. After a few false starts, young Zonk started to use charcoal to mark each snow passage within the maze and denote its destination. Her first find was old Ms. Blue Dress locked in horror's icy mask and Margot relieved her of her shell, literally limb by limb. Her Good Book, still in her grasp, came in handy for the morning kindling in the stove. After dinner, Margot belched a mist of a warm snow melt cup of water and said, "Yup, Mom. You were right. Skanky was the word I missed." They both had a giggle.

Weeks went by. The rescue team from both Redding and Medford were consistently delayed by continued heavy snowstorms. A plane was hired to locate the train and review the damage but a violent down draft tanked the plane into the mountainside killing the pilot in a small ball of fire.

The inhabitants in near the middle of the train were not as resourceful as the Zonks. Yes, they turned to cannibalizing their dead but soon turned on themselves in a feral last-ditch attempt at survival. Groups formed. Some on intellect and some on strength. It was all random and no one person could be trusted, no matter how dedicated to each group they were. The humans became what they always were. Animals.

The southerly flow of wind kept the Zonks' stove fumes pulsing in the surviving human's nostrils. After a few murders, they flung their vengeance on the Zonks and broke through the crust of snow, and slowly and simply swam their way through waves of rigid snow toward the caboose. Seven: four men and three women, all the passengers that were left, ravaged by the lust of hunger, attacked the caboose during the still of night.

Like mindless zombies they broke through the back windows. Nell's speed was not hampered by her drowsiness and she shot two people through the head instantly. The other humans recoiled back out of the confines of the train car. On the next attempt, the intruders brandished kitchen knives and an axe, and lunged forward. Nell once again shot two humans dead through their skulls. Margot wanted in on the action and Nell nodded in the affirmative. A large man busted open the back door of the caboose carrying a large iron rod, and Margot instantly pointed her revolver and shot into his left eye. She cocked her gun again but it was not necessary. He staggered forward a few steps and slowly knelt down on his knees, and pummeled face first to the floor. The last two overwhelmed the Zonks and wrestled them both to the bottom of the caboose. Nell looked at Margot, motioned with her eyes to the carbide lamp, and Margot knew what to do. She quickly wiggled free, grabbed the lamp, unscrewed the casing and poured the carbide into the full tea pot of water. Shaking it twice, she threw the pot into the stove, clamped closed the iron gate and Nell broke free, and she and Margot immediately dove out the windows into the deep snow. The water turned the carbide instantly into acetylene and the small iron stove exploded.

The morning brought the sun. Nell and Margot were huddled together in their own snow cave. The back of the caboose was completely destroyed. The iron fragments of the stove left no bodies but ground meat and splintered bone. A lone biplane flew overhead and then swung down low. He noted two survivors. An adult and a child.

Roger woke them both up out of a dream in a hospital in Medford, Oregon. He reprimanded them both on the use of English tea with milk.

The Cacophonous Mind of Emma Watson
by Opeia Zonk

"You can't save everyone. That is for the movies and is not reality. Most people can't even save themselves. If you can save one person other than yourself, just one, then you can claim success." — Ms. Watson

The scent of cat urine tanged the atmosphere around Ms. Watson's breakfast table. Marvin was there eating an overcooked crescent roll, but he ignored the brazened flakes since any food was good food and only a fool would bid farewell to such a gift. In his cup was a steaming swirl of rich coffee and cream, a combination that The Father would never let grace his lips. She also cooked greasy pork sausage with eggs over easy and her mouth expelled the dense smoke of cheap non-filtered cigarettes. These were his memories. Marvin cherished these memories. Ms. Watson filled his cup, and as in every morning, she said, "What is your VISION?"

Marvin Bartleby, at five, didn't know what she was talking about. His vision was of her, him, the Orphanage and parts of Baltimore. 'Smack' landed the rolled-up newspaper on his head. "NO! What is your VISION?" Eventually, a bubble of neurons surfaced to plead for oxygen and he realized she was asking him what he wanted to do with his future.

"I don't know!" 'Smack' landed the rolled-up newspaper.

"Again?" she yelled.

"I want to be my own person," he hissed through shut teeth that were buried in a sore head.

"Then THAT is your vision!" And that was his first breakfast with Ms. Watson.

She 'borrowed' Marvin for needed assistance in Baltimore to review yard and estate sales for her classic book collections. He took this time to peruse outdated computers for necessary parts. His most flamboyant find was the Interstellar Business Building's dumpsters where e-waste was not yet recycled. Just year-old processors and mainframe circuit boards were there for the taking.

Emma Watson was a doppelganger of her father, the great Reverend Watson of the South Baptist Church. Her father built from nothing a church, followed by a pre-school and then an elementary charter school. Reverend Watson was a great community leader and he seriously looked after his flock. He wore a black suit with a crisp white shirt and tie. Emma wore the same. He was big and overtly masculine. She was the same. He wanted his daughter to be a singer of Gospel Music. She wanted him to shut up. Music confused her mind. And there the comparison ended. Except for their love of collard greens, beans and cornbread.

The recipes, all, filtered down from her mother's side of the family, percolated in Emma. Emma's mother, unfortunately, succumbed to the frothing of the lard that coated her arteries and she died too young of a coronary disease. But the recipes were a past language unto themselves and she delved in to produce a language rich in wholesome spiced pinto beans, slathered bacon with onion and garlic infused collards, with the basic buttermilk pan corn bread with fried chitlins. And if your mouth does not water upon these words, then you don't know shit. And many people just don't really know shit. Most of them are Republicans.

Every Sunday, Emma would hold an evening dinner for her father. This night, she invited Marvin. Reverend Watson, at the head of the table, a bear of a man, uttered in a very low voice, "Mr. Bartleby, what exactly do you do?" And Emma quickly responded that Marvin had his shit together. Indeed, Marvin jumped up with apology and went into the basement, and retrieved a cardboard box full of mason jars – each containing his fecal waste. And it was all for the Reverend. Emma knew Marvin was on his way to success.

Author's note: Again, this was non-fiction. Marvin told me so much about his life that I wanted his beginning to have a story. He still keeps his fecal matter in mason jars in the basement of The Estate. He definitely has his shit together.

The Vacancy of Opeia

"The biological clock only has so many clicks. When it is done, there is no more winding." — Opeia

The titillations of menstruation broke down the stoic castle walls that protected her against procreation. Opeia, in her late twenties, wanted to breed. She could smell it and taste it and her senses were not wrong. It led her to a hunger that melted into irrational thoughts, but her desire was tantamount to foul reason and she visibly withdrew toward her complacency. There was not but Chester to meet any current males match, but alas, he was a pig and he did not smell a morel in Opeia's soul.

The turkey baster carafe was passed around what staff inhabited The Estate and the Noodle. Mannheim, an orderly now Doctor, wanted his Aryan DNA to inhabit the Zonks. He manipulated the sample to accentuate his genome donation. Opeia had a different idea. Not random but simple. She chose Marvin.

Marvin was pathetically nervous about this entire ordeal but Opeia was patient. He was shaking and was laid, floundering, on his own futon cotton queen mattress. She caressed his body and kissed him sweetly on his cheeks, face and buttocks, but that didn't appear to create the desired reaction. So, unlike the other female Zonks, she stripped down and mounted him, the timid bull that he was. Hormones being hormones, Marvin awoke with a massive initiative and it porked and plumbed the nodule of a singularity that would soon birth a new Zonk. The vacancy was now inhabited and the flashing neon tattoo on her mound's pubis proclaimed occupancy full. Marvin farted.

The Suffocation of the Trilobites

"There is no retribution for the infected conservatives. There is only consternation for the afflicted liberals. And I am here to fan the flames in the hearts of those liberal smoldering souls." — Margot

Margot was pounding her fist on a homemade podium in the far corner of a fishing warehouse, down by the docks in Seattle. The crowd was, by far, her largest at over fifty union members. The depression was in full force and impoverished people everywhere were looking for a message of solidarity and healing, and the Zonks were pushing the voices of Marx and Engels.

Many years before, Lenin and Trotsky (aka Bronstein) were on a similar mission in Russia. Their vision of a socialist Russia was difficult to implement. Then, a Georgian named Stalin, who had no intention of articulating the words of Marx or Engels, developed his private police force and took control of the government under the name of communism. It wasn't socialism; it was just a plain mass murdering dictatorship that was led by force, greed, fear and intimidation—much like the US Republican Party many years later. So, somewhere along the line, socialism got confused with communism and the latter was basically cruel dictatorships. The Zonks wanted to change the image of socialism by instilling its true message into the hearts and minds of the working class.

A large truck busted through the main door of the warehouse, and police and company loyalists arrived in strength. The owners of the fishing company did not want union bonding under any name and particularly those that sang the song of socialism. Margot was arrested for disturbing the peace but it was peace that was the seed she was attempting to sow. She had her first night in jail.

She came into consciousness on a concrete slab right next to a woman who was relieving herself in a porcelain toilet. The iron bars around the small room indicated to the young woman that she was incarcerated. There was another woman kneeling next to her, mopping her forehead with what appeared to be cotton panties. The panties were white but they were stained with blots of blood. Margot then realized that the blood was hers from her head. She attempted to sit up but fell back down. She was very dizzy. The woman on the toilet finished her ritual and looked down and spat on Margot's cheek. "Communist!" she said. The kneeling woman wiped away the expectoration and quietly said her name was Gilla.

Gilla Mostel was raised in Brooklyn, NY, to a middle-class Jewish tailor and her pious sewing mother. Mostel's was well known in the Jewish Quarter for inexpensive sturdy cloth, and expert design and sewing. The family lived above their clothing shop. Gilla had a singular mind and that mind was on being the best singer in the world. She saved all her money from assisting in the shop to buy the current records of Esther Walker and Mamie Smith. In the family bathroom, with floor to wall tiles, the reverberations were phenomenal. Unfortunately, Gilla was tone deaf. Severely tone deaf. Mr. Mostel funded various tutors and voice coaches but the young Mostel was genetically bound by the law of sonic numbness. What she heard when she sang in her bathroom was that of an alto singer like Clara Butt, but what the family actually heard was the scratchy hollering of a dying female that tripped and fell continuously in her endless echo chamber of a lacerating shower stall. Her father and mother begged her to go to school and focus on the family business, but Gilla was determined that her ears were not wrong and that the rest of the world just did not appreciate her nightingale song craft. She took all her savings and bought a ticket to the other side of the continent. Gilla went to Seattle.

With her passion and ambition, she was found at the fish market gallery hollering any tune that any passer-by would mention. Her memory for current tunes was immense. Soon, however, weeks in fact, she turned to prostitution to pay the bills. And again, unfortunately, she was worse at fornicating than singing, so her suitors were less than generous with their funds. She was eventually jailed on vagrancy and there she met Margot.

The Zonks don't forget a beating and Margot was not going to start to be benevolent. She shuffled off her dizziness and brought Gilla into the fold of her focus. Upon release, young Zonk took Gilla to her mother's herbal medicine and veterinary clinic on First Hill, and they began to formulate their futures. Dr. Nell's shop had bedrooms in the back with a little kitchen. Gilla's future was looking brighter. Well, if she could see it.

Early in her life, back in Brooklyn, physicians determined she had a recent, but unusually aggressive, form of macular degeneration. Odd for one so young and, sadly, her forecast was for complete blindness in a few years. This malady would not stop her to forge her destiny as a vocalist. Gilla's singing capabilities, as abhorrent as they were, needed one major thing. It lacked of marketing. And Margot had an idea.

Margot was talking but Gilla could not hear. She was looking up from the bottom of the water from Nell's clawfoot tub. Margot was scrubbing off Gilla's street stench. The Zonks only had so many senses to squander, and they could now only afford losing hearing when Gilla sang, so they did not want her filth-covered skin to suffocate their vision and nostrils too.

Margot was attempting to tell her she was going to be visited by a being from another dimension, and she sternly emphasized that she should be very polite to her at all times. This being could quite easily make Gilla's life a living Hell.

Gilla was asleep but she did not see Roger since she was not a Zonk. She saw a pan flute playing Martha that was a seventh dimension being that just received her PhD in human futility. She was vacant from any reality lately since she was tending to her pathetic meaningless tasks at fulfilling her futile goal at achieving her ultimate doctoral prize. She realized the task was futile, so she won. Dr. Martha emerged. Dr. Martha earned her due. She oversaw the destruction of many solar systems and even the eventual demise of Galaxies like MACS2129-1. Well, you have to go sometime.

Martha pointedly penetrated time, since she could, and moved with haste on the timeline. She met Roger at the Zonk Coffee Shop on Teegarden C just in time for Roger's cup of full steaming fresh jasmine pearl bud. It was an order that was late but so was she; exact time was just as fickle as it was for multi-dimensional beings too. When she materialized, some fool had put up a cement barrier that wasn't there over one hundred years ago. She skinned her knees. The impudent fuck! She composed herself and met Roger with disdain. "Must I?" she snorted.

"You certainly must!" was his response. And they began their blended tincture of imagination that was to become a truly coy event on earth.

Gilla was in a dream. Some woman was puffing poorly on a pan flute. She said she got it from an old Lebanese being for her recent ascension into Doctorhood. Her name was Martha from the seventh dimension and no, Gilla did not have to tell her anything about herself since Martha had already 'read' the book. Martha, patiently, as patient as she could be with the slugged soul of a third dimensional blob of flesh, told her a tale.

There was an old fisherman (the story actually started this way), and he was Etruscan from what is now Cosa, Italy. Daily, he would leave his village to scamper down the rolling slopes to a lonely outcropping of rock on the edge of the sea. The sea at this time was teeming with all sorts of fish. Even his poor eyesight could not dissuade him from plundering this flesh. With salt to cure, he would sell this sea bounty to his village and be a wealthy man. Well, relative wealth since the Etruscans generally married into wealth through noble family lineages, so the best he could really obtain was the line just nigh of absolute poverty. But that was a digression, as stated by Martha. Now, the old fisherman, even though historically he was very good at fishing, could not get a fish to bite at his bait. None. All the other fishermen rejoiced in the bounty of the sea but the old man could not understand why no fish would enjoy his line even though the bait was the same for all other men fishing in that water. He curled into a ball on the overhanging rocks near the sea and he prayed to his God, which at the time was actually Martha—without her PhD —though she was not a God but in the year 273 BCE, the fisherman could not possibly understand any dimension let alone the third one he was actually basking in. She heard his prayers but really did not give a shit about these mindless mounds of quivering meat. Beings don't even get interesting until the fifth dimension, well, except for the Zonks and that is why she was telling the story. So Martha, the pseudo-God, told the crying old fisherman to play on his strengths and forget his weaknesses. He did not understand, and then lightning struck his forehead from Martha's forced expulsion of nasal mucus and she yelled, "Be the failure you were meant to BE!"

The old fisherman, now completely blind from the lightning strike, still did not understand, but the next day he used his fishing pole to tap his way down to his seaside rock and began to fish. And fish. And fish. The other fishermen enjoyed his constitution and realized that he began to revel in his failure to catch anything. Indeed, every time he pulled up a line with nothing on it, he would yell to the sky and thank the Gods for not providing him with his want. The village people began to flock to the seaside to see the old man pull line after line of nothing but a bare hook and what would generally be a sign of sadness, he embraced in hilarity and danced on his rock, and yelled thanks to all the Gods—all that he could remember. The village took pity on him and began throwing coins of copper, then silver and then gold. His success was in his failure and his fame followed. He became the loyal Royal court jester in all the land since he, being a pathetic failure, was actually very funny.

Martha ended the tale on a foul note on her flute. She realized Gilla, doe eyed, didn't get the message of the story. So she shot out a sizzling bolt of snot between Gilla's eyes and left. Gilla woke up to see Margot on the side of her bed. Margot said, "Okay, this is what we are going to do."

Margot dressed her up in a thick wool black frock coat. She gave her some welding goggles that Margot picked up at a pawn shop. Gilla could not see out of these lenses but she couldn't see anyway so that didn't matter. Margot, from the same pawn shop, bought an abused dulcimer that was missing, at least, half of its strings. "But I don't know how to play the dulcimer," she pleaded.

"The fisherman couldn't catch fish either!" said Margot. The last item to adorn this Jewish soul was a walking cane. And honestly, she needed it.

She and Margot would early every morning saunter down to the Pike Street Market and take a prominent busking corner in the middle of the madness. And the madness was then amplified a very good deal. Gilla would holler out in her raspy voice, like fingernails on a chalkboard, and strum randomly on an out of tune dulcimer. Her welding goggles, and her black coat and timbre, made her look and sound like a blind Mary Poppins that somehow survived after swallowing Drano.

The black top hat that Margot placed at her feet became overflowing in cash and coin. Most people paid her to stop singing but a loyal few paid her to continue. And so it went on. A mob of maniacal humans daily met at this corner bifurcated on what was actually considered pure talent. And Gilla got rich. Well, relatively.

Gilla still lived with the Zonks in the back of the clinic but got a seeing-eye-dog, a Labrador named Fester. He had a leather harness and vest that stated clearly, he was not to be bothered since he was a seeing-eye-dog for the blind. He actually was a random drop off at Dr. Nell's Vet Clinic and he was quite incapable of being a dog for the blind since he, himself, was blind. But that was the stick. Gilla may not have invented it, but she sure did own it, and that 'it' was CAMP.

Margot needed Gilla for her next venture and that was revenge. No one messed with a Zonk and she was going to ride the point of the arrow right through the Seattle Police Department. Precisely the ones that beat her up so badly for sowing the seed of socialistic peace. The plan was simple. It had to be simple since complicated broke down too easily and they needed, on her budget, reliability.

A blind woman with welding goggles and a blind seeing-eye-dog bumped into the doors at the Seattle Police Department. Cordiality was awarded and that included a tour of the facility and a meeting with the Chief of Police. An inquiry led to the reality that the entire police department hired out Toy-Lem Chinese Laundry Service for all cleaning needs. Margot dug into the laundry business and she discovered that Toy-Lem ran a minor but lucrative drug operation on the side, and the police received kickbacks for the contract to clean the entire police force laundry. The scene was set, and even though they were both not Chinese, pity was pity during the depression years and two lonely thin bundles of rags, one blind with a knot headed bumbling canine, would not be turned away for mere cleaning duties.

The police garments came in special wax paper packages. Their underwear was marked by ink on the elastic band as to the owner. This was the prize. Initially they started off with oil of cinnamon, which was easy to obtain, from Wo's herbs just down the block. Impact was good but not sustaining since the oiled patch to the loin area of the undergarment looked like a urine stain. But then Nell had a better idea. From her laboratory, Nell extracted from various pepper strains pure capsaicin. She blended this into a hydrogenated cream that was tested at exactly one hundred percent pure. Nothing in the world could be technically more exothermic except for the blast of a welding torch. Margot and Gilla, at Toy-Lem's one weekend night, applied the cream to all the crotches of all undergarments for all the policemen in the Main Seattle Precinct. And then there was ignition.

The next week, nearly eighty percent of the Main precinct was absent from duty. An apparently rare strain of a blistering rash formed on the groin areas of all these men. A scientific investigation could not rule out a new sexually transmitted disease from the prostitutes in Chinatown. Many of these law enforcement officers were suspended for improper conduct, but the rest were to carefully skip the beat, bow-legged like a raw-hided whipped cowpoke, to air out their wicked sins on every block they walked. Police productivity fell by over fifty percent. Strangely, crime did not increase, but the majority of the Seattle population had some really good guffaws at the sight of these wobbling 'cowboys' in pain.

The Venting of Andromeda Wood

by Opeia Zonk

"Taciturn our voices lay. Silent but brooding. No more! No more! We will climb the mountain of mindless conservatives and arise to vanquish this stupidity from our Nation." — Ms. Wood, Ward Two

Ms. Wood was insane. Technically, she was clinically and mentally vibrant and crystal clear in her sanity, but her self-incarcerated body to this facility was to protect right-wing conservatives from death. She loathed, and rightfully so, Republicans. Ms. Wood never got close to fulfilling her ambitions to rid America of the seething pestilence of conservativism. She did, during a rally, vomit profusely on some flaming right-wing delegates. But that was it. Ms. Wood came in to the Zonk Farm of the Warped Noodle since she bit off the ear of North Carolina Republican congressman, Jack Waddell, during a campaign stint in front of the most popular social venue in Pittsboro. Judy Juggs and the Lactation Band were accompanying him for this voracious speaking tour on eradicating this land from liberals who wanted free education and free healthcare.

Covered in glandular secretions, Mr. Waddell said poignantly, "Free education and free healthcare are socialist constructs so that you can freely ignore the freedom that you already have by freely paying taxes to free the conservatives from liberal thinking. Your taxes are why I am here to protect you from the drivel of yourselves! I am here to be your hero to further the development of false productivity so that the degradation of society appears like a success." They all roared for his re-election. Ms. Wood, posing as a reporter, with her pen and paper in hand, lunged at the Congressman in an abrupt hug and succinctly bit off his right ear.

Ms. Wood, still chewing his cartilage while being processed into the Noodle, was smiling, tame and happy. And chewing. This cartilage she wanted to savor until the last dollop. The Zonks made it precisely clear to the staff of the Noodle that Andromeda was not to ever mingle with right-wing conservatives. Thankfully, and well planned, all of those folks were heavily medicated and securely locked up on Ward Three.

Andromeda was up to something. She was always up to something but this time it was very noticeable. She was too quiet. The much too much verbally raving and ranting woman was too calm; like the silence of animals right before a massive earthquake. Eni noticed it and she requested that Chester check in on her on random, but daily, intervals.

Chester reported to the Zonks that Ms. Wood was having secretive meetings with both male and female members of Ward Two. Ward Two was like all other Wards at the Noodle. The west wing was for females and the east wing was for males. In the center was a large communal area where both sexes could have food, conversation or play games. This was also the area where they received their medications. Ms. Wood, at night, was stealing the keys to the east wing and meeting with male members of Ward Two. Chester discovered this was not for fornication but verbal intercourse without lubrication. Their minds, under treatment, were not lucid enough to formulate rational conclusions. Or so Chester thought. Andromeda was also meeting with various sundry females in her wing of the Ward. Something was brewing. The Zonks decided to increase the dose of the medications on Ward Two, and just as a precaution, Ward Three as well.

Ms. Wood had two twin sons. Josh and Josh. They were identical in every way. She was never good with names and wanted to be sure she, at least, had a one hundred percent chance of getting their names right, even though her intended conversation with the correct Josh was basically 50/50. Josh and Josh grew up to be educated in engineering. One in wood and one in candy. Josh One, we will call him, was famous in this life for designing and building the most impeccable furniture, made of teak. He loved this wood. Resilient, heavy and strong. In fact, Andromeda was rocking in a chair made by him with this wood when she made her glorious proclamation. Josh Two, named for factual recognition, invented strawberry red licorice, thank God, to a deity he didn't believe in, since that anise flavored gummy crap candy stained the teeth and breath of everyone who ingested that charcoal excrement. And it was with this red colored candy that she wove her plan.

Latimer Bunk was the security night guard on Ward Two. He had keys to all the other Wards; in fact, he had all the keys to the entire building. Latimer was the only employee of the Zonks who was religious, and since by Zonk edict, all religions were bunk, it fit his last name so they kept him in employ. Mr. Bunk believed fervently in the pagan God called Zal. Zal was the leading deity to a small tribe on the island of Fiji. Zal was also the only God known to humankind that smoked Cuban seed Dominican Republic Rothchild Maduro cigars. Exactly like the ones that Mr. Bunk smoked. This coincidence was far too great to ignore, and Latimer became a tribal member and a vehement follower of Zal.

Years before, regrettably, young Mr. Bunk, during a vacation, traveled with the Tollbrook High School varsity football team to Mazatlán. His mother thought it would do him good since all he ever did was read very strange science fiction books on multi-dimensional beings. Roger and Martha liked Latimer tremendously. Allen Worple was the star quarterback and a sadist. Allen's ego was lauded about the former but was oblivious to the latter since he didn't understand the word, nor comprehend that causing pain to others was necessarily a bad thing. And he was going to cause pain on the chubby short pale book nerd since it gave him pleasure and steeped him in adulation amongst his future Republican teammates. Allen got Latimer very intoxicated on Mezcal. Allen was very concentrated that Latimer get the worm. It was necessary and manly, and Latimer desperately wanted to please his mother to become a man. He had many worms that day.

Latimer Bunk woke up on a sandy beach south of the main city in his swim trunks. He had no memory of changing clothes. He was beet red from blistering sunburn. The ocean was roaring but he could only hear the painful pounding of the Sumatran Gong players that inhabited his skull and were banging mercilessly on his inner eardrums. He tried to get up but could not. Upon inspection, he discovered someone had put a jellyfish down his trunks. Fortunately, this jelly's tentacles did not endorse themselves on his testicles but only on his right leg. This left his leg muscles stark rigid and Latimer, well, paralyzed. An old ragged blind fisherman with his fishing pole came up to him, tapped him on the forehead, and said in broken English, "Be the failure you were meant to BE!" Latimer did not understand and thought this man was crazy.

Young Bunk woke up again in a Mexican hospital in the middle of Mazatlán. Hovering over him was a very pretty nurse, Maria Klute, who was half Mexican and half German. She came from a long line of German Klutes. She told him he was very lucky since the jellyfish that stung him was deadly and if, by chance, it had entwined around his pathetic copulation organ, and she emphasized 'pathetic', then he would have been rendered sterile. But now, she stated, you are free to reproduce. His leg was healed eventually, and Nurse Klute would daily bring him a snow cone with rich red strawberry cream flavoring. She said this flavoring was well known in Mexico and it enhanced the vitality of 'pathetic' organs. She was not kidding. This flavor had an ingredient, illegal in the US, but vital for Mexico, that contained the ground up wings of the emerald-green beetle that contained terpenoid cantharidin—a very strong aphrodisiac. His recovery was rather quick at this juncture and his now portly blood-engorged organ was gratefully and daily relieved by Maria. Upon release, his epigenetic modifications to his genome were now burned into his soul and he would always associate the color strawberry red with pleasure and salvation. Latimer talked in his sleep and he often slept while on duty. Andromeda listened very carefully and her plan was complete.

One day, in the communal room, rocking in her teak wood chair, Andromeda yelled at the top of her lungs. Which was fairly substantial at 130 dB. Now that she had a captive audience, she hollered, "I proclaim the formation of the Nation of Teak, which is a group of women and men that are of liberal progressive minds that join in the rejection of all conservatives and conservative ideals. This group will denounce right-wing Republicans and purge them from this great nation. The Nation of Teak will embrace democratic socialist norms and policies, and assure free healthcare and free education for all citizens." Two people clapped but Ms. Wood did not know that they were applauding the fact that she had finally stopped yelling. There was a loud grunting noise coming from her left field of vision. It was Chester. Someone locked him up in the storage closet.

Wednesday morning, a box appeared. Security, the day shift, scoured the package. It just contained candy. The box was delivered at the foot of Ms. Wood's bed at eleven thirty a.m. She put this package into her teak made locker—made by Josh One. The parcel contained many plastic bags of Real Wood Red Licorice—made by Josh Two. The bags were transparent.

After dinner, Chester's suspicions were expanding, and he suggested a second round of medication for both Wards Two and Three. This action was performed.

Andromeda Wood, pretending to sleep, was sobbing in suppressed hilarity. The lights were turned off and Latimer sat down in his chair by the door and fell into a deep slumber. At midnight, Ms. Wood unlatched her locker to grab the parcel of candy. She and her female followers flocked around the snoozing Mr. Bunk and, at his feet, opened up the box that contained fresh strawberry flavored red licorice. Nudged awake, Latimer gazed down into the vast depth below his knees and immediately received a portly blood engorged organ. This time, there was no Maria for assistance, there was only his consternation and his will to survive. He flailed off his trousers along with his belt and keys, and began to inhale the sweet fragrance of impending love. Ms. Wood and crew disappeared to the east wing and released the male members of the new Nation of Teak. They combined to create a bizarre, heavily medicated, slurring and wobbling liberal force that jolted in a muscle pulsing tsunami up the stairs toward Ward Three. Their intentions, which were later haltingly parsed together by Chester, were that liberal Ward Two intended to completely annihilate conservative Ward Three. And they tried.

The door to Ward Three burst open at approximately one a.m. Armed with brooms, mops and Ms. Wood, equipped with Mr. Bunk's compressed can of pepper spray and truncheon, began the assault. Heavy psychosis medication affects depended on many variables. Weight and size were just two. Acclimation was also a factor. The initial battle was convincingly in line with the surprise assault of Ward Two members. Ward Three woke up startled and rebutted with some quirky defense. Both Ward inhabitants were under the impression that visual gelatinous hallucinations of mucus spewing walking lemon flavored cubical robots had taken over the Warped Noodle. They all began to fight, not for any liberal or conservative cause, but a real fight for survival. Someone heard down the stairwell Latimer yelling, "Zal is coming! Zal is coming!" And he did.

Ms. Wood discharged the can of pepper spray, but not able to aim properly, shot the entire can into her own face and only achieved temporary blindness and passed out. All the others, on both sides, eventually collapsed by sheer exhaustion in a failed flailing phonetic grunting frenzy. Not a soul was injured in any way. Zade often uses this incident during speeches to enhance the notion that all wars should be waged by the mentally incompetent. Oh, but wait, they are. Unfortunately, those wars had casualties. Dear, where was the heavy medication?

Many days later, Latimer sat down near the bed of a massively restrained Ms. Wood. He thanked her immensely for the red licorice. She just quietly smiled. Then, after several moments, he said, "Why can't you find some peace, some piece of common ground between Ward Two and those in Ward Three?"

She gazed at him with small, but bright, eyes then furrowed her eyebrows and stated in precise single words, "You can't negotiate with fascists!"

Author's note: Well, this too was non-fiction. It is strange, I find in this world, where truth and fiction fuse to form an odd reality. This realm, I am convinced, perseveres in the souls of the Zonks.

The Budding Joy from Marvin's Spigot

"Once again we somberly honor this day to remember the death of the Great Lady Badger Zonk but joyfully cradle this moment for the birth of Bootes into our home." — Opeia to the newly initiated Dangleberry class of students

Bootes was a handful. Like all Zonks, Opeia worked and breast fed at the same time. Marvin was the father but he did not want to take the lead. He was a Zonk by decree and he would always be there to tutor and mentor this very young squid. And he did. Bootes grew up to love him dearly.

Her first offering was a pre-digested spinach dark green turd that Opeia electroplated into a solid silver paper weight. This item still holds prominence in the Hall of Remembrance in the lower echelon of the Dangleberry Mansion.

Opeia was back in the lab. She had an idea. Eni and Zade were spending so much time in managing both the Noodle and The Estate that there was little time for much else, but both promised Opeia that they would assist her during the night hours.

Opeia was focused on phobias. Mental fears that afflict certain individuals. She wanted to weaponize one particular phobia and introduce its negative impact, but only on extreme right-wing conservative minds.

She initially considered ephebiphobia, the fear of teenagers, but in most extreme conservative families those parents already feared their children since all new generations have more liberal tendencies. Then there was coulrophobia, the fear of clowns, and here her idea was fairly sound, since the Republican President was one. But after some consideration, the President was already a Dictator and fear amongst his base was exactly what he needed. There was bathmophobia, the fear of steep slopes, but there again the majority of conservatives lived in the flat lands of America and had no slopes to fear. And androphobia, the fear of men, was examined but extreme conservatives were all homophobic anyway so what would be the point? Atelophobia, the fear of imperfection, was waxed too but, once again, Republicans honestly believed they had no deficiencies so that would be a waste. So Opeia finally settled on leukophobia, the morbid fear of the color white. But how would one weaponize this for the expected audience?

After much research, Opeia had a plan. Glaxkow Inc. was a media conglomerate that owned numerous smaller media outlets throughout the United States; specifically, in the rural Midwest and South. On an aside, over forty percent of their funding was through an endowment by Russian oligarchs. Money was money and that was the language of the conservatives. These TV stations were not cable and they filtered into the thirty percent of households that were basically uneducated whites, so these 'news' messages were deliberately controlled to manipulate this demographic. As Joseph Goebbels stated, "If you can control the propaganda, then you can control the people."

But one station that Glaxkow owned was cable and did reach a very large audience. Vixen TV. This TV station was of a particular interest to the Zonks. This TV station was controlled by some of the wealthiest people in the US and they directly rewrote news, and even history, to influence their ideals to shape the minds of the majority white viewers to false concepts. This vision was not new; it was basically to baffle the masses with bullshit and it worked. Vixen TV was the channel that spoke the Republican President's language—though he wasn't a Republican—but what was more disappointing was that the Republican congresspeople and senators were not Republican either. They all faded into the historical façade of the cabinets of Mussolini, Hitler, Stalin and Mao. This was now a dictatorship and the entire nation's media was Vixen TV. Joseph Goebbels was burning in Hell, thanks to Roger, but now Goebbels was laughing amongst the flames saying, "If you don't know your history, you are bound to repeat it!" Opeia needed assistance so she brought in the mind of Marvin.

Marvin was thoroughly famous on campus since the student body discovered that learning a mere two to three fourth-generation computer languages, could take them into the world and immerse them in upper middle-class wealth. Opeia sat down with a suckling Bootes and confronted Marvin with her plan.

Professor Marv loved the idea and the challenge. He went back to his lab and his mind began with a mull, then a ponder; it puzzled and reflected. Then the juices of his cranial lobes slathered in speculation until the light was not only luminescent but dazzlingly brilliant. He plopped into the now and realized he hadn't slept in days, and failed to show up for scads of lectures. He ran across The Estate yards, swam the pond, for whatever reason, and stumbled into Opeia's laboratory where she was found changing Bootes' diaper. The stench made him reel back with a jolt and he gagged. Through his ponderous gasp of an exultation, he exclaimed, "I've GOT IT!"

What Marvin had was an expanded understanding of frequency analysis. Not sonic frequencies but visual. If someone was well trained and compelled, that individual could hack into the server center of any TV station and modulate the visual frequencies to induce temporary phobias to anyone viewing the output of the TV. The temporary part was based on the recurrent viewing of the viewer. It was theoretical, but it was mathematically possible. Opeia was elated and wanted to fornicate right then and there, but Marvin was not able to generate that energy while Bootes was gazing at them from the crib. Opeia wanted Marv to focus his computer techniques on the phobia, leukophobia. And he did.

After a few months, he knew he had the particular frequency. He couldn't possibly test this computer visual frequency hack on the student body since they were Asian, Hispanic or Black and they all generally didn't like Caucasians anyway. He could not be the lab rat since he didn't much like humans in general. The Zonk staff of white people were out since if this worked, they could not be part of the Zonk team. So, he told Opeia that he was just going to wing it and hack into the Vixen cable channel and see what happened. And he did.

On that day, Marvin clicked the keyboard to type in the password WHITEWASH. His T5 line buzzed through various pipelines and servers, and landed into Vixen TV. That entire day and night the placid viewers were subjected to a mind-altering frequency that induced a solid phobia. But the next day nothing happened. Surely, there would have been paranoid waves on the streets with Caucasians fleeing from themselves in abject horror. They must recoil from their own hideous sight of their reflections in the mirror! No. Nothing.

Nothing in the news. The conservative whites were still the same shits as they always had been. Marvin had made a small error in his analysis. At the fifth iteration he claimed success but if he waited for the seventh iteration, he would have found the visual frequency he used did not have the correct amplitude. The phobia that he induced was not leukophobia but trypophobia, the fear of holes.

In retrospect, it was a semi-success. As noted in the data, young extreme conservatives did not breed at this time. They were all, to a person, morbidly afraid of holes.

Nell's Nefarious Merger

"Sometimes, conglomerates collaborate to coagulate." — Nell to Margot

Bulregard Matthes was wealthy but old. He was demented but his money kept him out of physical incarceration. He was harmless but annoying and Seattle just took him in as one of a number of eccentric people that flowed through the streets. His real name was Ezra Horowitz and he was part of a long line of lineages to the Rothchild name. He lived in a large mansion near Volunteer Park but only used one bedroom and one bathroom. He owned a mare named Funk that he kept in a stable in his garage. Bulregard, thankfully, didn't drive a car.

Bulregard was not English. He was more closely related to Trotsky as a Polish Jew than he was to John Manners as the Duke of Rutland, though he played the part of aristocratic English very well. Dressed as a major, a colonel or a general, depending on the day of the week, he was lavished with either a red, royal blue or gold uniform of the English Indian army. He carried a rusted Halberd, even though that instrument of war was not excessively used during the Indian Campaign; it didn't matter. He was insane.

He would ride Funk with all his pageantry of trumpets, flutes and horns that no one else could hear. Unseen confetti would rain down on his head. He would bow to their accolades at all his past triumphs, which were none, and the children would feed Funk apples and carrots upon her arrival, only to see her defecate road apples of her own making. It was wonderful. It was Seattle. Later, Republicans took copious notes about this man and his magnitude of influence. It all was brilliant in its inception and lunacy.

He met Nell on Funk near a street next to a coffee shop on Broadway; he went lush, she thought him extremely strange, and they got married. And the weirdness began.

Eccentricity attracts eccentricity like a pile of iron filings to a magnet. Polarities dominate. And they did. But, unlike most north and south projections, like encircled dislike in this case. That would be the meaning of eccentricity. And it was. Why couldn't our own country clutch this oddness and label it as sanity? The erudition of magnanimity procreated a form of taint that delved into a form of a necessity.

Margot was obviously upset. No female Zonk in known history ever married. Nell was calm but explained, "Yes, he is a loon, but now he is my loon and he has agreed to take my last name. Zonks have always been a tad odd and I see this as a grand addition into our family. And, of course, then there is his money."

"We don't need his money!" Margot said.

"This is a depression, Margot. Everyone needs work and everyone needs money," Nell stated resolutely. Margot did realize he was frumpy but occasionally said poignant phrases—as though the cloud of lunacy lifted suddenly and his eyes cleared, and out popped something intelligent.

"But I will not call him Father!" she said.

Nell replied, "He probably would not know what that meant so just call him Bulregard."

Dressed in his most opulent General attire, he opened the door to his mansion and a truck unloaded what little items the Zonks had. This house was huge by any Zonk standards, and Margot and Nell were to take any of the bedrooms and bathrooms on any of the three floors, just not the rooms Bulregard inhabited. The place really needed a cleaning and Margot and Nell got to work right away. Gilla Mostel stayed back at the Vet Clinic's backroom and kept that stead well groomed.

Margot suddenly woke up to realize how fantastic this situation was. She was always pounding the podium for socialist reforms in warehouses, basements and street corners, but now she had a nest for all the liberal progressive birds to roost. There was a huge dining room, offices, several bedrooms and bathrooms, and a large kitchen. This was a perfect haven for ruminating on constructive humanistic secular concepts. Nell smiled at her enthusiasm.

And then they came. Margot's reputation spread. Norman Thomas, Earl Browder, Gertrude Stein, John Reed, Edna St. Vincent Millay, Francis Farmer and on and on. Margot and Gilla would take notes at all of the meetings. A donation hat was passed around for food, liquor and cigarette expenses. These ideas formed a manifesto of a government for the people and by the people. The foundation became based on education, literacy and a sound secular philosophy. Margot was just amazed at being at the table with all these famous people during these cutting-edge political times.

Bulregard Zonk would enter into the fray with his Halberd and his medals sparkling. He would salute and bow to his patrons, and initially, Margot thought this embarrassing, but the budding socialist intellects greeted him with a round of applause and played on to his formalities in dementia. It all fit nicely into a small warm pocket of history.

That night, Bulregard yelled for Margot's attendance. Nell got to him first to make sure he was safe. He was in his bed, upright and pale. He motioned for Nell to leave as Margot entered his bedroom door. Bulregard beckoned her to get closer. He said, with some exasperation, "Look to the window and there in the reflection you will find safety and salvation!" And then, just as abruptly, he fell back down into the dense heat of his bed and fell asleep. Margot rushed to her mother, repeated the phrase, but neither knew what to make of it.

Nell shrugged her shoulders and said, "Well, mad as a hat maker."

The next day, Margot met with a young group of impassioned democratic socialists at the mansion, and gave them pamphlets and a revised copy of a new socialist manifesto. She sent them out to the streets of Seattle to market a new government agenda. At noon she had tea and pastries with the Ladies' Auxiliary and gave a rousing welcome speech. That evening she was again pounding the podium at the local Welders' Union down at the shipping dry docks. She was heartily received. Margot did not have the bus fare so she resolutely began to walk the five miles uphill toward home.

A group of financially backed conservatives had been secretly watching the socialist movement in Seattle. This swell was not good for business or their profit margins. Margot had to be stopped. They hired, at great expense for the time and for assured success, seven thugs. Armed with guns and knives their mission was to exterminate Margot Zonk. They were outside the Union Hall for Welders when she left and followed her up the street.

It was a typical Seattle spring night. Heavy mist was falling. On her fourth block, she was engulfed in a brown blanket and the boys smashed open the nearest door of a clothing supply store called Edna's Field. They made sports jerseys in all sizes for any team in the US. They threw her down amongst bolts of fabric and beat her in the blanket until she stopped screaming. The seven slowly unfolded the blanket and they were surprised that she was still conscious. They stuffed fabric in her throat and roped her mouth shut around her neck. She was wheezing hard to get enough oxygen through her blood-soaked nostrils. Margot felt weak and her vision was going into a fog. She looked up at the lamp light outside through a broken pane of window and saw the reflection of an old man on a horse dressed in a flamboyant gold uniform. He was wearing a ridiculous golden turban.

Bulregard and Funk crashed through the main window of the shop. Mannequins, jackets, wood and glass exploded to each side of the massive horse. The General had the Halberd in his right hand and a sabre in his left. The reins were nuzzled between his teeth. Margot fell back into falling fabric but easily saw Bulregard slash, pound and filet his way through the boys. The thugs turned and fired their guns. Over and over the concussions went. And then, after what seemed like hours but was precisely thirty-two seconds, the battle was done.

Funk was dead with seven bullets to her breast. All the boys, but one Buddy Bunk, the grandfather to Latimer, looked like gutted fresh fish complete with exposed entrails. The General lost his Halberd during the initial volley but he slowly crawled through the fabric and gore to eventually greet Margot. With his sabre he cut loose her rope around her mouth and removed the fabric from her throat. "Now that was a bloody good row!" he exclaimed, and like a falling pine tree, he pitched to his left on top of her body and died. There were five bullets discovered in his torso.

"The son of a bitch saved my life, the crazy loon!" Margot said to the police as tears poured from her eyes.

The lost Halberd was found in the lower intestinal track of Buddy Bunk. He survived to breed only through careful and expedited surgery. He bred during a conjugal visit during his life sentence with one Gabby Ghunt, his cousin.

The town of Seattle pitched in funds to have a grand stained-glass window made that had the likeness of General Bulregard saddled on top of a prancing Funk in various beautiful colors. It was placed in the front window of his mansion. The stained-glass window, today, is in an upstairs window of a Truck Stop in the mountains of Colorado.

The Necromancy of Sydney Gilman

by Opeia Zonk

"The mesmerizing allure of spirits can often play havoc with unstable minds." — Opeia

Sydney was a wizard. He had been one all his life. He came from a genetically lackadaisical and mediocre wizard lineage that stretched out for centuries across many nations and, to his knowledge, emanated from, then, a tiny village that was now called Varkaus, Finland. Of course, he had no memory of that time, just stories that were told down family gatherings during the traditional fireside babbles that he was fairly sure were shit.

He grew up paltry in the slum of Southside Chicago. But his family, since they were both witches and wizards, clairvoyantly told him it didn't matter since Southside Chicago would always be destitute. He was raised in crap. But crap was fertile and his seed was sown, and he grew. Sydney became a young man trained in the arts of pure magic, not illusion or trickery, but years of family, solid pagan, education. He was bullied, of course, and beaten, yes, but frail invisible flakes of dust inhabited the souls of those wicked and they all lost their testosterone as their testicles dried up like caraway seeds in a drought. All of them ended up as transient castratos that were too late in age to capture their lusty sweet soothing pure falsetto voices, and they inhaled their final future as slaves on Saltpeter-bearing ships coming from the northeast of India. Don't mess with a wizard.

He stayed ridged to his family philosophy and was very mum on any magical exploits. He worked as a produce manager, a butcher and a railway clerk but this just led him to the plastic life as a used car salesman in Oakland, California. He delved into a modest apartment in a building near Berkley. He sat on a bus bench on the corner near his abode and looked down. On the seat painted in black was the phrase, 'Bitch was a word designed by men to humiliate women!' and just below it was written, also in black, 'I am a woman and I sometimes am a Bitch and that should be respected!' Sydney thought, based on these statements, the world was a very weird place and then he noticed his bus was late.

Mr. Gilman didn't drive even though he could easily be equipped with a vehicle through Dasher Don's car lot where he worked. He could fly but hadn't since a child, and then only in the dark of night, since it would bring on too many suspicious eyes. So, like his family, he obtained the identity of just an average human soul. The only job he did turn down was selling Bibles since the hypocrisy would literally kill him. He did very well at Dasher Don's. Mr. Gilman was not only the best salesperson of this month but ever in the history of the car lot.

He was not a pontificating person but very soft spoken and, for a used car salesman, unusually factual in his presentation. Sydney was meek and mild tempered, and often nervously shuffled his feet and looked at the ground when speaking to customers. He genuinely proclaimed all the faults to the cars he was selling and freely admitted the change of gravel under the motor to hide the leaking oil. Sydney told them about the duct tape on this engine to prevent the head gasket from leaking, and the baling wire on this car to jump the broken voltage regulator box that was obviously damaged. They all stood wide eyed and aghast at the forceful wall of honesty that splashed across their faces. And just then, upon closing the deal, he would look each of them directly into their eyes and Sydney's eyes would then turn from a dark green to an orange glow—but only for a second. The customers suddenly grabbed his hand and shook it vigorously and with gratitude and much thanks, they signed the paperwork stating all the vehicle's faults and bought the car. And off they went.

To be a wizard today you have to be a master of the art of subtlety and Sydney was all of that. The spell he put his customers under was just a taint since he could not consciously burn the salad minds of people to purchase a car that he knew was crap. Sydney had a heart and that was his success as a person, but his failure at employment in most everything he attempted. The customers would eventually go home and the next day realize they had just purchased a hunk of junk car, but their signed names were on the deed of sale with the faults of the car clearly written out. They were legally stuck. This was all great and fine until a very nicely dressed gentleman arrived one afternoon and wanted to get his daughter a car for her graduation. The orange gaze appeared and the Oakland District Attorney just then purchased a 1988 Yugo in cherry red for his daughter. Two days later, police appeared and, literally, Mr. Gilman had to fly away. After several months, Sydney resurfaced in Norman, Oklahoma, selling Bibles.

Noticeably, this was problematic. He developed a nervous twitching in both of his eyes. The inhabitants of the houses that he would canvas were despondent to his malady and he stated that being imprisoned in solitary confinement for most of his life, his eyes were not amenable to sunlight. This, of course, was not a conducive positive statement for sales, but it did gently point out the direction his mind was going toward at this time.

Stepping out of a bus that was bound for Stillwater, he appeared at the front of a rustic farmhouse near the main highway; an old blind woman answered her door. She said her name was Gilla Mostel and she used to be a great singer during her time. "Oh, come in, come in," she pleaded and Sydney staggered his anorexic frame into a musty smelling room with dog excrement plastered in piles on the floor. She could not see his revulsion, and for his company she would naturally purchase a new King James leather bound edition with gold lettering if he would just sit and hear her 'soothing voice'.

"Of course!" was his chortled response.

Gilla paid him, ran her hand over the book, and whispered, "Just the first testament, you understand?" He didn't but it didn't matter since she began to careen into a gut-wrenching version of Gluck's 'Orfeo ed Euridice'. While he attempted to remain in control of his balance, she lithely tottered over, and behind her sofa, she pulled out a taxidermized Labrador dog complete with large white marbles for eyes, a plastic red wagging tongue, a vest that plainly stated not to bother the hound since he was a seeing-eye dog, and a very worn leather harness. Sydney began to think, through the rasping vomit of noise, that this just might be an hallucination. He noticed that the dog's feet were nailed to a large skateboard with a tether, apparently so she could walk this canine edifice down the road for a potentially rewarding constitutional. Then, still hollering, she gently lifted up the dog's tail and through some strangely devised mechanism in the dog's gut, a firm large tootsie roll candy appeared out of the dog's anus. When Gilla, still belching out reverberances, took a small nibble from the candy, Sydney Gilman lost his mind and ran out the back door, the screen door slapping behind him. He passed out from exhaustion in a cattle ranch pasture approximately two miles in distance.

Mr. Gilman awoke in the delivery area of a Goodwill store in Norman. Apparently, his saviors thought him worth enough for recycling. He hoped they got a tax deduction. With the money from the Bible he sold to the blind woman, he bought a light brown corduroy suit and a collared shirt, and he took the time to shave in the bathroom. What appeared upon exit was a very determined person. He looked normal in every possible way but his eyes glowed orange. Sydney could not hide any longer; he was now a very psychotic, but gifted, wizard.

He showed up at a fine home in the affluent, exclusive white neighborhood of God's Cradle. 'For Only the Flock of God' was etched into a sign outside the gate. With his orange eyes, he drifted through the security guards as though they saw no person at all entering. Sydney arrived at the stately home of Pentecostal Pastor Jackson (Jack) Thomas and it was Thanksgiving Day afternoon and Syd wanted to give thanks. Syd wanted to give thanks for the seven people around the seven chairs in the dining room awaiting grace. They all took him in. They really could not resist. He soberly placed on each of their plates a leather-bound gold embossed edition of the Bible of King James. He sat on the floor in the corner as the entire family gorged themselves on each and every page. When they were all done and very full, they all smiled and said their thanks for such a wonderful meal, and he left.

The next time he showed up was at the solid sound mahogany doors of The Zonk Farm for The Warped Noodle. His eyes were gray and he was calm. He was interviewed by the Zonks and they did not even doubt his magical powers, which left him visibly stunned. And Sydney Gilman was placed into the east wing of Ward Two. He eventually became a member of The Nation of Teak and he became a very positive influence.

During the aftermath of the altercation between Ms. Wood's left and the Republican's right, Sydney arrived. He was intent on knowing their mission's goals, and was respectful and attentive. Donning himself in a large white robe and carrying a hollow staff made of taped together empty toilet paper rolls, Syd commanded the room. His feet were adorned with slippers that were bright in color, looking like cartoon stuffed images of the yellow warbler—complete with little black eyes and beaks. He didn't walk but shuffled around to meet and greet the curds of the Teak Nation. The cheese would soon be ripe.

With papier-mâché, and using the most recent pages of the Bible, he stiffened up his hollow staff as if it was for use for a serious situation. Everyone spoke of his antics and most all the patients were afraid of him, especially Ward Three who thought Sydney was the Devil. The Zonks tried to calm Ward Three down stating there was no Devil just Republicans but that didn't appear to help.

Many nights later, neither Chester nor the Zonks suspected anything, but the Nation of Teak once again rose. No need for keys or issues with guards, the glowing orange eyes of Sydney led the way. Doors opened and guards were anesthetized by Syd's spells. There was not any ranting but a quiet slow stream of Teak members floating up the stairs. The main door to floor three opened without effort. Sydney Gilman magnificently stood in the middle of the room, pointed his staff to the ceiling and yelled, "Fitz Natal Freep!" There was a 'Phoop!' sound that shot from the end of the staff. Ms. Wood saw a bright swirling light like a small galaxy appearing on the ceiling. Several extreme right-wing conservatives, notorious for their evangelical platitudes and suppression of racial diversity, free education and affordable healthcare, all were levitated up into an upside-down toilet bowl that led to a vent shaft into a tin metal rectangular tube and out to an opening on the roof. The voices in the heads of their buoyant conservative carcasses rang with a sweet tone that stated now they were angels and they needed to fly. And they flew from the back topmost portion of the Warped Noodle down on a solid brick porch. The Zonks discovered that night that every one of the deceased had burned into their left wrist Isaiah 41. 'Do Not Fear for I Am with You'. And, apparently, he was.

That evening the Zonks met to agree that the Noodle needed expanding and a new building with very heavy security would be built. This building would be for the criminally insane and Sydney Gilman was the first inhabitant.

Author's note: From what I could gather from interviews from the patients, this was entirely true. But what firm truth can you judge from people that are insane? There were five dead bodies on the back porch of the Noodle that had fallen from the roof and that was a fact. When I attempted to interview Sydney, I swore his eyes glowed orange for a second, and…

Bootes

by Kohar Hakobyan

Translated from Armenian by Zackary Maxwell

The Strip of Ms. Mobi

"Around and around we go as history's pathetic war parade passes by and a preordained imminent arrival of another wave filters into our view on the horizon. It never ends." — Ms. Mobi

Laki Lukovich was a Russian ballerina at the age of five. She primarily played the lead child dancer in Swan Lake and the Nutcracker in her small town of Balakovo. She was nestled into the bosom of Yeltsin and he trained her across the country to exacerbate and dictate the power of focused communist youth. And she was very good at exacerbating.

Her illustrious career came to an abrupt close at puberty. Her mother's mother, Yurbitinta Laktatsiya, was genetically altered by the then Soviet Union to have an enormous nose. This was a state secret, but the future of the communist youth needed a method to instantly locate capitalistic sentiment and the great Russian scientists did as commanded. The Prominent Proboscis Karma experiment was awarded the Brezhnev Order of Necessary Emanation Detection. The PPK, not associated in any way with James Bond's pistol, were extreme engorged nasal organs for the red party youth to easily determine right from left where left, here, is right, and right, of course, is wrong. Young Laki, unfortunate for her career, inherited this wonderful malady. Initially, her dance instructors thought that this protuberance would merely enhance her performance since she now really did appear as a swan with a beak. But during a brief saunter flourish toward the end of Swan Lake, the young woman named Laki slipped due to the overwhelming forces of upper weight classical physics and she jolted downward only for the forces of nature to break the binds of blood capillaries in her snoot upon impact with the floor. The audience roared in hilarity. They thought this was some new comical twist of a classic opera. No, no, she was fired. The Russian world expired a sigh of relief since they all saw that ending coming—eventually.

Just as a note: a human nose has approximately six million olfactory receptors. The Russian genetic scientists cheered in exuberance when they discovered Laki's snoot had over three hundred million. Later, they found that Margie Funksteader, at the age of eighteen no less, in the outback of Birdsville, Australia, beat that olfactory number by one hundred million and she was discovered to have five thousand taste buds compared to an ordinary human's one thousand six hundred! No kidding. She knew exactly what beers were on tap in a pub that was twenty-five miles away. She said, nearly toothless, that this was possible because of her love of country, sheep and Victoria Bitter.

Destitute and semi-transient, Laki squandered enormous funds on costly custom nasal tampons. Fathom being able to acutely smell capitalism, conservatism, lies and dissent. The mind did not have a filter to drown out all that stench-filled noise. This drained her fortunes. The Russian genetic scientists took note. They were initially quizzically dismal for her outcome, but only for a second, then they got to work to beat four hundred million olfactory receptors per expanded snout. In Russia, like Texas, everything has to be bigger and better even though, in reality, it really wasn't.

There was a nocturne playing in her head. It was Chopin Nocturne Op. 9 No. 2. It was soothing and beautiful as she swam in her depression. Her future crushed by a mere genetically altered proboscis. "We are all just lab rats! she yelled. "We are all maggots for the State!" And she was right. Her cousin, Heldisk, was actually attempting to play the Chopin Nocturne on a WWII German dilapidated Bechstein piano captured at the battle of Konigsberg in their living room, with her nose. She also had been similarly altered under the state mandate genetic program. Her deftness with each plunge of her beak was amazing. This alone was worth something. This alone could save the family! And Laki began to practice.

Laki actually mastered Rachmaninoff's Piano Concerto No. 3 in D minor, Op. In between clinking the ivories with her swollen callused whiffer, she, in time, received PhDs in Mathematics and Theoretical Physics from the University of Moscow. Sadly, Russia was flush with various sorts of intelligent people and degrees were just rolls of toilet paper to brush away the detritus of expelled digested thoughts while real work needed to be done. Laki joined the circus.

The best circus in Russia was the Kuznetov Tribes. They were the most famous and profitable circus enterprise in all the non-NATO countries. The worst was owned by Oblonsky Traders and that was the most popular circus in all of known Russia due to its depravity of human pseudo-talented souls. No translations required. No language or dialects needed. It was all a visually apparent swirling madness of amazement and it worked. It worked in Moscow, Kiev, Siberia, the Urals and parts of Mongolia. It didn't matter. It was amazing in its pheromonal depth of depravity and the people swooned. They really did swoon.

Hector, a small person of frame, would drink a Draconic cup of strawberry cream elixir from the south of Mexico, and he would steel his lusty weapon to harness a team of young dead mules that he would drag back and forth across the stage. His tethered organ's strength was amazing. Really.

Artyom was not a great leader, but he could track anything, alive or dead, day or night, through any type of terrain. He would be blindfolded on a chair on the stage and an expensive item was borrowed from an audience member. The back of the stage was opened up, no matter where they were, whether in a desert, plains or mountains, and another audience member was told to go out there and hide the item anywhere in the distance. Upon the return of the person, Artyom, still blindfolded, would be given a count of three and on three he got up and ran as fast as he could off the stage, into the audience and, generally, right into the wall near the entrance where he knocked himself out. The crowd bellowed with laughter and most often, as in always, the hidden item was never recovered except by Artyom much later.

There was Kolya The Short, who was actually one of the best surgical minds known, but surgery just didn't pay like this circus did. He would stand in front of the stage in only his underwear and his assistant, Laki, initially, would give him knives that he would drive into his body. One after the other until his body appeared like a full pin cushion. Then he would slowly pass out from blood loss and the crowd hooted like no hooting ever. Being a surgeon, he knew precisely the spots to stab to miss any vital areas. They would sew him back up, give him a few pints of plasma, and he was good to go for the next stop on the circus tour.

Then there was Laki, adorned in an elegant long gown shimmering with jewels—actually it was a broken pane of stained glass from an old Russian orthodox church—and she lithely sat down before a piano, which was generally borrowed from the town school, and hands being bound behind her she smiled and nodded quietly to the audience. And then it happened. It was almost impossible to describe or even comprehend but her neck became immediately and instantly elastic while she pummeled the keyboard with her nose. She appeared as a rabid starving chicken at a keyboard full of grain. Using extremely rapid movements of the neck muscles, Laki flawlessly went through works by Stravinsky, Rimsky-Korsakov, Rubinstein and Mussorgsky. The audience cried, howled and begged for more. She played until her nose bled, and even then, continued until the keyboard was no longer visible as white and black but red as the color of the Nation. Coins and flowers were tossed at her feet. Laki became famous.

Like most Russians, Laki wanted to go to America. And she did just that. She saved all her money, bribed officials, and off she went to New York City, where she was promptly picked up by the US secret service and Laki Lukovich disappeared.

The US, for some time, knew of the PPK and Laki's genetically altered proboscis, and wanted one of their own. She was poked and prodded for months by scientists whose main goal was to engineer people's snoots, and those people would become federal agents and could instantly sniff out KGB, communist, or even ex-communist, perpetrators. But as it would turn out, in nature it is easier to recognize pheromonally conservative capitalists than it was to negotiate the hidden odorous highway of communists or ex-communists.

Federal agents gave her the name of Nobi Mobi and she was to be a stripper, even though her frame was that of an anorexic on laxatives; she agreed. They paid her well; she had numerous days off and vacation time to boot. The US NSA put her up in various towns and she would do her act and report back as to who would talk to her and where. It was easy and she was very good at reporting.

The 'Act' was when Ms. Mobi would scamper on stage, put an eight-track tape into a machine on a nearby stool, click the on button and out would pour from the speakers The Ballad of the Green Berets, by Sgt.

Barry Sadler. The song was exactly two minutes and twenty-seven seconds long so, Ms. Mobi had that length of time to undress. Being an eight-track player, it would start up again and she would then put her clothes back on. And then she would take them off and then put them on again. And on and on until the audience would boo her off stage or graciously pay her to stop.

After two years in the field, instead of a promotion, she was fired. No good leads or captures or any worthy intelligence came from this project. So Ms. Modi killed them. Well, not all of them, but as many as she could before they tasered her into unconsciousness.

What the NSA failed to understand was her heightened sense of smell was programmed for revulsion around any conservative leaning human. Which was most of the NSA, CIA and DHS. She was sick. Literally from the first step off of the plane into Kennedy Airport. She was throwing up constantly. Her anorexic frame was not that of a bulimia induced model but a genetically programed nose to ferret out conservatives. And now she was surrounded by them. So, after she was fired, she used her clearance to get into the scientists' labs and she poked and prodded them to death. Literally. Two were left alive since she smelled both were liberal, but four were mutilated with no chance of an open casket funeral.

The Zonk Farm of the Warped Noodle embraced her entrance. She was the second inhabitant to the newly built Ultra-Warped Noodle maximum security building for the criminally insane. They placed a piano in her room and were flabbergasted that with her hands chain cuffed behind her back she could play Wagner, Bach, Mendelsohn and Strauss with only her nose. But for the first few weeks all she played was Marche funèbre by Chopin over and over again like an endless strip. No one booed her off stage.

The Angel at The Foot of The Stairs

"From the blazing heat of a dry desert, if you could only take a
resplendent plunge into a cool oasis, then that is what flying feels like!"
— *Margot*

Out from a Stearman Model 75 biplane she sprung and ran into her mother's arms. She was no longer young but she was sprite and she just soloed her first plane flight. Margot was a junior pilot. But that didn't last long; like her addiction to shooting, she became obsessed with flying and she soon had her instrument rating, and became a full-fledged pilot. She flew for the Socialist Union of Seattle and made trips all throughout the northwest of the United States, ferrying members to meetings and speeches. Margot even got in the action and gave a round of talks to local politicians in her flight gear.

Her passion, conviction and energy were infectious and she became the poster picture of the movement. She offered up the opening rousing oration, for every local assembly. Margot Zonk was on a roll and she wanted to just keep rolling.

Unfortunately, for her nest of depleting Zonk eggs, she understood she needed to take time to procreate. At a fund-raising dinner at the mansion, she later passed around a glass carafe for all the male patrons. They took this vessel, one-by-one, and did the deed for extending socialist humanistic endeavors. Margot was at a wonder as to the wealth of celebrities' ointment contained in that jar. John Reed had died but he was replaced by Upton Sinclair. There were so many others. All, albeit, intoxicated. Stein humorously put a dollop of the juice in her gin and drank up. "That is the only orifice I will let you men have!" she said with laughter. That night, the baster plunger was pressed and the Zonk seed was again sown.

Margot's schedule did not stop while pregnant. The belly baby appeared to really enjoy it all. Barrel rolls, loops and Immelmann Turns simply spurred on a kicking frenzy of joy. Tacoma to Olympia to

Yakima, then to Kennewick and Boise to Eugene the child was gestated primarily in the air. But the message was sent. The World War with the Nazis was almost over and a new kind of political thinking would begin. A new world of vibrant smart people would lead the way for the future of the planet. Then Nell tripped.

The infrastructure of the mansion had been neglected due to more pertinent expenditures. The wood deteriorated in various areas and the carpet frayed. The latter was extreme at the top of the stairs to Nell's bedroom. She knew the hazard was there and routinely lifted her leg to avoid the issue. But one night she did not. Her slipper clipped the edge of the exposed carpet and she fell down the entire stair steps. Luckily, Roger was there to catch her upon impact with the bottom floor as he had done many times before. With no word to Margot, Roger took Nell to Teegarden B where she became the planet's sole Sheriff. But no animosity was to be had on this peaceful planet so Roger had her vacation on the ice planet of Barnard's Star B, where most mediocre Republicans were stowed, and at minus 275 degrees F, they froze solid. Nell would show up and shoot them. As many as she could before she ran out of ammunition. They couldn't die since they were already dead but it gave her great pleasure busting them into splinters.

Steve the Milkman

by Opeia Zonk

"I gave them a protein and calcium-vitamin D enriched liquid and they gave me their lives. It was definitely a fair trade-off." — Steve

Ed, to his friends, of whom he had none, was often busy being lethargic. He could not help but hurry to be late or run to be tardy. He was always going very fast to someplace like nowhere and that is where he liked it. Ed grappled with time only to know that it really did not exist, and delved into existence with just a broken toe through his stocking, delicately placing it in the vast cool liquid stretches of a place called reality but he knew that, too, was just fantasy. Steven Edwards was brilliant. Indeed, his IQ exceeded two hundred and twenty and most officials thought that way too low for his tested abilities.

The zone of Goldilocks applies to many areas in life. Exoplanets, for one, have a goldilocks zone of habitability for humans. Roger knows this all too well. Intelligence, too, has this sweet zone of Goldilocks. It is approximately between one hundred and fifteen to one hundred and thirty-five IQ. That is the luscious range on intelligence that is just right. Right to perfection—a perfection that doesn't exist in the third dimension with mass-based particles since perfection is infinity. Within this range of IQs, people inflicted are not smart enough to be bored. They are just smart enough to find focus and vision to solve problems that most people can't. They take notes since their minds will not store all that data. They delve into topics of conversation that plant the seed of hope and also doubt, that grows eventually to a hypothesis and then into a theorem. Collaboration brings condensation of minds. But Ed yawned at this truth. He already knew the conclusion. Ed, now Steve, became a milkman. Steve the Milkman was bored shitless.

Way before dawn, at the Utterly Drained Udder Dairy on the outskirts of Boston, Steve would leave with his milk van, completely retrofitted with a 440 Chrysler Mopar engine generating a whopping four hundred and seventy-five ponies. He would shave through a set of Michelins every week with reckless intent since his mother never used a condom during his unfortunate conception. But he was always on time and he was ready to deliver.

There were no conversations since he already knew what they were going to enunciate with their trifle of words that they could only puke out, and he would procure as an insult to his abilities. He drank copious amounts of spiced rum and smoked massive quantities of sativa. The world was full of maggots and he had to feed each and every one of them daily, but like all things, he grew tired of this too.

His girlfriend was Colitas Salisbury. She was a reformed prostitute, a reformed drug addict, a reformed Christian and a most stellar convincing perjurer. She was very good at knowing when to talk and when not too. Colitas was a mind fornicating manipulator. She was the best. She was the Mayor's butt slave and she always left a skid mark.

What is innocence but one that is introduced to a new concept? And Steve the Milkman offered nothing but new concepts. Ms. Salisbury was innocent until proven guilty.

The blazing glory of the four hundred and seventy-five pounding horses of a milk van coasting through the vibrant neighborhoods of Back-Bay-Beacon Hill, Central, Charlestown and West Roxbury to feed the rich, fat friendly pasteurized owners from the secretions of a lowly cow's udder. It was utterly fantastic in its necessity. Their coat of arms was stamped on their vests, coats and lapels. Those tribes of intellect that farm themselves out to fields of soccer, field hockey and curling. Yes, the delicate art of shoving a teapot full of cement down a frozen hockey rink with tenders that swept away the shavings of ice. It was life. But not in the life of Steve. They all had a badge of approval. A badge of narcissistic pride, but in this case, also a pseudo-intelligent coagulation of tribal gratification.

It all begins just right. Toddlers don't see sex or race or religion. Toddlers start just playing with others with no distinction other than they have some concept that the other toddlers are like them as a being. Then they begin growing and differences begin to matter. The toxins enter the soul. First it is male and female. Then, in equal measure, it is religion and race. These distinctions make a difference in origins and origins go under the microscope to families and those families, some, come from far distant countries. This gives a sense of pride to most, but also to others, a sense of purity so that that purity should not be diluted with another's family's blood for an irrational fear of some false contamination. Genetic diversity has always been nature's mode of extended evolutionary survival. That is a fact. Diversify or die. But somehow, and in some way, that message got lost with human tribalism.

We can't help ourselves! We want to be different, to stand out, but we yearn to be the same in our own little tumors. We beg to spread out unities, only later to fall victim to internal factions. Muslims to Shia, Sunnis and Shiites. Christians to Catholics, Protestants, Calvinists, Baptists, Episcopalian and on and on... Jews, Buddhism—it does not matter! The human mind cannot help but to weaponize anything to rid the planet of some different tribe, even though they are exactly biologically the same. They say, SAVE THE PLANET! But the planet has been here four and a half billion years, long before humans, and it will be here long after humans are nothing but dust and when none of their memories exist. So, what they are really saying is, SAVE THE HUMANS! But is that really such a good idea? Since we all are the cancer cells and our cities and societies are the tumors, then sanely, by what rationale would you want to save the disease called humans?

Ideally, we should all breed into a homogenous brown soup of wonderful people, and some try, but as a population this will not succeed. This is because we are forever bound by the dismal conclusion that we are part and parcel of some inevitable tribe.

This all was going through the mind of Steve Edwards when he woke up in his milk truck on the corner of Temple and Ivory. He was having a dream about a disease called humans. The engine was still running. That sativa was skunk. He looked down and there, staring back at him, was the lifeless corpse of Dick Van Goshin. His letter jacket had the insignia that was ripped off and in the hands of the milkman from the Boston University Academy. "He couldn't handle his milk," grumbled Steve. Dick was found convicted of rape in a fraternity house on campus. He was later acquitted through funds from his family.

"Everything, and I mean everything, has a price," his father smiled at the dinner reception for his homecoming from temporary incarceration. Then there was Don, Dirk and Gerry. They were all guilty of rape and molestation but curiously were let off without any jail time. Their bellies all now full of cow udder excretions, fortified with Vitamin D and a Steve enhancement from the refined castor bean, ricin. His failure was his collection of insignias from the jackets of the victims. This left a DNA trail to Steve the Milkman. The Milkman cometh and he went to the Zonks' Ultra Warped Noodle where he was warmly embraced. He was patient number three.

The Zonks, being sympathetic to his cause, had the entire band of Judy Juggs and the Lactation Crew perform just for him three times a year in his cell. Covered in glandular excretions, The Milkman would yell, "I LOVE THIS PLACE!" And he did.

Author's note: Steve was really quite extraordinary. His intellect and savvy could almost convince anyone he was sane. And in some ways, he was. He just chose a path to his version of sanity that was wrong for all others. The only complaint I have ever had with him, he being so brilliant, was that he could not pick out a tune on a piano with his nose.

The Ultra Warped Noodle

"The mind, the mind is the human weakness. Nature carved it from a stone of butter. It was solid enough to vomit pontifications of conservatism but was not soluble enough to meld into a mass of a firm foundation called reality." — Zade

Funding for the facility was initially an issue. But, from the grace of the Bank of England, the Zonk family properties of the Villas for Retirement were subsumed into the National Institute of Health and remained there for many years. Lady Zonk's model of aged care is still adhered to today. An endowment of several millions of dollars was given to the Zonk family and it filtered down to Chester, Opeia, Bootes, Eni, Marvin and Zade. They formed a committee and blueprints were designed, security was funded and staff were enrolled. Then, on a plot of land not far from the Warped Noodle, the ground was tilled and the structure laid for the maximum-security facility called the Ultra Warped Noodle. It was beautiful. It was just like one giant Nipple of Venus.

Venus didn't have a nipple. In point of fact, none of the planets in the solar system had a nipple of any sort. Roger checked. It was some Roman piss from the perturbation of paganism, not unlike Republicans' warped sense of democracy, that Venus became Aphrodite. And she had a nipple. Two. And there it stood.

Much like an Islamic mosque on Ex-Lax, there erected was a dome behind a cocoon of layered electrified wire with the tops of the rails covered in curly razors. Some idiot engineer installed a basketball court in the interior but it was never used since the incarcerated didn't play sports—they played minds. And a mind was not something you could re-create on the back of a gob of cement that was layered on top of gravel with a hoop!

Ada Place, always in the front row, raised her hand in Eni's Western Philosophy course. "Ms. Eni, I realize this is off topic and has nothing whatsoever to do with Zeno, but can I study Criminal Psychology?" And that is when it began.

Ada Place was actually one Ling Liu and was born in Xuzhou, China, to a single teenage mother. The mother died soon after due to complications from the pregnancy and Ling was put into an adoption agency. The Place family, nestled in the hills of Jemez Springs, New Mexico, were barren. Barren of intellect, since they were Republicans, but also barren of children because of a faulty uterus and one majorly damaged scrotum. The Places applied for, and eventually received, a plump one-year-old female who they named Ada after a premium bottle of gin that they drank in celebration of this wonderful gift from God.

Ada grew up rapidly and was the first in her class four years in a row. Much to the dismay of her educators, she often corrected them in class on any errors that were present. And, apparently, there were many errors present and she was sent to the Principal's office umpteen times for rude and inappropriate behavior. But the fact was she was just blatantly honest in a society that would rather bury itself in tact than in candor. She was eventually expelled due to bad behavior, a false charge, but it stained her being and she was sent home to be schooled by her mother.

Ms. Place, well, and Mr. Place, were impressive in their ability to intake large quantities of ethanol spirits and maintain an upright posture. Indeed, had they known about the Oblonsky Traders Russian Circus at this time, they would have been acceptable cast members. Unfortunately, they did not, and even though their circus days were never to occur, their parent days were soon drying up just as were her uterus and his lamentable gonads. The Places, glad to have Ada's company at home, drank two bottles of gin, a large Mason jar of homemade 'shine, two pints of rum and a chaser of what they thought was vodka but was actually water from the cat bowl. Someone belched and the other someone said, "Let's go for a drive." And they did.

Ada, sitting in the middle between mother and father, in a 1977 GMC short bed step side truck, was finishing up her proof of the Gauss-Bonnet theorem about surfaces in differential geometry, when a large boulder fell in front of the truck on Highway 4 going into Los Alamos. Mr. Place, driving, not particularly in the mood for rabbit-like reflexes, mashed on the brakes and made a minor collision with their front bumper and the rock. Ada, not in a seat belt, was thrown forward under her mother's legs on the passenger side and it was at this moment, three more boulders cascaded down the side of the mountain and crushed the cab of the truck to the ground.

The Places, in hindsight, did not feel any pain since they could not feel anything. They were inebriated up to their now mashed skulls. It took seven firefighters and three policemen with wedge bars, the jaws-of-life and a blow torch to retrieve the little girl. Aside from a few scratches, she was unharmed. She delighted in showing the firemen her theorem proof in the screaming red fire engine as it blazed down the road to Los Alamos, but they didn't understand differential geometry. The Zonks adopted her into the Dangleberry Estates within the next few days.

She was eleven that day in Eni's class when she raised her hand to pose the question. The Zonks, of course, said yes. She was given her own office and library access to any books on abnormal psychology, psychology, neurology, criminology or any other pertinent papers or works related to her topic of interest. More specific to her studies was the fact that she had three criminally insane people housed at the Ultra Warped Noodle that could be reviewed. And the Zonks let her.

The rooms in the Ultra Warped were large, with a bathroom, bedroom and dining areas. The furniture was gothic in design. The cathedral domed ceiling was etched with small thin bulletproof glassed windows to let in natural light. The walls and ceiling were all made of stone. For some odd couple, this 'cell' would make a really nice honeymoon suite. A thick iron door was the only entrance. The floors were dotted with throw carpets and the walls dangled with beautiful tapestries.

Sydney, the wizard, was the only real issue. He had to wear thick black glasses so that his glowing peepers could not manipulate the viewer. Sydney stated that he would not harm anyone at this facility but precautions had to be made. An orderly was always present to gag him if he uttered any spells, but trust being what it is, he was allowed not to be cuffed to an iron binding unit welded on the wall.

"I wish I could see you, I..." and his words trailed off. The orderlies put out a posh black leather chair in front of Sydney for her to sit in. Her legs dangled since they could not touch the floor. An orderly stood off to the side between the two chairs. "I wish I could see you, since I haven't seen a child in a great many years."

"I am not a child," stated Ada.

"Yes, yes... yes, but what I am trying to say is that I never in my life gave the little humans much notice." There was quiet. "They just didn't mean anything to me at the time and now they mean the future. So, what I am saying is I'd like to see the future." Ada smiled but realized he could not see that facial expression.

"I understand," she said.

Keeping notes with her notebook and pen, she went into a spiral of questions about his childhood, his early life, his accomplishments and concerns on existence. He patiently answered all her questions but it became apparent after about thirty minutes he was levitating slightly above his chair. The orderly would push him back down but he obviously was excited to converse with Ada and this forced him out of his chair. Zade eventually entered to intervene and stated it was okay for him to float around the room to answer questions. Ada was professional in her demeanor and presentation but toward the end of the interview, she fell silent and paused. "What does it feel like?" she said.

"What?" he was taken off guard by the question.

"Flying. What does it feel like?"

"Oh," he smiled. "It is like a million tiny needles that pierce your skin but you feel no pain but a strange warmth. And then you are buoyant and you can move around." He was quiet but there was no noise but breathing. "It feels great!" he proclaimed.

"Thank you, sir," she said and she got up to leave. Before she got to the door, she turned to him and said, "I wish I could fly."

He paused in the air and looked almost sad, and then whispered through tiny sobs, "Be careful what you wish for, Ada." The interview was over.

Ms. Mobi was not how she appeared in the newspapers. This menacing ruthless heartless killer was just a faint of a female that had a mere skeleton of a frame, and her head was adorned with a nose that was a serious honker. Ada thought she looked like a pale flamingo without wings and just as frail. She spoke in a surprisingly slow and low tone with a Russian accent that melted like the wax of bees during winter. Ada thought she could never fear this soul. How could she be capable of such deadly acts? Physically, she was a twig with an unrelenting nose engineered by scientists for what mattered at that time. It was not her fault that she was born with this inheritance. Ms. Mobi coughed upon entrance. Ada's smell was enormous but faint compared to those beings on Ward Three. She would have killed Ward Three outright for their suffocating stench. They talked and talked. About knitting and crocheting various garments for the children at The Estate. They spoke of cooking recipes differing from that of New Mexico alcoholics to that of rural Russia. Ada could play the piano, and very well, but paled to the nose of Nobi. They both played several duets. They spoke of politics and the Zonks. Ms. Modi expunged that if she could change time, she would have loved to be part of the Zonk Estate and that Ada was very lucky to be there. Modi was not remorseful on her genetic nose and said it gave her perspective in this madness of the world on whom to trust. And her nose was never wrong. They laughed. When Ada left, she looked at Ms. Modi and said, "I wish I could have a nose like you do."

Whereby Nobi said, "You do. You just have to listen to your senses."

Colitas Salisbury was sitting on the Milkman's lap. She was undulating back and forth to an unheard rhythm that pulsed between their loins. Ada knew of this motion since she had read about it in books. She just ignored the action. Steve was curious to her. He would look through her but not at her, like an owl looking through a morsel of meat. She was there but not really. Ada thought perhaps if they would finish their carnal lust, then the interview would go better but Steve was able to juggle both with elemental intent. The Milkman would often start and end her sentences. It was so reflexive that he did not notice it at all. Ada did. It was annoying. What mind was so bright to be in this being that could see through and converse with any of the planet's inhabitants without them speaking a word? His world must be a lonely place. A hollow place. And Ada said so. Steve gracefully stopped his motion with Colitas and pulled her off of his glistening stump. He sat solidified to his chair for minutes and he looked deep in Ada's eyes, and said, "Yes. The people of this world are hollow and so am I. I just see the lies and deceit in their body language—but I see none in yours. You must be very special."

She was surprised at his speech. Then, "No, I am just very young and haven't yet been tainted by the foulness of human maturity."

He smiled and uttered, "Keep it that way."

"I will endeavor," was her response. Such a wonderful mind if only he could train it to be harnessed for good. This interview, too, was over.

Ms. Place's paper was basically an analysis on criminal psychosis. But, deeper, she discovered that this group of non-functioning sociopaths were not unlike the Zonks. The Zonks just had control of their radical ideals and these people did not. The act of impulsivity always gave one away from the fine razor's edge of thoughtful sanity to that of insanity.

The Issue with The Squid

*"What should have been IN was now OUT. This is not right! No birth
in the outcome of Zonk history delivered such a travesty—so why
NOW?" — Margot*

Gilla Mostel was there at the birth and she felt around in the ooze with
her astute tactile fingers to determine, yes, the Zonk baby was indeed a
male. "The Gods hate US!" said Margot, who was a complete atheist but
she was ransacked with biological guilt on this fateful outcome. The
lineage of Zonk females suddenly expired. Margot wanted to call him
Canem Stercore but Gilla stated no, they should be kind and they named
him Tobias after Tobias George Smollett from the 18th century—a
Scottish author. Tobias Zonk it was.

The real issue was the serious funk of an odor emanating from the
freezer in the kitchen. Even on ice, Nell's carcass would have to be
addressed and soon. Bundling up the baby, Margot took off from Seattle
in the Stearman with Nell in the front and Margot flying from the back.
It was amazing how easy it was to breastfeed and fly at the same time—
unless, of course, there was rough weather or one was landing or taking
off. Changing diapers was another issue entirely and frequent landings
in small airports along the way had to be planned. Tobias loved the air
flights much better than any ride on solid ground. He never cried on the
trip, except upon landing, and when back in the air he was laughing and
gurgling all the time. Nell, decomposing and in the front seat, made
Margot gag along the way. Margot thought, and not to be rude but just
factual, that Nell Zonk never smelled good even during life. She had a
tendency to sweat much and always had a tang of a wet sack of very old
onions. But now, this was much worse. Margot thought about just tossing
her out in some random forest below, but she held true to her conscience
and Nell always liked Bryce Canyon in Utah. Even though Nell only saw
the Canyon once during a train trip so long ago, it was all she could talk
about in her mansion in Seattle.

On the fourth day out, with fair winds from the west, Margot set out from a farmer's field near Eskdale. By early morning, the Stearman was right above the Canyon rim. The sunrise was beautiful. It was a good day for a funeral. Nell's body was not harnessed in, but when Margot flipped the plane upside down, Nell's foot got stuck and she just dangled down from her seat. Margot righted the plane and rocked it back and forth, much to the amusement of Tobias, and then she tried again. Out she slid and down into the red and white cliffs of the Canyon. Nell was where she wanted to be. Margot turned her ship around.

A well-known Utah archer was napping on the Canyon rim that morning. He was bow hunting for the elusive and very rare Dixie Forest Condor. Elias Fidd was from Fruita in Western Colorado. He grew up on a farm that grew apples but he didn't like it much and was always out on the plains or local forests, hunting. Elias made his first bow and arrow at the age of six from a young pine sapling and his father's used guitar strings. He never cared for guns at all and prided himself on stealth and stalking to achieve his prize. Elias was very good.

He won his first championship match when he was eight, but being just a boy, they paid him off with a bag of marbles instead of money. Elias was pissed. The next year he won again but got paid cash since he threatened to shoot off the very perky nipples of the Mayor's daughter at one hundred yards if they didn't. And he could have. And they knew it and paid. Elias ended up eventually as a hunting guide out of Escalante, Utah, and he settled down into a small log cabin. On his off time, he would make his own Fidd bows and sell them to sports stores all throughout the west. Today, though, he was hunting the Dixie Condor.

Rumors abounded where rumors abounded the most and that was where copious amounts of various ethanol spirits, each at an assorted percentage of ethanol, were plied. And that would be Zion's Bar in Cannonville. Farmer Nolan was talking loudly to a lumber person from Oregon about a gargantuan bird flying just north of where they were. Elias was at the rear of the bar and could not help but hear. Nolan, severely intoxicated, said it was the Dixie Condor and he told the people in the bar, and told the reporters, that this bird was still around and it was so big that it could pull a horse off of the ground. This bird could mow through a group of pine trees like a scythe through a field of wheat. He saw it. He did.

Now Elias didn't believe this story a bit. But just what if this bird did exist? He heard the tall tales told to children to keep them to the forest paths or the great bird, Dixie, would pick them up and take them to her nest on a tall mountain top and feed them one-by-one to her nesting babies. Mr. Fidd didn't need the money. He wasn't rich by any means but money never pandered to his being, but what the archer did want was respect. He had already shot and killed every type of game in North America, dangerous or otherwise, with just a bow and arrow. This Dixie bird would be the feather in his cap.

"Respect isn't bought! It is earned!" his father would say. "You get respect by being the best at what you do and what YOU do is pick fucking apples!" Elias didn't like picking apples but he could shoot one off anyone's head at one hundred yards. Apparently, by his father's own admission, "That talent isn't worth shit!" To make matters worse, Elias was going through puberty and to appeal to his hormonal rushes, and since he was banished from archery, he was going to be the best at masturbation.

In the shed, early every morning, afternoon and evening, when he was not picking fucking apples, he was laying on a wooden bench and shoving the wasted cores from the apple press in the shed up his rectum to enhance a prolonged but continual orgasm. His logic, though sound, was later proven not possible by a scientist named Gretchen Zonk, that pressure on a man's prostate does not enhance the peak of an orgasm but just chops off the maximum pleasure amplitude in lieu of an elongated but medium frenzied pulse. But respect was needed and Elias was fanatical at his attempts. With five lubricated apple cores crammed up his throbbing anus he started again. And just at the moment of the inevitable launch, his mother entered the shed to find her son in the middle of an unstoppable train of glandular pulsing excretion frenzy. His splayed legs, and with a sack of grain to elevate his buttocks off the wooden bench, stoically portrayed an orifice twitching with a voracious appetite for used cores of apples. His mother screamed!

Doctors and psychiatrists followed. His father just gave up on believing he ever had a son. As small towns do talk, the townspeople from Fruita called him the Rotten Fruit from Fruita and no one would have anything to do with him. His mother gave him two options; she gave him back his bow and arrows and said the Monastery on the ridge outside of town was interested in having him. Momentarily, he was confused but understood the first option was the only option and that would be to take his bow with an arrow and go down into a dry creek bed and shoot himself. But suicide with a bow and arrow was difficult and he did not want to trade apple cores for blessed engorged flesh so he chose door number three. He ran away to Utah.

These were the dreams going through his mind while napping on the rim of Bryce Canyon that morning. He woke up on a grassy knoll surrounded by wild blueberries with sporadic pine trees. He looked up and way in the sky was what appeared to be a rapidly descending flapping large bird that was heading right for him. He slammed his head on a rotting stump just to make sure he was awake and this was not some part of his dream. Thunk! It wasn't. He looked up again and this mass of flopping feathers was nearly upon him. Like lightening his reflexes kicked in and he got off three arrows into Dixie as she was coming for his body. "You ain't gonna feed me to your fuck'n babies!" he yelled, but too late. Nell fell on top of Elias with a 'Whump!' and he was dead.

Bubba and Fritzy Ledbetter, from the great state of Arkansas, were on a hike on this canyon rim many years later. They were looking for a place to fornicate in the last light of an autumn season. The blueberries were ripe and they found joy in picking and eating all that they could. The Ledbetters were not married because they couldn't. They were brother and sister and they were in love. This was not acceptable except in parts of the southern US and they were hoping the Mormons in Utah would understand. They didn't. They came upon a grassy knoll with a patch of wildflowers. In the middle of the patch were two skeletons, one on top of the other. "They died making love," stated Fritzy. How the bodies through time were not strewn throughout the hillside by scavenging animals was not a mystery in their inbred minds. Roger was having a laugh though, since he was waiting for this moment. Nell, by the way, didn't care, since at this moment in time she was on Barnard's Star B blasting away at frozen Republicans and making them the little pathetic shards of ice that they were.

Vaya's Myopia

by Opeia Zonk

"God gave me a mind to see what I see. I don't need glasses to interrupt my true vision. My eyes see the truth and the truth is fucked up!" — Vaya

And fucked up it was. Democracy throughout the US, and indeed, the entire world was vaporizing in a pit of global nationalism. And this always historically led to a world at war. Millions and millions of people would die needlessly in the hands of governments that intentionally paralyzed their public with irrational fears of pains from a Hell that would never ever materialize. Truth would be bent into believable lies and the populace would run rampant to rally to a flag for a nation that really had ill intent on control of the people, through media manipulation. And lemmings they would become as lemmings did in all the histories of the past, but lemmings don't study history, they just eat, drink and fornicate out another litter of lemmings for the next generation. And thank God, since if they didn't, wars would eliminate all the lemmings and where would the world be? Free, actually. Free of lemmings.

Ms. Halabjaee understood this. She learned well from her father, who was a historian. All she heard at the dinner table at night over the Kurdish fair of her mother's kofta, kubbeh and dumplings, were his lectures. Dessert was figs, pomegranates and grapes. She loved these memories.

One afternoon near her town of Amedi in northern Iraq, a group of assassins was sent to kill the historian, Mr. Halabjaee, and his family. Apparently, his history, even though true, was not the history that needed to be rewritten by the rebels and he and his family needed to cease to exist. Halabjaee and his wife died, she on top of him to protect him from the bullets. Vaya escaped with her brother through a small tunnel and down the side of the hill. They soon joined up with the PKK, the Kurdistan Workers Party, and fought the rebels. It was easy to kill and

Vaya found it very satisfying. Peace was forgiveness, but she wasn't nearly there yet. Revenge soothed her salivating palate. Her brother died soon after from an infection from a bullet wound to his leg, but she did not mourn. It fed coal to her furnace of a soul and she fought on.

Vaya was a fierce fighter and her courage during conflicts made her a household Kurdish name. Vaya the Myopic was her title since she always wore thick plastic rimmed glasses and it made her look quizzically bookish and cute even though she was a vicious soldier.

Then shit hit the fan. While fighting for the US against the rebels of Northern Syria, the US gave into Turkish demands and the PKK was flanked by two opposing forces. They were at an unforgiveable wall on both sides. Sold out by US Republicans, the PKK was left to fight for themselves on two fronts. And Vaya was in the middle. The Jews suffered massively throughout history and they got their statehood called Israel. The Kurds paid for this ground with tens of thousands of PKK dead and with the permission of the US! Why did this not rank as a receipt for their own land and country! Why? They were sold out by the US Republicans. Those Kurdish deaths would be on their hands and theirs alone.

During a skirmish outside of Khaliloco, Northern Syria, Vaya was grazed by a bullet in her left ribs and one shot through her left shoulder. It was the glancing blow of a round above her left eyebrow that left her unconscious for days. Thought dead, the rebels stripped her naked and threw her into a ditch with the other dead. A passing US patrol scanned the area and determined she was still alive. Vaya awoke in an American airbase in Germany. Confused, she was violent and eventually secured by leather braces on her bed. She swore revenge on the US Republicans that sold out the Kurds. The Zonk Farm of the Warped Noodle gratefully embraced Yaya Halabjaee into their waiting arms. On Ward One— easily, she was destined for Ward Two—but the Zonks sympathized with her Kurdish needs and put her on the most rewarding Ward, Ward One. The first floor.

Less medicated and being astute, she chose painting as her artistic preference. Many took pottery since the red river clay felt so good on their bodies and they were seriously tired of smearing their own excrement for salvation. Vaya took to painting but did not use her anal discharge. She would paint on wood, stone, the floor, her 'cell', her laundry and her entire wardrobe. She painted. She just didn't give a shit about the type of a 'canvas'. But Vaya was myopic.

Yaya had glasses at the age of three from a UN mission to assist the Kurds. Four more frames followed throughout the years. It was through these glasses that she killed numerous Iraqi, Syrian and Turkish insurgents throughout her campaign. When she woke up in Germany, she gracefully purged herself from glasses and equipped her mind with just her natural vision of nearsightedness. It was a blessing to her art.

Thank God she had no access to Ward Three. She would have eviscerated them easily with a dull butter knife. But no, she stood like a pillar to her madness and bathed only in her memories of conservative destruction. Vaya wasn't rampant any more and she was quite stable in her juggling of the fastidiousness of her thriving mind.

She painted what she saw through myopic eyes. A scene from the communal cafeteria. A potato. An orderly smiling. A mop with handle that was apparently used to impale a Republican on Ward Three. All in non-toxic watercolors. All beautifully out of focus and all capable of being subsumed into the realm of impressionism. A blind man from the east wing dressed in brown rags and using a fishing pole as a cane tapped his way to her easel. He bent down to speak into her ear but unfortunately spoke into her prominent chin. "Be the failure you were meant to be," he sighed, then tapped his way into a nearby wall.

Author's note: Vaya was a treasure to the Noodle. We Zonks would let her leave the facility, with security, and produce art exhibits throughout North Carolina. She became locally famous. Without her glasses, however, she eventually got a seeing-eye-dog named Lulu. Lulu was absolutely blind but this added to Vaya's appeal. I think Vaya's point, as an artist, was that the blind were leading the blind, which was her statement on the government of America at this time.

Bootes's Desire

"I have been given the ring of the fisherman. From this, outside my dominion, I will let you all starve!" — Bootes

Bootes Zonk was not a typical Zonk. She was not a book nerd, nor particularly interested in science. She was a carefree spirit and the Zonks left her to her own devices. Which were many but most often including the demise of some animal. She wasn't a sadist, but she had a proclivity for rendering animals that were once alive to now be dead. She saw herself as a lone wolf assassin and her prey was fodder for the Dangleberry kitchen. She, and the people of The Estate, ate what she killed.

The homogenization of non-vegetable matter was disgusting. The plastic, the Styrofoam and the petrified slabs of meat strangled the fibers of her nerves and begged for an outlet of human normalcy. Society does not mean abandoning the instincts of humans relative to other creatures. Society does not elevate humans above other animals, nor does religion; it just blinds the remaining populace into a static void of putrid convenience and that medicates the mind into a sordid mass of pathetic tame digestion without any emotional consequence. "It is DISGUSTING!" her little mass of flesh would say.

"Labels, labels and more labels! This cancerous tumor called a society always needs labels. You are a girl or you are a boy. You are trans, bi or binary. You are straight, gay or lesbian. You are black, white, yellow or brown. You are a mulatto, blended, half-breed or mixed-race. You just call me Bootes or Zonk and if you don't know my name then just call me HUMAN!" Bootes was speaking to Chester. Chester replied with a 'gurgle and a snort' but she knew enough swine to understand he was calling her a Little Human. "No, no, no! Little is a label and could be construed to mean diminutive and therefore lacking. Just HUMAN!" Chester, chastised, gave out a loud SNORT and left for a wallow in the pond.

She was small for her age. It would be doubtful if she would grow past four feet eight inches. And she didn't. But size has its advantages, and for a huntress, that would be stealth.

The Zonks would let her be free. She would get up before the dawn, grab her rifle, one that was handed down through generations from someone named Thaddeus, and her fishing pole. Wearing hand-me-downs from someone named Margot: a leather dress, leather tight shoes and a leather flop hat, the latter fitted with an elastic band head lamp, she would go hunting. In her knapsack there were cartridges for her gun, fishing lures, a plastic wrapped pumpernickel chicken sandwich, a bottle of water and her favorite book, The Adventures of Badger Zonk. And off she went into the darkness.

Sometimes, students going from one classroom to the next would spot her in the distance running between the trees on the far edge of the property. But mostly, she was just invisible, and she liked it that way. South of the property of The Estate, through a field of corn and a barbed wire fence, was a large stream that meandered down and into a small lake. It was here, her private place, that Bootes built herself a 'fort' of old dead branches with patches of mud and grass. As dawn approached and nestled its orange brow over the eastern trees, she let cast her rod and reel and patiently waited. She would never come home empty handed. Whatever she caught, be it perch, catfish or bass, would end up in the kitchen at The Estate for a dish to be served that evening. With an old shoelace she would bind the fish through the gills and tie them alive to a stone in the water. Around noon, she would gut the fish with her four-inch bladed knife that she kept in her belt and sling the fish over her shoulder for an afternoon of hunting. The rifle was a basic single shot and she remembered the Zonk family saying, "If you need more than one shot to hit your target dead, then you don't need to be shooting." Today it would be a squirrel and two ducks. Pleased with her bounty, Bootes would scamper back home and go directly to the kitchen.

She, herself, did not know how to cook in this kitchen. Cooking, good cooking, was like chemistry and she had no mind for any of it. Bootes could cook on an open fire, but with no seasoning it was basic fare. She was content with being the huntress for the Dangleberry Estate and that was enough.

At eight a.m. the next morning, a private ambulance drove up the roundabout of the Warped Noodle and the driver and two orderlies unloaded a gurney with a small boy. He was strapped down, apparently, for violent behavior and was then whisked into the Children's Ward. The Zonks held council that morning to determine the future of this child.

From a library card in his back pocket, his name was Mitch McCabe. He had been found on the side of Highway 64 over a month before and had been treated at a private hospital for a serious head injury. Doctors there, allegedly, performed numerous surgeries on his head and brain and they put in a steel plate where his crushed right skull had been. Unable to work with him further, the doctors thought it best for him to be in the care of the Zonks at the Warped Noodle.

Initially, the boy was very violent. Groaning and gnawing at his sheets and, if he wasn't restrained, flailing his arms and legs toward any person nearby. But then, one afternoon, walked in Bootes. With a fishing pole in one hand and a sling full of fish over her shoulder she entered his room and said, "Hi!" Perhaps, she thought, she appeared to him like a small cyclops with her fish eyed head lamp attached to her flop hat. Maybe it was the fishing pole and some lost memory of a fishing trip. Whatever it was, though, Bootes was for this boy a calming influence. And so the Zonks put Mitch under Bootes' care. And care for him she did.

First, she had her father, Marvin, do a comprehensive computer background check on any families around that had the last name of McCabe. There turned out to be two. The one in Pittsboro did not have any children and the other was in the small town of Siler City. Hitching a ride with Chester, Bootes discovered that Mitch lived with his uncle on a small patch of land in the hills. Siler City knew Mitch well. They called him the bicycle boy since he made his living finding bicycles in landfills and fixed them up to re-sale to people in town. His uncle had been dead for years, but Mitch set up shop in an old barn on the property. Bootes went through this barn and discovered many bicycles in various states of repair. She also now understood this was where he slept and ate. But how did he end up on the side of Highway 64?

So soothing was Bootes for Mitch that after a few weeks she was allowed to take him out for walks. Mitch still could not talk but only audibly would expel a grunt. His walking was erratic and, in general, he could not control the movement of his arms. His right arm and hand, with focus, could be tamed and Bootes used this knowledge to focus Mitch in writing words on a pad of paper which he carried on a string around his neck. The first word he laboriously wrote on the pad was 'fish'.

Bootes grabbed her spare fishing rod and they both headed to the pond at The Estate. Within a half hour, Mitch pulled in, with some difficulty, five perch and two smallmouth bass. Slowly, Mitch was coming back to the land of the living. That evening in the dining hall, Bootes fed Mitch his fresh catch. Grilled fish with butter, lemon and fresh dill. Mitch cried. Not just because it tasted so good, but that he was unable to feed himself.

The next morning, Mitch wrote in his pad, Highway 64, MM 52. Bootes brushed his teeth and combed his hair. She said she understood and grabbed Chester for a drive down the highway. Eastbound to Pittsboro she found no mile marker MM 52, but westbound she did. Chester stopped and Bootes got out. About fifty yards east from the mile marker there was a large long tire skid mark and then an abrupt tear in the gravel and grass on the shoulder of the highway. Down a slight embankment was the crumpled-up frame of a light green bicycle. The impact on the frame, obviously from a vehicle, was the color of the bright paint of cherry red. Bootes took the bent frame of a bike and put it in the back of the maintenance van. It was apparent that Mitch was the victim of a hit and run.

Within the waning months of summer into early fall, Bootes took Mitch to her private place at the 'fort'. They both fished in the lake until the light of day turned to dusk. She would not let Mitch hunt since he was not physically totally in control of his body and would most probably hurt somebody or himself. But he was walking better and began to have much more control of his right arm and hand. During this time, he did not write in his pad much. Just 'fish' or 'eat'. They did not talk at all but he was very aware of Bootes's body language and knew when she was in a bad mood. He would awkwardly hug her during those times.

One afternoon, they both were eating in the cafeteria in the Child's Ward at the Warped Noodle. The TV was on a local news station channel. Suddenly, Mitch went ridged and with a flurry of focus jotted down on his paper pad, 'He Killed Me!'. Bootes turned around and there was Republican Congressman, Jack Waddell, giving a campaign speech and stating he would be at Ripley's Bar and Grill three nights from today, in Pittsboro, and all rounds would be on him. Now it all made sense to Bootes. Waddell was notorious for driving while intoxicated and he was always behind the wheel of his favorite cherry red Corvette convertible. He was never prosecuted or even charged since he was the local federal government's favorite politician.

Three nights later, Bootes borrowed Chester, who was up to his brain on a fresh batch of liberty caps. While he slithered the van down the dark licorice river avoiding massive rapids at every turn, Bootes decided to drive and ordered Chester to the backseat. How hard can it be? Well, one, her feet didn't touch the pedals. Tying blocks of wood to her shoes and sitting on two large phone books, she just managed to get the van into gear and off they went. Slowly. Very slowly.

Bootes arrived at the bar and she inspected the red convertible Corvette parked in the front of the establishment. The right-side bumper was dented in and scrapes ran down the front side to the passenger door. Judy Juggs and her band were screaming out an acid rock rendition of The Shadow of Your Smile. With a double dose of Oxytocin, the girls were at their best at drenching the pulsating massive crowd.

Chester and Bootes entered Ripley's. The speech was over and all of the rounds of booze were purchased. The place was packed and everyone was fairly well lubricated at this time. Waddell had already given his rousing speech about the negatives of a social welfare state and he was curled up in a back-booth blabbing to a group of high school cheerleaders still in their uniforms, on the benefits of the financial rape of the poor working class. They were all wearing buttons that stated, 'Wade in Waddell's Truth'. Which wasn't truth at all but overt lies that were glossed in a language that they could not decipher. Bootes understood that language. Being small and almost unnoticeable she jumped on his table, and pushed away those sequined adorned; she drew her knife and stabbed Waddell three times in his crotch. She whispered in his good ear, "Your noodle is al dente." And now it was.

In the following mayhem, she lost Chester. He was swimming in a nest of locust in a deserted African village. The locusts were consuming him. Bootes arrived from up the street to see that he had broken into a pet store and was writhing in a large aquarium with crickets that the store sold for people who owned lizards. She guided him from his African dream into the back of the van and she drove carefully home.

A few afternoons later, Bootes was with Mitch and she was feeding him lunch, although now his right hand could manage the task. On the TV was an announcement that Congressman Waddell, due to an illness, would not be seeking re-election. Mitch looked deeply into Bootes' eyes. That was all the language that he needed. He wrote on his pad of paper, 'barn'. The next day, without Chester at the wheel, Bootes drove The Estate van to Siler City and into the surrounding hills to his old barn. He anxiously searched through the detritus of his hovel and Bootes just sat down to admire a golden sprocket from a damaged bike. He grunted and grunted in approval. He found what he was looking for. It was a color polaroid picture of a small girl and a boy. Bootes gazed at this image. The boy was Mitch but the girl looked just like Bootes. After a few notes on the pad, it was apparent that Mitch's half-sister, Dora, was just like her. Half black and half white. And she had died of the flu long ago. Bootes wrote down on the pad, 'just call me Zonk and if you can't speak that name just write down 'HUMAN''. Mitch got it. He teared up and with much difficulty said, "Zonk." They both hugged and cried.

The Taxonomy of Tobias

"Mom, I don't think I am human." — Tobias
"Honestly, Tobias, I don't think any of us Zonks are." — Margot

Puzzles puzzled him. Tobias was obsessed with finding a solution to almost anything, which in most cases took him down a path of desperation that would not let go of his soul. He obtained an obsessed curiosity that, submerged in perseverance, pushed him through delirious mental tunnels that only exited to the realization that he was not smart enough to own the answer, even if he were lucky enough to stumble upon it. This depressed him; realizing he will never ever be, in his entire life, nothing but mediocre, rattled his psyche.

Margot was sleeping on the dining room sofa. She was with Roger and Nell on Teegarden B having a strong cup of Chinese Pu'erh tea while Roger and Nell imbibed on a mild oolong. Nell was amazed at how mature Margot had become. Roger wasn't paying attention. His eyes were on the new waiter named Chili and he was hot! Roger opened up his blue robe to reveal his muscular bronzed torso but Chili, refined in manners and disposition, stood like a tall glass of cool water, nodded a slight bow, opened up the fly on his trousers and proceeded to urinate on Roger's feet. Roger just laughed. Margot and Nell were disgusted and harmonized a response, "Roger, would you please stop it!" And when Chili was through with his bladder's evacuation, Roger got up in a huff and took the waiter to the rear of the Café.

"Mom, you've never had to raise a boy. No Zonks have. They are different. They have issues. They are weird."

"Margot, is he a Zonk?" Margot thought and she furrowed her brow. Quietly, she said, "Yes."

"Then that is all that matters."

"Mom, Mom!" Tobias was nudging her awake. Margot fell down a long tube from the Café on Teegarden B and fell promptly into her body on the sofa.

"Yes?" she said, irritated to have the conversation with her mother interrupted.

"I think that I am really an alien and that I have been sent here to take notes on humans and humanity and upon my death, I will go back to my people and tell them how screwed up this planet really has become."

"Tobias, you have no idea how correct you just might be."

Now that he was free to be the alien that he knew he was, he borrowed reams of paper and pencils from his mother's office and ran into the streets of Seattle to hide in corners of shops, bars and cafes to take notes on human behavior. He did not want to return to his planet empty handed and even though plagued by mediocrity, he would succeed in his mission assignments. Or he would die trying, which would just take him back to his planet anyway—so either way it was a winning endeavor.

Obviously, he would have to learn to fly. His planet would naturally have a different gravity and atmosphere but the basic elements of yaw, pitch and roll would be the same. As would straight flight, turns, climbs and descents. And he was convinced his planet would have spacecraft that adhered to this same physics. So he had to fly. And this appealed to Margot as a sweet bonding potential. Maybe this boy wasn't half bad at all.

When Margot wasn't ferrying socialists throughout the northwest and not, herself, pounding the podium, and Tobias not taking notes for his alien race to comprehend humans, they both were together flying the Stearman. Like Margot, he had insane focus, to the extent that all else did not matter. Tobias soloed within three months and had his instrument rating soon after that. Margot took notice and eventually bought the boy his own used de Havilland 85 Leopard Moth. It was the best day of Tobias' life.

The Moth took two passengers compared to the Stearman's one. The Moth had a closed cabin and the Stearman did not. The deal was, cut between mother and son, that he would take specific socialist lecturers to further areas north, south and east of Seattle. She would ferry the local folks within Washington, Oregon and Idaho. Zonk Airways had begun.

Zonk Airways began and ended the same way. Meager. But with no marketing or advertising and just by word of mouth, it didn't do so badly. Tobias chose the mascot for the planes to be that of a rabid beaver. Which didn't appeal to most anyone Caucasian but it distinctly got the attention of the Native Americans in northwest America, including Alaska. They called the airways the 'Crazy Planes', and aside from socialist lecturers, the American NW Indians were their best customers.

William Hatfield, Alaska Republican Senator, and his Russian wife, Olga, were in Seattle on a fundraising event. But it could have been called a razing event since it was out to tax big oil companies in the Arctic Circle, which were mainly on Native American land, and put those funds in a State trust for all the people of Alaska. Most other countries would fund directly their Natives since it was their land being used. But this was not for Hatfield. The money was to go to ALL the people of Alaska and bypass what he would later state as undesirable people. And now, Hatfield and spouse wanted to go hunting in their great State. They owned a spacious log lodge in Whittier, complete with everything but a dead animal head or skin. And Old Bill was going to make that deadness happen. He wanted the head of a moose, the skin of a bear and the body of America's greatest symbol of freedom, the scavenger buzzard in a tuxedo called the Bald Eagle. And the Hatfields wanted this NOW.

They called all chartered airlines from A to Y in the phone book. No one was available. Besides, a storm was coming through and it would be too hazardous. Senator Hatfield replied that he had put up with communists infiltrating the confines of the heart of American freedom and nothing, absolutely nothing, could be more dangerous than that. He flipped the last page in the phonebook and there it was. Zonk Airways. And he called. Tobias answered.

It would have been a cursed stain on the entire Zonk blood lineage if he would have said yes to this hunting trip. It would taint the souls of all living or dead Zonks for an answer in the affirmative. Tobias understood this all. But he was mediocre. He understood this, too. And he needed the money to staff a socialist gala at his mother's mansion. It all made sense. So he said, "Yes." Besides, his true alien planet would appreciate the notes on these human conservatives.

Tobias loaded their lean luggage and guns into the hold of the Moth. He knew that the Hatfields couldn't hit a barn door at point blank range and the clothes that they wore, and guns that they used, were not adequate for a hazardous region with dangerous game. But he was mute. Tobias had his Marlin 45-70 and his snub-nosed 44 magnum and that should just about do it. The Moth took off in clear weather from Seattle, heading into a storm over Alaska. Olga was wearing a mink stole but had on leopard tights and high heels. Old Bill was wearing nothing but a jock strap and hemp woven beach sandals from Harrods. Tobias flew up to altitude in the de Havilland and off they floated into a storm.

It was a slow trowel through strong head winds. Weaving and winding to Ketchikan, Sitka, Juneau and Yakulat. Tobias knew his course was off but he also had confidence that land would be near and Resurrection Bay loomed ahead in the rain, and down they went to Seward. There they rested for several days and Senator Hatfield and delightful sour Olga, full of liquor, wanted to kill dangerous animals. The apathetic pilot knew the only dangerous game was his two passengers and they only to themselves. But off Tobias went into the clouds once again to appease the lusty needs of the wealthy elite. The Hatfields were singing a song that he didn't know but apparently it was important enough for them to yell above the straining engine's whine. A sudden down draft came and they fell instantly a blistering one thousand feet. The Hatfields puked the remains of their stomachs on the back of Tobias. And then another down draft and the plane crashed into the snow on top of a mountain near Moose Pass.

Amazed at the fortitude of the Moth, Tobias unfortunately discovered his retching customers were still alive. She with her stole, leopard tights and high heels, and he with his lone jock strap, grabbed their guns and a bottle of Scotch and off they went into the blizzard to shoot anything that was more dangerous than themselves. Tobias covered the plane's cabin in a thick canvas tarp and started a small fire. He slept soundly through the remainder of the storm.

The local Chugach Native Americans found the plane and Tobias in a large heap of mounded snow. They freed the plane but it would not fly due to engine damage. They saw the fierce face of the rabid beaver and they concluded that Tobias was the pilot of the 'Crazy Plane' and that the Zonks were friendly to their people. And they were. Olga and Old Bill apparently got lost in the blizzard and shot themselves in an attempt to rid each other of a maddening charge from a dangerous beast. They were frozen solid and looked peaceful in their combined misery. Roger quickly put them both up on Barnard's Star B and Nell was there ready to blast them both into tiny shards of ice.

Trekking back to Seattle, Tobias kept his bent propeller and made it into a mailbox back at the mansion. The Socialist Gala, due to the Hatfield funds, went off without a hitch. Margot scolded Tobias for his poor choices but she did understand that sometimes you have to make wretched decisions with wretched people for a necessary recommended outcome. And he was very pleased with the copious notes he jotted down in his notebook on conservative humans. His alien planet would be so happy with these results.

The Lurid Lucid Allocations of Lucinda

by Opeia Zonk

"It is an evolutionary itch that you just have to scratch. And I am here to give you that itch." — *Lucinda*

Lucinda had no last name. She really didn't. She didn't exist except for the fact that she was alive. Her history was sketchy but apparently, under the influence of morphine, she was born from a prostitute in Prussia, now Poland. In her youth she made her way to become one of Hamburg's, well, most affordable courtesans. Her price point was very low but she made up for all of that through the volume of transgressions. And her voluminous desires were plenty. She was basically the Walmart of cunts.

She pined for her dead Leon, who died bravely at Konigsberg against the Nazis. She hated them but also hated what the communist Russians also did to her Jewish lover. They were all the same but under a different flag. She saved her money to go to America where decadence reigned supreme. But really, America was no different; a liberal party was attempting social change while a Republican party was pushing back to delude the workers into a false reality of success. Just like Russia. There was no difference. So Lucinda made a war on Republicans and communists. All of them.

Theoretically, it was amazing she was still alive. The navy sailors in Hamburg did the most to contribute. But a wealthy few in Philadelphia and Pittsburgh assisted to round out her wealth of diseases. She could not open up a beer bottle with any of her orifices, but she could suck a golf ball through a garden hose and did so on numerous occasions. She surmised through the War that she lost her Leon somewhere and some way. Strangely, it was later revealed that Leon died not by the hands of Nazis but by Soviet orders to kill the Polish Jews. Their mass grave is there in a mound near the Polish border today in a remote forest. Lucinda was out for vengeance for Leon and there wasn't a disease that wasn't known that she didn't contain.

At a Republican government rally she came with her hourglass figure and empathetic notions. She gave most of the Republican caucus members HPV, chlamydia, herpes simplex, herpes complex, gonorrhea, various forms of hepatitis, and syphilis. Lucinda was very professional in her delivery. It was wonderful; they didn't know the itch was there to scratch until Lucinda was already gone.

A federal marshal and his team caught her at the Waffle House in Harrisburg, PA. She was in the middle of seducing the right-wing soldiers of My Gun Club. The Warped Noodle took her into their care. Those inflicted itched for the rest of their lives.

Comfortable in her cell, she asked for nothing. Current medicines were available to treat most of her diseases, and those illnesses that could not be treated, medicines were available for the host to live with the disease through a fairly long healthy life. She wanted none of that. All she really wanted was something that the Zonks could not give and that was she merely wanted to share her itches with the Republicans on Ward Three. Lucinda showed no signs of violent behavior; indeed, she was extremely pleasant and even at her age still had the voluptuous physique, sprite smile and pixie flashing eyes that would seduce any man or woman into a gasp of awe.

She was eventually classified as 'safe' and let out on the grounds for walks, and she was introduced to many activities. She showed no interest in art, chess, checkers or bovine harassment. The latter, since this was also a ranch, became a pastime for the residents of the Noodle. No, Lucinda only showed interest in mushroom hunting, and since Eni and Zade were up to their necks in bureaucracy, she and Chester took the lead on the finding of mushrooms.

Chester took a great liking to Lucinda. She smelled of death and he knew she was dying, and he realized she knew it too, but that did not stop her from getting up each day and greeting all the people at the Noodle gently, warmly and with sincerity. And she really did have a passion for finding mushrooms even though it was the nose of Chester that snorfled out the small bloated fungi. The pair graced the kitchens of both the Noodle and The Estate with wonderful black truffles and morels. Lucinda ignored Chester's unfortunate side effect with morels since she had seen a great deal of engorged organs from various and sundry human males, as well as most all male farm animals. Her stage shows in post-war Europe were amazing to behold.

It was with a gain of trust that Chester finally let her in on his bounty of psilocybin-laced liberty cap 'shrooms. In his 'pen', which was actually an old office at The Estate, he and Lucinda sat by the hearth wearing environmentally friendly silk robes and on environmentally friendly silk rugs, and nibbled on these dried caps that gave liberty, while drinking the best brandy The Estate could offer. Which wasn't much but it tasted like apricots and Chester liked that.

They would often take 'trips' together, and this night, they were high on the seven seas. She holding his hoof and he her hand, they immersed themselves with the spray of saltwater from the prow of their frigate while a giant cockroach steered the vessel through rough water patches through razor sharp reefs. Chester's faithful cockroach was named Grub and he had fought by his master's side in large, but finite, altercations that, through time, left this wretch with an eye, two limbs and an antenna missing. But Grub was a cockroach and it wasn't easy to render them free of life, and he healed and held on and with a patch over his well-damaged eye, he became the executive officer of Chester's frigate named La Pook.

They had the wind to their advantage and they would make it just in time to the Isle of Dry Tortuga to recover the Lost Treasure of the Swine. Chester and his fair maiden, drenched in salt spray, sang the solemn tune of The Curse from the Dying Mudskipper.

The Curse from the Dying Mudskipper
The loo is the loo and poo is the poo
But the ocean is also known as Republican Stew
Eat well you shrews or I will cook a brew
From poo in the loo called the Ocean

The last phrase was hollered into the blazing wind while they both evacuated their bowels as a wave cascaded over the bow onto their bodies and pushed them back toward the stern of the vessel. They both laughed in their embrace knowing they added, if only a little, to the brew that was the Republican stew. This is where things got a tad fuzzy from the obvious definitions of dose and concentration. A nibble to Lucinda was a monstrous cud to Chester's maul. Taking body weight into consideration, Lucinda suddenly discovered Grub's sexual advances. Chester, taking note, and understanding their long, long friendship, pulled out his saber and cut off Grub's bobbing head. Grub hissed loudly and dove off the vessel into the surf of the Dry Tortugas. Astonished at the barren Isle with just an abandoned fort, and detecting no signs of any Tortugas, dry or wet—or even a hint of the Swine treasure, they both laid down in the sand near a small dune and huddled against the blistering coastal wind.

They both woke up on an environmentally friendly silken rug in front of a not so environmentally friendly hearth. They both checked out their environment to realize that they were on the floor covered in their own excrement. In between them, they found a large cockroach that was minus a head and its body, but was still moving. Curiously, Chester noted that the head of this insect had a very minute patch over one of its eyes.

Chester didn't notice his missing keys to The Noodle for the next several days. But by that time, it all was too late. Lucinda had snuck out from her room at night and quietly infiltrated Ward Three and had sex with all the males and females present. All but three were cured. One female and two males, all having compromised immune systems from other factors, died quickly. And so did Lucinda. Just a week later, and in the hoofs of Chester, she, loaded up with caps of liberty, sailed off on her own ship off the coast of Venezuela and was never seen again. Except by Roger, and later by most everyone Zonk, where he set her up to run a righteous bordello on Teegarden B where everyone was honestly disease-free.

Author's note: Lucinda was one of my best memories of the Noodle. She died from complications due to syphilis but she would have died from any one of her diseases anyway. She was very pleasant to be around and Chester loved her dearly. He gave up his mushroom habit for exactly seventy-two hours in respect for her. She was buried near the Vance Cemetery under the oak trees. On her headstone Chester had written, 'Lucinda. A hole by any other name still smells as sweet'. No dates. It was fitting.

The Tumultuous Times of Bootes Zonk

"How quickly they are to judge me by only their sense of vision. But their vision never sees clear enough through to find the clarity of my soul." — Bootes

Bootes grew up within the security of The Estate and The Warped Noodle. Eni's solar grid with Tesla batteries and Marvin's programming made it impossible for outside interference from State or federal entities. The facilities were there; they were off the grid and they paid their taxes. There were no complaints since the Zonk facilities were designed in a black box with no external inlets. And the Zonks like it that way.

Both facilities were very successful. The Warped Noodle and the Ultra-Warped were out of the box thinking that paid off for the mentally inflicted in humanitarian and necessary ways. The Estate still had the most inductees into high profile universities and tech schools throughout the US. It was with a one hundred percent success rate that the world took notice. Funds would come in but the Zonks were adamant to allow only under-privileged orphans into their curriculum. The funds were, however, necessary for a new wing on The Warped Noodle and the Ultra-Warped towers that would hold the most savage notorious mental criminals. The latter were designed for ultra-conservative right-wing murderous Republicans. And that would include the entire current Republican Senate—which had become a cabinet for a puppet dictator installed over the US, established by Russia. It makes one think how painful it must have been for Iranians to live under the Shah and Chileans to live under Pinochet (and many other countries). And now we Americans know. Funny how that all works out. For their business in the realm of Zonks, the future was looking very good.

The Zonks built a shed for the bicycle boy. Mitch had his own private place to work on abandoned bikes and he would laboriously re-fit them into a reliable form of functional art. The entire campus now rode on his bikes, which were free to anyone going anywhere on the Zonk Campus. Even Bootes.

Bootes was given by Mitch McCabe the McCabe special, which was a refurbished Trek 920 complete with rails for cargo. He wrote on his paper pad, 'You need to taste the pastry of the world'. She looked him in the eyes and did just that. In March of that year, she, with full panier bags of granola and water, a fishing pole and a rifle, took off from The Estate and wandered into America.

She headed north since the southern humidity was already creeping into her skin. She heard there was sanity in the north and she wanted to find it. Bootes stayed to the back roads and wove a trail through hundreds of years of history. Sleeping mostly in cemeteries, she considered these quiet safe places and, in general, they were. Honey, local honey, from obscure places along her trek became the focus of her desire. Each local bee colony feeding on a variety of local flowers made each jar contain a subtle taste that would be a memory for that odd place off the side of the road. When she had too many jars to carry, she would load them all in a box, each individually labeled with the place of purchase, and mail them back to The Estate. The students there would yearn to savor what Reidsville, NC, tasted like, or Martinsville, VA, or Naoma, WV, and on and on they came.

She would fish and hunt when she could. She did not have the proper State licenses but no one really noticed this little woman dressed like a strange leather-clad Native American on a bicycle. When Bootes got tired of the monotony, she would go into a random town to a café for supper and treat herself to a soda or ice cream. Only five times was she refused service with no reason given, but she was absolutely certain that skin color and prominent black features were the primary stimulant for such nausea. She would peruse local bookstores to look for copies of The Adventures of Badger Zonk but only found two at two different places, and those were in much bigger towns. Both times she would boast that Badger Zonk was actually Lady Zonk from England and she was her long ago relative. The bookstore in Muncie even let Bootes read the story to a very attentive circle of children and she took the moment to absorb in their intrigue and become Badger. Why not? She was wearing basically the same clothes and had a dagger too. Slashing in the air with her 'sword' and belching out orders to her crew, she stood proudly to fight the world and rid it from slavery. But much to Bootes' surprise, and confirmed by a mother's acknowledgment, was that most small towns did not teach the fact that slavery ever occurred.

Harassment was infrequent and in all the incidents the individuals were intoxicated, but they were savvy enough to realize that a very confident looking young woman owning no sense of humor and holding a rifle was not to be messed with. She was bitten by a dog in Kewanee, IL, while on her bike and her left leg needed seven stitches that she eventually received in Davenport, Iowa. That scar was to be her lasting memory on this entire journey after the honey was all consumed and gone.

Bootes sat down under a tree in a park that was on the Platte River in Fremont, NE. She jotted down her notes on her adventure and came up with a few conclusions. That America was mostly flat farmland or had rolling hills. There was no North and South that she was taught, but just big cities and little towns. The big cities had better education, more racial and religious diversity, and more liberal and progressive ideals. The little towns had less education, tended to be racist and intolerant of any religion but white religions, and were more conservative in their policies. She also wrote down that she was in love with Mitch McCabe. She had known this all along but just didn't feel it until this separation. And the farther she got from The Estate, the heavier her heart felt.

It did not go unnoticed by Bootes that she was in a town named after John C. Fremont. He was a US Republican Senator from California and he ran for President under the Republican ticket in 1856. He 'led' five expeditions into the American West and basically killed Native Americans or Hispanics that bothered him. Essentially, Fremont was an asshole. Upon leaving the town, she got off her bike well back from the 'Welcome To Fremont' sign and shot at the sign many times to make a happy face. Bootes was happy to leave his memory behind.

Days later, she wheeled into Greeley, Colorado. She had never seen mountains before and they were awesome to just view. She knew up in those mountains was a Truck Stop that would love to see her. Bootes called ahead and Great Grammy Gretchen stated, "Get your ass up here NOW!" And she did.

Bootes had to rewrite in her journal that most of America was flat with some rolling hills but starting here in Colorado, real topography began. And that topography killed her ass on a bicycle. But the views and the pure smell of the air full of ozone made every hurt of her leg muscles revive. A few days later, she pulled into Poncha Springs and sprang off her bike to run into the arms of Gretchen waiting at the front door of The Truck Stop.

Gretchen rarely visited The Estate since she, Monk Shin and Cornelius were busy reviewing and rectifying conservative right-wing nationalistic issues across the globe. But letters and photos kept them up to date on family and aging appearances. The Truck Stop was basically the same but older. Klondike was long dead but during the hilarious wake festival rejoicing her memory, the patrons passed a hat and enough funds were gathered to create a bronze statue of her sitting bug-eyed looking out on The Truck Stop inhabitants from her well-worn tattered throne. Her coronations still continued and her crown made of cheap beer cans was replaced every Wednesday night. The bookstore was much bigger. Shin's mini-mega church was also bigger. But the new addition was the Zonk Cemetery. So many truckers and Truck Stop patrons loved this Zonk atmosphere so much that they encouraged Gretchen and Cornelius to have them buried on the property. Gretchen purchased the lot behind Shin's church and an iron fence with a large iron gate was installed. There was just one catch. They all had to be cremated on Cornelius's newly designed pyre with multiple bellows. No one dissented.

Gretchen didn't know what to make of this little Zonk morsel. She had chutzpah and tremendous confidence for one so young. As if she had been through numerous battles and somehow stayed alive. She wasn't in need of anyone or anything and was quite aware of her independence. Gretchen's lab and Cornelius' invention room did not interest her. She had read many of the books in The Truck Stop but was only keenly interested in the Zonk family history. Bootes would later write the entire Zonk history and she called it, 'The Clan of the Cave Crickets'. Gretchen and the Zonk family surmised that the Cave Crickets were Hazel and Zazel. And they were correct.

Opeia could hear Grammy Gretchen's concerns in her voice on the phone but just stated, "Leave her alone and she will find her place that will benefit everyone." Bootes loved the biscuits and every morning Shin would supply her with many, all covered in greasy delicious gravy with butter. She noticed, because of her bike trip, her thighs were the size of small tree trunks and just as hard. The young Zonk took her bicycle up various mountain paths and loved it all. She never knew such freedom existed. Bootes found a bronzed plaque at the foot of the Falls of Atlantis for Manny Zonk but she never mentioned this to Gretchen, Shin or Cornelius for fear of it rising sad memories from the depths. She sat at these Falls and decided she should do what she was good at. And that was to hunt and fish. But first, she would need a bigger gun.

In North Carolina the game was just smaller. The fish, however, compared to Colorado, were mostly the same except for the rainbow trout and German browns. The Colorado deer were bigger than white tail. The Colorado black bear were bigger too. Elk, which did not exist in North Carolina, were huge. Then there were the cats. The lynx, bobcat and mountain lion. She bought herself a Sako Bavarian 300 Win Mag. More than enough for anything in North America. She also purchased a seven-inch blade Bowie knife that she secured to her belt. After sighting the rifle in behind The Truck Stop, she grabbed her backpack and fishing pole and disappeared into the mountains. Gretchen was just amazed at how such a small person could pack that amount of gear. But after looking her over in her Zonk family leathers and gazing at her stout legs, she realized Bootes really was a Zonk.

Days would go by, and sometimes over a week, but Bootes would always return pulling a Native American travois with her gear and the carcass of her kill. Elk, bear and deer were common. Geese and duck with fish were less common. Bootes refused to kill coyote, wolf or any cats unless her life was in danger and she made damn sure she was never in danger of those predators. Shin was flabbergasted at the plethora of the meat. He installed a larger freezer to accommodate these beasts and sadistically served up these exotic plates to the conservative curious patrons with his notorious five-star lava heartily spiced with dragon's breath peppers. The latter peppers acquired from a small farm in Tasmania. Those conservatives never returned.

She became a faithful follower to Shin's Church only because it wasn't really a church but a house of Eastern philosophies that tangled a web of Jainism, Sikhism, Taoism, Shintoism, Hinduism and Buddhism. Most of it flowed through Bootes' lifestyle. Except for killing animals, which she absolutely knew that humans were omnivores and would always be omnivores. No human could change what nature gave you over hundreds of thousands of years of evolution. Meat is not murder but life just feeds on life. And it has always been. But that doesn't mean one should relish a killing and the taking of a life. That is why Bootes always said a small prayer to her kills. "See you on the other side." And she eventually would. Roger would see to that.

Gretchen Zonk fell in love with this staunch crumpet and asked her to stay with them at The Truck Stop. They needed new Zonk blood to infiltrate the veins of this diesel and gas station monstrosity. They needed help. Bootes said yes but with one caveat. They had to set up Mitch McCabe nearby with his own bicycle shop. It was done!

There was no wedding per se, but Mitch was flown up from North Carolina via a charter plane and he was anointed in a ceremony overseen by Shin with Iberian bull semen. The bull, still alive, gratefully evacuated his gonads in the back of The Warped Noodle into a flask for this wonderful occasion. There was no president for this anointment but Shin didn't care since he was making this shit up as he went along and from Zonk history this tactic always appeared to be the path less painful. Mitch would take Bootes' last name and so another member of the Zonk Clan was to be had. Mitch Zonk.

The Invasion of the Zyerkons

"They are angry with me. I know. And I have kept perfect notes on all human activity but that apparently was not enough. Mom, I fucked up."
— Tobias to Margot

They were coming back from their Sunday weekly experience at Cornet Bay on upper Whidbey Island. This was the secret place only known to a few crab fisher people, to catch the maximum load of legal crabs upon high tide. It would not be a secret much longer. On the way back, near Deer Island, they would gratefully pick large mussels from the pilings from the dock and fill up a five-gallon bucket. Flush with a load of Dungeness crabs and a bucket of mussels, off they went via a ferry to their mansion. With a cup of melted butter with chopped fresh garlic and a pot of boiled artichokes, crabs and mussels, supper was on. This didn't appear to make a dent in Tobias' dour mood.

The Socialist movement was not going so well due to Joseph Raymond McCarthy, and now the US government was literally hunting them all down as if they were mindless bothersome cattle for slaughter. The federal government was at war with Communism and they didn't care that Communism wasn't Socialism. To the conservative mind it was all the same. They had to be extinguished like so many cockroaches. But cockroaches were hard to eradicate. So Margot and Tobias went undercover as Mormons. One of these Mormons went insane. But since all Mormons were insane, to Tobias, it just did not matter. The Zyerkons were invading.

Margot never really understood Tobias unless he was flying and only then, did he make some sort of sense. But recently he would miss his engagements for flight for a sweat-filled bed of cotton and a loin full of nervous twitches. It wasn't sexual but sheer fear of the Zyerkons. Tobias wasn't afraid of dying. God no. Any bush pilot that survived any of their colossal weather travesties would say death was a welcome event. No, Tobias was afraid of failure to his people on his planet. What

216

did he do wrong? Did he not take notes? Were the notes not specific to this drivel called humans? What? What was the issue? But the Zyerkons were not happy and they came. And Tobias, shit his pants. Over and over again.

Margot thought this was just some male thing having to do with a latent puberty issue. Roger refused to assist since he was having sex with a waiter named Chili. Martha was off destroying various unproductive galaxies just because she could. For this, Martha was given multiple seven-dimensional metals, but honestly, where could she keep them all? She went back in time and gave them to the Spartans so that they could melt them down for weapons and shields for their failed battle of Thermopylae. She would see them all on the other side. And she did.

Margot finally had Tobias hosed off with the urine from the circus elephants at the Puyallup Fair. This treatment didn't work but she could not, in all good conscience, put Tobias into the Lakewood mental facility near Tacoma and chose to treat him at home. Strangely starting with massive doses of the urine from elephants.

The elephants were from a Nevada Army installation near the Utah border. In a small valley that previously had the Pikes as scientists, the pachyderms were exposed to substantial doses of various radiation from a Uranium stockpile, all while pregnant. None of the young births were alive but one, a stock solid baby elephant named Titus, and he quickly disappeared from the base. The others were contained and their fluorescent urine was stored for the health benefits of one Tobias Zonk. He glowed but only at night.

The Zyerkons were a benevolent people with a single benevolent monarch named Thud. They resided on the planet called Gliese 667 Cc. They were peaceful. Very peaceful. But they could not handle, in anyway, lies. They just couldn't. And the journal reports from Tobias were obviously Republican blasphemy, and they, as a set of beings of the universe, had to annihilate the humans. It was necessary. It actually was necessary.

The invasion began in Corpus Christi Bay, near Corpus Christi, Texas. Why? Because that is where Thud's tentacle landed on his spinning globe of the earth when asked "Where, Boss?" Zyerkons appeared like humanoids and over hundreds of thousands of years evolved to be very adaptable and formidable beings. They had tentacles instead of fingers and a very robust outwardly protruding chest. Even the females, whose large breasts were regarded as the most alluring sexual aspect of any universal being in existence, touted their magnitude. Their spaceships went completely undetected since they looked like, in size and shape, to be that of live horseshoe crabs. Of which, off the coast of Texas, there were many. Beachgoers just ignored the invasion since they just didn't realize any invasion was occurring at all. You see, the Zyerkons were very small beings. About half the size of a small sugar ant. These beings, small as they were, conquered space travel, annihilated all known diseases, and invented an excruciatingly painful disintegration device known as the Phoot, named that since it actually made that noise when it was discharged. Thud was often quoted as saying, "Size does not matter in this entire universe."

The General's plan was to bypass the big city of Corpus altogether, head northwest, and flank the town of Odem on both the western and eastern sides and destroy all the inhabitants there before sunrise. They left their horseshoe-like spacecrafts on the shore of the north part of the Nueces Bay and a one hundred and fifty thousand-strong army marched quietly north to Odem. All was proceeding as planned for the first few hours and then the Zyerkons' fecal matter hit the proverbial fan when the army stumbled upon several mounds belonging to hundreds of thousands of fire ants. Texans know these small critters very well; they are extremely aggressive and inject their opponents with a very toxic alkaloid venom called solenopsin. Unfortunately, for the Zyerkons, this would prove fatal. The battle did not last long—exactly twenty-two minutes—but the valiant Zyerkons, not knowing even a word for defeat, fought to the last being. And that was Thud.

Thelma Gaak, clothed in just her bathrobe, exited her back screen door to her small abode, took a long drag on the first of her morning cigarettes and gazed at the fresh sunrise. She looked down on her cracked cement porch and there was this tiny ant writhing in pain. Ms. Gaak took another long drag off her smoldering paper tube filled with tobacco and was about to step on this creature until she faintly but distinctly heard the words, "Telak, Trak!" Which in Zyerkon meant "Save me!" Thelma Gaak did not know Zyerkon but knew enough to know that ants didn't

218

yell words. She got down on her knees and pushed her face close to the cement and through her far-sighted goggles, she peered closely at this creature. Now, Ms. Gaak was a tad over four feet ten inches but was plagued by serious back pains due to her enormous EEE cup breasts, which now, incidentally, fell out on the cement from her robe. Thud was amazed at the magnitude of the protuberances and quickly imaged that if she were just much smaller, she could possibly be his Queen. But that image dissipated quickly as he pulled the trigger on his Phoot. Translated later by Tobias, Thud said, "I am going to get you, you Republican son of a bitch!" Well, obviously, this was said in pain and passion since she was clearly a female and was no person's son. But luckily, he got the Republican issue correct since Thelma was a card-carrying extreme conservative.

The blast visibly hit a mole on Ms. Gaak's left breast near her nipple and it was instantaneously disintegrated. Thelma said, "Oh, Shit!" and with her right hand smashed the life out of Thud.

His last words were apparently, "Size does matter." That mole near her nipple, by the way, was malignant melanoma, not known to Thelma, and Thud had just extended her conservative and pathetic life for another forty years. Roger, making love to Chili in the back of a bar on Teegarden B, moaned.

Crud, Thuds replacement, contacted Tobias and plainly stated that irradiated elephant urine treatments were no long necessary, nor were his notes. The Nation of Zyerkons had given up hope for procuring any intelligent life on Earth since the effort would be entirely futile. Crud made it clear, "We don't negotiate with fascists!"

A PhD dissertation committee on some far away multi-dimensional planet yelled in unison, "We Told You So!!!"

The Towers of Babel

by Opeia Zonk

"I realize they are human and I realize that they are speaking English. But for the life of me, I can't understand a damn thing they are saying."
— Ada to Opeia

Ada Place became the lead psychiatrist for the Ultra-Warped Noodle. The new towers were constructed for the ultra-conservative murderous Republicans and Ms. Place called these spires The Towers of Babel. Yes, in reference to the Mesopotamian God, Marduk, but also to Genesis 11:1-9 meant to explain why two sets of people, identical in nature, speak different languages. And that, here, was the case. And, of course, the fact was quaintly said by Ada, "And those incarcerated Republican fuckers just regurgitate unintelligible BABBLE!"

The spires appeared much like that of Islamic Minarets and they were placed around the main building of the Ultra-Warped electrical fence like candles on the perimeter of a dome-like cake. Escape wasn't impossible just improbable since impossible required infinity and infinity did not exist with mass-based entities in the third dimension. But even if they got past the locks and the guards and the electric fence, the Zonks installed a series of genetically modified falcons that roosted on top of each spire but also throughout the campus of the Warped Noodle. These birds were altered just like Laki Lukovich's nose but also with very keen eyesight at locating ultra-conservatives. If any convict was found to be out of the spire and on the grounds the birds would instantly swoop down and remove the escapee's eyes. Because of this fowl modification, no Republican, middle-of-the-road or ultra-conservative would ever visit the Zonks. Ever. And that was just fine by them.

The spires were constructed with a single internal spiral staircase and each small floor was a small room that housed a criminal. Nothing spacious like the dome rooms but very Spartan like a prison cell. Ada remarked that even Feng Shui would not have assisted the Zonks' endeavor here for a peaceful and harmonious surrounding. Actually, the Zonks were fine with this conclusion. The floors of the spires had nothing in common with the floors of the main Noodle. The spire floors were all for murderous sane, or insane, Republicans. The only difference between Ward Three of the main Noodle and the spires was the fact that Ward Three patrons' machinations that led indirectly to an individual's death, were not overt but based on their lies and the irrationality of their diatribes. The death of the spire patrons' victims, however, were either covert or overt and were, if not directly by their hands, through indirect funding from them.

The Zonks did not believe in capital punishment. The Code of Hammurabi, as Gandhi stated, would leave the whole world blind. No. The best course of action, before Roger's hands would grab their souls, would be incarceration and scientific study. What made some people, rich or poor, as dumb as a sack of mindless hammers? What made them cause pain and death for others? Stanley Milgram's psychological experiments were a start for Ada Place and she wanted to try this out with the inhabitants of The Towers of Babel. Of course, the Zonks could just let them go, but the genetically engineered falcons would immediately render them blind— and then we'd get back to the stickiness of the Code of Hammurabi. Enough said.

The bottom floor of every tower was vacant and used for the guard's lunchroom, media center and game room. A small portion of this area now was formed into an area for psychological research led by Ms. Place. Marvin did the set up for the experiment and, intrinsically, it was simple. A small room with a door and wall was set up with an opaque window where a person from the outside could only see the silhouette of the participating 'victim' sitting down in front of a desk with a computer. The 'victim' would be wired to the wrist to receive electric shocks and the pain threshold would be registered on the computer before that person. On the other side of the wall was a volunteer. Generally, an orderly or nurse from the Noodle, and they would sit on a chair in front of a desk with a large red button and the 'dial of pain' on a console that had lights that would turn off and on due to the amount of pain that was received by the 'victim' behind the opaque window. Therefore, the volunteer could see the amount of pain that was being delivered to the silhouette of the 'victim'. In reality, no electricity was transferred to this prisoner but the convict was coached to yell and holler in serious pain when the red button was pressed. The lights on the consul in front of the volunteer would indicate mild pain at one to nearly death at the tenth light, and Ada was there to take notes and to encourage the volunteers to turn up the voltage on the dial. This was Stanley Milgram's experiment to the letter except for one unfortunate wire mishap where Marvin, distracted by the death of his beloved Emma Watson, who was found in her Baltimore Apartment with a rolled-up newspaper in her hands hissing out her last words to an unfortunate youth, "What is your VISION?" set the placebo red button to an actual RED button connecting a full moderating charge of electricity that would be delivered to the 'victims' who would instantly actually became victims upon the pressing.

After several attempts, Ada was stunned to realize that the 'victims' were so vocal and exact in their interpretation of being electrified. The screams of pain and resolute anguish were so sincere that she honestly thought they should attempt a career in acting. The other odd result, like Milgram's experiments, was that the volunteers that were hired to follow orders, did. Over seventy percent of the participant orderlies and nurses, schooled to ameliorate suffering and pain, continued to zap these people upon the orders of Ms. Place. Unfortunately, for the experiment, the 'victims' all died from complications due to death. Chester chortled. These spires could now be utilized to house his cornucopia of cherished caps of liberty.

Author's note: This was truly unfortunate and a tremendous stain flung on the entire institution of the Noodle's mental health record. We lowered the Global Citizen flag to half-mast around the complex but some unknown vandal replaced those flags, during the night, with a pig skull and cross bones. It was terrible. Chester belched.

Eni and Zade

by Janis Oxolins

Translated from Latvian by Zackary Maxwell

The Burial at The Mound

"The crest of our crust begins at innovation. We mire in the confines of politics that smother our souls but what we need is innovation in education to ameliorate this plague." — Monk Shin

It was early one November morning, when Bootes' and Mitch's tongues were swimming in a pool of saliva expecting Monk Shin's glorious biscuits and gravy. Bootes was not fishing or hunting today. There was a blizzard outside. Mitch had his hands full repairing and upgrading a new load of landfill throw-a-ways. After breakfast, Mitch started a fire in the fire pit central to The Truck Stop, certain that some weary travelers would need to warm up on this blustery cold day, and Bootes grabbed a book. She curled up on an old leather chair in the corner and opened up the book. It was titled, 'The Polarization of America'. "No shit," she said audibly to no one. Cornelius pulled up a chair. She noticed for someone over one hundred years of age that this ancient brilliant soul still moved about very well. His hair was long and silver in color. He was now wearing round glasses and looked like some wizard or professor.

"Can I show you something?" he asked. It was such a dreary day, and she didn't particularly want to continue reading a book where she had already lived the words, so she smiled gingerly and nodded in the affirmative.

She had been in his lab before, but it now appeared different. 'Clean' was the word she found floating in her head. He sat down on a bench and Bootes pulled up a stool. In front on an antiquated lab table was a large white porcelain bowl. Cornelius leaned his head over the bowl, lit a match, turned to Bootes and said smiling, "Presto!" and he dropped the lit match into the bowl. There was a huge flash with a 'whoosh'. There stood Cornelius, his face ash gray, his round glasses ash covered and his long silver hair singed in a circle around his head. The smell of sulfur and burnt hair engulfed her tiny nose.

Cornelius, though he could not see out of his charred lenses, turned to where he thought she was and said, "How was that?" And when these words came out of his mouth so did a billow of smoke. She couldn't help it. It was all so Zonk. Bootes laughed.

After he cleaned up, he came back to the table. His hair still singed in numerous places around his head but his face and glasses were clean. The smell of burnt hair was still emanating from his body. "You want to make some?" asked the centenarian. Of course, she was a Zonk.

They started off with something simple. Cornelius borrowed a box of Bootes' rifle cartridges, took off a few bullets and emptied the smokeless gunpowder into a small bowl. Bootes noticed that the burn rate was slower but also without all the smoke. Cornelius then took out some old vitamin plastic bottles and filled them up with varying amounts of gunpowder, put in a fuse, and taped the bottles up with varying amounts of duct tape. Bootes took notes. They then went out back under an awning, and since it was the season in the northern hemisphere, they put out three pumpkins in a row. Knife in hand, the centenarian carved out the stem at the top of each orange squash and put in a vitamin bottle duct taped explosive with the fuse sticking out.

Trust between this old man and the younger Zonk was not really great at this juncture, but she did as she was told and lit all three fuses and ran back behind the corner of The Truck Stop with Cornelius. Seconds later, and almost simultaneously, the pumpkins exploded. She didn't realize it until later, but she was jumping up and down in the snow and screaming sounds of success. She didn't know blowing crap up would be so much fun. Shin, upset from the rattling windows, looked out the back door to view three of his pumpkins that were slated for pies were now splattered and charred over mounds of snow. Then there was the sight in the corner of a very old man and a very young small woman dancing and yelling in a snow drift. Shin just said, "Fuck it!" and went back inside.

Cornelius, always the inventor, got suddenly serious and instructed Bootes to get her paper pad and review the notes. Looking over the blasted pumpkins like meat inspectors reviewing skinned carcasses, the two analyzed the impact areas. "What do you see?" whispered the old man. Bootes looked at her notes and noticed that the left pumpkin with the least amount of powder but the most amount of duct tape was basically vaporized. The middle pumpkin with the medium-sized powder charge with the medium amount of duct tape was scattered but the bottom was still there. And lastly, the right pumpkin with the most amount of powder but the least amount of tape was still blown up but a shell remained. "Good", the old man said, "It is compression that is key."

Both went back in the lab, hunkering over the beat-up table, and Cornelius said, "We cheated and cheating for a Zonk is not acceptable." Bootes didn't understand what he meant. "If you make something. If you invent it. You make it from scratch!" He said these words slowly and deliberatively.

Bootes just slowly nodded her head to the rhythm of the words that he spoke. "Got it," she said.

After the storm blew over, the next morning the old man and Bootes went on a scavenging hunt. The first item, charcoal, was easy. Shin kept several bags in the shed for summer grilling. The second, sulfur, was generally sold in chemical supply stores but Cornelius had the local pharmacy give him some for a potential flea remedy for animals he didn't own. The last, saltpeter, was the oxidizer and absolutely necessary, but since too many people were going around making their own black powder and blowing stuff up, that would be difficult to find. The key here was the word 'oxidizer'. It was to add oxygen to the burning mass to make it a more efficient explosion. Cornelius knew a welding shop in Salida that had oxy tabs for particular welding devices to add oxygen. He purchased many. After days experimenting with various amounts of all these ground-up ingredients, they both claimed success when one particular batch had the fastest burn rate with the least amount of residual waste. Both pleased, they packed this mixture in a pill bottle with cotton in the bottom and cotton in the top with the powder in the middle. This would enhance compression. With a fuse inserted and much duct tape, they went out in the middle of the night from the back door to the trash container, lit the fuse and threw it in. Hiding behind the corner of the building, the old man knew the final result but Bootes just had to peer around the edge of the wall just to see for herself, and what she saw was amazing. The bright flash and sonic boom were expected but the instantaneous shockwave that rippled through the drifts of snow and impacting her chest with such a force as to knock her down into the welcoming arms of a frosted pinion pine, was intense. All the windows of the back of The Truck Stop building were broken. Somewhere throbbing in her ears was Shin's yelling voice saying, "Assholes!" She looked up and there was Cornelius, tears in his eyes. She could barely hear him but he said, "Don't you just love to be ALIVE?" And she concurred. In fact, she had never been so happy. Freeing the bonds of too tightly attracted atoms within molecules was very similar to Badger Zonk's freeing of the slaves from their bonds. Freeing those tight bonds became an explosion of righteousness!

A few nights later, swinging slightly in her hammock next to Mitch, she slept hard. Fatigued by a two-day hunt tracking a very large black bear and bringing it all home, was too much. She was mentally and physically sore. She was poked awake by what she initially thought was Roger but she cleared her vision to see it was a very old man. The centenarian. He wanted to tell her something in private. So they both shuffled to his lab.

"I am dying. No, no, don't speak. Just listen. I have only a few more days. I don't want to be barbequed on my dual-bellow pyre and I don't want to be buried in the Zonk Cemetery. I want to be placed on a mound far away and I want to be exploded to bits so that nature's scavengers can take me away," Bootes nodded. She understood. The next day, the great Cornelius was dead.

Bootes conveyed his last wish to the Zonk family. There were some grumblings but they acquiesced to Gretchen's commands. The Zonks found a large mound just twenty miles north of Fowler, Colorado, in the eastern plains. The farmer there did not bother with the intrusion. The mound was a large knoll in the middle of a flat wheat field and on top was the carcass of one of the greatest inventors ever. He invented the Foreskin of Christ! And he was a hero to the Catholic Religion that he detested. The Vatican received annually 33.3% in gross sales. It was all wonderful.

Chester and Opeia flew into Denver to attend the 'service'. Eni and Zade were up to their noses in management back at the facilities in North Carolina and could not attend. There was no casket or pallbearers. Bootes and Opeia loaded up the old man's rectum with massive amounts of the powder that Bootes and Cornelius concocted. The tightly bound cotton pressured pill bottles were attached to a series of electronic sparking detonation devices whose wires ran out of his anus to a larger wire that ran down the hill to a box in the barn. They waited patiently. Monk Shin, sticking to the script, said, "Shit happens." The black adorned crowd huddle around Chester, Opeia and Bootes, and the three attached the positive lead to the charged car battery to set off the ignition.

There was a flash and later a boom. It took time for the concussion wave to travel down the mound to the mourning. Once hit, they now were mourning their mourning. Their teeth chattered and chipped. Cornelius was not vaporized. A small miscalculation in the mixture with the lack of cotton and duct tape caused a huge explosion but not with enough oomph. Parts of his body were found over a mile distance. The carrion did feast. And wasn't that the point? "Sorry, not enough compression," was all that Bootes said. But the Zonks were pleased with the results and hugged her.

The Frail Bonds Between the Branches on the Crispy Trees

"The crescent moon only reminds us of the cycle of life that surrounds us every day. It waxes and wanes and we are in between to deal with the forces of the tides." — Margot

Hans Gurp was from Teutonic stock. He could follow his bloodline generations back to the Great Field Marshal Blucher. And like Blucher he ate meat and potatoes. Anything green was the sign of infection and it certainly was not going to be on any plate for him to eat. As a result, Hans, like his wife and children, were quite bulbous. Their large house was on several acres in the foothills of the Cascade mountains outside of Seattle. It was elegant and could easily be confused as an upper-class domicile from Prussian 18th century history. The inside of this hovel was just as garish and appeared like a mahogany-beamed cathedral complete with rare pieces from a museum. All the paintings were 'originals' and all were of the Gurp family in various ridiculous costumes and assuming poses. The vase on the table by the stairwell was exquisite in detail and possibly Cretan in design but upon viewing the bottom of the pottery, it was clear this container was made in China and purchased at Walmart for three dollars and fifty cents. Not including tax. Yet Hans would swear to his visitors with the sincerity of an ox that everything adorned within those walls were all priceless family heirlooms.

Hans made his fortune in meat. Specifically, pork, and that only in the form of sausage. His Prussian family recipe went back hundreds of years and to this day, it was a firm secret held in a vault behind the bloated portrait of his rotund beloved pale son, Hanzie. In fact, known only to Hans, the ethnicity of this extremely wonderful recipe was not Teutonic in origin but African American from one Bella Jefferson of Demopolis, Alabama. Basically, Hans' fantastic sausage recipe was stolen. After the war, a young Hans Twerp traveled from his hometown in Germany called Braunfels and jumped on a ship in Hamburg that was bound for New York. As with all timetables after the war, the ship was late and chubby Hans went into the nearest café to find something to eat. Not noticing the red lights, his next meal would be that of a very fine vagina owned by a woman with only a first name. Lucinda. Lucinda gave young Hans more than just affection but an infection that he carried laboriously across the Atlantic and into the early parts of his life in America. Misery led this robust youth looking for a cure. From Syracuse to Grand Rapids to Pascagoula to Montgomery and finally to a small town of Demopolis, Alabama, where Dr. Jefferson, direct out of Howard University, father of Bella, cured the young Twerp with salvarsan, penicillin and a touch of arsenic. Dr. Jefferson, pleased with his salvation remedy, sat down with Hans and said, "Change your last name. It would be better for you in this land of America in the long run." And he was right. Twerp became Gurp and, actually, nothing changed. Roger went through the timelines on both last names and Hans still ended up just as pathetic.

While he was recuperating from his illness in Demopolis and rejoicing in his emancipation from near death, his appetite grew and he became a regular patron of Bella Jefferson's BBQ. What Ms. Jefferson's family discovered was that if you slow cooked pork ribs on a grill using the family sauce recipe for over fourteen hours and, separately, cooked down neck bones in the family roux for four hours, and combined all this boneless meat mass into a grinder and put this masticated pulp into the cleaned-out intestine of a pig, with a ratio of 60/40 pig fat to meat, then heaven would enter your soul upon ingestion. And it did. Outside on a large plywood board was painted her slogan. 'Do you want to know what a piece of Heaven tastes like?' With, ironically, a painted face of a very happy pig.

Hans, now Gurp, became addicted to this tubed flesh and broke in early in the morning to the BBQ establishment and stole Bella's recipe. Why not? Was he not Aryan? Was he not chosen to understand the subtleties of the nuanced palate? They could not possibly appreciate this mixture and most probably stumbled blindly upon it like a bear in a forest playing with its pecker. This belonged to him. Yet he stole it. Regardless of his pride in Teutonic superiority, he fled Alabama with remorse and guilt and ended up near Seattle. He quickly started a butcher market, and with this absconded list of ingredients, he became the northwest King of the Gurp sausage. Hans became very wealthy. But he stole.

Guilt weaves its tendrils like thousands of mating writhing squid into and on the neurons of some neurotic brains. Hans' brain was baked back when he was young by fundamentalist Lutherans. If Lutherans can be fundamental. The slapping of his knuckles with rulers. The verbal psychological torture of being much less than Lars over and over and over again. That bratwurst was really 'brautwurst' that literally meant 'Bride's Meat' and he loved them so much that the church deemed Hans as homosexual, which led to years of non-lubricated persecution. The pressure was building and the only release was more potatoes and sausage. But the sausage was stolen and he was eating stolen sausage and it was just becoming all too much.

The cork popped in Hans at approximately one a.m. in the morning. He hadn't slept. He was sitting in his Prussian family leather-bound royal chair, direct from IKEA, and decided to wake up his entire family. Girtha, Hanzie, Gretze and Hans all went out of the house, and on their manicured lawn, sat down for a family prayer. Hans, holding hands with his family in a circle, prayed audibly to God to relieve him of his sin. This misery that tormented his being throughout his useless life. What could be done? "Show me a sign!!!" And then came a sputter from the clouds.

Margot was just returning from a socialist soiree in Spokane when her plane started to cough repeatedly over Snoqualmie Pass. She pumped the fuel mixture richer but that didn't appear to solve the issue. As with Seattle most of the year, it was cloudy with misting rain. The floodlights of the plane went on as soon as she cut through the lowest cloud layer at two hundred feet. What Margot saw was a large clear spurge of rolling land mingled with pine trees and a large house with a circle of kneeling people on the front lawn. "Wiccans probably," she said when the engine quit. With little velocity, she came down hard and decapitated the entire praying Gurp clan. In just a nanosecond the Aryan Sausage King and his family were just a memory. The splatter blinded Margot's goggles and she careened into the house through the bloated portrait of Hanzie, exploding the vault containing Bella's secret recipe. The secret was now safe with Bella.

The Stearman was no more. Margot was found lodged in a large Grand Fir tree with a charred branch through the right side of her body. Her right lung and assorted organs were all a mush. Miraculously, she lived for another three days. Tobias flew back from a job in Ketchikan, Alaska, to see her at the trauma center. They cut the branch but did not remove it since they thought she would die instantly due to blood loss. There she was, impaled. Gilla Mostel felt her body and face for a 'visual'. Margot told Gilla to travel to Oklahoma, "They would like your singing voice and music there." To Tobias, her last words were, "You are NOT human. Do you understand? You are a Zonk!" And she rolled over to die in the arms of Roger.

Roger set Margot up on Teegarden B as a stunt pilot. The inhabitants of the planet were very curious about this antiquated bi-plane and its pilot. Of course, they had spaceships to ferry them about the galaxy, but this plane and pilot brought back a renaissance of the real tangible essence of primitive flight. Margot Zonk became a legend.

The Tale of the Tyrannical Toot

by Opeia Zonk

"I found a pond. The swans were white. I found another pond. The swans were white. Thousands of ponds later and nothing but white swans! But I am absolutely sure the next pond will contain a black swan. I know it!" — Ted Toot

Bootes gave birth to a little baby girl maggot named Cygnus Zonk. She was beautiful in a maggoty sort of way. Mitch was petrified with the fear that his damaged right brain would somehow affect his semen and produce a brain damaged child. It didn't. Cygnus was wonderful in her glorious ooze. Cygnus Zonk came into this world. Like Bootes, she was tiny but mighty and screaming out all the small volume of oxygen contained in her little lungs.

Mr. Toot, on the Richter Scale of assholes, was a twelve. Even though the scale only went up to ten, and no earthquake on Earth ever exceeded that, Toot was a twelve. He was a DC lobbyist for a firm maladroitly referred to as 'The Liberal Leftists for Progressive Policies'. This was funded by the ultra-conservative company uniquely and erroneously titled, 'Parents for the Planned Nest of the Motherly Neighborhood', which trapped young single white pregnant teenage girls into their web of deceit and convinced them through 'therapy' to marry fundamentalist Hispanic Catholic migrants that the now right-wing government would then expel across the US border to a country that would be plagued excruciatingly with Caucasian genes! And they say conservatives don't know science. Well, stop thinking! They don't! It is all a racist plague.

Ted Toot lied, cajoled, stole, desecrated, tortured, terrorized, brutalized, blinded and murdered to solely uphold the wholesome family values of the Republican party. He, himself, was the epitome of those values. Ted, however, wasn't always that serene.

Lumberton, Texas, was a sleepy little town just north of Beaumont. If your nose was calibrated to the humidity just right with a southern wind you could almost smell the sea breeze through the forest of pines. The inhabitants were all white Christians and they made a point about stating so to anyone visiting from outside the city limits. Gerald, the grocery manager, always was smiling at the entrance of his store and warmly shook your hand. If he did not know you, he would put his hand on your shoulder and lead you to his office, and ask about your faith and your family. That was, of course, if you were Caucasian. If not, you were politely ignored until your patience dried up and you went away—like an electric fan blowing away an unpleasant odor. The city was not famous for anything. Nothing whatsoever. No inventor came from this town. No sports player. Ms. Dillson, the eighty-seven-year-old former owner of the grocery store, made headlines in the three-paged Lumberton Express, when she claimed to have been raped multiple times. She suffered from serious dementia so this story was taken quizzically by the Sheriff. Pastor Roy was sent to her house to console her only for her to jump up and rape the Pastor with a candlestick. Had the Sheriff taken the time to have Ms. Dillson checked at a doctor's office, the lab results would have shown that she had semen in all three main orifices in her body. And that semen belonged to one Ted Toot. The only other whispering stain of gossip that surrounded this town was Ollie Graystone, a gay boy in high school who was found hung by his neck from a pine tree in the park, and Chester Longly, a black retired blacksmith who, somehow, while walking his dog, got his leash snagged on the back bumper of a passing truck and he and his dog were hauled down the road to their eventual deaths. Both were ruled accidents. But both were caused by Ted Toot.

Mr. Toot was plum full of passion. Unfortunately, the passion was all hate. Mostly self-hate. But he would never admit to any of that. The only real joy he could obtain was by causing pain in other people. And the only people that understood this passion became his 'friends' and they all had the same thing in common. This hate. But this hate would never go away, it just sat in their stomachs and grumbled to be fed. And the real focus of their hate was boiled down into a melting pot and that material that settled to the bottom was called 'change'.

Tiny Toot towns all over this country, where everyone knew everyone's name and everyone went to church on Sunday and that church was a Christian church, was a Toot town. And the only race was white. Where science was not trusted but faith was the healer. Then there was change. Change was race. Change was religion. Change was LGBTQ. Change was science. And the people of the tiny Toot towns became afraid of this change. To control this change, they had to control their media and their local educational systems. They had to keep the local populations ignorant of the expanding world. And they fought this true knowledge with their grumbling hate to thwart this change. Ted Toot and his friends found a home for their small-minded belief system and that was in the Republican party.

After years of loyal service, he brutalized his way up the chain of command into the warm arms of Margret Johansson—the fifth wealthiest woman in Texas. Ms. Johansson came from a small town called Alice, Texas. Which, by the way, has the best sweet tea in all of the entire state. Her money came from oil. Which one might think natural due to fracking of the subsurface shale in this state, but in actuality, it was her husband's silicon-based oil lubrication invention that found a home in sexual activities throughout the Planet. This made their wealth secure. By a strange and unfortunate possibility of infinite realities, Roger uncovered that just IF the Zyerkons were successful in their attack on Odem, Texas, their westward and eastward push would have eradicated both the towns of Alice and Lumberton, along with Ms. Johansson's and Ted Toot's lineages and this freak'n chapter need not have been written. At all! Damn fire ants!

After way too many minutes held in the bosom of Ms. Johansson, it became clear that Ted had an Oedipus complex. Margret, too, was smitten and it wasn't long before Mr. Toot was renowned as 'The Fixer' for many prominent Republicans working under this new US dictatorship. Mr. Toot's first mission assignment was to annihilate all the Zonks.

Ted took two of his best 'friends', Zed and Fred. All were heavily armed with militarized weapons that expended multiple rounds per the pull of a trigger indicating later to the Zonks that these individuals should, based on Zonk lore, not be shooting at all. The plan was for a night push through the southern fence of The Estate and Zed and Fred would flank left to the Silk Barn, and Ted would flank right to the school cottages. They would attack the main Estate at exactly one in the morning and shoot anything that moved.

Upon fence penetration, at midnight, the silent alarm was sounded throughout both The Estate and the Warped Noodle. Eni and Zade, armed with sniper rifles, ran to the roof. Marvin, through communication links, indicated through infrared sensors, that there were three humans approaching from the south in an east/west flank formation. And then things got sort of screwed up.

Zed and Fred got lost, and somehow, through the brambles and fences, ended up in the back area of the Warped Noodle. The security falcons, immediately sensing conservatives, quickly flew down to remove their eyes. Their screams disturbed a very old Iberian bull who rose slowly from his bed of leaves and charged the meandering hollering humans. Disemboweled, Zed and Fred were no more. The bull, tuckering out his last tucker, satisfied, lay down and died. Ted, hearing the sounds of an apparently successful skirmish to his west, ran over the gravel driveway and launched himself directly through The Estate's kitchen window. Ada Place, finishing up her nightly snack ritual of tuna on rye at the kitchen's counter, jumped up, and her inner Wushu kicked in. Literally. Ted's nipples were removed in a flourish and he was subsequently completely emasculated. With his trachea crushed he fell to the floor gasping for air. Chester, late as usual, took a pre-mauled ball of the caps of liberty from his mouth and shoved a hoof full down Ted's esophagus.

The banner waved bravely in the breeze as the band played a merry heroic tune. Ted Toot's pride swelled and tears seeped from his eyes. The tears blinded him temporarily only to clear and see the US dictator embrace him on the platform to the hordes of a cheering crowd as The Dick placed around his neck the Presidential Medal of Freedom. The cheers roared in patriotic bliss to the point of pain. He grabbed his ears and fell to the Dictator's feet. He looked up and there was just an orange bloated man laughing hysterically as spittle dripped down on Ted's forehead. He was hot. He was very hot. He was on KELT-9 and he was weaving his burnt entrails into a never-ending basket.

Author's note: I really wish this was fiction but sadly it was not. What can I say but life sometimes really sucks?

Cygnus and Titus

"Don't you see your face in the lake? Like today, it is all still. Your reflection is pure and real and it is you. Don't be afraid of it. You cannot fear true reality since it is all a fact." — Cygnus to Titus

Little Cochetopa Creek fed into a series of small lakes just northwest of Mt. Ouray. Up a long forest path, through tall timber, Cyg went by the old Gooseberry Farm that was now broken down and weathered. The old farmer's wife waved, bent over her seat on the chicken crate and popped in her ass a longneck beer. A 'fitz' and a 'spritz' later she winked at Cyg as Cyg crawled up the path to go fishing. The farmer himself, long dead due to a bizarre mauling by a supposedly rabid castrated beagle, still baffled authorities. Cyg stayed clear.

The rusty plaque that was stamped into a Douglas Fir tree halfway up the trail stated, 'A dream is nothing but life. Thaddeus'. Cyg smiled. These were her family's woods.

She went down a hollow into a glen with a small lake. It didn't appear to be there before and perhaps she was the first human to discover this vast tiny place. She carried her rifle, handed down from Thaddeus, a single shot .22, but it wasn't for big varmints like her mother hunted but just little ones. Her fishing pole was her mother's, too. Made of bamboo with twill twine and covered in shellac. It was hardy and true. Then a small elephant showed up. It was glowing a bright mild green.

The elephant was the size of a large dog but no bigger. He was radiant in his radiance. He forced himself between the trees to the edge of the lake. Cyg was unperturbed by oddities. She was a Zonk. "Howdie," she said. He grunted in response and much to his amazement she ran to embrace him into a huge hug.

He said his name was Titus and he spoke English fluently. The elephant said that he was born in a large laboratory in a valley in Utah and that many other glowing elephants were born there, too, but none survived. Humans put him in a truck and took him north to a border town between Utah and Colorado near La Sal. It was there where he escaped and went east into the Rocky Mountains. Several days later, he smelled a little human girl. And now he was here. "I am very hungry," he said.

"What do you eat?" said Cyg.

"Why, little girls, of course."

She smiled brightly. "Then I will be your meal," she giggled. "But I will not go quietly or easily. I will make you work for your dinner. You must, you see, since I am a Zonk." Now it was Titus that was smiling. Irradiation did something to this elephant. It stifled his growth and made him glow green but it increased his speed and strength. He could easily pounce on this human and rip off her head but she was so odd that he found her incredible.

"How about a fish instead?" he said firmly. Cyg sat down on a log next to Titus, hooked up some bait, and tossed in the line from her pole. Fish it was.

Titus proceeded to talk about the Battle of Waterloo. Did she know of this event? She nodded in the affirmative. "Man's inhumanity to man is historic and conflicts between humans will never ever end," she said proudly.

"Why?" whispered Titus.

"Because the human animal is basically very stupid. It really is amazing that they have gotten this far evolutionarily."

"Did you know Napoleon was not engaged at the Battle of Waterloo?" She did know this.

"Yes, he could not sit on his horse during the battle since his hemorrhoids were inflamed. He was in a doctor's carriage up on a hillside during the entire battle."

"Do you think hemorrhoids cost the French the battle?"

"No, silly. Wellington with the help of Blucher and the Prussians outnumbered the French. The French would have lost the battle anyway," she retorted.

"Sixty-five thousand people dead in two days. And all for nothing," Titus sighed.

"I told you they were stupid," said Cyg. And then bit a fish.

Titus was amazed at the focus and mechanical precision Cyg had in pulling this fish out of the water, gutting it, starting a fire, cooking and then harvesting wild mint on a nearby hill to garnish the dish. The trout tasted awesome. But then again, Titus was hungry. "Thank you but I now must go," he vaulted.

"No," she smiled. "You will stay with us. You will be safe with the Zonks." And so it began.

The Hemlock Trees and the Hives

"You disgust me. You are filth and a pestilence to all humans! I detest your very existence! You are nothing to me. You are less than shit... (pause) But there is something about you. Something odd. And I find that fatally attractive." — Sarah to Tobias

Sarah Cox wanted nothing to do with cocks. Nor vaginas for that matter. It was all just human organs and they got in her way. Ms. Cox was an apiarist. She was not a human but a bee, and a queen at that. She lived on a small plot of land just north of Mount Baker in northern Washington State and owned thousands of bees in bee boxes. Ms. Cox made pure Alpine flower honey. She loved bees and she loathed humans. Which was understandable since she, herself, as was said before, was a bee. A Queen. Ms. Cox even wore a crown.

But being a bee in the body of a human had its issues. She was trapped in what she loathed. She wanted out but she could not do that. This was her Hell. She sold her honey, really the finest bee product in America, to the people down in the bottom land in the city of Mt. Vernon. She hated them and they hated her but it was all good since she was able to survive to be with her bees.

Tobias was working as a pilot for a behemoth mining firm called Techtonics. This firm owned thirty-eight percent of all mining operations on the planet. Copper, feldspar, lithium, silver and gold (and many other minerals) were mined by this colossal firm. They paid very well for Tobias' work and his work was treacherous. A graduate from the School of Mines in Colorado came up with a bizarre idea. Trees that grew in the mineral-rich soils, through osmosis, sucked up those minerals. If the tips of these trees could be harvested via a low flying plane, then they could be analyzed and mapped to reveal particular areas that could contain a wealth of needed minerals. But whom to choose for a pilot? They would have to be crazy and they chose Tobias Zonk. This scientist at the School of Mines invented a scoop device that contained a razor-sharp edge that hung like a sharp spoon below the belly of the plane. The serrated bits of the top of the trees would then be put into the backside of the plane through the momentum of the flying craft, with coordinates mapped by the pilot, and the harvest returned to an airfield for later analysis, and mineral data could be mapped. Several previous 'great' pilots tried and died. But Tobias was not 'great'; he was crazy. Techtonics bought Tobias. He was known throughout the northwest as the most brazened bush pilot ever. All said he was dead, he just did not know it yet.

The mining company bought and re-fitted a Piper Super Cub with the razor cutting device on the bottom and a holding pen in the back. Tobias tried this plane out on the slopes of Mt. Baker with some success. He would gun the engine quickly for the harvest cut of the tree tips. The other dead pilots most probably slowed down for the cut and the friction of the tree cutting stalled out their planes. That was their mistake. Tobias came down hard, fast and confident. Tobias took off from a small field near Marysville early in the morning. The plane was strong and was used to this mountain area. The Zonk pilot felt a drag on the frame but that was obvious since the serrated cutting device hung low on the belly of the craft. His mission was to test the tree tips in and around the northwestern slope of Mt. Baker. He was ready.

Ms. Cox, shaking off a hard night's sleep, pulled on her yellow poncho with black stripes made from alpaca wool and put on a pair of woven beach sandals that she bought from a Native American from the Kenai region in Alaska. The sandals had a tag that stated they were from Harrods but she was sure they were really Chinese knock offs. Aside from the poncho and sandals she was absolutely naked. That was her way. Bees didn't wear clothes either. She left her cabin to tend to her bees. Today the bees were uneasy. Ms. Cox erroneously concluded that the bees, being hypersensitive to vibrations, were distressed due to the seismic variations in the ground from the volcano, Mt. Baker, where they lived just slightly north. But no, it was Tobias and his plane.

The Super Cub came down hard and fast on the tips of the trees. One particular mountain hemlock branch pierced the floor of the craft and gutted the wires for the rudder and ailerons. Tobias, the consummate bush pilot, did not flinch. His sphincter, as was recorded much later, never constricted. Death was welcome. He came down on the boxes of bees just below stall speed. Crashing, he destroyed the entire bee colony and almost Ms. Cox with the impact. Drowning in honey and the carcasses of bees, he acquiesced and decided to forego the living, and planned for an early eternal nap. Roger was not there.

Sarah Cox dug him out of a mess of wreckage covered in honey and dead bees. He was dead. He had inhaled a massive amount of honey. She used her fingers to dig out the bee-secreted mess from Tobias' throat. She tilted back his head and breathed into his lungs. She performed CPR for several minutes until he coughed his way from Teegarden B to Earth. Tobias was not happy. Nor was Sarah. She was pissed. Her entire life had been extinguished with one pathetic crash of a plane. And all because of this fool. She hated him and he her. He was dead and now he was living. They soon loathed each other to marriage and had a son. Nine months and three days later Cornelius was born. He was a greasy shit but he was a Zonk. And that is all that mattered.

The Dead Trash Can

by Opeia Zonk

"How do you say goodbye as debris to the one whose mission was to say goodbye to debris." — Eni

It is strange, possibly obsessive, what humans fall in love with. For some people, it is old cobalt blue bottles; for others it is tiny miniature trains; some bladder control and then there was Eni—she was in love with a trash can. Now, granted, she has had the trash can since her early days in the US at The Truck Stop. She bought it at a discount store and there it was in the back, all by itself on an empty shelf, alone for all the world to see. Basically, she felt sorry for it. There were trash cans back at The Truck Stop, but aside from the clothes on her back, she didn't own anything. So she bought this trash can. It was hers.

It was essentially just a plain-woven small basket from what appeared to be thick light-yellow straw. It was about eighteen inches high, cylindrical and tapered slightly at the bottom. The basket had a plastic liner sewn into the rim. Probably manufactured by some poor soul in Bangladesh but that poor soul, obvious by the crafting, took pride in their work. Not a weave was out of place and for ninety-nine cents it was a bargain.

This tightly wound 'can' was the antithesis of Eni. She was clearly carefree, independent and thoughtful. The 'can' was mostly vacuous, slightly jaundiced and really uptight. To compare this trash can to a Republican was pertinent but Eni knew that would be unfair to this basket. At least this basket had a purpose.

This trash basket held a prominent place in the corner of every bedroom Eni had inhabited since it was purchased. The Truck Stop, The Pony Express, The Dairy Farm and now The Estate. But as with all things in this third dimension, entropy always wins and degradation, as slow as it is for some entities, creeps its way through like so many tree roots through an old asphalt parking lot. Zade started by making subtle comments. "Get rid of that damn thing!" But Eni would ignore her. The basket, now paltry and frayed, wobbled upon any debris entry. The stoutness was gone and the plastic inner lining had long gone the way of the other trash. Gravity, a weak force, over time claims many a victim and the straw bindings were just giving out. Eni considered shellacking the entire basket and making it resilient to the elements but that would be akin to embalming a dead person in an attempt to thwart nature's natural design. No. Just one more day. And that day lasted into weeks and months. And then one evening, Eni entered her bedroom and the trash basket was gone. In its place was a green plastic container with a large yellow happy face painted on this side. "Merde!" she screamed.

Eni found Zade in the back of The Estate. Zade had made a small fire from dead brambles and branches. There she sat looking into the orange blaze. Beside her was the dilapidated trash basket. It was plum full of adult diapers from the Warped Noodle. Eni was furious over what she considered an invasion of her privacy. Zade looked at it as a motion toward sanity. "It is just a fucking straw basket!" shouted Zade.

"No. No it is not. It is a memory and it is very hard to watch a memory fade." Zade grabbed the straw 'can' but hesitated to throw the mass into the fire.

"You do realize these are all diapers from Republicans on Ward Three?" Zade said.

"Fuck you, I don't care. Give me back my basket." Eni was in tears.

"I can fix it," said a voice in the darkness. Eni and Zade turned. They could not make out the figure flickering far from the flames of the fire. "I can fix it," the voice repeated. Like an apparition, the flannel-clad nightgown and rabbit fuzzy slippers of Ms. Betel appeared. She was from Ward One at the Noodle.

Ms. Ruby Betel was from a southern Amish village in Pennsylvania. She grew up plainly as plain as the Amish would let her be plain. She actually lived on a plain and that helped with the plainness. But Ruby was genetically predisposed with an endocrine imbalance in her ovaries that increased her androgen hormone levels. She was hirsute.

She was covered in hair. Her face, her chest and back. The only area spared by the growth of a hair was her forehead. As a furball, she was cute, but as an Amish woman she was considered unfortunate. Ruby had a quick mind and was top in her class on all subjects. But the male elders did not know what to do so they insisted that she be hidden and kept a secret. And so she was.

Ms. Ruby eventually escaped since it is fairly easy to escape from Amish villages. It is much more difficult to get in. And that was a fact. Her curious condition was discovered in a train station in Philadelphia and she joined the Marcos Brothers Traveling Circus. There were no Marcos brothers but just a circus derived from the mind of one Alex Goldstein from the Bronx. Ms. Betel was just another oddity among other oddities that were paraded around to make normal people 'feel' normal when, in fact, those 'normal' people were quite insane. Alex Goldstein understood that. That was his sense of humor. Mock the pathetic by individuals that appeared more pathetic which in fact were not pathetic at all. But the 'normal' pathetic people didn't get the rub, since they were pathetic, and the oddities got it but failed to sell it since, well, the audience was pathetic. Ruby did make some money, though.

It was a quarter past never when the morbidly obese woman gelatinously rolled her way into Ruby's train car. And then it happened. She introduced Ms. Betel to the cordless hair trimmer.

Ms. Betel spent the night and most of the next day with the gelatinous maiden and they shaved and shaved and shaved. What appeared was, yes, a mound of hair, but underneath was a pristine porcelain waif who was absolutely beautiful. With a tad use of shaving cream and a razor, the sculpture was complete. Ruby was radiant.

The Circus fired her outright. Even though beautiful, she wasn't odd, and odd sells. Kicked off the train in Des Moines, she took her savings and traveled back to the south of Pennsylvania to her Amish village. They did not recognize her. But when she grew back her mane they understood. Ruby was home. But Ruby was home with a rechargeable cordless hair trimmer and eventually she was found out. The Amish elders would not abide such betrayal of her using modern technology and electricity and, with much consternation, she was banished from the village forever. Before she left, Ms. Ruby Betel went to the woodshed and removed several roughly honed pine fence posts. The village woke up the next day to find the elders still elder but each with a stiff splintery fence post up each of their asses. And hence, Ruby was introduced to the Warped Noodle.

Zade was trembling. Her hand was on the basket full of adult Republican diapers. "I can fix it," said Ruby once again.

"What can you fix?" asked Zade.

"The basket," Ruby said while shuffling her feet into the dirt.

"What did you do in your Amish Village?" Eni quietly said.

"I was the weaver," said Ruby. Zade emptied the basket of diapers into the fire and gently handed the basket into the hands of Ms. Betel.

Days later the trash basket was new. Rewoven with straw and dark bamboo strands and it stood rigid with a new removeable linen liner. Eni hugged Ruby and then Zade. Life just takes so many weird turns.

Authors note: Ms. Betel died soon after this meeting. Her batteries went dead on her cordless and she found in the Noodle's utility closet an old corded sheering set which she unfortunately used in the bathtub. She accidently electrocuted herself. But through the enormous zapping, not a hair was left on her body. I am sure she would have appreciated that.

The Carnivorous Cadaver of the Mighty Pachyderm

"I don't know how to describe it. I love flesh." — Titus

"I should be dead. I know this. The amount of radiation given to my pregnant mother was enough to fry most all things on this planet. What perverse mentality considered irradiating the fetuses of pachyderms? We were, and are, beings of this planet. You thought us less because we were not you. You were wrong. We are we and you are you, and we belong to this planet. At least for now. Now I am mutationally altered. I will never be what I was supposed to be due to human interference. I will always be small and I will glow but I also am now very intelligent, more so than humans, and extremely strong yet small. And now I, unlike all other elephants, I want to eat meat. I am a carnivore." And Titus rejoiced.

Cygnus was reading a new synopsis on Machiavelli and the unification of the Italian states into a republic when Titus barged into her room. Swinging from her hammock, she said, "Yes?"

And Titus said, "I need meat!" Bootes evidently had her focus on flesh before she understood Titus' carnal flesh-bound lust. She gratefully expanded her dominion to encompass Titus in her fleshly bound endeavors. They became perpetual partners. And the meat flourished.

Titus just wanted the organs. It is with the organs that came all the vitamins. Iron, folic acid, chromium, copper and zinc with the liver. The kidneys contain proteins and Omega 3 fatty acids. The brain, antioxidants. The heart is rich in folate, iron, zinc and selenium. The tongue is wealthy in vitamin B12. But the real muscle meat was for Bootes. And she did not complain.

Cygnus was correct. Titus became a necessity to the family Zonk. He became a Zonk. He was welcomed into this family. Titus devoured the concept of the Zonk life. Free education and free healthcare. It was what was necessary. It was what was now.

The Mutual Bonds of Loathing

"There are several levels of love just like there are of hate. One must choose from the former or the latter, or like my family, a strange mixture of both." — Cornelius.

"Poppy Tobias never flew again after that crash and Mom never raised bees. They both gave something up for their mutual loathing. They bought a small house east of Seattle in the foothills of the Cascades. It had a few acres and we had a large garden. For me, growing up, it was a paradise." Cornelius was speaking into his new tape recorder. He wasn't an inventor yet. He wanted to be a reporter. He wanted to be Clark Kent.

Poppy took a job as a welder and Sarah dove deep into domestic bliss and tended the house and garden. She loved being a mother. She also started baking. It became her addiction. Sarah set her goal to make the best tasting biscuit in all the World. And after several years, she achieved perfection. Though she never wrote the recipe down and kept the ingredients and measurements strictly between her ears.

The one thing Sarah really loved about Poppy was his devotion to the Socialist message. In time, she would embrace this too. Poppy never thumped a podium in front of a labor union but he did thump the table every night at dinner. Sarah smiled when he would become reverential and Cornelius, wide eyed, soaked it all in like a sponge. The anti-social nature of the young Zonk was most likely inherited from Sarah. She still could not stand being around any other humans but her son and husband. And the boy took mostly to his room when not in school. He, like his mother, did not have any friends. Cornelius learned to really enjoy being by himself.

The first time he broke his leg was early one morning when his parents were still asleep. In his white tee-shirt he had taken his mother's clothes pins and pinned a bright red sheet on his back to his shoulders. He climbed the ladder to the roof. Cornelius knew that to fly was, in essence, easy. To obtain a low Earth orbit all he had to do was achieve a sufficient velocity so that he would constantly fall toward Earth yet just miss it. He ran the entire length of the roof and launched off. He didn't miss the Earth.

This led him to his first invention and his second broken leg. While convalescing in his room with his leg in a cast, he pondered. Putting pencil to paper he designed an enormous sling shot made from surgical tubing. The two ridged pine trees in his front yard would be the stems of the slingshot and the tubing, well, while he was having his cast procured on his leg at the Redmond Hospital, he noticed large dumpsters in the back with surgical waste. Including surgical tubing. After several months and many trips to the hospital, he had over fifty yards of tubing. This tubing, doubled, would be just enough between the two pine trees for his experiment. Early one morning, Cornelius securely tied the tubing to each tree. He put a pillow in the middle of the tubing to secure his back. Still in his cast, and with red cape pinned on, he pushed back and back until he thought the tubes just might break. And off he flew. He didn't miss the Earth this time either. Luckily, he did miss the neighbor's fence and 'flew' into a field full of cattle. He miraculously missed these bovine critters too and then skipped over a pond like a flat stone into the forest on the other side. Here, Cornelius tumbled in the soft ground, his shirt snagging a root, and he was thrown into a pine tree stump. With two broken legs, and going nowhere soon, with pen and paper, Cornelius created his second invention. A rabbit snare.

The concept was simple. Take a young sapling, bend it over without breaking the main trunk, tie a thin rope to the top of the bent tree and stake the rope to the ground with the rope having a lasso at the end. With a thin string tied to the stake, Cornelius would be yards away. With the rabbit in the lasso drawn with bait, the string pulled to remove the stake, the rabbit was wonked up and caught hanging helplessly for harvest.

It was well into fall before the casts were off and his legs were healed. Cornelius took his rope deep into the forest to find a portly sapling. He pulled it over with much difficulty and secured the rope to the top of the young tree. He then staked the rope to the ground and made the lasso at the end. Burying the stake and lasso in dead leaves, it showed no trace of being there at all. But Cornelius, being Cornelius, forgot the twine string to set off the trap. He ran deep out of the woods to get the string from his house. As fate's river was to certainly flow that day, Oskar Milfen, a convict, a three-time loser on anti-Semitic convictions, working on a prison road crew was resurfacing a nearby route area with asphalt. On a call from nature, Oskar asked to go into the forest to rid his lower bowels of digested matter. The guard agreed. Oskar had other plans. While in the forest, Mr. Milfen got on his hands and knees and scurried briskly through the trees while covering himself with the fallen foliage. Just around the next few trees, and with a 'twack' and a 'twang', Cornelius' trap was launched and the lasso caught Oskar right around his neck. The force of the upward pulling portly young tree not only broke the convict's neck but also decapitated him instantly. The young Zonk, running over the ridge through the forest with string in his hand looked over the gore and said through clenched teeth, "Oooh, shit!" He turned around and quietly but quickly made his way home. Cornelius never mentioned this to anyone and it didn't appear in any local media. He checked. "But it was a great idea," he said softly to himself.

Cornelius went off to the University of Washington in Seattle. He initially studied Mechanics, Physics and Logic but ended up in a college in Arkansas. But when he left the home the home life fell apart. Poppy and Sarah's loathing for one another did not have Cornelius as a deflection any more. They remained married but Poppy left on a long, long road that eventually ended in Texas. Sarah stayed in the house and took up raising bees and she became very well known locally for her honey. Poppy, taking the long way to Texas, played a card game somewhere in Alaska and won a dilapidated Truck Stop in a remote area of the Colorado Rockies called Poncha Springs. This Truck Stop would later play a very important role in the lives of the Zonks.

The Cauldron of Yichun

by Opeia Zonk

"This is a direct example of the repercussions of bullied youth who eventually forge this scalding path toward retribution." — Ada Place

There was a new inhabitant to the Ultra-Warped Noodle. This one was not for the spires since he wasn't a Republican. No, this one was special and Ada took special care of him in a large room in the dome. He, like Ada, was Chinese but from the Fujian Province. Like Ada, he was adopted by white parents, but in his case, wealthy conservative Christians who didn't particularly want a boy from China but wanted more to make a statement to their church that they were enlightened by God's policies. The boy became more of a strange bobble on a necklace to be shown but not heard. He was not loved but tolerated and his value in being was his wealth in Christian forgiveness. This boy's name was Yichun Zhang. When he was old enough, he refused his given name of Asgard Davies.

The Georgetown Vargus prep school in upstate New York became his prison and his Hell. This school was founded by Latham Vargus in 1868, who was from the first Klan of the KKK. Vargus' idiocy was only outweighed by his sadism and he created this prep school to be devoted to wealthy white elites that all contained the bluest of bloods. Ridiculously, Zhang's blood was also blue, just not Caucasian blue, and for some asinine reason that difference made the schoolboys hate him.

(Author's note: Actually, the most pure of bloods, not tainted by Neanderthal, Denisovan or Homo Erectus DNA would be the people of Central Africa. Black people NOT white people have the purest of bloods. And like any other human, it is both red and blue depending on oxygen or no-oxygen, respectively.)

Yichun was beaten, brutalized and raped repeatedly by these gold insignia patch-wearing prayer-pledging vomits. A day with just verbal abuse was like a calm breeze before a tornado. After school he privately enrolled in a local Kung Fu school that taught Hung Gar. And he focused and focused. One day the Master pulled him to the side and said, "Where does all this anger come from?"

And Yichun said, "From wealthy white boys."

The Master understood. But he said, "Be very careful." A month later, Yichun was confident and ready. Three large white boys came at him from the field yard. Within minutes he had rendered them all unconscious. But a second rush of other boys overwhelmed his capabilities and they beat him to near death.

"You have to understand that genetically you are inferior. You will always be less than that of a Caucasian," said his parents. "You just have to take it and learn your place in society."

"Fuck you all," he replied silently.

Georgetown-Vargus and Chesterfield-Taylor were the two top teams in the Water Polo Championship for northern New York State. At the flip of a coin, Vargus was the host in their new Olympic-sized pool. The pool bleachers were packed due to the fact that Chesterfield was only thirty miles away. And far in the back, on the uppermost bleacher, solemnly sat Yichun Zhang.

Georgetown-Vargus wanted the green leaf award for environmental consciousness, so they installed an extra-large, gas-heated non-tank water heater. This was for the main pool, but more specifically for the new sauna and the innovative heated relaxing therapeutic pool. Yichun took the liberty to bypass the sauna and therapeutic pool and put all the heating coils into the main Olympic pool. Although the players noticed the difference, it was so warm and soothing no one bothered to speak up. At near half time, a button was pushed on a remote and the temperature went from a balmy 95 degrees F to 320 degrees F in just a second. Both teams were boiled alive. Apart from the boiling sound and piercing screams, the bleachers were full of aghast horror-stricken wealthy white faces. The bodies, bobbing to the surface in the scalding water, appeared like blanched wieners split at the seams. In the last upper row, a Chinese-looking young man was laughing so hard that tears were streaming down his face. The Ultra-Warped was ready and welcoming.

Authors note: He was definitely a challenge to work with. His scars ran deep. We love him and are diligently working to reverse the mental damage due to social bullying.

The Supple Curiosity of Cygnus

"It comes around, these genes. It is all there mapped out in the genome. A family can never escape the destiny of blood. I felt sometime, and in some way, some Zonk was going to come around to fill my shoes." — *Granny Gretchen*

Albert Shin was the great grandson of Monk Shin. He showed up at The Truck Stop one day and appeared cautiously out of place. A glowing small elephant was snoring on the floor and a bronze statue of some type of monkey was seated on a carpeted pedestal in the back. The fire pit had no fire. It was quiet. An elderly woman came down the stairs. She had long silver hair, goggles on her eyes and a white lab coat that, in black, stated 'Zonk'. He was in the right place. The elephant farted and stirred. The gas emanating from him glowed light green. "So you must be Albert," said a clear voice from the bookstore. The voice was from Cygnus.

Roger convinced Cyg that this was necessary to continue the Zonk clan's dominance on this earth. The Truck Stop was necessary but age was inevitable in humans and these people needed to be backfilled to embrace the Zonk vision. Cyg chose Albert. Even though Shin left his wife and family back in Atlanta on that fated past of the death of Swiss orphans, Ms. Shin loved the outcome. She quickly remarried a REAL Chinese man who made her walk seven steps behind him and treated her like shit. She was proud to have such a man. This, she was craved to say, was the definition of a true man. She groveled and cowed and smiled at her new male prominence. She was now a true Chinese woman. Albert had too much of Monk Shin in him. It wasn't so much of being westernized as being true to his Eastern philosophical beliefs. Albert, too, was a great cook and studied all the five-star recipes of the legend Monk Shin.

Monk Shin appeared from the kitchen, arms covered in flour, and said, "Shit." He was old but never looked more than forty years of age.

His hair, white as snow, was the only indication of Shin growing old. In his autumn years he spoke simply, in one word grunts. 'Shit' and 'Fuck' were the most prominent. But there were others that trickled through the broken rocks of his mind. With a nod and an indication to move into the kitchen, Albert became a Zonk.

Shin's muse had just recently expired. Monk Skeeter, on the top of Mt. Antero, died suddenly due to suffocation by his girlfriend, Ms. Skank. She, sitting on his face during cunnilingus, through her haze of sativa, received his rapid body jerks as indications of pleasure that were actually his last wretched attempt to gasp for oxygen. He died. But, noted by Skank, in death Skeeter wore a Cheshire smile with frosting around his mouth and beard that would make a glazed donut proud. Skank needed a job now. She waddled her way down from the top of the mountain and became Albert's semi-trusted assistant in The Truck Stop. Skank had a black pearl in a zip lock bag stuffed up her anus. The author doesn't know why? He is just making this shit up as he goes along. Leave it alone!

Along the smooth sides of the inner hourglass are microscopic ridges that hinge and stall the falling sands of time. Depending on the glass the sand falls at a different rate but that rate is minimal in comparison to human time. But that minimal rate adds up to consequences in results. And Cygnus was that falling grain of sand.

Cygnus would become a scientist. She would graduate with a degree in Biopsychology and Epigenetics followed by a PhD in Structural Neurology. Dr. Zonk was now solid. But she was sweeping a dining room near a fire pit at The Truck Stop. She was home.

And Kittens Do Scratch

"Love is not love as we know it. It is a constant re-scaffolding of the interior frame that builds a relationship. Over and over again it has to be addressed or the scaffolding breaks down. Love is the glue that keeps this platform of twine together." — Opeia

Eni and Zade were both finding their match. They were both going through menopause and both going through separate hormonal rollercoasters that they thought could possibly rescue them from the itching banality of life. They were horny, hot and sad; the last gasps from two dying breeding female bodies.

Then came Igor Frunze. Italian at birth but raised soon after in a suburb near Zurich and then in a German borough called Nagold. A small village with southern Catholic German leanings. The people there had an annoying habit of being addicted to tobacco. Some of the elderly of Nagold would chew the tobacco leaves, spit the contents into a single udder of the dead small cow, and shove it deep in their ears for a long-lasting smooth tantalizing buzz of nicotine. Clearly, there was little else to do in this quaint German town.

Igor was seriously handicapped by being excruciatingly handsome. And he used this terrible handicap at every possible moment so that his career would flourish. He became top in his class, not for fortitude, reason or intelligence, but through good looks and a blistering smile. He pretended to give a damn about rules, regulations and honor. He dated copiously and feigned compassion and sincerity just to use humans as tools to build a better ladder to success. And success to Igor was fame and fortune. Roger hated Mr. Frunze since essentially Frunze was a three-dimensional heterosexual Roger. Roger could have had Igor Frunze eradicated then and there but Roger knew the end of this story so bided his time with another luscious morsel of a waiter, Karl, on Teegarden B.

Mr. Frunze, soon to be Dr. Frunze, received his Master's in Psychology at the University of Stuttgart and then his PhD in Behavior and Cognition at the University of Gottingen. Many amorous professor relationships later, he squeaked by near the bottom of his graduating class. But he did graduate. He was passionate about Freud but only because Sigmund reminded Igor of himself. Freud was a failed neuroscientist and so created his own science, psychoanalysis, so he could be the master of talk therapy. The science was just as ambiguous as the Christian Bible and it is this vagueness that still feeds the longevity of this flawed 'erudition'.

The Goebbels School of Conservative Propensity out of Austria recruited Dr. Frunze to be a mole. They needed this mole to infiltrate one of the most secret organizations on the planet. The Zonk Farm of the Warped Noodle. With the Doctor's doctored resume, it was a Doctor too good to be true. And Igor was that Doctor since being that Doctor was going to be extremely lucrative.

Generally, shallow was easy to spot on the Zonk radar, but the hormone spigot being as it was, fog trundled into the brains of Zade and Eni. Chester, Marvin and Opeia found it excruciating to view the fawning spectacle of these two, soon to be biologically dead, females over this obviously pathetic Doctor. But when not drooling over the Muffin of Stud, the two women were found digging their crotches into the bark of any nearby available oak tree. The female occupants of the Warped Noodle were such a randy bunch.

It all came to a head when Eni discovered Zade giving head to Igor in an unoccupied room on Ward One. Being Zonks, they could have had communal coitus, but things being extremely heated always tend to boil over and they did. Hair was pulled and eyes were jabbed. Gnashing teeth were displayed and it all looked like some circle of Dante's Hell. Bloodied and bruised they were motionless on the floor. Igor just sat on the bed and laughed at the spectacle and then he excused himself into the arms of a passing nurse who escorted him into an adjoining vanity closet. Apparently, Igor was not that vain since his pants were still unzipped.

Eni and Zade did not look or speak to each other for days. Work went on as usual. Both thought of forgiveness. Both were reasonable scientists. But the swells of hormones dragged both through the surf into the unrelenting wet sand. They bobbled on the waves waiting for some relief.

That relief came in the form of Marvin. Marvin scanned The Estate and the Warped Noodle for frequencies. Particularly, the ones that should not be available to anyone at either of the Zonk facilities. Cell phones were not allowed and only land lines could be used. Yet, on a late Monday night, Marvin picked up a signal from a cell phone. It was emanating from the basement laundry room at the Noodle. The attached number to which that cell was calling was listed in Austria. Marvin hacked in to the feed and Dr. Mole was discovered. It was time for the Zonks to dance. And dance they did.

Ada Place got a call on Tuesday from Eni and Zade. Her rounds at the Ultra-Warped had only a slight modification. Ada understood. On Wednesday, Dr. Frunze got a call from Eni and Zade stating there was an emergency issue in Room One of the Ultra-Warped Noodle. They both accompanied Igor through the electric fences and the main iron door to the room. They unlocked the door and let in Igor but suddenly slammed the door shut, locking it and trapping him in.

Sydney was in the corner in the dark. His eyes glowing orange. There was a sound of a 'zap' and Igor was now a beautiful, and very handsome, carrot. His face, eyes and mouth were there expressing a very startled emotion. Igor would have loved to see how beautiful he was if a mirror was present but only the glint from the sheen of the metal top of the hamster cage being removed gave him a bit of a view of an orange thin gloss. The hamster slowly devoured the screaming carrot root tip first. Sydney graciously wiped away the carrot's orange tears of pain. He put his head slightly in the hamster's cage and caressed the carrot as it writhed. "Never, ever, fuck with Zonks," he whispered. And soon the hamster was full and happy.

Eni and Zade, upon leaving the building, held hands like children and began to skip back to their offices. They might be reproductively dead but they were far far from death.

The Torch and Its Passing

"The placebo is only effective if you don't know it is a placebo. And only then is it twenty percent successful. But if you were terminal, would you put yourself in the hands of twenty percent? Of course, but only if you knew it was a real drug and not a placebo. And Republicans are terminal." — *Dialog between Cygnus and Gretchen*

Gretchen's laboratory was expanded into Cornelius' old lab. Cygnus took her place behind the beakers, scopes and pipettes to initially assist Gretchen but that didn't last very long. Bootes got into the fur business. Since Monk Shin did the butchering of her beasts the fur was usually sold at a lower price for it to be treated and processed. But Bootes decided to cut out the middle person and she now processed her own hides. The revenue was a necessary boost to The Truck Stop's bottom line.

Monk Shin, with Albert, kicked in to recreate Grammy's Better Battered Buttered Biscuit. Gretchen had the where-with-all to actually write down the methodical recipe. The Truck Stop was doing well but the years had not been kind. Monk Shin's Church was still overflowing but age plucks a chicken one feather at a time and then eventually you just realize you are old.

Cygnus was in the lab with Gretchen. The Republicans had formed a US Dictatorship and there was no time to lose. Historically a right-wing militia would soon be formed and they would be used to suffocate any ideas of liberal progressive thought. Hitler had his brown shirts, Stalin had his NKVD that later became the KGB, and Mussolini had his youth group called the Blackshirts (Camicia Nera). Look it up; this crap isn't made up. History, for the ignorant, always repeats. Which basically means, for humans, it always repeats. Gretchen understood that to formulate a CRISPR Cas 9 gene variant in humans to make them more like Zonks, would take years of lab work and experimentation. They didn't have the flexibility of time.

'If you want it bad enough, you will get it. If you didn't get it, you didn't want it bad enough'. —Old Zonk Family Saying

And what Gretchen and Cygnus wanted was a disease. One that didn't exist but one that had certain devastating side effects. What Gretchen and Cyg concocted in the lab that night was a plague of enormous virulence. With test tubes, beakers, Erlenmeyer flasks, Bunsen burners, vast chemicals and tremendous confidence the two scientists, in Level A protective clothing, left the laboratory early that morning with a tiny stoppered vile containing the virus patheolibropatheticus-Z1 or PLP-Z1. The Z was for Zonk and the 1 was the hazard class on how many times you'd have to be exposed to the virus to get the disease. This virus was incredibly infectious. The laboratory statement was clear. Dr. Cygnus Zonk plainly described the virus as a possible catastrophic pandemic of global proportions. This virus would infect a person and lay dormant with no signs of the disease for fourteen days. In that time, that infected person could easily infect other people just by expelling the air from their lungs.

The facts were severe. What was the mortality rate? Zero. Did the disease maim, disfigure, impair or in any way shorten a span of life? No. Then what the hell was the issue? According to Dr. Zonk's report, if the virus infected a right-wing conservative it would irreparably turn this individual into a dyed-in-the-wool, true blue progressive liberal. With a dormancy period of fourteen days before any signs of liberalization, the entire country would go bright blue in just a matter of months. No more Republicans. Ever.

With the help of satellites, fiber optics and servers, the news of this unfortunate plague ripped through the world like a fire in a dry wheat field with a strong summer wind and the air containing a relative humidity of three percent. And that was bad.

This did not mean there would be no more yin and yang. No. There now would be just a democratic socialist government with a side that viewed rules and regulations in a more theoretical way versus the other side of socialists that were more pragmatic. There would still be two, three or more 'sides' just under the umbrella of socialism. Just like the rest of the industrial world. But this virus also had one other grotesque side effect. It made the inflicted incredibly wealthy. Almost overnight. Silence.

The only thing that right-wing conservative persons loved more than being a starched white shirt white Republican was money. And even a hint of increased funds would draw the red moths quickly into the burning flames of blue. And these flames burned so hot. Because flames that were left, as Roger knew, burned that way. And they did.

Certl Horvat, the kindly ninety-three-year-old woman in a small cabin in Jasper, Colorado, came down with the first case of PLP-Z1. To the reporter she stated that she felt a warm sensation in her stomach and suddenly, as if an angel was motivating her muscles, she pulled down the portraits of Reagan and the Bushes and threw them all into the fire. The next day, she received a post in the mail that stated she was worth 2.5 million dollars. Now, these were all facts. Ms. Horvat read the morning paper about the disease but had slight dementia. She put into her oatmeal that morning red pepper flakes instead of milk and butter. Hence the warming sensation. She was a Jewish refugee from Hungary and when she was a tad younger, she had taken all her savings and put the funds into stocks of a small company called Apple. She forgot all about this, naturally. So, of course, she was surprised about the post in the mail. Due to the sublime psychosomatic effects of the new article, she was now a staunch socialist. And she remained that way until her death.

Hysteria turned into elation and in the history of humankind there was never such a need to obtain a disease as PLP-Z1. Everyone wanted it. Even the liberals. The next reported case came from a very unlikely source. A small elephant that was glowing green at a Truck Stop in Poncha Springs, Colorado, apparently was a carrier of the virus. The elephant, though seriously infected, did not become a liberal or gain any wealth but just glowed a radiant shade of green. When touched, the elephant would give a grunt and the poor soul whose hand touched the thick hide was bound for a life of profound socialistic beliefs and garnering insane wealth. The lines of humans into The Truck Stop were fantastic in length.

Titus was disgusted by the conservative attention. Their touch to his flesh revolted him. He could easily tear these pathetic humans apart and devour them whole. But Gretchen and Cyg calmed him down with colossal amounts of spiced rum and pleaded with him to be nice. He was. Actually, a prolonged direct contact to his body was lethal due to his radiation exposure. Mutations would occur. But, for the most part, since through the divine graces of Roger, the people that touched Titus were conservatives, to the Zonks, it just didn't matter.

As with all viruses, like a good orgasm, there is a swell and a peak then a shudder and a calm cool pastiness since that temporarily nurtured virus was now sleeping in the 'wet' spot. Eventually, after almost a year, it was discovered that there were no real liberal leanings to the victims and they received no greater wealth than those not infected. But on the flip side, due to the increased patronage of The Truck Stop, the Zonk bottom line increased by several million dollars and exactly eighteen percent of the 'infected' Republicans were now devout progressive liberals. Sometimes life is just so odd that way.

The Moribund Lethargy of Dante's First Circle
Stories Compiled by Zackary Maxwell
Translated by Zackary Maxwell

The Moribund Lethargy of Dante's First Circle Segments
The Estate, the Noodle and The Truck Stop
by Azad Baksi (Kurdish)
Maggots Everywhere
by Enukuha Ozonlins (Latvian)
Vexing Vixens of Valhalla
by Banoz Aheng (Kurdish)

The Estate, the Noodle and The Truck Stop
by Azad Baksi
Translated from Kurdish by Zackary Maxwell

The Gulley

"There once was an old river named Fanfa. She was, long ago, a brave river that fought many battles to become what she was. Then a drought came and she dried up. Then some rains would fall but it was not enough for her to claim her old fame. And then no rains. She was just an old dry gulley. But that dent in the earth had long memories that would one day come to life." — Chester chewing on liberty caps talking to Marvin near his wood fire

Chester Zonk died at 7.43 a.m. on Thursday, the 9th of February. He was very old for a porcine. Roger saw to that. It just was his time. He loved a goose once. The goose loved him back. But they were not a genetically compatible species. They tried to have sex but they could not breed. All they had was intelligent conversation. But in time, that was enough. The goose, back in Curdsville, KY, died at the same time and on the same day. The day Chester died, there came a severe drought to North Carolina and all the local rivers near The Estate dried up.

The funeral was encapsulated by love for this Zonk. He wanted his body to be consumed by The Estate's children. Life does feed on life, even with one so honored. He was ceremoniously cremated on a pile of logs using the Cornelius method of bellow enhancement. He was rendered into ashes. The ashes were put into a large batter of buttermilk pancakes and the whole body of the school, not known by them, had a tad of Chester. He was happy on Teegarden B eating the refuse of the slovenly race of beings called Barkazones. Chester was so necessary that they gave him the title of Refuse Coordinator. The Barkazones were such a filthy race of beings that they should have been extradited to various mega-galactic cesspools. Like Canis Minor. But their influx of massive funds to this planet convinced all that the Barkazones' trash was very welcome indeed. The Barkazones were much like wealthy Republicans on Earth.

At Café Zonk, Lucinda was at one table with her legs up high and her dress pulled up. She was fanning her crotch which was blistered and red. Not from any disease, since Teegarden B was disease free, but from elemental friction. Friction was still a factor on this planet. As on planet Earth, she didn't like conservatives and the visiting Barkazones reminded her too much of Republicans and Communists. As it turned out, a Barkazone, under extreme duress, would die in a flash of light and a puff of pastel pink smoke. These beings would come under this type of stress in the midst of human sexual congress, and for Lucinda, congress was in session. From the windows of her brothel, it appeared like some radical broken holiday light decoration with random flashing lights and pink emanating fumes. It was eerily beautiful to behold.

Dr. Martha was on vacation from her seven-dimensional tour of galaxy destruction. Some high falutin' member of her dissertation committee discovered that Galaxy Messier 109 appeared too much like the Sculptor Galaxy. Obviously, it was a mistake and all universal mistakes in any dimension had to be rectified. So, at a flip of a seven-dimensional coin, Messier 109's time was up. Now, granted, all Dr. Martha had to do was tweak the galaxy's parameter a scrunch and with a few massive blasts of direct cosmic radiation and Messier 109 would look different and there would be no loss of anything. But the Barkazones were from Messier 109 so the odds were stacked against this spiral of conservative shits. Dr. Martha, with a flash, disintegrated the entire spinning blob. All that existed there now was a large intergalactic pink cloud of vapor. A vacation was needed and now she was having a hot cup of pearl jasmine tea with Roger.

Roger brought up Earth. Martha yawned. Nationalism was raising its ugly head in many various countries and some had already established faux but dangerous dictatorships. This always led to war and millions of humans would… "So?" Martha interrupted. "Earth was a failed experiment from the beginning. It will always be a failed experiment in all other infinite histories defined in all other realities. It was meant to be that way as an example to all other evolving beings on all the other growing planets to not be like EARTH! Mothers and fathers on all those other planets tell their children, it you keep acting that way you will end up like humans on earth! And the kids get it! They shut the hell up! Earth is good for one thing and that is as an example for all other planets what NOT to be!" A Barkazone entered the café and demanded a stool at the crowded bar area. Barking and shouting he insisted on having somebody's stool.

Roger walked up to this gentleman and said, "Do you see that wonderful woman there at that table…" and Roger pointed to Martha. He nodded. "She just annihilated your entire galaxy, Messier 109," Roger said with a wry smile. Horror melted into his face and with a howl of anguish there was a bright flash of light and then just a small pink cloud. Roger sat back down.

"Roger, sometimes you can be so cruel," Martha giggled.

Chester walked by and stopped at their table. He smelled of rotten Be-Bak (Barkazone-flavored root chewing sticks) and Barkazone excrement. He did not miss Earth or humans but he did miss the Zonks terribly and the school children. Was there anything, at all, that they could do? Martha loved Chester. She loved him long before he was a Zonk. She looked at Roger and Roger said, "Well, it is really up to you."

Martha said, "You do realize you can't go back as a pig?" Chester nodded in the affirmative. So with a wink and a nod, Chester disappeared.

As most know, time, in other dimensions greater than three, is just a physical reality and you can walk along its axis just as a third-dimensional being moves through space. So, upon Chester's death and his short stay on Teegarden B, years had gone by on Earth. And it hadn't rained a drop since Chester's death. A large goat waltzed through The Estate gate early one morning as though it had been there all its life. It went up to a recently planted rose garden. A sign said, 'Chester's Rose Garden'. The large goat curled up near a small rose bush and fell asleep. It began to rain.

The Trout

"Just because you want to die doesn't mean you should. You need to look more closely within yourself to find that spark to kindle that flame of desire." — Bootes to the Trout

Just west of Ruedi Reservoir in the Rocky Mountains were the succulent ripples of the Fryingpan River. Slowly percolating down the mountains, it was home to many wonderful trout. Lester was one of these trout. Lester was seriously tired of life.

Chrissy Thompson just won the Republican 3rd congressional district of Colorado. She was a white Caucasian born in a small farm west of Grand Junction. She had blond hair and blue eyes with distinctive dark brown eyebrows that she twerked up her forehead left or right to enhance her point of verbal view. Her face was always a pasty non-gloss caked smear of heavy off-white makeup. Chrissy was a fraud.

Chrissy Thompson was really Cecilia Rodriguez from Guadalajara, Mexico. At the age of six, with her uncle, they crossed the Rio Grande into Texas and worked as migrant laborers. They eventually settled down on a plot of land near Fruita, Colorado and grew apples. Cecilia knew one thing and she stuck with it the rest of her life. She wanted to be white. When she was old enough, she dyed her hair blond. Blue contact lenses followed white makeup. She strived hard to lose her accent and began to mimic the vernacular of the Caucasian schoolgirls. Cecilia Rodriquez was no more. She was now Chrissy Thompson. The uncle was gravely disappointed in her choice of a race to be. If he spoke to her in Spanish, she would pretend not to understand what he was saying.

The uncle bought this apple farm cheap. The local people of Fruita thought it was cursed. Previously owned by the Fidd family, the apple and subsequent cider business was very good. But rumor had it that the Fidd boy lost his mind and was found shoving lubricated apple cores up his rectum. The Fidd boy apparently ran away and the Fidd family just gave up on the farm. Farmer Fidd took his own life by injecting heated mayonnaise into a vein. Many years later, Ms. Fidd heard they found the Fidd boy dead, apparently while making love to some woman on the rim of a canyon in Utah. "At least he died happy," she stated to a local reporter.

"But did they find any apple cores in his butt?" The reporter just did not have that information.

The uncle knew much about curses. And he also knew they were great in purchasing inexpensive properties. In no time, with little assistance from Chrissy, the apple farm and its cider business were back up and running. On her 16th birthday, the uncle celebrated by getting Chrissy an elegant dress, of course in white. That hot afternoon, the uncle set out to prune various trees on his farm. He went to the shed, but upon opening the door, there lay Chrissy on a wood bench with a sack of grain under her buttock. She was furiously masturbating and her rectum was chock full of lubricated apple cores. Apparently, she heard about the curse too. The uncle, clutching his head in anguish yelled, in Spanish, "White people are so messed up!" Chrissy Thompson ran out the door of the shed and into the town of Grand Junction. She would never ever go back to the farm. She went into town and became a Republican.

Chrissy worked herself up the political ranks. She wrote policy and passed legislation that would prohibit local farms and businesses from hiring undocumented laborers. She would pass laws that would reduce taxation on the wealthy. And she would push forward a bill that would slash public education funding. "You have to keep stupid people stupid or they just will not vote Republican!" She said this in private just after she attended a very successful fundraising event at Thatcher Middle School.

Congresswoman Thompson, being a migrant herself, knew the illegals and the illegal routes. She personally was there when many were incarcerated by local and federal forces. There were always pictures or a video taken with an exquisitely dressed Chrissy nearby with a gun, holster and belt. She was tough on crime. The press loved her.

But her numbers started slipping the next year. Chrissy was under stress. She lost most of her hair—not to stress but to over bleaching. She now wore a platinum blond shoulder length wig. She needed a new angle so she decided to become an angler. Now, Chrissy never hunted or fished in her entire life. But many Republican Coloradoans did. She needed their votes. With an entourage of twelve trucks loaded with fishing reels, rods and cameras, Thompson was off for Fryingpan River. Chrissy was so confident of a successful fishing experience, she invited Channel 4 with their live action feed service to show real images of her as an avid angler. This real-time feed would go directly into the houses of thousands of conservative homes in the Rockies.

Bootes was camping at the base of Sloane Peak near the Fryingpan. Mitch tagged along since he needed a break. She already had, the previous day, a successful fishing venture. The cooler was full of trout. But she wanted one more day. The beauty here in the Rockies was extraordinary and she wanted to inhale every inch of it. She got down to the river before the snoot of the sun would rise over the mountains. Mitch was at camp and would tend to the fire and clean up their cozy habitat.

Bootes made her first cast of the morning into the babbling stream. And then Lester showed up. Lester was a twenty-three-inch-long rainbow trout. He was only two years of age. Not old enough for senility. He swam right up to the foot of Bootes Zonk. Lester wanted to die. Bootes was aporetic. The art of fishing was to weed out the lesser intellects of the species. If Republicans were trout, then trout would be extinct by now. But what Bootes gazed down on was a valiant beast. She gently pulled him gasping out of the water. Lester had thirteen hooks in his body. Most were in his mouth but some were in different areas of his torso. Eight had weathered fishing lines that contained lead weights. Three of these had weights over two ounces in burden. It was obvious to Bootes he was a fighter and he loved his life. But now not.

Young Lester, when hooked, developed a tail-fin kick. Most probably genetic in origin but this kick was not present in any other fish. It produced a gut-wrenching snap that would always eradicate Lester from the line but unfortunately leave the hook and, sometimes, the line and subsequent lead weight in place. Lester was tired.

"No," said Bootes. "You are to live. You are a Zonk." She meticulously and carefully removed all his hooks and weights. She calmly washed him off in the stream that was his home, kissed him on the snout, and set him free. He looked back just once. He wanted to remember this human. Lester was grateful. He swam down the river into the waiting hooks of Chrissy Thompson.

Congresswoman Thompson had set up shop just west of where Bootes was fishing. She cascaded out of her SUV wearing the standard appropriate angler attire of leopard print tights, an actual mink stole, a Gucci blouse and leather high heels. She garrulously spoke to the cameras and her assistant handed her a fishing rod. She paused a pregnant moment to look down at this odd device but suddenly came into character, and with a broad smile, her team of assistants sauntered down the slope to a large granite flat rock overlooking the river.

The plan was simple because simple was all she could understand. Ten other assistants with fishing rods, along with Chrissy, would cast their lines into the river and proceed to catch the largest trout they could. Once caught, Chrissy would then cradle the fish for the trophy shot, no matter who actually caught the fish, and the Channel 4 news crew would zoom in for the final media moment and she would deliver a quick blab on fishing and gun rights for Americans.

Ms. Thompson's fragrance that day was Gruterry Musk Eau De Toilette direct from France. This was extremely expensive perfume made from the glands of mating (or excited) badgers. This dense musky odor pilfered the forested hills and into the nose of Mitch Zonk. Curious, he went to investigate.

Chrissy and crew had just cast their lines into the river. Just by extreme luck, her baited hook hit the water. She turned, wobbling on her high heels, and smiled at the cameras like she had completed this task many times before. And then a snag. Just by a remarkable event, her hook snagged Lester. Lester, fasting, was not in the mood for a meal. He had just been saved from ultimate death by a very kind human. But as the tendrils of fate would swim in the vast tepid waters of a cesspool, Chrissy's hook snagged Lester's tail muscle. The hook, in his tail, incapacitated his genetic tail-fin kick. Chrissy, never feeling this sensation before, overreacted and yanked viciously back—sealing the hook and the fate of this fish. Uncharacteristically of an avid angler, she didn't use her reel. She briskly walked up the road until the fish was dragged flopping on the flat granite rock. Walking back down to the river, the cameras were flashing and she hugged the fish to her breast. "I do this all the time," she lied. She pulled out her knife and from the throat to the tail she slit the writhing beast. The entrails spilled out onto the rock beneath her heels. Mitch just made the crest of the hill to look down at the commotion. Bootes, looking down the river to the retinue of people, noticed Lester lying dying on a rock. She ran down the river to be with him. Behind Mitch lunged three male badgers from the forest with their heads and loins swarming with heated bouquet of hormones from Ms. Thompson's Eau De Toilette. Lester looked up at this woman that had just gutted him. She was smiling, holding a knife in her hands. With a thrust and gut pulling tail flip he plunged the knife deep into her right eye. She bolted upright still smiling an idiotic smile. She leaned back and slipped in the entrails of Lester. At that moment, three very horny male badgers contacted her body. They began to gnaw and hump. The furry mass tipped over the rock and into the succulent meandering river with a plop. The cameras stopped flashing but the Channel 4 News feed continued live streaming. Bootes and Mitch made it to the flat granite rock at the same time. Lester was trying to speak but Bootes and Mitch didn't speak trout. But what Roger later translated was, "What a BITCH!" And Chrissy was. Lester laid his head down and died.

Congresswoman Chrissy Thompson of the 3rd District of Colorado floated down the river, placid in death with her contorted figure. Her makeup, oil based, still managed to be removed by the philandering badgers and the impact of the river rocks. Her wig gone. Her blue contact lenses gone. What was viewed on Channel 4 live streaming at that moment was a seriously destressed dead human appearing like an elderly disheveled bald hispanic woman submerged in a river. Which she was.

The Casserole and Kassandra

"No, you have to believe me. Really. Now! It is all death. I am not kidding." — Kassandra to the Zonks

Kassandra Tak came from Harvey, Michigan, which means she had white skin, big boobs and a bouffant hair style. Her car was a faux wood paneled 1966 Vega. She wanted to breed but the local boys wanted diversity and preferred their melanin roasted dark. They wanted to spread their seed, but her haven, moist as it was, was just not dark enough. Kassandra cried.

Ms. Tak was infested with a hideous plague that forced her brain cells to rapidly truncate her neurons to her throat and force her to state true things. She could not lie. As a result, she could not be a Republican. Her family, obviously troubled by this issue, forced her truthful mind into a mental institution where they would systematically shock her brain into a series of peaceful yet poignant lies. She just could not do it. Kassandra went insane.

Mentally destroyed, she was sent to the Zonk Farm of the Warped Noodle. She was warmly received.

Walking toward the Silk Barn, Opeia noticed a goat with huge horns. The goat was about the size of a large dog. It was calmly snoozing in Chester's Rose Garden. Opeia approached quietly and sat down by this snoring goat. It slowly opened up its gold-colored eyes and Opeia immediately knew it was Chester. He had come back in the body of a small Pyrenean Ibex. Martha's sense of humor did shine through. This particular mountain Ibex had been extinct since the year 2000. And, well, now it wasn't.

The rest of the Zonk family wasn't so sure but when the goat meandered into Chester's old office like it had been there a thousand times, took off the lid of a jar containing his caps of liberty supply, took a mouth full, and then went on a 'trip' grunting away—they all nodded their heads, yup, this was Chester. Zade and Eni were pissed since Roger could have given them a heads up. But Roger was out on Barnard Star B with Nell. Nell had run out of frozen Republicans to blast to slivers of ice so Roger was on an emergency run to restock the entire planet.

She had this irritating quirk, Kassandra, of always being right. But her claims were so ludicrous and bizarre that no sane person would believe her, so she was ignored. Besides a random aggravating left jolt from her head neck muscle, possibly due to the electro-shock therapy, and a habit of eating bugs, Kassandra was very beautiful. In an upper Michigan sort of way.

Opeia, too, had eaten insects back in Nevada at The Pony Express. She loved the crunch and digestible protein. If only humans would get over what they thought was 'gross' then famines would be shortly eradicated and humans would then feel confident enough to breed more, and then all bugs would be eaten and famines would return. Life sucks that way. But today there were bugs. Many of them. And Kassandra and Opeia ran throughout the fields of cattle in the back of the Noodle to collect as many as they could.

Two and a half pounds later, Kassandra and Opeia arrived at the door to the kitchen at The Estate. The bag of bugs was put into the freezer for a slightly humane death. The Ibex had a steel wok with oil already heated up for the occasion. It was still awkward for Opeia to call the goat Chester, but she squeaked out, "Are you ready, Chester?" Chester grunted. In went the garlic, then the chopped onions followed by the insects. Lightly browned and on the plate garnished with parsley and serrano pepper. Salt to taste. Kassandra loved this Zonk family. And the Zonk family loved her.

The Goebbels School of Conservative Propensity in Austria was not deterred by the absence and non-returned calls of Dr. Igor Frunze (Dr. Mole). They sent into the Warped Noodle two more highly trained individuals. These two were caterers and they represented Zesty's Food Service.

The festivity was the annual gala for the Warped Noodle. The first Thursday in April, that year, was the fundraiser. Food was brought in from diverse catering services representing the finest foods from many countries on Earth. Invites were many and the new West Wing of the Noodle was opened to a spectacular expanse of cathedral ceilings, waxed mahogany floors and an ebony wooded band stand. Tables with silver utensils and china crockery graced the perimeter of the dance floor. All dictators and Republicans politely declined the event since, literally, their eyes or their lives would be on the line. But Hollywood, Europe, Britain, Australia, China, Japan and Bollywood with all the actors and directors showed up in droves. Many countries from Africa and South/Central America attended. Southern Democrat politicians, few as they were, did also attend. Iceland, Greenland and the Galapagos Islands were errors on the invites but they showed up anyway and were welcomed. All these countries and US states wanted to establish similar institutions for the mentally ill. They wanted to glean this Zonk knowledge and apply it into the entire globe. And the Zonks were open to freely expose their facility and grounds to all. All that the falcons didn't blind.

The Casserole, or really Casseroles, were of the Toulouse-style cassoulet by the famed New York Chef, Antwone Gogol. This was complete with pork skin bundles, beans, duck confit and sprinkled with breadcrumbs. Goebbels' assistants injected each dish with a potent dose of a string of amino acids that folded over into a three-dimensional shape. This was the Creutzfeldt-Jakob disease. These proteins, called prions, were one hundred percent fatal to the victim. No cure. The dish that was infected could be cooked to burnt charcoal and the disease would still be viable. Austria's Group of Conservative Propensity was fixated to literally wipe out the Zonks and their patrons. Still, the dish by the way, not poisoned, was fantastically delicious.

The band was Suds, Tripe and Grits, an all-female local bluegrass band that were the masters of the banjo blues polka. Stella, on washboard, was the lead singer and an eclectic entertainer. Lori was on pots and pans and Vicki on bass banjo rounded out the music. Kelly on string bass was sick that night and chose to flick her throat with her index finger into a microphone behind the stage to mimic the thunderous lower notes. Because no band member had any 'real' training, the noise that came out of this mass of incontinent sound reeled the listener into a kaleidoscope of cascading dissonance like many vital instruments being thrown down a long and never-ending staircase, snorting and begging for relief. The one star in all this cacophony was Stella.

Stella Horath and her brother, Ferd, grew up in a dirt mound that used to be a temple just outside of Cartersville, Georgia. The State, not the country, and if you don't know what that means then stop reading this book and go masturbate to any God or Gods that you believe in since you will need it for your survival. Stella and Ferd, abandoned by their parents, went out one night and dug a hole in the Etowah Indian Mounds. There they stayed for years until they were discovered by their nephew, Pluton. Pluton, not into a ménage á trois, since he really didn't know what that meant and wouldn't care if he did, killed Ferd. Ferd, having absolutely no thoughts of defiling his sister, preferred calm farm animals for loin relief and died needlessly. Stella killed Pluton while he slumbered in a slumber. But what Stella had inherited, unbeknownst to herself, was a phenomenal kidney pressurized grunt and a good prophetic intense bladder blast of focused urine.

The 'Act' was that after the initial introduction of the harsh dissonance of the pseudo-chorded musical arrangements, a crate of doves would be let loose. The doves, startled by the discord, would fly to the many overhanging chandlers, then Stella in her short tartan skirt, without panties, would dance around chaotically and then kick her leg high up in the air and squirt out a precise and accurate bolt of urine to knock the doves, one by one, off of their perches. By the end of the night's festivities, the food and drink consumed, the spastic dancing expired, all would be covered in dove excrement and Stella's urine, and the audience would go wild with applause. Why not? The US Dictator had to go all the way to Russia and pay for this type of treatment. An auction of various items made by the inhabitants of the Warped Noodle then followed. Checks were written and the evening would conclude. Vaya's paintings were most desired and brought in millions.

But the evening had yet to begin. People were just pulling up in their electric and hydrogen-fueled limousines. One famous couple arrived in an antiquated Stanley Steamer. Albeit slowly. But apparently that was the point. The local press was addicted. Stella was just recovering from her alcohol-induced stupor, which was necessary to refill her crucial bladder before her performance. And then the caterers entered. Chester, the Ibex goat, did notice something odd when the Zesty Service van stopped at the rear entrance and two gentlemen wearing tuxedos carried dishes through the door. But they were also wearing face masks and triple coated PVC gloves. Perhaps this was a Zesty gag but the well-honed horns of Chester acted like antenna to trouble so he followed them.

Suds, Tripe and Grits were already ripping into an incoherent version of Tchaikovsky's 1812 Overture, and Stella, with each 'canon' blast, would kick her leg high with a grunt and nail a dove off of its perch. The party was on. And then Kassandra came in through a side entrance, jumped onto the stage, and yelled, "You are all going to die!" The band stopped playing and the patrons instantly became silent.

She was whisked off stage by Eni and Zade to a near wall. Kassandra told them what she had seen in her mind. Poisoned casserole dishes. Zonks, being Zonks, believed her. Zade looked at Chester and he knew what was wrong.

The Zesty caterers did not suspect a thing when the horns of a large ram gored out both of their posteriors simultaneously. Their facial expressions were of surprise and dismay. With Casseroles and Zesty caterers removed, the band played on and once again the party was on.

The Zesty caterers were no longer zesty but they were not dead. So Eni, Zade, Opeia and Chester escorted them to the Dome of the Ultra-Warped Noodle into Room One. Sydney was most happy to accommodate. After the Zonks left, two 'zaps' later and with trailing tiny screams, there was one really fat and happy hamster.

The Castle Rock Ranch

"There is a persistent rumor that a small elephant is about. A midget elephant that is supposedly very rare. I want this elephant in my collection. I want it to be known throughout that by killing rare species we also can preserve them." — Dr. Pus

The Castle Rock Ranch was up and across the Arkansas River from The Truck Stop on a high plateau east of Salida. The entire nipple of this large knoll was a cattle ranch owned by Alex Pus. The 'nipple', in the center, was a large pillar-shaped rock that looked like a turret to a castle, hence the name of the ranch. Dr. Pus was a doctor in hunting, tracking and killing. He was the best at what he did through perseverance and determination. Which probably meant he was abused in some way as a child. And he was.

His mansion lodge on the top of this mammoth knoll was a testament to his prowling abilities since it was lumped full of all the rare taxidermized fauna that he had rid from this planet. "I kill so I can preserve the animals I kill!" This was his bellow. Insane as that sounds, he was correct in his mind since that mind was entangled in insanity. Dr. Pus even killed the last of the Spanish Pyrenees goats, which Martha gracefully resurrected into the life of Chester. "They are NOT extinct. They are merely waiting for your arrival for a Wednesday morning viewing." And like the workings of a Seth Thomas clock, he would open up his doors exactly at eight a.m. to a plethora of local school children to view his menagerie of stuffed animals that he had rendered lifeless. This was his 'gift' to a new breed of hunters that could possibly comprehend that killing was a greater good for the longevity of rare animal species. But, sadly, in death, this was the last place to view those extinct species.

Dr. Pus was right about everything since he had written his own world history and pushed that narrative on as many children as he could. These children, sponges all, soaked up the visuals and the words and went home calmly accepting of his new world order. It only took seven seeds to sow faith in a soul in Christianity. Seven seeds to sow. And on the seventh, the human would be a believer in Christ Almighty. And like the immutable Christ, Dr. Pus planted many seeds that fathered many extinctions.

Titus had been on a hunting trip with Bootes. They had just returned to The Truck Stop in the maintenance van with an immense carcass of a bison in the back. "Don't ask," she chirped at Monk Shin. Actually, the bison was from Taylor's Buffalo Ranch south in the valley between the Wet Mountains and the Sangre de Christos. This was a real bison since Americans tend to get names mucked up. There never has been a buffalo in North America. Ever. Buffalo are in Asia and Africa. And Taylor knew that but still called his ranch a 'Buffalo Ranch' since Americans just don't get much of anything true.

"Why attempt to confront truth to a frazzled mind?" he would say. But Titus and Bootes did not get this bison from Taylor's property. This bison escaped from a tear in a fence and he left to go wandering up and over a range of mountains.

The Zonks were hunting east of Crestone at the foot of Fluted Peak. It was a brutally cold October night but Bootes was not to fear. The small green glowing pachyderm created his own warmth and they were perfectly balmy in their tent. The next day Bootes took the lead but quickly Titus sensed something a few hundred yards to the south. "What is it?" Bootes inquired.

"I don't know. Possibly a bull elk. It is nothing I have smelled before." So Bootes turned south and cautiously zig-zagged her way through the snow. Titus, never circumspect, blundered after her.

Out of the mouth of Titus came, "Wait…" But it was too late. The charging bison flew out of a group of trees toward Bootes. Bootes, sensing sudden impact, fell over in the deep snow. And then there was a flash of mild green light and it was all over.

Digging herself out of the snow and looking out, there was a horrendous splatter of blood and the carcass of a bison. Titus was just finishing up with what remained of the organs. "Never had a bison before. It is very good." He smiled but the blood on his lips and ears made him look like a small green drag queen pachyderm. Bootes leaned back, looked in the sky, and laughed.

Monk Shin had never had bison meat either. But it became the staple during the next week for The Truck Stop as 'The Special' in the form of burgers and steaks. Because of the severity of the cold, Monk Shin put a large grill over the internal fire pit. Patrons could either grill their own meat or have Monk Shin do his 'Chinese Extraordinaire'. This became very popular.

After the Wednesday night Coronation of Queen Klondike when the fire was dying down and the people had all gone home, Gretchen locked the doors, threw a rug over a seriously passed out elephant, one that polished off an entire case of spiced rum, and the lights were turned off. Only the throbbing of the diesel engines from the trucks warmed the air like the pulsing beat of a mother's heart to a fetus in a womb. All was quiet.

Very early on that Thursday morning, small muffled explosions could be heard. Victoria Skank was in Albert's room busy copulating and they were the only ones awake. "All I can remember is the thumping of quiet detonations and whisper silent hisses. And then a crunching of weight on the stair steps, a blast at the door, a bright light and pain to my body. That was it," Albert told the police.

Ms. Skank said in her husky voice, "And I didn't even get to orgasm."

The sun rose to find The Truck Stop paralyzed since all the Zonks within were paralyzed. It took over eight hours for the stun dart venom to wear off. Apparently, a very efficiently trained crew blew the locks and rushed The Truck Stop. The only thing that was missing was Titus. He was nowhere to be found.

The Truck Stop alarm never sounded. Since Titus was part of the family, the system wasn't necessary. He could literally sense anything for miles around. But in his state of inebriation, he was a Zonk that was vigorously zonked. And now he was gone. Bootes and Cyg called Marvin at The Estate. Marvin hacked into a military satellite and zoomed into the Colorado Rockies but no radiation signature was discernible. It was like the elephant just disappeared.

"Boo!" said Dr. Pus as the lid of a lead-lined cargo case was opened. There in a mass of duct tape was Titus with only his eyes and snoot protruding from a ball of adhesive strips. People carried him to a large metal table and laid him softly down. The metal was so cold. "I am obsessed with fine rare animals. I always have been. Now I have you. You are one of a kind, or so I hear. So your addition will be most welcome indeed." Pus pulled out a long carving knife. "But first you have to give me something. You have to give me your life." He smiled. Titus's eyes bulged. His long proboscis went rigid like the reproductive organ on a seventy-year-old man who just overdosed on Viagra. And a blast blew forth that broke all the windows in Dr. Pus' ranch. A sound so large that it cascaded down from the ranch house through the trees and down the mountain into the waiting ears of the Zonks at The Truck Stop. They heard a mind-deafening 'WONK!'

Bootes, Gretchen and Cyg grabbed their rifles. Shin and Mitch grabbed kitchen knives. Albert and Ms. Skank grabbed each other's loins and proceeded to return to copulation. The Zonks rushed up the eastern slope of the mountain behind Salida, and upon the crest before the 'nipple' they saw in the distance the Castle Ranch. Dr. Pus and team, temporarily anesthetized by Titus' blasting burp, grabbed cutlery and Dr. Pus stabbed into the undulating mound of duct tape.

The Zonks luckily were late—much thanks to Roger. Any closer and all that would be left of them would be overcooked strips of bacon. The blinding green flash of light and subsequent concussion vaporized everything within a three-hundred-yard circle. Even thirty seconds later, the ground still rumbled and a large mushroom cloud appeared looking like a humongous Amanita phalloides. The Zonks, covered in dirt, snow and tree branches, dug themselves out. Down a wandering path came a mildly green glowing elephant. "What is for lunch?" he asked.

The Wanton Worries of the Worry Warts

"Humans are pathetic. It is obvious to me, anyway, that all of nature embraces this fault to the extreme for all these beings on this Earth. Their persistence in existence is indisputably disposed to being deplorable. I have no idea why. But it does make me laugh." — Roger

Luyten b, more commonly known as GJ 273b, rotates around a red dwarf star. It is very Earth like and is only 12.2 light years distant from Earth. This is where Roger laboriously dumps the patron saints of beings that worry.

To worry is to be radically concerned. It is a pre-programmed message in humans due to evolution's vagaries. To worry has apparently kept humans alive throughout history many times so that this gene is now procreated to manifest itself in the consistent blatant panic of humankind. If only worry was to be blended with strong reason then all would be well. But unfortunately, worry blinds any reason and hysteria follows. Sometimes benign crazy and sometimes outwardly violent.

Petulant Petunia Posh lived in Peach Springs, Arizona. When she was young, she was originally from Havasu City and her mother there was a nurse at the hospital. Her mother, Tiff, was neither reasonable nor rational but she did suffer excessively from obsessive compulsive disorder (OCD). Tiff worried about everything. The food that they ate, the water they drank, the air that they inhaled, and being a nurse, any contagious pathogens. Tiff's 'partner', and father to Petunia, was accidently suffocated by a dry-cleaning bag while sleeping since Tiff was convinced that a crow that just passed by had H5N1. She was now convinced he would never transmit that disease ever. And he didn't since he didn't have it to begin with.

Tiff and Petunia Posh constantly wore modified Level C uniforms with a full Tyvek suit, booties, nitrile gloves and a face mask with attached HEPA filters. Lack of sunlight made their bodies lean in

Vitamin D. But Tiff didn't care. She and her daughter were paranoid but alive.

Petunia didn't know life outside of that suit except for when she was in the 'bubble'. It made the kid non-social, since there were the possibilities of rips and tears, and play was not permitted. Being a teenager, though, it was excruciating. Doug Kram, the son of the local dentist, was young Ms. Posh's boyfriend. They had been 'dating' through a large plastic bubble that Tiff set up in her backyard with Petunia on the inside. Small exterior and interior holes fed into full latex gloves so they could 'touch'. Conversation was muffled but what else could one do? Kissing was allowed but no nibbling was possible due to the possible rupture of the bubble. And then there was always Tiff standing right before them the entire time with a dry-cleaning bag in her hand in case Doug got out of control.

Two nights later, Tiff came home late. She was just in a hospital room with a Canadian who was returning from a catering job in North Carolina. He tested positive for Creutzfeldt-Jakob disease. Tiff, always prepared, got the nod from the head nurse to comfort this man. And she did. The last thing he whispered to her was, "Don't eat the casserole. It is a little off." Supposedly, he being at the Warped Noodle gala and being a caterer, he had taken a tiny spoonful of the Toulouse-style cassoulet by Gogol. Knowing the morbidity rate of this disease, Tiff's skin, under her hazardous materials suit, crawled. After his death, she panicked, and still in her Tyvek suit, face mask, gloves and booties, hurried home. She wanted to reduce the possibility of exposure to other humans and decided to use the backdoor of her home as an entrance and run to the shower room.

Upon entering the backyard, however, there was Petunia in the bubble attempting to copulate with Doug, who was pulsating on her lawn like some demonic disco dancer. His feeble attempts at introducing his engorged reproductive organ through the arm holes of the bubble into the internal connected latex glove, then into Petunia's waiting vagina was heartbreaking. And Tiff was literally going to break someone's heart.

Her velocity was much greater than his, since his pants were down to his ankles, and on a sudden urge to retreat all he proceeded to do was trip backwards. Tiff lunged but Doug's gravity pulled him quickly to the ground and Ms. Posh missed him completely, only for her to land on the water sprinkler device behind him. The impact of this sprinkler with Tiff bruised her ribs and cut a deep laceration into her suit. She looked down and screamed. She ran to the back porch and grabbed a dry-cleaning bag. And then she slowly marched up to Doug who was still on the ground and in shock. Her eyes flashed red. Not because of some potent Hella-ish apparition inhabiting her body, but because Mr. Quigley, the neighbor, never took down his Christmas lights since he was a lazy asshole.

"Mom! Mom!" came a muffled cry from inside the plastic balloon. Tiff bent down over Doug, kissed him on the mouth, then put the bag over her head, tied it off with a string, and leaned back. Minutes later she was dead.

Days later, Doug Kram was found in a dumpster in the back of a grocery store with a dry-cleaning bag over his head. His wide eyes and mouth were frozen in a clear verbal cue stating, 'Why???'. Obviously, Petunia Posh could not take the chance of her mother's kiss being contaminated.

Ms. Posh resurfaced in Peach Springs, Arizona, and opened up her own HAZMAT shop complete with every protective suit from Class A to Class D, air cylinders, filtration devices, masks, suits, gloves and boots. This was followed by a cornucopia of testing kits to discover anything as small as a gas leak or any number of biological pathogens. She was ready. But Peach Springs, being just one thousand in population, was not.

She went door-to-door in her suit, mask, filters, gloves and boots and she spoke to the great people of Peach Springs. That all it took was a random insect, bird, bat or worm that could carry disease into this town. That depending on gestation, random tourists who did not even appear sick, could easily bring in a disease and kill them all. A town hall meeting was arranged. The local sheriff decided to close down all roads leading into Peach Springs. Petunia made it clear that outsiders were the filth and venom that would eradicate these good citizens. Posh's store outfitted everyone in town with HAZMAT gear just like she wore. This included a twenty-eight-ounce spray bottle containing a twenty percent Clorox solution with distilled water.

Charter Bus 277 out of Los Angeles was lost. This motor bus contained forty-three people who were primarily from Guam but many were from Kiribati and Palau. 'See America' was the friendly slogan on the brochure. And so far, the people of America were very friendly to the people of Micronesia. The bus was headed to the north rim of the Grand Canyon but unfortunately made a wrong turn at Kingman. They didn't know they were lost for several miles since the Micronesian people were so festive. Singing songs and drinking. They had just come from the Mexican border and these people had a genuine hankering for mescal. So lost they were.

Just exiting Truxton, there was a road barrier that stated 'No Entrance, Quarantine Area'. But, naturally, this didn't apply to them since they didn't have any ills and had drunk enough mescal to be immune to most anything. The bus driver concurred with the passengers and drove over the barriers. The town of Peach Springs was dilapidated in an antiquated sort of tone. The Micronesians pressed their faces on the windows in the bus to see this rural American town. Besides an obvious western appearance and vegetation, this could be a small town in Guam. No people were on the streets. In fact, no person was present anywhere.

Charter Bus 277 stopped with a grunt at the town's only grocery store. The people of Micronesia staggered out. Petunia and the Sheriff scattered and the town inhabitants were hiding behind buildings, walls and broken-down cars. What they saw through their plastic masks were people that were not from this country. They spoke English but they were not American. They were clearly infected with some disease by the way they walked and slurred their words. They had to be attacked in order to survive. At the 'funk' from the Sheriff's flare gun, the sparkler went up into the air. The Micronesians erroneously thought this is how Arizonans greet their tourists. With a firework display. And then the rush occurred.

Hundreds of good citizens rose out of their seclusion and attacked the bus. All the tourists saw were humans covered in white suits, masks and booties spraying them with sprinkler bottles full of acid. Actually, it was not an acid but a base, but who is to quibble during duress? The Micronesians did not disperse but congealed into a mass that rallied behind the bus. Eyes burning but focused, one yelled, "Fuck these guys!" and in mass they ran into the white-suited crowd. The occupants of the town, realizing the tourists' infection had turned them into a ball of rage, fled. Petunia was first, then the Sheriff and then all the rest. Off they went down the edge of the sheer cliff face of the canyon into the abyss of Roger's waiting arms.

"Fuck Americans! They are so weird!" said one Guamanian. And he was right. They were. But he was an American too— so that made the statement pathetic. After the tourists were checked out in a hospital in Flagstaff, the doctors stated they had never witnessed a group of people so free of external microbes.

Luyten b became full. Full of worry warts. Why, you may ask, didn't Roger put them on a disease-free planet like Teegarden B? Because Roger knew they did not deserve it. They did not produce anything good—just panic. And panic needs to be contained.

A Door Shuts and One Opens

"You can knock all you want on the door of heaven, but no entity ever will answer. It is that silence that is the gift, since life is so full of noise." — Roger

Gretchen receded into the light of a late full moon on a Monday night. She was found a few days later by Titus and Cyg behind a granite razor ridge that exposed a field of alpine flowers. She was curled into a fetal ball with a book in her hand that was titled, 'The Adventures of Badger Zonk'. It was open at page thirty-three. The first paragraph stated in quotations, 'No one has ever defeated a Zonk and no one will ever defeat me'. But death has its own rules. The Zonks all gathered around her and agreed to just leave her be. The next spring that same field had twenty times the number of wildflowers. It was glorious to behold.

Victoria Skank gave birth to a slimy pink piece of stuffed manicotti. Albert named him Zot. So Zot Zonk was born.

Cyg took over the entire laboratory including Gretchen's. Bootes had already moved her skinning operation into Cornelius' lab. Aside from Grammy's biscuit and Monk Shin's food, the Zonk Bookstore was a close third in popularity. Structural additions and a second-floor balcony were added to the store to make way for another condensed array of amazing knowledge, bound tightly in literature. Victoria wore the baby in a cloth satchel around her front so she could breast feed and do her work at the same time. It was springtime in the Rockies and The Truck Stop business was booming.

Getting a wild hair, as Zonks tended to acquire this bulging strand, Cygnus bought twenty-five acres of land near the southeast slope below Pahlone Peak—close to where Cyg found Titus or the other way around. She and Titus decided to venture out to this area and, well, dig a hole. Bootes tagged along just in case an elk, deer or bear might appear. That evening they made camp near Green Creek.

They were greeted in the morning with a thick mist. Bootes went south up along the creek to hunt and Cyg, with Titus, went west up the slope. The younger Zonk took out a map and a compass and she was fairly sure she was smack dab in the middle of her property. It was time to dig a hole. She pulled from her backpack a pick and a shovel and she started to dig. And dig. And dig. Titus yawned. "Is this going to take long?" he enquired.

Sweating, she looked up and out of breath said, "Yes, this is just a start of a very long process. It is called mining." He yawned again and she noticed. "Well, what?"

"Stand back," he grunted. She did. "No, much farther back." She backed up several yards. Then with a 'snort' and a 'honk', his proboscis became rigid and out flashed a blinding green light, and the slope of the mountain now had a large deep hole in it.

"Shit," she said.

"Yes, shit indeed." he replied.

They entered the cavern. No retaining structures were needed since Titus' green blast solidified all the surrounding rock in the hole. With a few more 'honks' and 'snorts' the two were deep inside the mountain interior. It would have taken modern humans with modern equipment years to obtain this engineering feat but with one radioactive elephant it just took twenty minutes. What they found was amazing! Strands of silver, nickel, gold and cobalt. It would be the latter that would bring home the bacon. Titus smiled at Cyg. "We are in the mining business," they both said harmonizing. As they waltzed down the side of the mountain beaming, there was Bootes near the creek bending over a fire with roasted deer kabobs.

Herbie's Absolutions

"Touch is so important for humans. It is a reflection of trust and understanding. It is upon that contact that true conscious feelings can occur." — Herbie Newt

In a typical brownstone house in German Town, a suburb of Columbus, Ohio, stood the pillar of a true progressive liberal family. Doctors Ed and Lorraine Newt were progressive liberals who fought for justice, free healthcare and free education. Freedom meant freedom for the masses and liberty meant liberty for all people. Republicans modified these terms to mean freedom and liberty for all finance. Not people. It was money that was to be free and liberated. So much for everyone else. Their son, Herbert, became the devil.

No, not the Devil since he, she, doesn't exist. He just thought he was the devil since he had an ongoing issue with Christians. But it has never been reality that mattered. It was only the perception of that reality that mattered and that perception was really screwed up in Herbert.

"You need treatment for your anger," stated Dr. Pugh. "Historically, there has been nothing wrong with Christians. Ever. You need treatment and you have no idea that what you are saying is vile and excessive! Damn you for second guessing God Almighty! You will die. I foresee it all. And you will be eaten raw by the rabid teeth of demons!" Herbie farted. Herbie disappeared.

He showed up weeks later impaled on an electric fence surrounding a top-secret research facility in a valley in Utah. Herbie was peculiarly attempting to get into this facility. He was pronounced dead on the scene. But with no identification papers on his body and since it was late at night, the local security merely put him in the building in Room 121 near the basement stairs. This area had not been used for years and it was naturally cool. A fine place for a carcass. The scientists would just have to deal with him in the morning.

Room 121 was a notorious place. It was the place where scientists exposed pregnant pachyderms to extreme high levels of radiation to induce possible mutations. This was the birthplace of Titus. Herbie's heart was not yet able to rid itself from life's tangible noose. It was near silent but it wasn't dead. Hours passed and the slow beating of the drum got louder and louder. Herbie stirred to life at three a.m. He sat upright. He was on a metal table in some sort of lab room. The smell of burnt hair and skin were nauseating. He tried to stand but the floor appeared to be like a trampoline. It was undulating up and down. The weary carcass pitched himself off of the table onto the floor and he staggered. It was so cold. Weaving back and forth he clutched the wall to steady his body but his legs did not respond to basic mental commands. Herbie fell onto a countertop that contained many buttons and levers. As gravity sucked him to the floor, he frantically grabbed the countertop and his hand fell upon a lever. But he was weak and gravity was stronger and he hit the floor but not before pulling the lever all the way down.

Lights and gauges flashed on. A thin beam of green light shot out of a protrusion in the ceiling that focused directly on the table that he had just fallen from. That was partially lucky otherwise he would have been nearly killed twice in one night. But radiation unfortunately has a tendency not to stay focused for long and a tinge of green laced his body's perimeter and Herbie passed out.

He woke up in some type of cylindrical room. He saw faces pressed to four separate windowpanes looking in. Herbie was naked and some soul had taken the time to clean him up. The stench of burnt skin and hair was gone. He felt ecstatic, or no, more like static electricity was tickling his torso. The lights were dimmed to near darkness. Perhaps the scientists wanted him to sleep now. So, shutting his eyes, he dreamed of his favorite food. Bacon.

Voltron stood on top of an enormously tall plateau overlooking an expansive sea of squirming ants. The ants were attempting to climb the walls of the steep cliff. Ants upon ants piled on each other and pushed up the rock. They were trying to reach Voltron. The ants were all chanting 'slleb elgnij' over and over again. Voltron suddenly realized he had an imposing erection. He was overcome with embarrassment and grief. Why now? Why was he cursed with such a stalk? Relief was begging.

He grabbed his cumbersome member and spunked off sparks into the vast abyss below. 'Slleb elgnij' was the sad reply from below. Closer and closer they climbed like some impressive slow impact of a trudging train.

Their cute tiny faces appeared over the plateau's rim. One, then two and then many more. They came to consume Voltron, who did nothing but spunk sparks from above that randomly killed thousands of innocent ants. Now was the time. Now was the reckoning. The wave of ants spilled forth. The impact would be swift. Voltron turned. His eyes were pouring forth tears of compassion. He opened up his arms to embrace the on-coming hoards.

Simultaneous to the collision of the cresting wave there was a tremendous flash and explosion when millions of high amp volts rang through the fathoms of this sea. Voltron opened up his eyes and what he saw was a solidified ocean of bacon strips. He earnestly sat down among the piles of fried pork and began to nibble the edges of one that was very burnt. Delicious, he thought. Then it came to him. Their chant. The 'slleb elgnij'. It was nothing but jingle bells spelled backwards. Indeed, Voltron guessed and chuckled it probably was Christmas. And what a nicer gift to receive than endless mounds of bacon. "Merry Christmas, everyone!" Voltron said to no one. Over and over and over again it echoed in the void below.

"Merry Christmas, everyone!" stuttered out of the mouth of Herbie. His eyes opened. Leaning over him was a female scientist in a lab coat. Her name plate said, 'Shut Up'. Her hands were a dazzling bright blue since they were covered in gloves with a triple coat of PVC. "Ms. Up, can I have some bacon? I am starving?" He reached up to touch her face and with a flash and a loud ZAP she became bacon. Well, not actually fried pork, but a human charred carcass that resembled burnt bacon. Dead Ms. Up fell on top of Herbie. He was horrified. Was he still asleep? Was he in a dream? With a solid 'thunk' and his head colliding with the wall of his cylinder, it was clear he wasn't. He pushed Ms. Up to the floor. Her ears still had sparks emanating from them. Her deep emptied black eye sockets sang a paralytic version of Bach's Brandenburg Concerto No. 3 in G major. Mr. Newt was not well. He teetered to the locked door, and when he touched the handle, there was a flash of light and an explosion. The door was no more. People ran in various directions. Some scientists. Some security guards. Young Mr. Gallo, a recent hire to security, pulled his gun and shot. But the bullet on impact simply turned to vapor. Mr. Newt looked down and he was embarrassed to find he had an erection. He sat down to relieve this impending issue and upon peaking, sparks flew out and any human that was unfortunate to be spewed upon turned immediately into crispy 'bacon'. "Sorry!" he said. Over and over and over again. "Sorry about that!" he mumbled to the mounds of the friable dead.

He found a tweed suit, a shirt and a pair of trousers in a professor's office. Boots he would glean from a locker in the security area. As Mr. Newt would discover, it was only his hands and excretions that could apparently deliver a shock. In the locker room he found PVC triple-coated gloves and put them on. He calmly walked out of the facility and 'borrowed' a car and off he went to find a revival. Herbie really did have an issue with Christians.

George Whitehead was from Rough Common near Canterbury in England. His father, a mason, was a blatant drunk and often beat the boy for no reason. But, surely, there was reason in his rants when, while beating the child, he would often say to the rhythm of the lash, "The only gold you will earn in this lifetime is behind the pulpit. It is there you can bark the word of Heaven and cheat from the poor their last wretched farthings!" George Whitehead, at the age of twelve, would become a self-educated Minister of God. He never actually took the time to read the Bible, in any form, but he knew valuable passages and with his voluminous stage presence and Hell-bound dictation, he soiled the underwear of many. At least those that could afford under garments. The trickle of money eventually broke the financial dam and Minister George would take his 'show' to the United States of America. The land where people actually thought they were free.

In a very used Ford Econoline Van, and with three faithful followers of the Lord, he plunged through America, setting up his vast canvas tent and chairs to the roaring crowds filled with God's Love. Whitehead would literally take your last penny. "It all adds up you know," he would state later. "And now through my blessing they are rich without guilt!" Tears were shed and people would faint from the power he gave through his voice of gravel. His intelligence would not be diluted by stupidity and he stayed away from large northeastern coast towns and the entire mass of Long Island due to the density of the Jewish population. The south was ripe but he needed more. His gallivanting canvas tent punctured a hole in the Mormon west. He set up his yurt in Fry Canyon, Utah.

Twenty-three kindly folk ventured into this tent. Not many. "But it just might pay for the gas," said the devout Minister. Usually, he promised a 'free' Bible to every attending person but a 'blessed and signed' copy would cost a mere fourteen dollars. Is that so much to pay for a ticket into Heaven? But for this measly crowd, he sold the 'blessed and signed' copies for seven heavenly dollars each. And he got it.

The sermon was a rapture. All hollered and wept. George, it needs to be said, was a charlatan. But he was a very good charlatan. And then came Herbie Newt. He wandered into the tent, took off his gloves and sat down in the back. George, a professional, sensing a non-believer, stopped short and peered into the back row. He said, "Stranger? You are no stranger to God. He knows you well. Come and lay your hands on me so I can take away all of your sins." Mr. Newt slowly stood up and walked to the stage. He turned back to see the smiling glowing faces of the pious of Fry Canyon.

Stepping on the stage, he leaned into the Minister and said, "I absolve you from stupidity." And Herbie embraced George Whitehead. With a flash George was 'bacon'. Nineteen total mounds of sparking debris were discovered by law enforcement under this canvas tent. All of them, according to Mr. Newt, were absolved of their sins.

Three more revival absolution barbecues later and Herbie was surrounded by law enforcement near Plano, Texas. The Zonks were sent in by charter jet and then helicopter. Sydney, with black goggles, was in tow. An orange gaze and the hint of a 'zap' was noted and Herbie Newt was encased harmlessly in non-conducting rubber. Mr. Newt would now be the fifth member in the Dome of the Ultra-Warped Noodle. He was warmly received.

Zot's Unique Ability to Do Nothing in Particular

"Zot is such a fragmentary child. Even for a Zonk. He shows an interest in absolutely nothing. And what is his issue with walking into walls?"
— Cygnus to Bootes
"Does it really matter, Cyg? He is a Zonk. And that is all that matters,"
Bootes sputtered this through a mouth full of cheddar cheese. And so it was.

Titus was initially annoyed by Zot. Zot would randomly, but frequently, hug him and often pulled his tail. Titus briefly considered blasting this child into vapor but then he would 'huff' and just stoically take it. Zot really could not help himself. Titus was this small green glowing elephant that was incredibly cute. Though Titus loathed that term he really was cute. Zot, however, was not. Later he would be considered handsome, but now as a child, he was obtuse in mind and spirit.

And there was the fact that Zot walked into walls. Ever since he was a toddler he just cantered into any solid frame. Initially, the Zonks thought this comical but after a few years it was a tad disturbing. Cygnus checked out his eyes. They were fine. He could see like an eagle. She then checked out his mental capacity. For his age, his brain was functioning just fine. So Cyg thought this was basically cognitive. Zot actually believed he could walk through solid mass. The Zonks would let him just be a Zonk.

In time, Zot and Titus became inseparable. Zot went to the mine with Titus. Zot had all his meals with Titus. Zot even slept with Titus. And Titus didn't mind. The older Zot got, the better they could communicate, and Titus began to love this child. Titus taught the boy classic literature. From Balzac, Zola, and D.H. Lawrence, to Poe, Dickens and Chaucer. On and on it went. One afternoon, outside of the mine near Green Creek, Zot said to Titus, "Why can't I walk through things?"

"Because you are just a biological mass of connecting cells and that ending blob of mass cannot move through any other form of mass," Titus quietly snorted.

"But if I modulate the frequency of each of my atoms precisely to the frequency of the other mass, then I should be able to pass directly through." Titus was baffled by this statement.

After a pause, he said, "Yes, but how would you obtain this frequency modulation capability?"

"You, Titus. It has always been you." Titus thought about this. Obviously, the boy had been walking into walls since they were together. Even as a toddler. So, perhaps, the proximity to Titus' radiance could possibly be feeding this poor child's dilution. "I just need a snootful to align my atoms. Would you do this for me?"

Titus grimaced. "This could kill you, son, and where would I be without you in my life?"

"I won't die, Martha told me so."

"Who is Martha?"

"She is a very kind person that has issues with blind fishermen."

"Don't talk nonsense."

"She created you!" Zot cried.

Titus went and puddled in the creek side and pondered. This was so odd it was most probably correct. He ambled back with brows furrowed. The creases in his forehead appeared as long perforated dimples. "Okay," he said. There near the babbling creek, Zot knelt down on the lush wild grass. Titus, still with furrowed brows, placed his proboscis on the forehead of Zot. "Ready," he whispered. But before Zot could say yes, a small 'poot' came from Titus snout and a mild green haze engulfed the boy. The glow only lasted a few seconds and melted away. Zot opened up his eyes.

"Is that it?"

"Yup," chortled the pachyderm. Zot stood up, looked Titus in the eyes and walked briskly into a towering pine tree. With a 'plunk', Zot was knocked out.

Looking up, he saw a pool of blurred faces. He was in his bed. The nose of a glowing elephant was removing a thermometer from his mouth. "How do you spell lucidity?" came a soft voice.

"Titus," Zot gargled.

"He's fine," said another voice. They all shuffled away out of the room except for the elephant. The door was quietly closed.

"Why didn't it work?"

"Because you have to 'feel' it," said Titus. "You have to turn it on and that takes energy from your mind. You just need to find the switch to turn it all on." Now it was Zot that had the furrowed brows.

Weeks went by. Titus taught the little Zot to ride on his back. They would hunt with Bootes or build dams in the creeks. These dams would create small pools that they could bathe in. At night, in these pools, Titus would look up and instruct Zot on all the known constellations. Astronomy was now the mental fuel of the month. Astronomers were the ultimate historians. The nights in the remote Rockies were dark and this was critical for star gazing. The Zonks purchased a large telescope, computer and camera and placed it on top of The Truck Stop. Finally, something that opened the door of interest in Zot. The viewing of eons of history in the passing of ancient starlight.

One dark night, staring into his scope, Zot 'found' Teegarden B. He had no idea that one day he would live there. It was only noticeable in the dip in the neighboring stars' luminosity. But the signature was there. Roger was there with Karl. Roger did not like this viewing intrusion and flipped his middle finger to Zot. But no technology was yet available to discern such a rebuke on Earth. Zot saw nothing. But he did hear his mother's scream. Crystal clear, through the cold night air. Victoria, while cooking bear meat, splattered the fat on her apron and it caught fire. Albert, luckily, was there and put a blanket over her to put out the fire. She was singed but unharmed. Zot just appeared through the ceiling and connecting walls to rush in for assistance. Zot Zonk could walk through walls. When filled with adrenaline, Zot Zonk could walk through anything.

Ada's Love

"I did not know a person could feel this way. I saw them all, all humans, as lumps of flesh that I communicated with. They were just there. Lumps. But Herbie changed all of that. — Ada Place

Years ago, in Xuzhou, China, Dandan Liu was found destitute in an alleyway near a tin-covered shack. That shack was her home. She was dying from malnutrition. This occurs throughout the world in various places. Mostly due to poor nutrition from lack of available food. Dandan did not have this issue. She had food. She just wanted to be a supermodel.

She came from a very wealthy family but that did not enhance her biography. A poor waif from dead parents was her narrative. Her anorexic body crawled on the stone-covered streets begging for morsels of food that she inhaled but would later regurgitate with a smile. With her chin covered in bile mucus, she would look to heaven and laugh, knowing that some deity would save her and make her in control of her own destiny. She would be a supermodel. But this supermodel had some serious issues and skinned up knees. This supermodel was dying.

The deity was the nation of China. It came swooping down to 'rescue' her from her imminent demise and put her, with many other unfortunates, into a science program. Her name and identity were gone. She was fed and made healthy again. She became a Rubenesque cherub. Beaming with life and energy she bounded against her bed restraints. How could she be a supermodel now with all this girth? Food was introduced to her through a funnel. She gurgled and coughed but it was no use. Then fourteen days from her last period, irradiated semen from hapless deck hands from the confiscated pirate ship, Laka Vette, was injected into her uterus and a baby was eventually born. That baby would become Ada.

Dandan Liu did eventually walk the catwalk. Ironically, to the disco music of 'I Will Survive', Ms. Liu, glossy-eyed with pin tip pupils, overdosing on opium, staggered down a plank and into a blazing hot crowd of adoring flames. The experiment was deemed a failure since no positive or negative mutations were apparent. The unfortunate mothers were exterminated. Liu's baby was put up for adoption in America.

"It is exposure, exposure, exposure. Humans are like lab rats. They have very limited attention spans. They can't hold a decent conversation without soon blurring off into a tangent. To stay relevant in this business, you must be verbally and visually available at all times. At all costs. Once you lose their attention, then you never existed at all." Herbie was talking to Ada Place in Room Four.

"So you want to be a serial killer?" Ada queried.

"No. Hell no. I was given this gift to stop lies. Christianity is nothing but lies. A pilfered and plagiarized religion that was rewritten to placate the masses of mindless fodder." Ada never looked down at her notepad. She didn't write down any notes. She was mesmerized by Mr. Newt.

He was charismatic and handsome in a rugged way. But she did not get any hint of manipulation like some others in the Spires or the Milkman. Ada honestly believed the only thing Mr. Newt wanted from her was good conversation.

Months went by and Ada's professional demeanor evaporated like condensation on a soda can in a blast furnace. Talk sessions turned into pearl jasmine tea parties. Tea parties turned into the readings of Yeats, Frost, Plath, Rilke and Pound. To alleviate the depression from the words of the depressed poets, they turned to amorous machinations. And that was tricky.

Rolling around on the sofa, Herbie really enjoyed this tiny bit of China. She was small but she was nimble. And what she lacked in experience, Ada made up in knowledge from vast amounts of erotic literature. Mr. Newt knew all his excretions were electrically deadly. His saliva could easily kill a human upon expectoration. So he knew no open mouth kissing would be possible. But Ada dove in to consume his lips like a starving peasant ravishing a twitching dying rabbit. He tried to stop her but he could not. He, in vain, attempted to dislodge her grasp and push her free. But she persisted and contact was made. Saliva was swapped. Herbie's eyes grew wide expecting the worst. But there was Ada, thick rimmed glasses and all, staring right back at him. Her lips and face were glowing orange.

Finally, Herbie wrestled free. "What. Are you insane?"

"No," she smiled. "I am horny." And she was.

"But why aren't you dead!?"

"I have no idea. Perhaps it is love," she said. She was so adorable that he bent over and kissed her passionately. Again, her lips and face glowed orange but nothing else except a sheen of sheer pleasure. Rounding the bases, the ball players stripped down and Ada played with his neck, chest, buttocks and balls. Cautiously, Herbie took off his gloves and lightly caressed her. She glowed orange in every place he touched. "It tickles like small static electrical pulses," she mused.

"Yeah, well, one tickle for you turns everyone else into bacon strips," he stated.

"Well, you don't need bacon when you can have Chinese pie." And she jumped up and sat on Herbie's face. Her loins turned bright orange and she quickly peaked from the extraordinary pulse of ecstasy. "Damn," she hissed. "I have never felt that ever before."

Herbie grabbed her tiny frame and mounted her on his twitching log. "Here goes everything!" he said through pursed lips. Suddenly, sparks flew from below and the small Chinese woman lit up bright orange. He arched his back in a wave of arduous relief and she passed out into his arms flopping like a fish out of water. Mr. Newt frantically held the small frail body and laid her down on a blanket on the floor. "Ada? Ada?!" She shuddered awake and smiled.

"Shit," she said as steam vapor exited her mouth.

Opeia, Zade and Eni chastised Ada for fraternization with an inmate but they really did not care. They were curious as to why she was not dead. Many studies later and it was apparent that Ada obtained an accidental mutation that protected her from any form of electrocution— no matter how many amps or volts. She could easily bleed from a scratch but she could not be shocked from electricity. Ada and Herbie became engaged. Chester managed the jamboree.

The Zonk Mineral Company

"It was really ridiculous how this all came together. I don't believe in luck. I think a person makes their own luck. But, honestly, fate lined up the Zonks and it just happened." — Cygnus Zonk

Roger was wincing while urinating in a metal bowl in the burrow on Proxima Centauri b. Gretchen was not there. She was windsurfing on a lake of ice on TRAPPIST-1e. Roger's head hurt. Not the head between his shoulders but the tip of his penis. Knowing disease did not occur on Teagarden B, he was mentally attempting to retrace his steps throughout the universe. "Karl and Chili had to be clean." He gagged. There was that fling with Bana on Wolf 1061c but he was so sincere on his cleanliness. "Take responsibly for your own actions!" he said abruptly to the stuffed castrated beagle on the shelf. One of the canine's marble eyes popped off and rolled out on the floor. Roger gazed upon this desiccated body of the dog. It slightly resembled a dried squid with four tentacles. Five if you included the tale. Martha appeared with Hazel and Zazel. The latter were in a lazy 69 in the hammock, munching happily on their fir lined 'trees'.

"Why so glum, Roger? Life is good. I just annihilated three distinct species of arrogant beings on Teegarden C."

"Yes, I know. That was my planet."

"Sorry," she said. "Well, Roger, they just did not give a shit. They had to go. The positive energy was just not there."

"Thaddeus was on that planet." He winced again as urine was forced out.

"Oh, I saved him. He is a Zonk. No Zonks can be harmed in any way. I told you that."

"But he will be lonely," he winced.

"Oh, no. I thawed out a group of pathetic Republicans on Bernard Star B to keep him happy."

"You bitch! That too was my planet. Would you please not interfere with my work? And Thaddeus would really hate them."

"I know, but he was becoming a bit bored of his surroundings. I think this will liven him up." Martha saw that Roger was in immense pain. "Here," she said, "Let me help you with that." And with a nod, his 'head' was clear and he was free from pain.

"I didn't need your help," he sighed.

"I know, but what would we do without each other," Martha said, turning to vapor. Hazel and Zazel continued on their resolution, rocking in the hammock, to obtain some ultimate conclusion.

Zot was late. And now being mature enough to extract reproductive fluids from his minor hose, he focused on nothing but extraction. Titus was waiting at the mine and he had entirely no patience for puberty. "Get the HELL up here!!!" Titus trumpeted. The words avalanched down the valley and off of trees into the back of The Truck Stop and up the stairs and into the bathroom, where Zot vibrated on his porcelain stool.

"Damn you!" he pathetically yelled back. He was looking at the beautiful breasts and the delightful smiling faces of the Himba Tribe from Namibia in an ancient National Geographic magazine. He thought they curiously looked much like Bootes but Bootes rarely smiled.

Off Zot ran up the valley to the Green Creek Camp. The initial large canvas tent turned into a large shed with bunks and a stove. The processing plant was just down from the main mine entrance. It was small but it was enough for the flow of ore. The Zonks were not attempting to capitalize on the market but just be efficient enough to be profitable. Huge growth was not in their plans.

But the Zonks had two things that worked really well together. They had a nuclear elephant that could blast through anything and they now had Zot who, at a whim, could walk through anything. And the two worked really well together. Except for today, since Zot ran up winded with an obvious banana in his pants. Titus grimaced. "Let's get to work." And they did.

Zot would slither through rock as easily as most sober humans through air and he would mentally map out various veins of ore that he would literally run through. Returning with this knowledge, Titus would blast, or not blast, depending on the finds, into this rock and the valuable ore would be extracted. No technology on Earth was like it.

The valuable ore would be in mounds around the processing cabin. Inside, slowly but methodically, Cygnus extracted the fine metals from the ores. Silver, nickel, copper, gold, but most important, cobalt. Cobalt depletion throughout the planet was imminent since demand overruled the supply. With a steady stream of this mineral, they could inject the market with needed technology, and in so doing, reap the financial rewards. The rest of the minerals were smaller in volume but it all added up. The Zonk Mineral Company was born.

More land was purchased and a gravel road introduced. An occasional monthly truck would arrive at the processing unit and loads of the fine minerals were burdened on the axles and off they went and money would flow in. The income funded a complete makeover, in spurts, of the entire Truck Stop. Re-walled, re-shelved and re-vamped, inside and out, The Truck Stop re-gained its former magnificence and then some. A professional skin flautist, Hubert Saugen, was hired to replace Thaddeus' unique abilities. Thumper became Tapper since Hubert always wore the best Italian leather shoes. Business was gracefully erupting. Literally.

The Issues with Porter and Berlin

"Lies, lies, lies. The truth is nothing but lies! Don't believe it! If you let truth in your head you will be forever doomed by the plague of reality."
— *Senator Wiley (R), Mississippi, Ward Three*

"They are the best, you know? They speak to me personally like a well-paid mistress. The songs are sugar in my head. I truly love them both." Republican Senator Joseph Wiley from Kosciusko, Mississippi was speaking to Ada Place on Ward Three. He was speaking about his love of two music composers. Cole Porter and Irvine Berlin. He stunk of fish since he ate bountiful amounts of only the freshest ocean cuisine. It cost the Noodle an un-godly amount of funds for swordfish, albacore and mahi-mahi. But it was apparently worth it all to keep the Senator from Mississippi relatively sane. Wiley thought all other foods were contaminated with liberal tendencies and that the notorious progressive virus had yet to make its way into the ocean depths. He was not correct. He obsessively drank only bottled water that was unopened, and imbibed pure grain alcohol only through a funnel inserted into his anus. Joseph Wiley was a very fastidious person.

He spoke to God daily. Just through his mind. He did not want some middle person priest to muddle things up so he preferred direct contact. And God had him do 'fantastic' atrocities. The first time he was caught in a felony was at the Izaak Synagogue in Poland. He serenely pattered through the beauty to spill random squirts of lighter fluid on everything he saw. Unfortunately, he failed to use the last ruminates of his fuel to fill his Zippo lighter. With no flame, security easily wiped him away like some odd turd. Wiley secured the vote after his ample release from a Polish jail to win the incumbent Republican win for Mississippi. Again, he was disposed to callously spewing flammable liquids onto a Lesbian float during New Orleans Mardi Gras. Caught, Queen Bull Dyke, a 430-pound Samoan, easily tossed his frail body to the second floor of the Hotel Isle-De-Lis, where he was smothered by New Orleans love. Later, necklaces still dangling from his neck, he was drooling and warmly received into the bosom of the Noodle.

Joseph, Joe to all the friends he didn't have, was finishing off a large plate of swordfish. The high mercury content of all the cumulative ocean fish he had eaten throughout his daily life finally went to his head and it was destroying what little sanity he had left.

Thursday night, he could not sleep. He appeared greatly agitated. His radio was blaring out a medley of greatest hits from Irving Berlin and Cole Porter. Dancing and singing he leapt up on the tabletops and began to urinate and expectorate at anything that moved. Security called Ada Place to intervene.

The lights were shut off by security and Xenon gas was fed through the overhead vents of Ward Three. After several minutes the hooting and hollering fell silent. After a few hours Ward Three was back in business and Joseph Wiley was in a small conference room with Ada. "What appears to be the issue, Mr. Wiley?"

"Well, I just want my music played and I want everyone to enjoy Porter and Berlin," he said.

"What if the other patients don't like Porter and Berlin?"

"Nonsense, you chink cunt! What would you know of America! Porter and Berlin are the epitome of America and American values," he gargled.

"What values would those be, Mr. Wiley?"

"Shit, woman! White Christian values and a love between a man and a woman!" whined Joseph.

"But," Ada hesitated. "Cole Porter was a homosexual and Irving Berlin was Jewish." And Senator, Republican, Joseph Wiley finally popped a cork. His face transformed into a melting rubber mask of hate. Noticing this ubiquitous metamorphosis, Ada stood slowly up. But Wiley's charge was too quick and too much and Ada was thrown on the floor, being strangled by this Republican Senator who was chock full of Christian family values. Joseph heard behind him a 'snort' and he immediately turned his head. There, rearing on his back two legs, was Chester, and his horns came crashing down.

Senator Wiley came to consciousness on the top floor of Ultra-Warped Noodle Spire Two. He was just in Spartan surroundings on a bed of straw with a bedpan on the floor. The speakers on top of the ceiling were purring out the calming sounds of an ocean shore. Wave upon wave would slightly rumble through his head. The iron door creaked open and there on a mobile steel trestle rolled into Wiley's domain, lay a thirty-pound blue fin tuna. Frozen solid. "How would you like this cooked, sir?" asked the security guard standing wide-eyed for an honest response.

"Up your ASS!" yelled the Senator. Wiley grabbed the solid tuna by the tail and swung it widely. He clocked the guard out of the cell into the stone wall rendering him not available for retort. Wiley went up and out of the top of Spire Number Two still clutching the tuna. Attached to each spire was a metal cable that docked into the top of the center neighboring dome structure. Apparently, this was engineered to ground lightning strikes for all buildings. Joseph, being right and Christian and blessed by God himself, threw the frozen carcass of the fish over the wire. With one hand on the tail and the other in its mouth, he slid down the metal wire moving quickly to the Dome. Friction is a physical attribute that is normally ignored by the human population until a person actually falls down at even a slow speed. The fish, though frozen and solid, was suddenly cut in half by the ridged metal wire due to said friction just above the Dome. And Republican Senator Wiley from Mississippi came crashing through a vent shaft into and above the sparking and fornicating arms of Ada and Mr. Newt.

"Fuck!" said Herbie when he looked up to see a man falling at him with a tuna cut cleanly in half in each hand. Ada jolted to the side, still glowing a bright orange. A large 'FRATZ' exploded. Impact occurred and Joe was nothing more than a pile of sparkling detritus. The smell of burnt fish was abhorrent.

The Proximity to Contusions

"There are molecules that are way too tightly bound. They cling together but don't necessarily like being together. Like Republicans and peace. They secretly want relief. I am here to give that relief and to assist them in freeing themselves from their deplorable bonds." —
Bootes Zonk

Bootes was fishing along a creek just south of the mine. She took it upon herself to supply food for Zot, Titus and Cygnus. Mitch shut down the bike shop, just for this day, to spend time with her. He also liked to fish. His left leg and left arm were still not in balance but over time he was able to manage much better. For him, this day was a vacation. They sat still on the creek edge counting the surrounding mountain peaks that were covered in soft lactation. A strange figure of a man, one covered in oiled rags, eyes soft white and obviously blind, scrabbled through some brambles. He was holding an ancient fishing pole.

This man, using his fishing pole as guidance, tapped his way through the foliage and over the creek to stand beside Bootes and Mitch. The Zonks were puzzled. It was like looking at a Monet painting and there in the middle of the lilies was a baked potato complete with chives and butter. This potato tapped deliberately with his fishing pole to get nearer to the two. Looking up into the sky, pulling onto his long face, he opened up his toothless mouth and said, "Be the failure you were meant to be." And he just meandered away through the forest and dissolved into the green.

Mitch got up and abruptly followed this blind person but, apparently, he was much quicker and Mitch found no trail to follow. The blind man was gone. "What the hell?" he said to Bootes upon return.

"Zonks are afflicted with this sort of thing. Try to get used to it." Just then she caught a fish.

Turds do roll downhill. Yes, but many things, due to gravity, would also roll down a hill, but here near the east base of Pahlone Peak, turds did coagulate. Those solid forms of pre-digested expelled matter came in the shape of ultra-conservative businesspeople wanting a piece of this burgeoning mineral action. The Zonks were not receptive.

"You are a sick fuck and you need to be eradicated along with your half-breed brethren. You never could amount to greatness since your life was failed by messed up breeding. You all need to die and let the real men take over this farcical parade you call success," Major Balthazar speaking to Cygnus though a megaphone up from the valley below. The local authorities attempted to ameliorate this confrontation by stating the historical fact that no person ever succeeded in altercations with the Zonk family. But Balthazar had no ears for this closure.

Bootes and Mitch had just returned from fishing to hear the news from Cygnus. They were in the bunkhouse. Bootes said, "We have the high ground. They will most likely attempt a large push up from the valley with flanking maneuvers from both left and right. What we need is some really dense fog. And when the weather doesn't produce this ingredient, then we will have to make our own." Smiling, she got up and walked up to the processing shed.

Major Balthazar was a history buff and enjoyed the success of the Zulus against the British at the Battle of Isandlwana in South Africa. Indeed, at his ranch, he had an actual Assegai spear and cowhide shield from that Zulu-English 1879 altercation. The plan was simple since simple was all the thug-hired miner army would understand. From the valley floor they were to march in a line. The right and left sides in cadence with the center mass. At the first Zonk attack, the center mass of thugs was to quickly retreat giving the Zonks the mistaken impression they were winning. The Zonks naturally would rush after the retreating mass of thugs in the center, only to be flanked left and right from the both sides of the valley. Caught in between, they would be crushed. This is what the Zulu Chief, Khoza, called the Claw Defense. If it worked against the British, thought the Major, it would work against the ignorant Zonks.

Bootes came down from the processing shed carrying a crate full of what looked like tin cans. "If nature can't provide dense fog, then I can," she grinned. She told Titus and Zot that at the first sign of the attackers, she wanted Zot to push a can into Titus' snout. Titus, with a 'snort' would

306

blow the can down into the valley and it would explode on impact. "Keep this up for a ninety-degree spread on both sides of the valley and below."

"I could just kill them," smirked Titus.

"Yup. But where is the fun in that?" Cygnus retorted.

It was such a nice morning in the Rockies. No breeze and cool air. The only voices one could hear were the language of this little stream of water. The sound of a newborn baby blowing bubbles from its mouth. Then, two hundred yards below, came men with guns and tactical gear. They came up at the Zonks in a line. At one hundred yards, Zot loaded a can into Titus' snoot. Like a mortar launcher, with a mild 'fonk' noise, off the can went. Systematically, Zot and Titus blanketed the valley with dense smoke and it rose up above the sides of the valley.

Major Balthazar, in the middle lead position, used his megaphone to have his 'troops' advance. With the heavy smoke, no person could see past a few feet. Up the slope a small green elephant trumpeted, "Charge!!!" But the Zonks just stood still. No Zonk charged. And that was the plan. The Major, suspecting an offensive, went into the Claw Defense and retreated his men in the middle.

After a minute, Balthazar on his megaphone yelled, "Flanks to the middle!" and the crushing Zulu Claw began. But there were no Zonks in the middle. They sat peacefully up near the mine listening to the madness undulating out of the thick mist below. The left flank met the right flank stock dab in the middle. With zero visibility, each flank thought they were fighting the Zonks but were instead fighting themselves. Gunfire and explosions erupted from this cloud of vapor. The Major, sensing victory, turned his center mass of thugs around and moved back up the valley to finish off the Zonks. In so doing, however, he finished off his own men.

The next morning, Mitch and Bootes went to the creek to do some fishing. A breeze tumbled down the peaks above and pushed out the battle smoke. The carnage below was great. Of the fifty-five initial combatants, only eighteen lived to tell the tale. Scarred and bruised they retreated into their cars below. The Major, impaled on a bayonet, had the strength to strangle the life out of the Zonk he thought he found. His face was in the creek with his megaphone for a hat. "And to think, I didn't have to blast anyone," grinned Titus.

Maggots Everywhere

By Maahir Ghazi

Translated from Kurdish by Zackary Maxwell

The Parthenon of Idiocy

"Secretly they belch out their blasphemous fabrications. Humans are such invertebrates. Why is it only a fraction of us can see through this debris?" — Eni to Zade
"We are Zonks." — Zade's reply

"The tomato is God's gift to a garden. With the right soil and acidity, it is tart, juicy and vibrant. The cucumber is, at best, a bit puckish but could easily be reeled in with a shave or, at best, pickled in a jar. Now the zucchini appears a tame animal but only at first. If you turn your back on this beast, she will raise her head and bloat to a log that you will just have to ingest in many forms. Carrots are docile wimps, and fed the correct minerals, they will be as sweet as candy. Onions! It's Walla Walla sweets for me. And grown correctly they are not hot in sensation but actually are sweet. Garlic, leave them alone. They don't like attention. Nor do potatoes. Pole beans and Chinese snap peas finish off the lot but just ignore them with impudence. They enjoy the callus abuse." Chester was giving this lecture with a bunch of new students to The Estate in the new expansive garden.

Cloise Dart was a fresh recruit. Average size for her age of eight. Long glistening dark hair rolled down her neck to the center of her back. She never wore a ponytail. The tumble of hair created a black waterfall over her shoulders. She was very happy here. But she was also very blind. Born with an ocular enhancement, she was blessed to not see anything. She 'felt' everything. Sensory expansion made her taste, touch, smell, sound and perception very astute. Cloise would make a high-toned click in her throat that would reverberate off surrounding near objects and like a porpoise through the deep sea, she would navigate her field of sound through the air. "In time you will get used to it," she cheerfully said to Chester. He stared blankly into her blank eyes. No focus but there was recognition. Chester liked this child.

The goat, with eyes closed, clucked and chirped to his spleen's desire but always ended up bonking his head with some solid structure. A fence post, a wall, several boulders and finally a pond. He surfaced to a laughing girl, "You need to listen, silly. It is all there in the sound." He submerged and laughed in bubbles under water.

Ms. Dart wanted to be a horticulturist and with her positive attitude, the Zonks let her soul plant her seed into the soil. And she did. Cloise Dart became the head gardener for The Estate.

As nature tends to balance all things, if something is taken away, then something else is returned. Ms. Dart just did not know what that 'something' would become. Then, quite extraordinarily, a chance occurrence provided the opportunity to raise its noble head above the profound dirt. On a misty Spring morning, alone in the garden, Cloise was planting the early year crops. She was disturbed by a mingling sensation in her lower intestinal tract. Could it have been Chester's out of season shrimp scampi? Or Kassandra's clandestine raid on the Silk Barn to harvest Bombyx mori moths and make them into that quiche? There was a grumble and a slight spurt. She panicked, raised up her dress and dolloped a marble size ball of fecal matter into a hole that she recently dug containing three corn seeds. Several grumbles and spurts later she filled up all the holes containing seeds for this year's novel crops. With now light and variable winds in her colon, she curtsied to her garden and left. Clicking and clucking she went back to her studies.

Within a month, with much sunshine, pure water and great gardening care, the crops sprouted. Days from their first exposure to the surface, they grew to enormous heights. It was as if some super vitamin had been introduced to these seeds. Soon after another month, the garden was overflowing with produce. The Zonks were amazed that through Ms. Dart's diligence, they had a bounty twenty times that of any previous year. And what was most curious, was that when Cloise walked through the garden to greet her massive plants, they would appear to follow her slowly through her stroll. She clicked and clucked and bent down to pet her corn, whispering into each leaf something no one else could hear. The garlic reached out to tickle her leg. The cucumbers made perverse suggestions and she locked her kneecaps to prevent entry. The tomatoes would unnaturally swell with redness and purposely brush her nipples as she passed. The Chinese snap peas would feign indifference upon her passing, but would quickly plunge lustfully and twine their vines in her dress lace near her buttock and pinch. "You shits," she would say with a giggle. Chester, on inspection, noted that when the fruit of these plants was harvested, they didn't die. They just produced another fruit in its place. A perpetual garden with perpetual fruits. It was astonishing.

The Zonks were baffled and bafflement ate at their minds like ants on a slice of a cool strawberry on a hot day on a sidewalk in Denton, Texas. In a query with Ms. Dart, they gleaned that her fecal matter could possibly lead to this perplexing occurrence. Opeia asked for a sample and received a large jar full of brown marbles. Analysis indicated that a messenger RNA modification through this waste was inoculated into each plant that gave it added growth, increased productivity, reproducibility and, interestingly, a possible personality. Yes, a plant with a possible conscience. How did a blind orphan girl from Topeka, Kansas, obtain such an ability? Chester did comment that her stools were nearly identical to his. His were like a spilled bag of rusty wet ball bearings. The Zonks told him in unison, "Chester, shut up!"

The only serious regrettable outcome was that all of these luscious fruits tasted like shit. Nature has its limitations and if you increased one essence then another item needed reduction. In this case it was productivity and taste respectively. But the Zonks, being Zonks, did not necessarily identify that taste aspect as a loss but a possible gain. It was all how the populace defined taste. And taste was subjective. Subjectivity could be manipulated. It was all in a frame of mind and that mind could be altered with marketing.

"Besides," stated Cloise. "I have given these organisms a conscience and in so doing they are now perennial. They are living and they are my friends. They might wither in the cold but they will not die. Not in my care. They are my children." And these children prospered. The Zonks now had mounds of fresh fruits so they needed to get this harvest out to market. But how?

Opeia said the scientific analysis showed that all the produce had high contents of vitamins with antioxidants, sugars and fiber. Despite the bad taste, this produce was very healthy to eat. Eni suggested fermentation. "We could make wine, beer and liquor from this stuff,"

Marvin said. "What we need is an overwhelming online marketing campaign and inundate the web with Zonk Fruits and Vegetables! Healthier and more heart happy than any produce ever!" The business was on.

A large shed was built just south of the Silk Barn. This shed was divided up into a distillery, a winery and a small brewery. The distillery produced Zonk Vonk, a pure grain alcohol that tasted like elephant excrement. A case of this liquid was sent up to The Truck Stop and Titus concurred. Zonk Wonk was a heavy red wine loaded with tannins that had hints of cinnamon, coriander and bat guano. Then there was the Zonk Bonk, an IPA craft beer that could easily take paint off of a 1940 Buick, with notes of aspen bark, chain saw lubricant and Arctic tern poop.

Marvin staged 'tastings' that he named exotically as Chateau de Noodle's Wine Extravaganza, Chester's National Beer Rally and Bulgakov's Spirit Festival. All were held in the back of the Warped Noodle and all patrons of Ward One and Two were invited to participate. The inmates all ingested these fluids to much grief. They gagged and threw up. But a quick clearing of the palate with Chester's Russian blintzes with mixed berry sauce and the incarcerated smiled and voted five out of four thumbs up on all entries. The press took note. The products, five thumbs up printed on the labels, were all sold out in just a few days.

Immediately, doctors throughout the US were proclaiming the instant health benefits from consuming these Zonk fluids. Weight loss was prompt. Margot Miller of 325 Salina Dr. in Grubner, California, went from four hundred and eighty pounds down to eighty pounds just by inhalation alone using a glass of Zonk Vonk. The word was out. The Zonks, giddy, just made the nation love the taste and smell of shit. And it sold volumes.

Opeia, always the scientist, never left her lab. She used more of Ms. Dart's moist marbles to do further studies. Perhaps, just perhaps, with the positive results in plants, that human inoculation could possibly make that individual more animate, and better yet, instill a conscience. But how would you get humans to eat excrement? Even if it was for their own good? "Chocolate!" said Chester. And chocolate it was. A seventy percent cocoa mix with heavy cream and light sucrose percolated in

Chester's kitchen. Down went the marbles and out came balls of confectionery. A smattering of powdered sugar and it was bonbons for the elite. And the elite would be those people without a conscience on Ward Three.

After dinner that night, every person on Ward Three was to have dessert. Not their usual colorful gelatinous cubes but Zonk Bonbons. A chaser of a shot of Zonk Vonk would be offered. Not uncharacteristically, the men, being too macho to gag, consumed the entire morsel without complaint. The females, devoted, knew Christ was with them during this journey but made faces of disgust. The warm glow of the Lord on imbibing the Zonk fluid made them calmly swallow the mush. A rosy hue permeated their beings. But what the Zonks did not understand was that you can't jumpstart a dinosaur into a realization of reality without a consequence. This consequence was rage. How would anyone like to know that their entire life was shallow and fed by greed, irrationality and lies? And know for a fact that this was absolutely wrong. The onslaught of this concept overloaded their minds with the understanding that they were nothing but parasites feeding on the masses. Not the symbiotic beneficial bugs that take and give, but the disastrous feeders that bleed the national body to death. They now urgently loathed themselves and all people that brought this knowledge to them. Ward Three rushed the guards with a tsunami pulse of hate. With much scuffling, two insane Republicans filled with rage found an exit and they wanted to kill anyone. They jumped the fence in the back of the Noodle and made their way through the dark to the back Estate's southern fence. They stopped. In the still of the night, they silently heard the sounds of a bizarre chicken. A large chicken. It clicked and clucked its way through the garden. In the light of the moon, they saw the chicken caressing the garden plants. Lude things were occurring with the cucumbers. The Republicans were going to kill this chicken. They had to. The two attacked this clucking being but the garden came alive and the vines and the corn, tomatoes, pole beans and even one garlic plant severed their necks rapidly. Blood oozed from their carcasses. Blood that was full of iron and minerals. The plants, using osmosis, enjoyed it all. Cloise Dart sighed in relief since she was pleasantly enjoying a randy zucchini.

And Pteranodons Do Fly

*"I think flight is a secret plonk in our family blood. Some of us just love
to get off of the ground and view the people below as what they are.
Mindless ants!" — Cygnus*

Zot was on top of The Truck Stop. He was looking at the Andromeda
Galaxy. It was beautiful. He took many pictures with many filters to
outline an amazing portrait that was so vibrant even a human, passing by
in a spacecraft, could not discern. That is because cameras can 'see' at
wavelengths that we cannot. Zot knew that Andromeda, in four and a half
billion years, will collide with The Milky Way. It will form a massive
new elliptical galaxy. Humans, thought Zot, will all be dead by then and
some other being, if they are intelligent enough, would have to rename
it. It would most likely appear as a potato. But potatoes would most
probably not be around then either so some alien will probably call it Irk
since Irks on Teegarden B look just like a potato. "Our sun will run out
of fuel at this time too," he said to himself. "It will swell up and burn the
atmosphere off of Earth and toast everything to a cinder. And the
Universe will laugh, dance and rejoice since the madhouse will have
burnt down and taken with it the scourge of mankind." He sighed. "Then
another planet will evolve, another being just as idiotic as a human, and
it will all begin all over again. Again, and again."

"Sounds depressing," said a rough noise behind him. Zot turned
around to see Titus. "But it is not. It is funny in its absurdity and
predictability. The Universe obviously needs predictable absurdity." Zot
nodded.

The discord sounds of hammering, sawing and welding revealed
themselves early in the morning. This repetitive melody emanated from
the lab of Cygnus. She was building a very large glider that looked like
a Pteranodon. "The idea just popped into my head," she said to Bootes.

"Yeah, well sometimes I think about shooting myself, but I don't do it!" she replied. Feeling that hostility would not lead to anything creative, Cyg smiled and continued to work.

The concept might have benefited with better engineering, but be that as it may, out in the back of The Truck Stop, with a twenty-one-foot wingspan married to a deep airfoil camber with a dual tail was the glider. The wings folded up for transport. Below were a cradle and a harness for the pilot. Direction could be controlled by pulling on left and right metal cords that manipulated slight variances in the tips of the wings. Cygnus' helmet was constructed with a large fin in the back and this acted as a rudder during flight.

Beaufort and Castor Nolan were on a summer vacation from Cannonville, Utah. Even though Utah had the mountain vistas, the colorful canyons and bountiful carcasses of fine wild animals, it just didn't have a bison. The Nolan brothers, sons of a serious drunk but great storyteller, Farmer Nolan, paid fifty-thousand dollars to Taylor's Ranch to 'accidently' let out two bison from his Buffalo Ranch in southern Colorado. "How would you find them?" said a concerned Taylor on the phone.

"Don't worry. We Nolans can sniff a mouse fart in a hurricane." And apparently, they could. The brothers showed up in Salida, Colorado, on a very warm early summer day. Their sniffers indicated that the bison were most probably south of Methodist Mountain. The next morning, Sunday, mouths laced with fumes of mescal, and worms digested, the Nolans set out to be the master hunters that they were. They were proud NRA members since birth. They were Republicans, but they didn't really know why. Probably because their father was one.

Cygnus, Zot and Bootes laboriously hauled the glider up the slope. It wasn't the weight, since Cyg used a strong lightweight metal called Chromoly. The fabric was just parachute silk painted dark like a Pteranodon. It was the girth of the mess that had to be dragged up the incline through trees and brambles. Around stumps and roots. "Careful, careful. Don't tear the silk," Cyg warned.

"Bitch," whispered Bootes. "All this for flight." Sweating, they made the summit and locked in the wings. Donning her finned helmet, she strapped herself into the harness. She toggled the metal left and right cords for wing deflection. She attached last minute ideas that were hollow rods that connected her heels to the two 'feet' of the flying lizard's tail. This would hopefully assist in lift. "You are a shit, you know!" said Bootes when she kissed her.

"And you, Mom, are a cunt." Cyg smiled. Zot and Bootes easily lifted her and her craft off the ground. They pointed her west toward the sun to take advantage of the young thermal air from below. And off she went.

Beaufort and Castor were defecating. Probably as a result of the spiced chili that they consumed the night before at May's Café. Like most things in life, the entry is much more enjoyable than the exit. They were grunting and groaning under a pine tree. A shadow appeared and quickly went away. Perhaps, a low flying airplane but there was no engine noise. It was all quiet except for a mild breeze through the pines. That meandering breeze brought the stench from Castor's delivery to Beaufort and vice versa. "Damn, bro, bury that thing!" said Castor.

"Fuck you," gritted Beaufort. The passing of the stools was painful.

Out on the clearing the large shadow appeared again. It faded again suddenly across the grass. "What the hell?" said Castor.

"Yup," retorted Beaufort. They staggered out in the field. Their pants were still around their ankles. They looked up and there before their own disbelieving eyes was a colossal bird swooping down upon them.

Castor, bringing up his gun to his shoulder, stuttered, "It's the Dixie Condor!"

Beaufort levelled his rifle up to say, "We will be rich!" And they fired. They continued to fire until all their bullets were expended.

Cyg was in heaven. She had never felt so free. Light as a feather and floating over the trees. She spired back over the peak to see Zot and Bootes waving at her. Down the mountain over an open field, she flew. Banking back and diving down again. She saw two male humans appear in the middle of the clearing. Their pants were down to their ankles. "Poor gays. They just can't find a place to make love!" she yelled. The noise of the wind through her helmet was deafening. Cyg banked the bird again. The two men appeared to be doing something with large sticks pointed at her.

She felt a drag on her craft. Something was wrong. Then another and another. Cyg checked her lines and they were functioning. Something else was amiss. The bird was descending too rapidly. Pulling the cords, Zonk attempted to level off the craft into the clearing. The two men just stood there and did not move. The glider came down with a rush and she pushed with all of her leg strength on the rods connected to the tail. This pulled the Pteranodon up from an imminent crash but it also promptly decapitated the two men. "Fuck!" she yelled.

Luckily, the warm morning created a gust of thermals and she gained altitude. She swiftly steered the craft over the mountain and headed back home to The Truck Stop. But just over the back of the gas station building, the wings collapsed and she sank into the canvas tent of Monk Shin's Sunday sermon. Dangling from high up above, Cyg looked down. The Monk was pissed. The congregation all howled, "An Angel from God has appeared!" Cyg lost bladder control.

"Holy ointment!" bellowed someone below. And they all began to bathe in the falling yellow liquid. Cyg looked at Monk Shin with eyes that pleaded forgiveness.

The Nolan brothers' sniffers must have been off that day. The bison didn't go north, but south to New Mexico. They were found, allegedly, near Taos, weeks later in a field.

Lackadaisical Lumberjacks Create Hazards

"I am full of whimsy." — Chester
"Then bear down and grunt." — Replied Cloise

Ms Dart and the Goat were rolling around in the dirt in the garden. The plants were spastically following their every move. She felt his face. "Why touch me?" Chester said.

"Sincerity," Ms Dart prompted.

"I am being real," the Goat curiously thought.

"What is real?" said Cloise. They had both just taken a handful of caps of liberty and were gradually falling down a foam paisley-covered staircase into a dense blue forest.

The forest wasn't actually blue. It came from a dim light behind the trees that made the timber appear blue. "You are blind," said a tree to the Zucchini.

"Yes, but I have vision in sound," acknowledged the dark green fruit.

"And you, Potato, do you like being a tuber?" The Potato opened up its golden eyes to focus on the blue-hued tree. "I don't like this dream. Can we have a re-boot?" the Potato queried.

"No!" the forest empathically stated.

The Potato and the Zucchini waded through the forest and brambles, hand in hand, to the edge of a steep cliff. A voracious vegetarian appeared in the ferns. Its eyes glowed with lust and hunger. There was no escape. Only death. But the vegetarian lurched forward and the tuber and fruit fell from the cliff. It was the only way out. Descending, the Potato and Zucchini reached out and grabbed a lonely protruding vine. This halted their fall. They laughed but looked below. Down at the bottom of the cliff was another vegetarian. It was looking up and licking its lips. They could not go up and they were destined by gravity to go down. Both up and down were fatal. The Zucchini realized that the vine they were clutching onto was a large strawberry plant. And there, right there, was a ripe opulent red fruit. The Potato picked it off. He took a small bite. He put the rest into the open mouth of the Zucchini. They chewed until they cried. It was the best and sweetest fruit they had ever tasted.

The bright pulses of chainsaws brought them back to the blue forest. The trees were in pain and lamenting. The lumberjacks told the Zucchini and the Potato that demand for toilet paper was up. Money was to be made. "Stand aside!" yelled the manager. They did not move. The Potato was churned into a giant latke and the Zucchini was serrated into a moist bread concoction.

"I told you I did not like this dream," said the tuber as he was eviscerated.

The Mother's Movement of The Bowels

"The dark green poop is the dessert." — Cygnus exhaled

The light large manicotti pasta noodle stuffed with cheese emerged to a gasping existence. She took a lung full of air and she began to cry. Reality was just too much. It is with most humans. From a warm and stable environment to abruptly enter the frigid arms of Earth and they greet you with a slap on the behind. Tears and yelling follow. That is the beginning. And that is the best that life gets unless you are a conservative Republican who steals from the sodden waifs that intentionally drown in lies. They harvest their produce to enhance their wealth and their golden piss will trickle down to feed the masses.

The baby was called Lyra Zonk. She was pug disgusting in a visual sense but aren't they all? Zonk loins produced a luscious entity. It was a girl Zonk from Zot and Cygnus to the world. "Now to work!" hollered Cyg. And off they went.

The Passing of The Pomegranates

"Pompous paisley porcupines mashed in a jar all squirming to be set free. But the lid was on just too tight, so they all were pickled in their pee." — Chester singing to his art class

The Zonks had a meeting at The Estate. The school's curriculum needed revamping. Philosophy, chemistry, mathematics, computer software development and engineering were all good and great, but The Estate was just weak in some areas. So the Zonks agreed to build a culinary school and adjacent to that would be a large room with a glass ceiling for the new art class. "I would like to teach the cooking classes," Chester announced.

"We thought you'd say that," Eni snickered. "But, no. You are going to teach the art class." Chester was astonished. His face made such a frown that they all laughed.

"I know nothing of art," he pleaded.

"And that might be to your advantage," said Opiea.

Months went by and all was prepared. Since Eni had a background in chemistry, and cooking was basically chemistry, she would teach the culinary science courses. The building, full of the finest stoves, ovens, cookware, freezers and cupboards was all shiny stainless steel. All ingredients, from around the world, were stocked to supply the students with any global recipe they could possibly mentally muster. "So, what would you all like to cook for our first class?" Eni smiled.

"Eggs and bacon!" was the predominate response. Everyone nodded their heads but one.

"Chicken tikka masala with garlic naan," said Cloise.

"Masala it is." And Eni pulled out an Indian cookbook and they all gathered around.

The new art class building was amazing. Every stool had an easel. The walls were shelved with numerous paints, brushes, colored powders, resins and oils. Canvases of all sizes were in the back against the wall.

Large pads of think white paper were in stacks on the floor. The center lectern was elevated and off to the side of a large wooden platform in the middle of the room. All the stools and easels were surrounding the platform like American Indians surrounding a wagon train of intrusive settlers. The wagon train was Chester. He was nervous. Opiea visited the class that afternoon and what she saw was mild chaos that resulted in a multicolored goat and what appeared to be finger painting. She pulled Chester to the side. "Try still life objects."

Ms Dart came in the next day to the art class, clicking and clucking. She wanted to assist Chester any way she could. In her arms she carried a basket of freshly plucked pomegranates from her garden. She went from stool to stool and gave each student a pinkish fruit. "With pencil and paper pad only, draw this fruit as best you can," she announced. Then Ms Dart sat down on a stool in front of a pad of paper on an easel and she began drawing.

After over an hour, Chester said, "Pencils down." He began to parade around the area with his grunts of 'oohs' and 'aaahs' as he reviewed the students' work. Then at last, not expecting much, he came upon Cloise's drawing. There on the paper was an absolutely exact replica of a pomegranate. So vibrant in black and gray hues you could pull it off the paper and eat it. "Shit," he said.

Ms Dart looked up and said, "Can we now do nudes?" The class laughed.

Setting Bounds with No Boundaries

"I didn't think motherhood would be like this. This is far more challenging than I imagined." — Cygnus to Bootes

The new Zonk was much more than a handful, since mutations are what they are, and Lyra, like Zot, could toddle through anything. If she didn't want to be held, she simply disappeared out of their arms and on the floor she appeared. So, even if you could catch her, it wouldn't be for long. And what would be the point? She would just scurry through the walls to the kitchen through the refrigerator to get her milk bottle. Zot would find her sometime later curled up by Titus to get warm or nestled in the bosom of Victoria, as her grandmother would exhale a cloud of burnt sativa. So Cyg made Zot the disciplinarian. "You and you alone will have to set Lyra's boundaries!" Zot, not given to be any task master, was mostly a rule breaker too, so he let little Lyra generally do whatever she wanted. She always showed up somewhere.

Rumors are most usually more interesting than reality. They have always been. The rumor that the Zonks were incredibly wealthy was relative to the amount they paid out for most of their bizarre ideas and how successful those ideas became. So it was a roller coaster of failures and triumphs. But, honestly, compared to most people, yeah, the Zonks were fabulously affluent. They just did not act or look like it. And rumor had it, the Zonks kept all this money in the catacombs beneath The Truck Stop.

Sergeant York was literally a sergeant in the Marines. At one time, he was quite fit and led an explosive team into various battles in Iraq and Afghanistan. He was very good but ridiculously insubordinate and for every stripe he earned, one would eventually be taken away due to his complete inability to shut the hell up. He lived impoverished up on a dry hill seventeen miles north of Westcliffe, Colorado. His abode was a lavish dilapidated trailer complete with exterior exposed fiberglass insulation, bent aluminum frame, flat tires and a hose attached to a red pump that was used for a shower and often for potable water—if the well wasn't dry. York cried when he was melancholy and he was often melancholy when he either listened or read anything negative about the US Dictator. "This is the greatest, most winning country ever, thanks to this guy." The sergeant was not correct about many things and this was one of them. He wanted to win and to win was to believe in the almighty presence of this US Dictator.

Alone at night behind his shanty, around a roaring fire, he was gingerly getting lit on a cheap beverage loaded with ethanol. Sitting on a large chunk of feldspar and quartz, the sergeant gazed into the flame. He just stared and stared at the licking tongues of Satan. The tongues were speaking to him. At least he thought they were speaking to him. "Be you," spoke a voice coming from the fire.

"What?" York groped for clarity.

"Beeee yooouu!" it said.

"Be me? Of course I am fucking me."

"No, no, nooooo. Be the failure that you were meant to be," said the voice. Sergeant York stood up abruptly and ran around the other side of the fire. There on the ground was sitting a very old bald man covered in rags with eyes that looked like hardboiled eggs. He was holding a wooden fishing pole.

"You ass! You scared the crap out of me!" The old man slowly got up and shuffled into the darkness.

"Failure, shit. What I need is a success—and now." So the Sargent stewed, planned and drank copious amounts of Fizz Walter's 100% grain alcohol. The plan was simple because that is all he could possibly understand. His plan was to break into the catacombs of The Truck Stop and steal all the money from those liberal lecherous ludicrous bastards, and put it to work making this great country white and Christian again.

The sergeant was no fool. His time in the military, if anything, taught him idiocy and much patience. The latter seemingly lead to the former. He didn't know why. York staked out The Truck Stop. He took notes on the Zonks' arrivals and exits. He made timetables of their precise moves and activities. What frustrated him the most was that the Zonks' movements were entirely random. No patterns whatsoever. So late one night, he looked at his reflection in the mirror of his disintegrated Willy's

Jeep with the neon red glow of a restaurant sign in the background and said, "Fuck it." And he did.

The timing was coincidental. Most probably due to Roger messing around with the Zonks' third dimensional medium. Bootes and Titus were out hunting. They were told two bison from Taylor's Buffalo Ranch escaped and they needed trackers to find them and bring them back in. "Screw that!" said Bootes. Titus snickered. "Bison is such a good meat. Why waste it?" They headed off in the maintenance van south down the valley. Cygnus and Zot were rocking back and forth in their hammock. Monk Shin was in Bootes' lab rolled tight like a burrito in a new bearskin rug. Albert and Veronica were delightfully grabbing their loins and copulating.

"Do you know that since God is love, then I just made God to you?" Victoria muttered.

"Shit, girl, you are so profound," licked Albert on her lips. Lyra was nowhere to be found.

"She'll show up. She always does," whispered Zot to a concerned Cyg. Her breasts hurt and milk was seeping out. "Why waste a good thing?" And Zot went to work.

York went to work too. Like the stealth soldier he was, he breeched the back door of The Truck Stop. The first door to his left—and he was very lucky—was the door to the basement. The Sergeant, flashlight in one hand and a Colt 45 in the other—no, not the gun but the malt beer—slithered down the stairs into vast tunnels. Hours later, he discovered no money. No hidden anything. Just shovels, rope, paint cans, archives of Zonk paperwork and a rusted bazooka. Tunnel after tunnel he scoured. And then, at the end of a long passage there was an iron door. The Sergeant cranked on the handle and it easily opened with a long laborious creak. There, from his flashlight beam, was a large heavy metal safe. York was a demolition man. He brought with him a pound of plastic explosive and a detonator. He was a professional. But before the mess, York instinctively pulled on the handle of the safe and it gradually opened. In the feeble light, he gazed on an empty safe. All that was there was a small baby drinking ice cold milk from a baby bottle. In her other hand was a seven-inch knife that Lyra had 'borrowed' from Monk Shin's kitchen. Instantly, Lyra plunged the knife into the throat of Sergeant

York. He grabbed his spurting neck, yelled, "Jesus!" and staggered backward, tripping over several boxes. The flashlight fell on the floor and in its light dancing on the walls there was a hint of a baby disappearing through the safe and into the walls of the catacombs. Lyra showed up after all. She always did.

Chester's Visible Ebullience

"It has literally been a lifetime ago, but the affliction has persevered."
— Chester's apology

Eni's cooking class was slogging ahead with minor successes and mostly overly brazened catastrophes. One glaring wonder blip on the culinary radar was Ms. Dart's al dente spring pasta with sautéed morels in heavy butter and morel cream sauce with fresh ground garlic, oregano and cracked pepper. Without assistance from anyone, she created this masterpiece. All applauded and she bowed graciously to the sound, and grabbed her drawing pad and waltzed and clucked to her art class.

"Well, class," hawed Chester. "Cloise brought up an idea that is pertinent for all art students. We must uncover the musculature of the physique, the forms and shades of the body, the head, neck, arms and the legs. We asked the staff and gallant Ms. Vaya Halabjaee, a serious painter in her own right, has agreed to be your nude model for today." A hand went up near the back of the class.

"But why her?" said a voice.

"Because she said yes," Chester admonished. "But, sir, you are already nude. Why not stand proudly on the platform yourself and be drawn as the courageous being that you are?" Chester tightened his pupils to focus on the voice. It was Cloise Dart. "Damn," he thought. But his ego just would not let this idea go. He was courageous. A painting might come out of this and be placed above the mantle in The Estate. People would come years later and gaze upon this magnificent ibex and know he was an outstanding figure of the Zonk clan. Chester would be remembered.

"Ah, okay." he stuttered.

The ibex was an elegant beast. Small, but his gigantic horns and tight-muscled torso plainly announced strength. He took to the platform. The students began painting, and some drawing. Chester rapidly discovered how difficult it was to stay stock still for such a time. While he was lamenting his decision, small hands were feeling his body. They were the hands of Ms Dart.

Chester stood rigid. "I am a professional. I am a professional. I can do this," he thought. She felt all over his body from his tail, tummy, back, neck and then his face. The goat smiled. He knew she could not see that smile but she could feel it and she did. Cloise smiled too. Then, instantly, Chester smelled the enticing aroma of morels that lingered on her hands and fingers. He snorted to get this odor from his nostrils. He began to choke and cough. "Sorry," he said to the class. The goat felt a stimulating experience arising from below. There was a large noticeable bloat and an expansive desire promoted itself. Chester the goat, like the pig, loved morels and it showed itself in a profound way. "I am a professional. I am a professional. I can do this!" he said aloud to no one in particular. Cloise's clucking and clicking produced a big smile. Her sonic vision ascertained a large growing mass. She did not know about the morel and Chester issue. She thought it was her touch alone. She touched the protrusion. Chester passed out.

Roger and Martha, on Barnard Star B, were laughing so hard they too almost passed out. "Martha, it is you that is cruel," Roger sputtered.

"I couldn't help it. I couldn't. It was such a Chester thing. It had to be preserved."

The Nautical Notables on Lake Zonk

"It was a dark and stormy night." — Captain Pitt
"Shut the hell up!" — Titus

One long weary cold night, during Hanukkah, the Zonks, non-religious, lit the standard menorah. It was on a shelf above a bronze monkey with a crown in a Queen's chair in the back. It was also cold. The central fire pit was ablaze and that helped a tad. Titus was glowing warm and most people just snuggled against his body. He loved the attention.

Blasting from an open door came a barrage of snow, wind and Captain Pitt. He stood in front of the small crowd, pulled himself erect, solid and tall with his skipper's hat tilted to one side, saluted and promptly keeled over into a pile of snow and dust. His Meerschaum pipe was still smoldering and hanging from his lips.

"Check. One, two. One, two, three. Are we there yet? Please, somebody?" announced a dry voice.

"I am here," the egg sang. And he was. Fallopian tube communication would be years away, but Dr. Green thought it was about time to try.

"Hello, young ruffian," the Doctor announced through the speakerphone.

"I love you," the egg said, hesitating over each word. Captain Don Pitt was in the egg. And because he was in charge, he was dynamic. He sailed down the tube, fighting stiff currents and out he popped into a cavern, floating. Eventually, the Captain lodged onto the wall of this dark place and there he stayed for several months. Dr. Green spoke to the Captain at various times, always after some annoying undulation, and they got to know each other quite well.

The Captain did not want to come out into the world. He was a captain and captains needed to be in fluid. He was in fluid. Warm humming fluid. And he had this friend he could occasionally talk to named Dr. Green. But out he came. He was pissed. But he came out.

There was a man there named Mr. Pitt. The Captain didn't recognize his voice but the voice stated clearly that Mr. Pitt was his father. The baby's eyes opened wide. There was Dr. Green behind Mr. Pitt. Dr. Green was smiling. The Captain was jolted by a spank to his buttock cheek.

"Mom? Were you banging Dr. Green during office visits when you were pregnant?"

"Yes, son," she smiled, intoxicated. "And he would always talk to you afterward on a tiny megaphone through my vaginal opening." "Ahhhhhhh ..."

"Ahhhhhhh!" said Captain Pitt, awakening. There was a small green glowing elephant stomping on his chest. He was covered in an enormous amount of melting dandruff. Someone was polite enough to drag him over to the firepit.

"Who the hell are you?" penetrated the green elephant.

"Why, I am Captain Pitt at your service, sir!" said the tall man on the floor. His lanky frame spangled around and stood up. He gathered his hat and pipe and sat down in front of the fire. His legs didn't appear to hold enough muscle to keep up such a figure. But they did.

"So, Captain. What are you the captain of?" Zot enquired as he pulled up a chair. It was a droll evening and there really was nothing else better to do so the Zonks gathered around to hear a tall tale from a tall sailor. Except for Titus. The sailor man just stole his social vibe and he went to crawl under a faux Navajo rug.

"Laka Vette was a sweet bird," he said, not quite sober but certainly not ethanol related. "She was my fish, you see." They didn't and he saw that on their faces. "She was my ship." And the Zonks all sardonically raised their eyebrows and nodded.

"And where is this ship?" Zot pondered aloud.

"She is a scrap heap in Dandong, China. They took her away from me while I and my crew were politely pilfering indiscriminate vessels throughout the China Sea. You see, China had an issue with pilfering and I swear to God I have read all the regulations and I have never come across anything negative about pilfering. Nothing!" The Captain's face was in anguish. "They took us." Now crying. "They took us and did things to us." He paused. "They made our testicles radioactive!" The Zonks sighed.

Titus farted and under the rug quietly said, "I know the feeling."

Captain Pitt became a common feature at The Truck Stop. When he was not sleeping in his car outside, he was wandering around the bookstore or bothering Monk Shin and Albert for food. When an early spring melted the mountain trails, the Zonks had a surprise for the Captain. Up past the Falls of Atlantis, where there still was a bronze plaque dedicated to a once frozen Manny, there was a lake. It was not large but Bootes convinced US Fish and Wildlife to stock the water here every year with trout. And they did. Years ago, the Zonks came here to camp. It didn't have a name so they called it Zonk Lake. But, in point of fact, it did have a name and it was called Bear Lake back in 1859. Apparently, a trapper, Frederick Pu, saw a bear there having intimate relations with a hollowed knot on a tree stump. The author of this book was that bear. But since the lake name wasn't listed anywhere except in an old book on a shelf in the basement of a cement building in Denver, it didn't matter. It was Zonk Lake.

On Zonk Lake, the Zonks built a tiny replica of a Viking long ship compete with a sail, rudder and two side oars. On the side of the vessel was painted, 'Laka Vette'. The Captain was in tears. Shaking with excitement, he took the helm on the prow. Titus was in back, steering with the rudder. There was little wind but the sail did fill and it ambled out into the middle of the water. "Port!" he bellowed. But the small craft continued forward. "I said, port, man!" the Captain hollered. Titus, not a nautical beast, turned to the right. "Port, goddamn it all! Port! You fucking runt of a beast!" And then Captain Pitt dissolved in a flash of green sparks.

The Zonks all shrugged their shoulders. "Don't mess with a nuclear pachyderm," said Zot. They all went home. Bratwursts were on the grill.

Who Feeds on the Carrion-Eater's Carrion?

"There is nothing more satisfying than this meat. It is sweet. Did you know that? Sweet to the taste. They live their lives as right-wing conservative bastards. Sour souls among the living. But their meat is wonderfully sweet." — Bob Blakely, Ultra-Warped Noodle, Room Six.

On the back steps of the Blue Ridge mountains, overhanging the valley of Oakridge, Tennessee, was a grandiose wood cabin about the size of a single car garage. Seven people lived in there. The smell was something ferocious. Like an impacted tampon after several weeks or phenomenally good cheese. Most visitors thought they had walked into Hell. Montgomery Blakely thought this was Heaven. Not only was it his Heaven but it was his home and the six other inhabitants were his brothers and sisters. Being the eldest, Montgomery had to make something out of himself but not being schooled, his options were somewhat limited so he became a chiropractor. Dr. Monty Blakely had arrived.

No one in Tater Valley knew what a chiropractor was but they did know what a doctor was supposed to be and Dr. Blakely did not quite fit that description. His only tool of the trade was a large club that he had fashioned out of a branch of hickory. When he was called upon for a service, no matter what the complaint, he would say in his deep booming baritone, "Where does it hurt?" And the patient would point to a knee or shoulder or foot or any part of the body and Dr. Blakely would wield his club and fiercely bring it down directly on that spot. The resulting pain would be so great that any previous pain, and with it the complaint, disappeared. It was a miracle. Although the illnesses in the valley increased during the Doctor's tenure there, complaints were completely eradicated. Feeling his job was complete and his methods were successful, he moved on to another valley to apply his trade.

Valley after valley he whacked his way through the mountains of Tennessee. After some time, rumors spread and he was not able to find even one measly grievance. "I am just too damn good at what I do!" he exclaimed and decided to settle down and raise a family in a small town called Rugby. He found an old widow with no teeth that did some amazing things with her gums that, Dr. Blakely suspected, her father had taught her when she was young. They married and had one child. They called him Bob, since it was something simple; it was also a palindrome and upside down it spelled 'pop' so, the mountain folk way of thinking was, he might be a good father. Bob did not turn out to even be a father. He became a murderer. It was cheaper.

Dr. Blakely took his lean savings from whacking and he bought house after house. The subprime mortgage rates were incredibly low and realtors were barking to buy more and more and more. And he did. Dr. Blakely was going to be the Rent King of Rugby and he and his family were going to do nothing but live on that rental flow of funds.

Bob was charming. Indeed, one could say he was very charismatic. He obviously did not get this from his over-salivating mother, and the closest thing to charm Dr. Blakely had was his ostentatious bedside manner phrase, "Where does it hurt?" just before causing even more pain. So Bob was convinced he was adopted and his parents, thinking this was amusing, did not dissuade him from such thoughts.

Bob's life was wonderful. Living in the country was pure. He fished and hunted and swam in deep creeks. Even though he was very affable, he rarely socialized and preferred solitude in the forest. And then a crash occurred. Not a physical crash but a virtual one and all the houses his father owned, and still owed hundreds of thousands on, fell in value. Greed was the basic cause. And that greed specifically came from conservatives. Money was far more important than the wellbeing of humans. Wracked with monumental debt, Dr. Blakely fell into a deep dark depression. He didn't move from his dining room chair for days. Attempting to help, his wife brought him his old hickory club. "Perhaps you could go back to whacking?" she slobbered. Sensing an opportunity, she slid below the table, undid his trousers, and began to use her gums.

Staring blankly into space, Dr. Blakely took his club, whispered, "Where does it hurt?" and brought the club violently down on his head.

He careened backward in his chair, with his wife still attached below, and he fell into the shelf behind him. This shelf held up an old, but trustworthy, large RCS Zenith TV, which subsequently fell upon his head and electrocuted them both. Bob, later walking in with a string full of fish, dropped to his knees and wept. Bob went insane.

Wherever greed was, Bob was going to kill it. Whenever money was more important than the life of a human, Bob was going to kill it. But that was just not enough. Bob knew in nature death was just another cycle of life. To really kill something, you needed to render it down to basic matter that only had enough nutrients for bacteria to ingest. You had to consume the kill and relinquish it into a turd. Bob Blakely went on a feeding frenzy.

A month later in New York City, Bob dined with a multitude of bankers. The entrée was always the same. He wasn't discriminating. As long as they were greedy conservatives, that was tasty enough. Nature limits humans from too much excess. It always does. The police eventually visited Bob Blakely for questioning. Being pleasant, he offered them a kidney pie, "Fresh out of the oven with fried onions and brown gravy." Warm to the stomach, the officers could not refuse. Detective Tyson even took the remainder home. On analysis, the kidney in the pie belonged to one missing banker, Carter Morgan. Bob Blakely was interred into the warm cradle of the Ultra-Warped Noodle.

Sailing the Seas of Brie

"Peace is relative. Did you know some soldiers in a war find peace in war since they are not bound by their nagging partners or dealing with bill payments? Peace is everywhere. My peace is alone on the water."
— Lyra Zonk

After the vaporization of Captain Pitt, the Laka Vette was still a viable craft. She was maintained and often used by Zot and Cygnus. Titus would occasionally haul her out on the shore and the Vette would be repainted with wood sealant. Her oak hull would last for years. Lyra, when she was about six, took the helm and daily sailed the lake—when it was not frozen, of course. On summer days, on brisk seas, she sailed back and forth across the lake. She initially was not a natural, but practice does make average, and Lyra did become an average sailor. But average or not, she loved it and it made her happy. "But what am I to do with my Zonk life?" she muttered to a passing trout. He did not answer but flipped up his tail fin in her wake. Perhaps, she thought, to say, 'Piss off!'. Lyra would be a legitimate illusionist since she was the illusion. But exposing her innate abilities and capitalizing on them, did not appeal to her. "What do I love other than sailing?" she enquired to a toad on the shoreline.

"Cheese," said the toad. She stood up hastily, nearly falling out of the boat.

"What?" she replied, incredulously. And out stepped Titus from behind a large tree stump.

"Cheese, I said." And cheese it was.

It made sense. Ever since she could remember she was addicted to whole milk. The fattier the better. But cheese at The Truck Stop was rare. The selection was cheddar in sharp or mild. But she read of countries that had ethereal fare that would melt on touch of tongue but smelled of rotten decaying beaver. Ones that oozed off the plate like molasses in winter but tasted like the buttock of a dying infant with dysentery. Rounds of compressed curds that glop on serration like pus on an itched scab on a wounded soldier, that smelled of gangrene. She wanted all of this. And she was going to put the Zonk name on all her products. Lyra was going to make the best cheese ever.

The Zonks built an addition to Monk Shin's kitchen. This was going to be the Zonk Cheese Factory. The family ordered all known books on possible cheeses throughout history and Lyra got to work.

Her first cheese was complex in its manufacture and flavor. But Zonks loved a challenge. Lyra's initial effort was a large batch round of Serra da Estrela. A Portuguese sheep milk cheese coagulated using Cynara cadunculus thistle. She did not want a runny product so she let it cure for several months in an earthen pot with a bamboo lid. With much fanfare, Monk Shin was chosen by Lyra to expose her first effort. The centenarian shuffled over to the countertop and put his right hand out on a wall to steady himself. With his left hand, he grabbed the pot lid and, with a flourish, pulled it off. And immediately, with a similar augmentation, he staggered back and pitched forward, colliding with the shelving, jolted his entire body twice, and pitched to the floor stone dead. The stench was captivating in its grasp and literally ripped the air from out of the Monk's lungs. Bootes knelt down, and giving what normally would be, Shin's eulogy, said, "Shit happens."

Lyra was found days later by Zot. She was a shivering mess in an underground aquifer three hundred and ninety-five feet below The Truck Stop. In his head lamp he saw a sobbing child. He hugged her. "Time to go home. Besides, and for your information, your cheese goes very well with white port wine and grilled vegetables." Zot walked her through the rocks and the walls and put her to bed. He kissed her on the forehead and said, "What about doing a Munster d'Alsace next time? I understand it smells of rancid male armpits after an Olympic workout." Lyra smiled.

Lady Lydecker and Her Rings of Destiny

"Listen to the metronome. Listen. It is an inflection of your central core. It is the pulse of your heart. Listen. Now look. Open your eyes and see the rings." — Lady Lydecker to Chester.

There was no usual ambulance, police security van or even a strapped down gurney. In came an impeccable waxed white Bentley and it stopped precisely at the foot of the stairs of the Warped Noodle. The staff thought this was a VIP visiting, possibly from Arabia, but the driver got out, elegantly strolled to the passenger door, and out came Lady Lydecker. She was decked out in a tight white leather dress dazzled with platinum ostrich plumes. Her feet were covered in peccary moccasins derived from the Guarani Tribe from Paraguay. Only two pairs were in existence. Lydecker dispatched the other owner by making her swallow the footwear, including the tassels and beads, in one gulp. Accentuated in makeup and donning the headdress of Nefertiti, she sauntered into the entry as though she literally owned the entire place.

She insisted that the entire staff and Zonks bow to her. Which, reluctantly, they did. Escorted into her secure 'villa', she stated that she was not satisfied by the surroundings but was glad, "At least it is white."

Lady Lydecker was the queen of fakes. She was captivating but mentally caustic. She did have a unique talent to mesmerize anyone to do her temporary bidding, including robbery and extortion. She, herself, would not do the crimes but her mentally feeble sods would execute the atrocities and, if caught, would wake up in a jail not knowing why they were there. She was voracious in her appetite for money. The Lady's net worth was over four and a half million dollars, with funds that had no relevant source. Lydecker, aside from her constant need for nicotine, needed only money to live and she would get this through manipulation, and ultimately murder. Real work did not appeal to her.

Young Dorka Lydecker grew up in an impoverished Roma nomadic camp between Pisek and Trebic in Southern Czechia. She was born in a wagon and grew up in that wagon for many years. Back and forth across the country they went entertaining with music and dance for any passing coins that were available. Her mother, a buxom woman, not her breasts but her front teeth, was a poor fortune teller but a great hypnotist and she would paralyze the minds of the unfortunates that ambled into her tent, and they walked out pleased as punch that they just gave every cent that they owned to this kindly old woman. But the victims of this charade often came to their senses, and hence why this caravan of entertainers had to continuously move about.

The youthful Dorka learned all she could from her rabbit-toothed mother. Though she didn't inherit her teeth, she did obtain large protruding mammary glands that she accentuated with the compression of a tight corset. Her mother, always the conniver, thought that a dangling watch on a chain or a jewel on a necklace was just too stale for as illustrious a beauty as Dorka, so the mother pierced her daughter's nipples and inserted rotating silver rings. From a marketing standpoint, this was genius. Dorka, always the opportunist, mesmerized her mother, then the entire tribe, stole all their money and went off to London to become an angler for much bigger fish.

It became all too apparent that skimming money from a wealthy gent was all too easy but her spell was only temporary, and eventually they would catch on. So she started her illicit group of nefarious individuals which she, herself, would hand pick from the slums of the city and induce them with mental paralysis, and have these people do horrible crimes. All for looking at rotating silver rings attached to nipples on enormous glands while a tick tock of a metronome would putter close by. The latter, her addition, to distract momentarily just before she exposed her glands.

The local constables caught a hint of fraud and soon London was just too hot to live in any more. She bought the title of Lady Lydecker and sailed for New York City. Through city after city she expanded her wealth while keeping her fame unnoticed. The Lady remained mostly in extortion and robbery. But she sometimes dabbled in drug trafficking. Murder was an unpleasant by-product of the latter, but she quipped, "Money stained red, can be washed." The most unfortunate side effect of her mind-numbing ability was that it only lasted for approximately three hours. After that, the victim was rendered conscious and remembered nothing of any event. A brilliant detective, Vart Stumpel, from Kansas City, using a data mining process on many different computer servers, nailed Ms. Lydecker to the crimes. The Zonks were wary but did their jobs. Lydecker was received with cool hands into the Noodle.

Multifarious attempts to expose her rings in her 'villa' to orderlies almost succeeded in escape so she was bound, literally, with a brass brassiere with a combination lock that had a code only known to Chester. Chester was sent in to admonish the inmate for such escape attempts. Lady Lydecker was sitting on her bed next to a nightstand that had a large Seth Thomas metronome. It was pumping away a dark marimba tone exactly to the heartbeat of a Pyrenean ibex. She offered Chester a warm chamomile and valerian root herbal tea. Her beauty and the inflection of her voice intoxicated his being. The door was closed and Chester began his reproach for her behavior. Her voice melodiously road up and down like a small vessel in a mild swell. The swell was at the same pulse as the beat of the metronome. Up and down. Up and down. It must have been the tea, he thought. His mind was like an Irish shoreline in winter, spring, summer or fall. Wet and foggy. Lydecker pulled from her pocket a necklace that had a large quartz crystal spinning to and fro. Back and forth it went with the sea. Chester's eyelids were like lead weights and every lurch from the sea swell added to the weight. "I would like to remind you that you can't mesmerize anyone..." He coughed. "Code? What code?" And it ticked and tocked. "Code. Oh, that code," he whimpered. His chin hit his chest. His face was just too heavy. Babbling through gurgles, he told her the code to her brass restraint. She removed her metal brassiere and asked the ibex gently to look into the rings. Round and round they went. His eyes laboriously opened. And then the door swung open wide and the lights flickered.

A fist like a stone of marble, with clicking and clucking sounds, leaped up to land a haymaker on the Lady's chin. She reeled back from the impact, looked directly in the eyes of Cloise and said, "Look into my rings."

Cloise said, "I am blind, you BITCH, and don't fuck with my BOYFRIEND!" And Ms Dart proceeded to beat the literal crap out of Lady Lydecker until she was unconscious. The Lady, lying in a pool of her blood and excrement, twitched in anticipation of another blow, but it did not come. "From now on," she punctuated to Chester. "I will take over this inmate. Understand?" He did.

Smoke'n Ace and Bootes Zonk

"There are times, like these, that require people to step up to the plate. To acknowledge their attributes and find their hidden weaknesses. It is times like these why we are here. Ms. Zonk, draw your gun." — Ace McCandle

Direct from Buna, Texas, came Ace McCandle. His father's real last name was McClod but Ace did not take to that name very much and modified it based on his favorite TV character, Stud McCandle, sheriff of a nondescript western town in a desert. Stud was fast. He was accurate. And he was dumber than a rotted stump in a marsh and that was how Southern Texas liked their portrayals. Stud was a hero.

Ace wanted to be that hero. He wanted to be Stud. Ace had a poster of Stud on his bedroom wall in his parents' 'renovated' double wide. He ejaculated to his poster several times a day. Not because he sexually wanted to be involved with Stud, but because he wanted to just BE him. Simple. Ejaculation meant melding. Swapping fluids. He was just swapping melding fluids with Stud so that he could possibly be him. It really made sense in a South Texas type of mind. Ace bought a gun.

Young McCandle practiced with his revolver every time he could, and over several years, he became thoroughly proficient. He could clear his holster in a blink of an eye and discharge the weapon at any target within fifty yards, and hit it dead center. Every time. Ace joined the police force as a Deputy for Port Neches, Texas, and during his first year alone he shot and killed three people: Amy Wagner, 27, for cussing; Daisy Bunker, 87, for not using the crosswalk; and Nat Vend, 67, for littering. He was brought to trial for excessive force but each verdict exonerated him. Ace's defense was simple. "Come on, Judge! I am Texan!" The juries and the press loved Ace McCandle.

Now, Sheriff McCandle moved to McAllen, since he heard there was a crisis on the border. He looked into the mirror of his decrepit apartment and adjusting the badge on his shirt said, "I'm gonna personally clean up this Tex-Mex shit once and for all." Which meant he was going to kill a bunch of people and use fear and intimidation to create what the Catholic Inquisition called Pious Necessary Rigidity. Apparently, referring to the spines of people when the Inquisition passed through their towns.

Ace was awarded many opportunities to practice with his revolver on moving targets during this time. Of course, none of them were shooting back so it wasn't quite fair, but fair didn't play into the mind of a man who was representing the law. From McAllen, to Laredo, to Eagle Pass to Del Rio the bags of bodies were stacked up like cords of wood. Eventually, the news of this barbarity floated up to The Truck Stop and the Zonks just had to step into the fray. On a slow morning, with only four dead, Sheriff McCandle received a note. It read, 'How about picking on someone your own size? —Bootes Zonk. Noon, Thursday at The Truck Stop parking lot. Poncha Springs, Colorado'. And this was a bit funny, since Bootes stood four feet eight inches tall and Ace was six foot five. But size doesn't necessarily mean height, and in this case, it meant virtual 'balls'.

The Sherriff could not pass up on this exchange since his macho meter was cranked to fifteen on a scale from one to ten. Ace took a well-needed vacation from leading his transient victims during instantly planned bullet trajectory analysis, to meet with destiny in the mountains of Colorado.

Bootes, unlike Badger, Nell or Margot in the Zonk family, could not shoot a pistol. A rifle was her weapon and she had never shot a human before. She had no qualms about the issue since Ace McCandle was notably lower in status than that of a mere maggot, but she was positive she could not out-shoot the Sherriff of Del Rio with a short gun. She would just have to use her rifle.

Doubt was a terrible thing even to a sturdy confident soul. But doubt did creep its nasty vines through the mind of Bootes. She did not show this in any way, and would die before she complained, but her confidence was slightly eroded. "We are Zonks! And this has to be done," she told the small crowd in the parking lot on a late Thursday morning.

At precisely eleven forty-five a.m., a bright red Cadillac pulled into The Truck Stop. Out stepped a tall lanky body with a sheriff uniform, a

Texas star, wearing a belt, holster and an ivory handled revolver. His eyes were squinting by being blazed by the Texas border sun, and his grin exposed yellowed teeth from a life of chewing tobacco. He appeared much taller since his hat added five inches to his overall height. The sun was to his back which was in his favor. Ace was surprised to see at the other end of the parking lot a small black woman who held a rifle that was almost as long as she was tall. He would have laughed but his Texas manners got the best of him and he just saluted her with two right fingers from the brim of his hat. Bootes nodded.

The clock hit noon and they both just stood there looking at each other. Ace broke the silence and stated the typically boring phrase from his TV hero Stud McCandle. Silence. Ace, quick as a snake, pulled his gun. Lyra, underneath the parking lot the entire time, shot up through his body, grabbed the barrel of his revolver, and pulled down. McCandle, looked down, and bewildered at the sight of a young girl protruding from his pelvis, pulled the trigger. At the same time, Lyra looked up and said, Texan style, "Howdy!" The bullet entered his groin and ricocheted off of the asphalt parking lot and re-entered his left ass cheek. Since he was reeling back from Lyra's visual, the bullet then entered his left lobe of his sorely unused mind and out it went just above his left eye. Profuse profane words attempted to formulate on his lips but the nerves were just not cooperating with his vocal cords. He fell back on the hood of his car. Pulling the trigger in a last gasp at retribution, Lyra aimed the gun toward his right ostrich-booted foot. Dead center. The Sheriff did not flinch. He could feel no pain. Ace McCandle was dead.

The US Dictator wanted to personally sue the Zonks for this tragic occurrence. But since Ace, literally, shot himself, all courts ruled this unfortunate event as an accidental suicide. All Texas flags flew at half mast, except at the border, since some vandals apparently jacked the flag to the top. Spray paint on a section of a border wall stated, 'Tyranny is no longer legal here at the border!'. And it wasn't.

Vexing Vixens of Valhalla
By Loosig Zakaryan
Translated from Armenian by Zackary Maxwell

.

The Stumpel Proclamation

"I hereby announce that the Stumpel Agency and Zonk Enterprises will team up to facilitate a crucial need in eradicating madness from the world." — Vart Stumpel to Zonk Enterprises

The Stumpels were paltry folk from the farm fields of Kansas. Wide open expanses of nothing but wheat. When a small bump became present, like the two-hundred-foot knoll in their backyard, it was labeled as a landmark of great interest. You could stand on top of this knoll and look in the vast distance and see, well, more of Kansas. Flat fucking Kansas. There were many Republicans in Kansas since the people there did nothing but bitch and moan about issues that they were not capable of determining any solutions for. So they stuck with bitching and moaning, which are the hallmarks of all great Republicans.

The youngest of the clan, Vart, was considered retarded since all he wanted to do was read books. So, being polite parents, they took him to church where the nuns repeatedly beat him, and his calluses grew to be muscles and he began to work in the field. Albeit, with a book in one hand and a hoe in another. At the supple age of nine, he performed on his parents' porch in the light of a fading moon Shakespeare's Sonnet 18. Prancing in tights, speaking an ode to a young man's beauty, disrupted the minimal thoughts of the farming family and, once again, he went to church to be beaten by nuns. Nuns, one must say, who were themselves closet lesbians, but the Almighty loved all who loved themselves. Or something like that. Vart returned from the Holy mastication chamber to be venerated by the sweat on his brow as he plowed the fields of wheat.

Vart did not grow up being pious, but he did grow up being pissed, which is basically the same thing if a person welcomed sanity enough. He went to college, much to the dismay of his parents, and he graduated top of his class in political science at Brown University. He went into the FBI Academy, was processed at Quantico, Virginia, and out came an agent. Working from the Kansas City field office, he was a primary in concluding many unsolved cases. The Lady Lydecker case was just one. Vart started his own agency with loyal dedicated officers that wanted to clean up the madness that had gripped the globe. The Stumpel Agency was born and, partnered with the Zonks, they would resolve the issue and exterminate all the deranged vermin. Or, at least, house them safely at the Noodle until forever.

The Zonk holdings unified into a conglomerate. Each entity unified into a whole. The Truck Stop, The Estate, The Zonk Farm of the Warped Noodle, The Ultra-Warped Noodle, Monk Shin's Church and the Zonk Mine were all combined financially. Albert and Victoria would command the Church and the kitchen. Lyra, the cheese factory. Zot and Cygnus would run The Truck Stop. Bootes and Titus would run the Mine and continue to hunt and fish. Chester, Cloise Dart and Ada Place would run the Noodle and Ultra-Warped Noodle. Opeia and Marvin would run The Estate. Eni and Zade would assist when needed but were basically retired. Vart would network with Marvin to scour the data feeds to ferret out the lawless pests. Everyone had a focus and their combined vision was to eradicate global madness.

Geli Raubal was a cherub youth. Plump to the touch with cherry puffed cheeks, she sashayed into the dining room with a delicious pink tutu and thick hips that rasped when she walked from the nylon friction. She bowed like the princess that she was and quickly severed the swollen jugular veins, oblivious in surprise, of her parents at the dining room table with a kitchen knife. Bleeding to death, she curtsied before them and pranced her way to the kitchen for a bite of her mother's fresh chocolate swirled marbled cheesecake. Geli finished the whole cake herself. With a burp she bowed deeply to the gore around the main table and bid her farewells.

Geli was named after Geli Raubal. She was the nubile tart who was the predecessor to Eva Braun (Hitler's girlfriend). Both had their doom but Geli was susceptible to vague suggestions. She was young. Hitler like her to squat over his face as he laid upon the floor. Many historians used this information to say Hitler was insane. He was insane. But the Zonks often squatted over their lovers' faces. This was called fellatio, cunnilingus or exercising a heightened olfactory thrombosis. This did not matter to the Zonks. What did matter was that Hitler was insane and he used his youth for sexual exploits he couldn't obtain from anyone else. Except for the author, but I wasn't there at the time. Indeed, had I been, the war would not have ever occurred. Sad about Roger's time travel. Roger just shook his head. Seriously, at this time in history, Roger was having a plate of buttered irks laced with liquid vitriol and just passed out. Shit really does unfortunately happen. His, 'Sorry', though sincere, was just not enough to cover the damages. Geli, Hitler's girl, apparently shot herself in the chest at twenty-three and died, though the simple truth is much less tangible.

Geli's, not Hilter's girl, method of dispatch was a seven-inch kitchen knife with a solid teak handle. Well balanced and razor sharp for cutting even the toughest of cuts. If only steaks, mutton and pork were on the menu, then all would have been fine. Geli, however, preferred human carotid arteries to lacerate. After every such event, no matter where the fracas would occur, she would always acquire a local cheesecake and consume the entire delicacy in one sitting. She lived off the funds she liberated from her severed 'families'. But one after one, families would take her in. How could they resist such a charming cute muffin of sweetness? And the outcome would be the same; she would curtsy and bow low after the onslaught, and with a smile, leave, locate and devour a cake made from cheese.

Marvin thought to cross reference cheesecakes and kitchen cutlery, but the population exposed on the computer was that of the entire continents of North America and Europe. Obviously, people use knifes to cut their cakes. So Marvin decided just to simply plot each and every carotid artery severing on a large digital map with times and dates of each incident. The Strumpels' team thought this was incredible that she would blatantly leave such obvious bloody breadcrumbs for them to follow. But she did.

Based on data alone, her festival started in Stillwater, Oklahoma. Then Broken Arrow, Oklahoma, and through the fertile lowlands of the Midwest. Every fifty miles, she would stop and search for an older couple and plead for assistance, and their answering the door was the beginning of their end. Plotting the incidents did not give any hint of a logical path. It was in an eastward direction but the motion was erratic and often looped back upon itself like a blind dog with half a nostril attempting to find a bone that he'd buried eighteen years hence.

But the fifty-mile radius was enough to narrow down the slaughter. It was just a matter of time before the agents would eventually gel knowledge between the murder locations and eventually distinguish a perpetrator. And this arose in Carmi, Indiana—a small town just west of Nowhere. Indisputably, there was a town called Nowhere, Indiana, and all the populace there were nobodies. No one amounted to anything and they liked that life just fine. The author of this book lives there now.

Knocking on the screen door of Gladys and Elbert Findley, Geli curled her strawberry locks with a finger and blew a big bubble of pink orally kneaded gum. Old man, Elbert, bounded to the door. "Much energy for one so old," thought Ms. Raubal.

"Are you selling Bibles per chance?" he quickly interjected.

"Ah, no. Why?"

"Well, I have over two thousand seven hundred in my possession and you just can't have enough, now can you?" He smiled.

"Ah, no. Not enough." She smiled back.

"What can I do for you, my child?" His gaze lowered through the screen of the door.

"How about a blow job for twenty?" she said, chewing. Not surprised, he gracefully opened the door and said to enter. She did. His name was Minister Findley, retired, and he had received many blow jobs in his life but never from one as plump and sweet. She demurred her reaction but stayed on course. "Where would you like it?" she quietly said since she wasn't exactly sure they were alone in the house.

"On my man chair," he boldly exclaimed. "But I don't know why they call it a man chair when my wife often sits in it and she is not a man." Geli looked up into his eyes and slowly nodded. He sat down in a plush worn leather chair.

"Where is your wife?" she enquired.

"Oh, out. You know women. They like to go out." She smiled. He pulled down his trousers to expose the minute sausage that had been left out on a hot day in a dry desert on a park bench. "Blow away." He grinned. She bowed her head and simultaneously grabbed her knife from a fold in her dress. It got stuck on a thread on her belt but with a tug it came free. Geli pounced but not before Gladys plunged her knives, two five-inch razor sharp blades, into both sides of Geli's neck, cutting the brain's main blood supply. Ms. Raubal drunkenly stood up and turned to see her attacker.

Before her eyes rolled back into her head, she saw a polite smiling gray-haired woman holding two bloody knives who said, "Do you want some tea?" But Geli didn't. She died and fell to the floor. "Well, now that we know what is for dinner, what do you want for dessert?" the wife cackled.

"How about cheesecake?" said Elbert.

Stumpel and Marvin's case went cold. Literally, the temperature of a room in Carmi, Indiana, in a late Spring. The perpetrator of these crimes was never found.

The Stipulation of Pu

*"I have been through the sands of the Gobi. I have survived as-Sudd,
the swamplands of Africa, and I have surfed the frozen ridges of the
Patagonia glaciers. But all I really remember in my pathetic life are the
mountains of the Rockies."* — Frederick Pu

Duyi Pu was from a mountain village in the northwest Hunan province. Ideal for a youth with cliffs to scale and caves to spelunk. He did it all. At the age of nine, he joined a British expedition in the Gobi Desert looking for the gigantic Mongolian Death Worm. Apparently, they found this large non-arthropod invertebrate beast since no person returned but young Mr. Pu. Rumors preceded him to the populace and stories of this massacre were profound. Yellow acid and electric shocks hammering from the mouth of the creature dissolved a knowledge of this fateful expedition. Young Pu said, "Bullshit. This crew was totally unprepared for desert travel and were suffocated by an intense sandstorm." But they looked perplexed at the truth and laughed and spit on Pu for being so correctly ignorant. Tragic stories, false as they were, brought in more gold to Mongolians than they could ever dig in a decade. The Death Worm lived. Pu decided to flee obtuseness and went to Africa to be a guide.

Overtly sanguine about his eleven-year-old posture, he delved head over heels into being a guide for a flock of Germans hunting an elusive and rare Sudanese Kharr water buffalo. This buffalo did not exist, but the poor countries were getting wise as to what existed or not. Tall tales of long tails brought in a bounty of money. And Kharr, the size of a medium Amish barn, roamed in swamps and killed and ingested anything in its path. No bullet or spear could penetrate its hide. Canon balls would only bounce off harmlessly. Powerful explosives would only disrupt his lope but he would soon recover to march through his realm. "How do you kill this beast?" asked Werner Helsenbach, the lead German, in a perfect Prussian lilt.

"We drown it!" said Pu confidently in his safari tent as though he had performed this task many times throughout his young life.

Water in the Sudanese desert to purposely drown a potential colossal prey was basically preposterous. But just one hundred and fifty miles north of Juba sat a festering pimple of a massive swamp called as-Sudd. And there they went. Supposing that the Amish barn-sized mammoth would coincidently just show up, they did not question. Germans wanted results. They did not want to be bothered with hypotheticals.

After a copious rain deluge in the swamp, they dredged a large divot in a tepid marsh. Over fifty feet in depth and much more in width. Enticing aquatic plants were scattered throughout this basin and all that was needed was one Kharr. The beast. Fanning the fumes of the aquatic foliage with pumps of huge palm fronds that the local Sudanese, well paid by German standards, floated into the air. Day after day the fronds were fanned, but nothing came from the sand dunes in the desert.

One afternoon, in the distance, a mile at least, stood the monstrous animal. Snorting and coughing it pawed the ground. This was the time and the moment for the Germans to bag their prey and they were ready. Pu was ready. He held a trip rope hidden in the desert sand that would trigger a mass of nestled figs in nets, which would subsequently collide with the beast, snare his legs, and pull him into the drowning pool. And the monstrosity came running.

It ran and ran, bellowing as it scrambled through the brush. But, bafflingly, like some optical illusion, the closer the monster came the smaller it appeared. By the time it got to the edge of the swamp, it was no bigger than a moderately sized house cat. With all the force it could muster, it rammed its head and horns into Werner's right calf. He winced. "Fuck. That hurt, you shit," he said to the small buffalo. "This can't be Kharr? It can't be?" he said incredulously to the Dinka tribal chief. Pu, translating, said it had been a bad several years and the great mighty Kharr could not get enough to eat so the Gods shrunk him so that he could still live.

"Come back in a few years. He will be great again." Pu laughed but only to himself. The Dinka had such a wonderful sense of humor. But oddly enough, Germans being Germans, they did come back after a few years only to discover the great and mighty Kharr, still the size of a cat, had been stepped on by a donkey and killed. Pu wasn't there for that expedition. Pu really had enough of exaggerated tall tales and sailed off for Patagonia.

He arrived in Rio Gallegos, Argentina, on one of the few days a year that it rained. Soaked to the skin, Pu bought some supplies and asked around if there were any mountain treks through Patagonia. The locals briskly pointed toward the pub called La Marfa. Entering the bustling stead, he edged his way through the people to the bar and ordered a Mate. Pu noticed a group of people in the back of the smoke-filled room that stood out in dress, attitude and volume. They were drinking ample amounts of some ethanol-laced product. "Shit. Americans," he sighed. Weaving his way through the patrons and prostitutes, he eventually landed on their table. "Sorry for the bother. I am a guide and I am looking for an expedition." The Americans hesitated, but only for a minute. He was Asian but curiously appearing Indian enough that he just might be needed.

"Why not," said a large man in the middle, leaning back on his chair. His black beard hung low from his chin. "Harry," he said, holding out his hand.

"Duyi Pu," smiled Pu, returning the grasp.

"Yeah," he returned the smile. "Well, we'll have to work on that. I think we will call you Fred." And Duyi forever from that time on was called Fred, or later, Fredrick Pu.

The Americans had a small troop. They were well stocked in all foods, clothing, ropes, harnesses and horses. Fred relieved them of ample material and loaded up his much worthy mule. The Americans laughed at his choice of transportation, but Fred bowed low and said, "It is better to have half an ass than no ass at all." But, point of fact, a mule was much heartier than a horse. It was solid, steady and could survive severe heat and cold. It could carry much more weight but the mule was just not fast. But fast meant nothing in the mountains and the Americans had much to learn.

Around their campfire that night, Harry told the troops where they were going and what they were after. It wasn't gold or silver or any lost Incan gems. It was the elusive Meh-Teh. This was a freak in nature in the form of an eight-foot-tall albino gorilla, except that he walked exclusively on his rear two legs. Enormously strong and ferocious it was considered one of the world's most dangerous beasts. "Damn it all. Not again," whispered Pu to himself. "You sure you don't want to look for lost Incan treasure?" said Pu.

"Listen, Fred, if you don't have the guts for this you can back out at any time."

"Ah, it isn't my guts that is an issue but the noodle between my ears. And my pasta is telling me that this is going to be frolicking fun, enormously worthy, and an adventure that will ultimately be pathetic." But Pu translated 'pathetic' in his native Mandarin and luckily the Americans didn't understand Mandarin. They all laughed. Later, Pu looking up to the vast cloud of stars and said, "Here we go again." To no one in particular.

The map indicated they were to re-stock supplies at Torres del Paine and start the climb to Tyndall Glacier, and then move directly north in search of this creature. They were to travel in a zig-zag pattern to increase the likelihood of discovering this beast. "It was a good plan if you were attempting to capture something that was real," thought Pu bitterly. But capture wasn't in Harry's plan. He was going to kill this animal, have it stuffed and present it to the New York Historical Society for a very large sum of money in return. Pu didn't care about the money but he did care about his life so he slept with both eyes open. A trick he learned in the Gobi.

They found a trail of very large furry footsteps in the snow. Each foot had four extended claws. Based on the size of the feet, the creature could easily stand eight feet in height. But Pu, analyzing a print, furrowed his brow and said, "But the depth into the snow isn't deep enough to justify the needed mass the creature must have."

"Shut up, Fred, and track. That is what you are hired to do!" So Pu tracked and tracked. A late heavy Spring snow detonated from the bowels of the sky and blanketed the slow-moving troop across the glacier. Pu, in the lead, hesitated. He 'felt' something odd. It was a tiny warm updraft from below. Visually, no one could see anything but white. But Pu 'felt' it. He stopped. Harry said, "What is it?" thinking he found the creature.

"It doesn't feel right."

"What? Fuck off!" And off the troop went, into the white, and down a three thousand nine-hundred-foot sheer ice cliff they flew. Pu stuck his hand into the white and felt the rim of the cliff. The tracks led directly to this point.

Four individuals were left in the expedition including Pu. They made camp as best they could. Late the next morning the weather cleared. Pu got up first and quickly walked around to shake off the cold. When his eyes thawed, he noticed the horses had all frozen to death. Only his mule was still alive. Realizing he had the only mode of transportation left, he bundled up his gear and left. The others would easily overwhelm him upon awakening. The mule was the only way out.

A week later, down out of the snow and mountains, Pu arrived in a Selk'nam Indian village. He knew the language to some degree. They told him that the Meh-Teh was just a story they told their children to make sure they never wandered too far from the tribe. It was very effective. A young teenager, Tok, in the tribe would take two half wooden barrels and cover the bottoms with seal fur and attach walrus tusks as claws. Tok heard of the dumb white people that searched for a fictional being. Tok wanted to make it real so he strapped his feet in the half barrels and walked across the glacier to the cliff edge. He didn't think the white man was dumb enough to walk off a cliff. Tok was wrong. "Yeah, glad I am not white," said Pu to the Chief.

Years later, Pu learned that gold was found in this region of Patagonia. The Argentine and Chilean farmers hired mercenaries to kill the indigenous people so they could have access to their land. Of the three thousand Selk'nam people, less than five hundred remained after the genocide. Many of the survivors were put into slavery or circuses. And all for money. Tok died by being shot in the back. All the bounty killers were well paid and none were convicted of any crimes. Such is life.

But currently, that night, camping under the stars, Fredrick Pu began thinking about America. It was 1851 and the western America mountains were boundless areas yet to be explored. People were moving in from California to the east and from the Midwest to the west. In the middle were the Rocky Mountains. And there is where Fredrick Pu would make his home.

"It was a fascinating time to be alive," Pu said to a Denver reporter. "It was a relatively short trip from Patagonia to San Francisco. There, I was not treated well. People from China arrived in droves but those that became merchants fared better than those that were conscripted, basically as slaves, to work on the railroads in the mountains. Thousands of Chinese died for those simple two parallel strips of iron that roamed through the west. It was progress only for the purpose of money using what the white man thought was an inferior race of humans. I was successful because I spoke fluent English. Better than most Americans. And I was amiable and the white people thought amiable was submissive and there was nothing more enjoyable than a submissive Chinaman. I was harassed and spat on, and abused physically and verbally. But I had money and bought a good mule and supplies and off I went into the mountains never to return." The reporter stopped writing to wipe his brow. "Would you like some tea?" said Pu.

"No, please continue," offered the reporter.

"I just turned thirty, or so I thought, age vanishes during a life full of adventure." The wrinkled face afforded a smile, looking deeply at nothing in the distance. "The mule and I became fast friends. He was not racist in the least but I think through time he began to hate white people. He occasionally kicked one when I came into a town and for no reason at all, at least that I understood, but one that he could not say." Pu ached as he rose from his chair and went to a cabinet to pull out a map. "See here," he pointed. "I spent a lifetime in these peaks. The Sierra Nevadas up to the Cascades. The Rockies from Canada down to Silver City, New Mexico. The Native Indians primarily left me alone. They thought I was odd. I looked like them and could speak most of their languages but I had no tribe. I was alone. I think they felt sorry for me. I didn't care. I hired out as a guide mostly to white settlers that wanted to go from the east to the west in the most optimal manner. But weather didn't often permit that path. Occasionally I tracked nefarious criminals that wanted to use the mountains to disappear. I found many. They all chose death to captivity. I completely understood as I assisted them on their journey." He painfully turned around to gaze at the reporter in his eyes. "But here," he slammed down his finger. "Was where I found peace." Pu didn't see where his finger landed, but the reporter pulled out a magnifying glass and leaned into the map. There, in tiny script, it said Bear Lake.

"I named the fucker," he garbled. "I did. I was hired by the Federal government to find a large grizzly bear that was possibly in the Rocky Mountains of Colorado. There were few grizzlies in the Rockies at that time. So I thought this another hoax." Pause. "But a tiny woman from the government came up and said, 'Please, Mr. Pu, we need to find this bear. He is my friend'. Baffled, I stood. And looked down at this creature and said, 'one stipulation, I will go if it is real'.

"Oh, sir, it is definitely real." So I went.

"I tracked the beast for several weeks up and down the Southern Colorado Rockies. I ultimately came upon a lake and there was this bear. He was a lonely beast and he kept having sexual interludes with a hollow knot on a large tree stump. Did you know other animals could be homosexual?" he queried the reporter. The reporter shook his head embarrassingly in the negative even though he too was a closeted man lover. One had to be during this time. It wasn't safe but only in the acting or musical dance professions. Pu saw this in his eyes. "Oh, whatever." Pu babbled, "Obviously, the scientists wanted the bear for experiments to understand his sexual preferences." Pause. "Well, I just could not do it. You are what you are at birth and that is that. If you don't understand that then you are a fool and should not be allowed to breed." Silence. Fredrick Pu looked down at the reporter and he tilted his head. "At least I named the lake after him." The reporter nodded. Later that week, in a wooden stable outside of Lamar, Colorado, Fredrick Pu plopped over dead in a batch of hay. He was surrounded by a pack of young wild mules.

The Reanimation of Herb's Lament

"I have discovered that the more I think I know, the less I really do. It is a painful realization that we all must live with. If you don't get it, then you never will and need to find a quiet place and just die. Please, for the sake of humanity, do. Oh, and on the way to your demise, don't breed either." — Herbert Newt

Ada Place was 'interviewing' Mr. Newt. Large orange sparks were emanating from their loins. She and he were jolting to the voltage culminating in a momentous climax. A symphony of crescendos exploded into an orange glow and silence. Saliva vapor exited her mouth like dense cigarette smoke. "Howdy, to you too?" she looked down to say.

"Gracias," he whimpered. "You have abducted my soul." And she did. Literally.

The squids came out months later. Obviously not expected. Lean at birth but robust in nature. Twin girls. Velda and Vanora were expectorated out of a warm hole into this Universe. They laughed upon entrance to this grand bazaar and did not need a slap on their behinds for a conscious breath of mostly nitrogen. The only curious nature of these children, noted by the nurses, was that when they opened their eyes an electric bolt of mild lightening would be produced. It was not fatal but it was very painful and it had to be mitigated. Ada and Herbie concurred. The girls appeared to enjoy each shocking event.

The kids were cocooned in a carved-out niche from Herbie's unit. It would be their nursery. They were excluded from socializing with anyone but their parents—at least for now until methods could be generated to establish other potential arrangements. "This is why we don't fornicate with inmates!" hissed Eni to Ada.

"Love is love," said Ms Place.

"Well, I once fell in love with an artichoke but I just could not fit it up my cunt! So we called it off. Get it!"

"Ah, no. You should see our sparks. We fit rather well," Ada smirked and left in a huff.

The huff became a puff and the puff became a cloud and it had to be reconciled. Chester called a meeting and it was resolved. Ada and Herbie were to become Zonks and as Zonks they had privileges beyond most, and as a family they needed acceptance. The Zonks, Eni included, accepted them. Zonks they were.

Velda and Vanora grew up to be pranksters. They had to be, of course, they were Zonks. They zapped each other randomly much for their amusement. Sparks were a hallowed tale from the nursery. Giggles followed.

The V girls, as they were called, were inseparable. Being virtually identical it was difficult to tell them apart so they were just called V when a person referred to either of them. Through their father's tutelage, they learned to control their zapping abilities, the voltages and the amplitudes. The latter was particularly important since high amps would mean certain death to the receiver of the zap. They were eventually normalized into The Estate school system, and aside from some brief and painful altercations, the student body soon realized that taunting or bullying the V girls had serious implications.

They both showed a typical Zonk love of science, particularly chemistry and physiology, and they both begged Opeia for the use of her lab. "Certainly. But I want to review your plan." So the V girls disappeared into the depths of their dorm room to plumb their vision.

As it turned out, just that week in the jungles of the Congo, seventy percent of the team of botanists studying local tribal plant medicinal cures all died from a virulent deadly mutation of malaria. Their deaths were so quick that most nations put a travel restriction on this part of Africa. Velda and Vanora devised a strategy. They would produce a mosquito repellent so effective that any human awash with this ointment would never have a bite to transmit any insect-borne diseases. This would save thousands, perhaps hundreds of thousands, of lives every year. "It would have to be organic," said Velda.

"Naturally," Vanora smirked.

"No processed chemicals and it should have a lotion base that would hydrate the skin."

"Obviously," Vanora nodded.

Scouring through The Estate library, they both simmered the possibilities throughout many nights. They eventually boiled down the potentials to one Nepeta cataria plant, or more commonly known as catnip. This plant naturally produces nepetalactone, which is a very effective repellent mostly for mosquitos. They laughed. "We have a plan!" Opeia approved this vision immediately. Off to the lab they went.

Cloise assisted in the garden and soon the V girls had a small mountain of plants from that member of the mint family. The key ingredient they were after was terpenoid nepetalactone and this oil could easily be extracted through steam distillation. The difficult part of their process was to emulsify the oil with a mild lubricant and still keep the effectiveness of the repellent's nature. After several attempts, they finally succeeded, and the girls applied the lotion on their arms and stuck them into an aquarium full of female Anopheles mosquitoes. Not one set foot on their skin.

Marketed as Zonk Ointment, and independently tested in various laboratories, this became a minor achievement in prohibiting malaria to spread. Three research groups, during the following month, focused on Africa: one from China, one from America and one from the United Kingdom, and all were supplied with this Zonk lotion. Initial results were amazing. No crew member got a single mosquito bite. But fate would stir the nostrils of the feral and all three exploration teams lost contact with their nations.

Rescue parties were subsequently sent out by all countries only to find each team completely dismembered and scavenged. Further testing on the lotion determined that what was repellent to the pest insect was a naturally magnified addiction to felines. Any person wearing this lotion in the wild, and some streets of France, would be mauled to death immediately by cats—be they lions, cheetahs, leopards or so many others. A scientist from Baltimore, testing the lotion in his neighborhood, lost an arm to house cats alone. After all, it was called catnip.

Velda and Vanora were devastated. Curled into a ball, they embraced each other on the floor of their room and cried. Little bolts of lightning shot from their eyes on the carpet and walls, and burnt holes everywhere they looked. When they calmed down, their room appeared like a smoldering piece of swiss cheese. Zade entered. She knelt down to hug them. "Welcome to being Zonks," she whispered.

The Infinite Lust of Hubert Saugen

"I am immensely proficient in one instrument only. And this talent, by the grace of God, was given to me personally by my uncle, the Rector of Runkel." — Mr. Saugen

He walked into The Truck Stop immaculate. He nodded to the patrons as if he knew them. His shoes were Italian leather with spats; his three-piece suit was an original Armani; his shirt was Anna Borelli; his hat was a Homburg; and his spectacles were rimmed with tortoise shell. Socks: none. His name was Hubert Saugen.

Tall and agile of frame, he enquired as to who the owner was to be. Albert came from the kitchen in his apron covered in burnt bear fat grease. "Yes?" he said, perturbed.

"I came about the enquiry for the replacement of a Thaddeus Zonk," was his overly polite reply. Cygnus and Bootes scampered down the staircase as best they could at this age and greeted the applicant with much aplomb. Bowing and nodding, he was giddy with this response. "No, no, no. I am not worthy of this."

"But yes, you are. Your reputation is immeasurable."

"Nonsense. I just am a good musician." They housed him in a small room on the second floor. A cotton futon, plain chair, wooden desk and a dangling LED light were his only companions. He did not complain but nestled himself into the goose down blanket and fell fast asleep.

The Saugens came from Limburg, Germany, just slightly west of Runkel. Hubert was 'blessed' repeatedly by his uncle, the Rector of Runkel. The Holy's tag name in the trenches was the uncle's moniker, the Rector of Rectums. And he was. He became known through this segment of his divine territory as an anti-horticulturist since he de-flowered so many ignorant youths. Hubert was one. Youth Saugen liquefied into a person whose talent lay in the flute of the skin. Hubert Saugen became a professional.

362

Jurgen. Jurgen came to his mind. In a fog it was long ago but the boys bonded in a room of stone-covered walls. He was Hubert's friend. His only friend. His only desire. The world was mad but they had each other. They were orphans left in a wash of orphans after World War II. That was the war after the one that was to end all wars and that one only succeeded in causing the Second World War. "Humans must love wars since we always appear to be in one," said Jurgen to Hubie.

"Yup. But let's make sure we don't end up in one," he replied.

In an internment camp outside of Frankfurt, his uncle came to claim his nephew. But Hubert would not go without his friend and he was very insistent on this issue. But looking up, there was a priest who gazed down upon this Rector of Rectums so the uncle reluctantly nodded in the affirmative. They made a room in the basement of his Catholic sanctuary and it was to be their home for many years. The walls perpetually sweated moisture. It smelled of mold and dirt. One wall had a rack of very old wine hidden behind a dirty canvas curtain. The uncle was careful to not let the Americans liberate this aging liquid. The boys, however, did. Boys being boys.

"To be a great musician you must practice, practice, practice!" said his Uncle. "And you, my son, will be the best skin flautist in the world," pontificating while pulling down his trousers. "Practice away!" He leaned back in his large leather chair. Five hours a day was the bare minimum. The choir elders needed servicing, too, as did most wealthy donors. Jurgen was needed, and quickly the two became a succulent tag team that would eventually shake the pillars of Heaven itself.

Jurgen and Hubert were caught imbibing the fermented nectar of the grapes. Aged and delicate, they had no concept of the intensity of flavors that bathed their nubile palate. They only knew that it made them temporarily pleasantly dizzy. The uncle plodded down the moist stairwell. "Well, well, what have we here?" Strapping them both, bottoms up on wooden stools, their naked buttock cheeks stained red from the moonlight glaring from a tainted windowpane. "I vacillate in my necessary need to use Vaseline, so I won't." He pondered. Parting his robe, he smiled; he had much business to do before the rise of the sun.

Years of this wonderful abuse created two phenomenal musicians. Talented in oral movements and nerve pressure finger placements that only a few on this globe could possibly master. Then a war appeared on the horizon.

The Arabs were strangling the Israelis and the Israelis needed expansion. Pressure built up and the Six-Day War occurred. Jurgen, hearing the tension months before, stated to Hubert one night that he had to go. "But why?" a perplexed Hubert gawked at his friend.

"Because I am a Jew," he said. "You would not understand. My family died in the camps and I was hidden. My name is Jurgen but my last name is Feinstein. I am Ashkenazi. I am sorry, my lover, but I have to go." And he did.

And he died. At the Battle of Ammunition Hill in Jordanian-held territory. "He was not a brave soldier," stated his commander. "But he provided amazing stress relief to the battle weary and wounded. He just had a knack of putting smiles on men's faces."

Hubert attempted suicide when he received this note. A shoelace and ambition were all that was required. But Uncle received him into his arms and said, "Not now. I need your orifices." At least he was needed and kneaded he was.

Saugen released himself on his own recognizance upon his Uncle's passing. He practiced his trade throughout Northern Europe only to land in Philadelphia. Because of his choice of instruments, he was compelled to work in areas of ill repute. But Hubert made up for this in his tone of dress. He would then, as now, dress immaculately as the outstanding gentleman that he was.

"Batter's up," was muttered into his ear. His eyes fluttered and he strained to focus on the voice. It was Cygnus. "There is a line of people waiting to see your immanence," she explained. He nodded, and with elegance in tuned to a righteous diva, he clothed himself and with much well-earned pretension walked down the stairs to the men's room to go to work. Thaddeus had a farm boy's charm and innocence, but Hubert made up for all of this by his precision musicianship abilities. It was the difference between a Volkswagen and a Porsche and the truck drivers took note. Business was booming.

The Plumber Who Could Not Plumb

"The hoe handle is a unique device that, if viewed in a different perspective, does miraculous relief. Yes, it is a hoe. But using the other end it becomes a weapon against intestinal disorders." — Mr. Law, professional plumber

The plumber was well known in the southwest of Texas. He was born in Ciudad Victoria, Mexico, but was raised in Reynosa by his mother's sister. Learning the plumbing trade at an early age, he applied his craft voraciously since the fat content in most dishes equaled the best tasting. It still does in point of fact. Fat was craved by our homo sapiens ancestors, since thousands of years ago it was so hard to find, and that programming still exists in us all. And that fat clogged up pipes. Enrico Lopez was prone to expedite his response time. He was known for quick and efficient service. And he was the best.

Mr. Lopez's tools at the time were simple. Humans like simple. That is all most understand. Enrico used explosives. Compressed gun powder charges of his own design were essential. Then, for stubborn clogs, Anfo. The latter a mixture of ammonium nitrate and diesel fuel. It never failed.

The populace applauded Enrico's efforts. His work not only, extensively, undid the clog, but it destroyed major portions of the antiquated sewer system that was already in place. This forced government officials to service these pipes and update them to modern standards. Everyone was happy except the Governor of Tamaulipas. He banished Mr. Lopez across the border to the US so he could succumb to the fates of the migrants.

At the border, they literally kicked him back to Mexico. This tennis match ended abruptly when the tennis ball fell into a coma. On wakening, Enrico discovered a deal had been made between the US Dictator with the Republicans and the Mexican government. The US would take Mr. Lopez in exchange for two liberal progressive media manipulators, sisters Clare and Nannie Beagle. Lopez didn't know the Beagle sisters and the Beagle sisters didn't know about the explosive plumber. They just met once, about halfway on the bridge going across the border. They did not exchange anything but a glance. Enrico did notice that they looked jubilant as though they had won some massive prize. On the American side, Lopez was taken into custody and was grilled repeatedly by Republican politicians. "Why do you blow things up?" "Do you want to blow up Americans?" "Are you a member of any illicit terrorist group?"

"I am a plumber. That is all. I just want to practice my trade," pleaded Enrico.

"No, asshole. All you will ever do here is pick melons!" Enrico made a mental note never to like Republicans. They were always uptight and made facial expressions like they were all constantly full of a painful gas that they could not possibly expel. The ACLU stepped in and his future radically changed.

Mr. Lopez became an American. Enrico, just in his twenties, went to school and became a lawyer. He thought this position was one of importance and power. He changed his last name to reflect his position. It was a poor choice. Enrico Law made more in one week as a plumber than a lawyer did in a year since he was plagued by a conscience. "What a fuck'n waste," he said. And Mr. Law gave up law and went back to plumbing.

Explosive plumbing in the US was not a welcomed method. Generally, in most areas, the infrastructures were basically new and intense rapid concussive expansion due to molecular ignition was not necessary. So, Enrico turned his attention to the thriving ranching establishments.

As destiny alights on a shoulder like a butterfly that someone had been chasing for years, Enrico Law got a call from a rancher just south of Uvalde. The white clover and rich alfalfa that late Spring caused his entire herd of cattle to have bloat—a gas build up in the rumen. They would all die if relief was not administered. "Why hire a plumber?" Enrico enquired. "Because I can't freak'n afford a veterinarian!" Vets, treating bloat, used a very large needle and jammed it into the side of the suffering animal. If the right place was punctured, then gas would hiss out of the needle and eventually the pressure in the rumen was gone. But this was expensive and time consuming. And this farmer did not have the money or the time.

The plumber showed up the next morning in his much beloved weathered GMC truck. In the bed was one lonely hoe with a recently shellacked handle. The farmer had the cattle lined up at the fence. From a tub of petroleum jelly, Law grabbed a handful and lubricated up the handle. He gracefully pumped the wooded rod into the ass of the first bloated cow. With the rod fully immersed inside the bovine's cavity, Law rapidly undulated the hoe in a circular direction and with a large 'whoosh' pulled out the lubricated mess. Gas came out at such a velocity that it blew off the farmer's hat. The stench temporarily blinded them both. Coughing and laughing, the farmer said, "Damn. You're hired!"

"Just something simple we Mexicans figured out with cattle." Mr. Law, covered in bovine discharge, beamed.

Enrico, the plumber, got to work. For half the price and time of a veterinarian, Law could de-bloat a herd. And half the price was still a great deal of money. Enrico Law became wealthy. Every rancher in southwest Texas wanted his services. This was not such good news for the area veterinarians. They, in turn, complained to their Republican constituents and they swooped down from their lofty Capital. Within days, black sedans with black windows pulled up at the Law abode. Black-suited white people with black sunglasses exited the vehicles.

"Mr. Lopez. We meet again. What a joy this is," said the Republican Congressman.

"It's Law, not Lopez."

"Oh, so you changed your name to potentially escape prosecution?"

"Ah, no. I just changed it."

"I knew you'd eventually be trouble, Mr. Lopez."

"Law."

"Law," the Republican snidely corrected. "What you have done here is break the law, Mr. Law. And you are going to jail."

"Ah, no. I didn't break any law or laws."

"And how could you possibly know?" The congressman enquired.

"Because, since I saw you last, I went to college and got a degree in criminal law. Hence, the name change. I am well within my rights to work in this manner." The Republican Senator blanched like a boiled navy bean. He nervously twitched and his face made bold distortions. What Republicans hated more than progressive liberals was a well-educated Mexican. His scowl was incendiary as he rose from his chair. He lowered his now red eyes and motioned for everyone to leave. Without a word, they loaded into their sedans and left in a cloud of dust. Enrico smiled.

A few days later, a farmer found Enrico in his dry drainage ditch. He was beaten, stabbed and shot. But, remarkably, he was still breathing. No knife wound or bullet puncture disrupted anything vital. The impacts to his skull, however, left lasting damage. When he gained consciousness, he was not a well man. Enrico Law popped a cork.

The plumber vanished in the dust and mesquite. Texas state and Federal Republicans were often found unconscious and randomly molested. In every case, a splintered hoe handle was protruding from their posteriors. The sharp offshoots of wood shards caused internal infections. No deaths ever occurred but the afflicted were absolutely miserable for several months. The perpetrator was never discovered but the farmers in southwest Texas knew the criminal well. They would get together every Thursday for breakfast and laugh their asses off. Calmly, one afternoon, Enrico Law (now back to Lopez), waltzed into the confines of The Noodle. He was warmly received.

The Nightlight in The Closet

"I realize I have met you both a thousand times before. And every time it is always, shall I say, a shocking experience. So let's get this over with." — Roger to the V girls

Snoozing platonically as they always did, both curled into a ball, the minute beam of a nightlight oozed from the closet, grazed their covers and a shadow emerged. The twins both opened up their eyes simultaneously to review the shadow in the doorway. It mumbled some non-audible words and instantly the girls shot bolts of lightning from their sleepy peepers into the form. "Shit!" it yelled. "Every damn time!" "Stop, I am Roger. Certainly, somebody must have told you about me?" The girls giggled.

"Sorry, Roger," they harmonized.

And the girls did know about Roger. He wasn't a god but a fifth-dimensional being, but relative to their pitiful three, he was basically a god. All Zonk females, even if they hadn't met him, knew of this being. "Sorry, Roger," they repeated.

"Yes, understood. But you always zap me in my groin," he lamented.

"Well, if you'd tie your robe on entry, we would have nothing to stare at but your beautiful face." They did have a point, he thought. He grimaced in pain as he sat down on the floor.

"Listen, I tell you this now since I always have told you this now and it makes a difference later in time." He hesitated to make sure he had their attention. He did. "Dark clouds will be in formation years from now and it is vitally important that you two assist the others to combine their abilities to build a defense."

"We don't understand," they chirped.

"No, no, not now but you will. You see I am planting the seed now so that it can germinate and bloom in the future. Just remember my words. Okay?"

"Okay," Velda and Vanora replied. He stood up and moved toward the closet.

"Remember," he said sternly.

"Remember, what?" they giggled.

"Oh, you shits. You are Zonks after all." And Roger turned to vapor.

The Wailing Horn of Titus

"It is not always a sad song. Indeed, some tunes coming down the valley are very upbeat. There was one just last week about this time that made me want to dance." — Zot to Lyra while he was looking at Hoag's Ring Galaxy

Up from the valley floor at the entrance to the Zonk mine sat Titus in the clouded haze of a blue moon. Through his snoot he was slowly playing Chet Baker's 'There Will Never Be Another You' to a smiling Bootes. He liked to make her smile since she rarely did. "Fuck you," she said to him.

"So, you can read thoughts?" he pried.

"No, I can read faces," she grinned. He continued to play.

Peeling off melodies from an onion made of glowing green 'brass' there came Miles Davis, Jon Faddis, Dizzy's 'Swing Low Sweet Cadillac' and a screeching finality of Maynard Ferguson that sent all forest animals in opposing directions—except for some very angry eagles and owls that did not need the competition.

The next morning was a Sunday. Monk Albert, unnecessarily nervous, was leading his first congregation. The canvas roof was repaired from Cyg's locally appreciated, but singularly unwelcomed, plummet from the skies as an angel with bladder issues leading people to flock in to see if another sign from God would appear. It didn't. Hooting and hollering were not typical sounds emanating from a Buddhist temple. But they did. The sounds were more like a black Baptist revival from the deep South. Monk Albert personally apologized about this to the Dalai Lama but gave in to the overwhelming positive vibe. Chinese, as with all white Americans, have no rhythm, and Albert plainly exposed his failings. But the congregation loved his humorous attempts, and this became his opening fanfare to his later mumbled chants with burning swirling incense.

Lyra succeeded in producing a batch of Munster d'Alsace. She passed a fresh cut loaf around The Truck Stop loiterers, and gagging and vomiting proliferated. She was pleased. It took a hearty constitution to handle these abrupt fragrances and pungent tastes so she started a class with patrons in the back. She began, thankfully, with mild cheddar and mozzarella on lightly sea salted garlic and dill crackers. A baby step with really great cheese is often prescribed.

Later, perched in her empty aquifer cavern, she struggled to sleep. Deep below the bowels of the Earth from The Truck Stop, Lyra found solitude. With only a head lamp for illumination, she looked into the clear water below. There, scuttling below, was a blind albino cave cricket. "Howdy," she said with a corresponding rapid echo that nauseated her senses. It was cool here. Above was a ponderous dry ninety degrees F and open windows and fans had to be used. She curled into a ball and through the reverberating walls of this small cave she heard the tantalizing tunes of Titus' 'brass' horn. The song was 'Stella by Starlight' by Miles Davis. She fell soundly into a slumber.

The light blue glow of phosphorescence lured from below. It painted the walls a pastel hue. A body hovered from above. It was Roger. "I know you," she said quietly. He alighted on a stalactite and looked down.

"You are not going to disappear?" he muttered.

"What is the point? You always find me in the realm of infinite realities." He smiled.

"There are black clouds looming," Roger uttered.

"Cut the shit, Roger, we know this through the network of Zonk. We are all going to die if we don't jam together for the final cricket game. Is that it?"

"Yup," he coughed.

"Well, don't worry; in a deluge of realities, how many have we failed?"

"Eighty-nine percent."

"Shit," she said.

"Yeah, shit. So pay attention." She did. The swinging tune, echoing through the cave, was Bix Beiderbecke's 'Riverboat Shuffle'. Titus played on.

Cloise and Chester's Repine

"Gargling would help. Just lean your head back and let me stick my fingers down your throat. Stop gagging! Shit! Just take it to the purge. What is your issue?" — Cloise to Chester

The newlyweds were squirming on their honeymoon in Cloise's garden. The plants were undulating with their twitching bodies in rhythm to an unheard tune. Chester wasn't twitching from a feeling of ecstasy but of suffocation. He inhaled an imbibed ball of liberty caps and it was stuck in his trachea. Cloise was doing what she could but she herself was under the influence of the mushrooms and was having a difficult time communicating with this throbbing inflated ostrich. She chopped the large flightless bird on the back of the neck and this only caused the bird's eyes to bulge out. She hit the bird on the back with a rake and that just caused this dying fowl foul to faint. Then Cloise, in a last-ditch effort, plunged the rake handle into the bird's stomach and out popped a mucus covered ball of wonder. Gasping for air, Chester said, "If our honeymoon trip starts out this bad, then it can only get better." And he kissed his bride and popped the mucus covered mushroom morsel back into his mouth and chewed.

The jungle was lush. Perhaps, overly so. The young doctors had never seen so many shades of green. They were funded by the US Government's Office of Defamation and they were to eradicate dysentery in the BaKa tribe in the Congo Basin. They canoed up slow moving arteries that fed the main river that fed the land. Doctor Chester and Cloise both had advanced degrees in bad taste so they were uniquely qualified for this mission. And something definitely tasted bad in the heart of this jungle.

The BaKa tribe were a proud people and they would never ask for assistance for any issue, not from a neighboring tribe, and certainly not from another nation, and definitely not the nation called America. But the unfortunate truth was the BaKu tribe was sitting on land that had the

373

most abundant and rich deposits of cobalt. The world needed this mineral for computers and phones that led to social media websites, that spread lies like butter down a metal playground slide in Tucson in July. So America needed lies and hence they needed cobalt. But the BaKu tribe was suffering from a bout of terrible dysentery and this kept the people from gathering ore. So the US sent their leading scientists up the river to get the near-slaves from dying so that they could basically barely live to gather ore. It was a win-lose situation but it was all how you spun the tale and Americans were great at spinning tales. "We are saving these people," the US Dictator proclaimed. "Mineral? What mineral? We don't need no minerals. What we need is the tribe healthy and happy and going back to useful, very labor intensive but cheap, waged work." Later, in private, he acknowledged to the Vixen Press, "Listen, we rape the tribe so that they can rape their women. It is a win-win."

And here came Drs. Cloise and Chester, up the meandering acrid river to the boundary of the BaKu. Stepping across the threshold of these great people, the doctors sluggishly mired through a dense mud-filled creek to reach the village.

As it turned out, Cloise and Chester were not needed at all. The Chief of the tribe had his PhD from Harvard Medical School in Pathology. He utilized pygmy elephants to shoot scalding herbal medicinal water up the backsides of the impaired. This cured everyone. Indeed, after a welcomed dinner, the Chief explained that they knew the United States was exploiting them and they had to passively retaliate. He did this by making a batch of poorly cooked cassava which created the dysentery. Perplexed, Cloise and Chester just gawked at the Chief, speechless. The next thing they knew, they were strapped naked on trees and disemboweled. So much for being passive.

On rebirth, they both flowed out into the dirt of the garden. The plants were still swaying to music that only they could hear. "Listen, Chester. Let's get something straight. The next trip we take will be an old-fashioned physical trip in a car or boat. Get it?"

"Got it," he coughed.

Punting Down the Arkansas

*"A vacation? Where are we going? Yes, I would love a vacation. I
don't remember ever having one of those. This will be great. Lisbon?
Paris? Istanbul?" — Lyra to Cygnus*
"Pueblo." — Cygnus's reply

"Pueblo! Pueblo!? Pueblo is just down the mountain! What kind of shit
vacation is that?"

"It is how we get there that will be different," Cyg mumbled while
chewing through Albert's fresh bear fajita special, complete with bean
sprouts with a ranch style dressing.

The tickling sensation began in the fingers and then the palms. These
two pairs of Zonk hands were not accustomed to the constant pounding
of a hammer and chisel. Calluses formed, much to the delight of Zot and
Lyra. They were used to moving through matter and not physically
manipulating it into a shape. Bootes and Cyg just laughed. They had
calluses to spare. Pine was all there was, so flexible and lightweight was
the only option. They built two eighteen-foot crafts using the
specifications of the local Native Americans. Well balanced and sealed,
they were fine canoes for an even-tempered river. And the Arkansas was
just that for this year. Slow run off from the mountains kept the river
down and this was just excellent for a long vacation.

Cyg, Bootes and Lyra were in the first vessel. Zot, Mitch and Titus
were in the second. They had food and camping equipment for at least
one night. Depending on their journey, that would be enough. They
entered the river just south of Buena Vista near Johnson Village. Monk
Albert and Victoria drove both maintenance vans to unload them on the
riverside. "We will pick you up in Pueblo when you call." Albert smiled.
They all saluted the Zonk Salute, which was the middle finger of each
hand extended upward with the other fingers curled down. Titus just
honked. Off they went.

Their first noted attribute to this triumphant journey was that it wasn't triumphant at all. It was akin to having aged intercourse without lubrication. Laborious and painful. They had paddles but stopped to cut thin poles down for punting. It was that type of river this year. Boring was not a word used by the Zonks since that directly implied a lack of wanton imagination. Which they did not have. But this trek was seriously having the family re-think this term. Bootes took this time to fish and she caught a bounty of trout. Lyra brought a book by an obscure author titled, 'The Chronicles of Zonk' which she delved into and found the stories curiously similar to her own life. But the rest were dull to their nuts. Titus, after playing poignant blues tunes on his 'horn', started to randomly vaporize rabbits on the shore. Cygnus and Mitch prayed a Buddhist meditation for opulence. And opulence is what they received.

A plethora of moisture appeared over the collegiate horizons like a burst from a pent-up bubble of dark clouds. And it rained. The torrent was unprecedented and the Zonks covered in bear fat greased canvases, layered themselves to repel the primary global forces.

The torrent started slowly after. It was a nudge that became a push that became an immediate flush. The Arkansas was having a bout of the rancid cassava BaKu purge. And down they flowed.

It wasn't exactly a rollicking adventure but one of fright and controlled panic. Titus went to the back to use his snoot as a rudder. Zot and Mitch were on paddles doing everything they could to avoid exposed rocks. On the front boat, Lyra was using her punting pole as a rudder, while Cyg and Bootes were on paddles. What was generally a very calm part of the river erupted into rapids of two, three and fourth class. Fifth class being the worst and almost not survivable.

Weaving in and around several pillars of rock, the first canoe made it through by sheer luck, but Zot, Mitch and Titus made it around the first large chunk of granite only to be caught in a sudden reverse eddy that slammed their canoe into another outlying boulder. The pressure of this flow was immense, and Mitch, using his only good arm, pushed with all his might with his paddle on the rock, but this only succeeded in tipping the craft over and they all fell out. With much flailing, they all pulled themselves up onto another large rock that covered them with cascading waves. Titus, immensely strong, grabbed the canoe, drained out the water and put it back into the river. He frantically looked at Zot and Mitch and said, "Screw this shit!" And he turned, and with a series of green blasts, vaporized all the rocks in the river for over one hundred yards. Quickly, the river became calm in this region of the flow.

"Thanks," said Bootes as Titus and the others pulled up alongside of them on the shore. They tied up their boats and sat down on a sandy area and had lunch. Lunch was Bootes' fresh caught trout.

"Should we go on?" Mitch enquired.

"As I read this river, we have a real rough patch through the gorge around the next few corners, but after that it is quiet all the way into Pueblo. With Mr. Blaster here," Cyg gazed at Titus, "we all should be fine." They all loaded up and, "Once more into the breech," touted Titus, and off they went.

Around the next corner, they went under a highway bridge and things changed drastically. The river was mashed between two towering sides of perpendicular cliffs and exposed rocks pushed out of the bubbling cauldron, like enormous teeth from a hungry dragon. These were class five rapids. Survival depended on the clarity of the canoers, and these few Zonks were definitely left in a fog.

Far in the distance and high up above, was the Royal Gorge bridge. This was the bridge where Thaddeus took his last fateful flight. Light green blasts were shaving off the dragon's teeth but there were too many and the velocity of the river was too great. Waves were pounding them from all sides but Titus did not falter and kept focused on pulling teeth from the river.

Eventually, they just gave up and clutched on to each other and over the falls they went. The canoes detonated in fractured splinters and their bodies washed up in an eddy on the southern shore. Zot and Lyra fared the best since they merely disappeared into the wet boulders, resurfaced from the bottom of the river and swam to shore. Titus was Titus and he didn't have a scratch. Cyg, Bootes and Mitch were beaten and weathered on a lone rock outcropping. Lyra swam up and said, "Mom, for a first vacation, that has to be one of the best." But her voice fell silent. She looked down and Bootes was cradling Mitch's body. His head was caved in.

Bootes didn't cry but leaned over him, hugged him tight, and gave him the Cornelius eulogy, "See you on the other side."

Spit from above came raining down from the humans on the bridge aloft. Oddly enough, this was the same exact place that Thaddeus landed many years ago. Titus crawled out of the water and, feeling the spittle on his body and looking at Mitch being covered in spit, was filled with rage. He looked up to the bridge with his glowing red eyes and his erect proboscis. He was about to let out a massive vaporizing blast to blow the bridge and those humans into atoms. Cyg, sensing this issue, quickly grabbed Titus' snout and squeezed. It filled up like a balloon and out his nostrils exited a tiny 'fitz'. "Damn you," he snorfled.

"Yes, damn me," she nodded.

There were no handicaps on Teegarden B. Mitch had the use of all his appendages. He forgot what that freedom felt like. Roger set him up with his own bicycle shop, the only one on the planet, and he became rightfully popular. Most of the inhabitants didn't know how to bike. So Mitch taught them one by one. He formed a club and his thigh muscles grew large like that of the trunks of small oak trees.

Tactical Twisting Tushies

"I believe it was my idea initially but, really, Cloise took off with the riff and made it into a song. I didn't think it would gain legs but it did and off it went." — Chester

The tactile senses of a woman with no sight knew the right buttons to push for a goat's amorous conclusion. It was the throbbing patter of rain on the late evening's windowpanes, like a random wash of a hose that lured them into a sleep. He softly snored and the reek of feta would overwhelm most people, but not Cloise. She woke up and covered Chester up with a cotton sheet and stood up in the light of the kerosene lamp. Her body tingled. Looking out through the window she felt the pulsing beat of the rain and knew her garden needed the moisture. "You are beautiful naked," said the voice in the dark with golden eyes.

"So you don't like me with clothes on?" she pursued.

"No," he softly said. "Actually, I think it would be lust to put a picture of your naked body on every month of a Zonk calendar."

"Interesting." She beamed. And so it began.

It didn't take much coaxing. With the new heavy taxes imposed by the Republicans on the Zonk Enterprise, their intent to strangle them out of America, funds were seriously needed. The great female photographer, Franny Bee, was contracted from New York and flown down to ascertain the possibilities. And they were many. Raw material is what this photographer needed and the Zonk Estate, and soon the Noodle (and Ultra Warped), would not disappoint. The Zonks could not afford much but this insightful person that captured exact images just settled for ten percent of the total sales.

Franny whored in with her entourage and lived with the Zonks for over a month. Clicking away, staging shots, capturing the essence of insanity and the life of a schooled orphanage. And all the teachers and inmates were naked. Vaya Halabjaee, the Kurdish artist, was wanting to be nude since Chester started his art class. This was her moment. She arrived on set sans clothing, except for a scant see-through white veil. She tittered in excitement and sat down on a stool. An easel was brought in with paints and she was instructed to paint her emotions. She did. The cool metallic stool tinged her labia and she painted Pegasus with an erection. All was captured in mellow yellow light.

Ada and Herbie were apprehended in a moment of rare public rich explosion and Ada, enhanced, look like a naked smiling Chinese worker in a smelter plant pouring a thick molten hot alloy metal. Orange sparks everywhere. What beauty. Eni and Zade got into the action while swimming in the pond, being swarmed by brightly colored Koi augmented by their human honey-painted naked bodies coated with fish meal. Exquisite. Laki Lukovich, hammering away with her mammoth snout on a freshly tuned keyboard, and shimmering with her bare body laced in olive oil, as she pounded out Toccata in C, Op. 7 with the rapidity of a horny woodpecker. Hirsute in certain areas, she did require a trim before photos commenced.

The first female Zonk Calendar was distributed with much confidence. It sold out fifteen times in the first year. It made millions. The title was: The Monthly Mundane Menagerie from The Madhouse, Vol. 1. Franny Bee optioned a male calendar at fifteen percent and the deal was on. Travel arrangements were made for Franny and her crew to dabble at The Truck Stop. All were game.

Zot was flamboyantly glowing through the fireplace flickers. Monk Albert, marinating an elk steak with garlic and mushrooms, smiled for the lavish digital canvas adorned with only a tawdry apron. He farted and it was captured in a 'whoosh', unheard by the digital image but caught in a flourish from the back side of his canvas drape. Hubert Saugen was caught post-glandular extraction and he looked directly into the lens, smiled, and wiped his chin. Random inebriated truck drivers eagerly stepped up to assist in the project.

This too was a global hit. With the final December month electrified by a naked, as always, Titus; as he 'honked' and 'snorted', green sparkles affected his shiny heinie and this was quite alluring to most salivating mammals. His wink of a brown eye caught the attention of many and he became the Stud Bull of The Zonks.

Zot's Zipper

"Really it was by accident. I was on the roof behind the telescope attempting to find the Sagittarius Dwarf Spheroidal Galaxy. Titus was up at the mine playing 'Stardust' by Hoagie Carmichael and Lyra asked me to dance. We twirled and I hit the scope's tripod. I looked into the view finder and there it was." — Zot Zonk

During the early morning, a couple with their young son stumbled from their hike down from the western slope of Pahlone Peak. Looking up, the humans were in awe upon discovering a light green glowing elephant at the entrance to a cave playing 'Night in Tunisia' with his trunk. The boy looked at his parents and said, "It's the Grinch."

"No, it's not, Honey," said the female. The boy scrambled up the rocks to attempt to touch the creature but he only succeeded in ruining Titus' wonderful finale. Titus looked out through the opening of the cave and stared at the trio.

"There are graves with your names on them missing bodies. Please go find them before I assist you all in inhabiting those plots." They scampered down the trail.

"How absolutely rude," said the man.

"See, I told you it was the Grinch," mumbled the boy.

That same morning, Zot received a reply from the Central Bureau for Astronomical Telegrams. Zot Zonk discovered a completely new comet. The press named it the Zipper, since when Zot was later interviewed, he said, "That thing sure is zipping along at a great velocity." A picture of Zot and Lyra smiling and dancing in front of the telescope on The Truck Stop roof, made the front page of the Denver Post.

"You're famous, Pop!" she said, hugging him.

"Fame is fleeting, now get back to studies."

Actually, Martha set up the entire celestial orb concept. It was to be a symbol to the Zonks as a premonition of what was to occur. But Zonks, being Zonks, were far too well educated to delve into superstitions and took the comet as a really dirty ball of ice. Which it was.

Fame was fleeting and The Truck Stop got back to business. The winter was over and the mine was reopened, and this meant Titus and Zot had other things to do than play music or look toward the heavens. Besides, The Zot Zipper would not even be visible to the naked eye for a very long time. It was quickly forgotten.

Lyra, escaping the torrent of literature from Monk Albert on Eastern Philosophies, dove to her cavern for a nap and a snack of what she called turd stick casseroles. The latter being Albert's lunch fare called Yang Rou Chaun, or mutton on a stick covered lightly with sesame seeds. Looking at one, it became apparent why Lyra named them the way she did. With just a head lamp illuminating her grotto, she sat down softly to ingest the 'turds'. "Looks good," pierced the quiet. Looking up, Lyra saw the blue fluorescence of Roger hovering.

"When was the last time you ate?" she asked.

"It has been a long time. I mainly just drink…"

"Pearl Jasmine tea," she interrupted. He rolled his eyes. "You know, if you float down here, I won't have to gaze up and see your wagging wang."

"Is that what kids call it now? A wang? It doesn't sound particularly scientific." He floated down.

"Oh, it is. It comes from the ancient Chinese word, Wangafide, which means a fleshy protuberance that often becomes an irritant."

"Really?" Roger blurted incredulously.

"Nah, I just made that shit up," she smiled.

"Zonks, why do I bother?" he shook his head.

"So, what's dangling?" she asked.

"Martha, my seven-dimensional accomplice, sent the comet as an omen of ill tidings."

"How prophetic!" Lyra squeaked.

"It is, so would you please pay attention." She nodded in the affirmative. So, after a tedious monologue, which she repeated, he bid farewell.

"Wait," Lyra said anxiously. "What was your last meal that you ate?" He hesitated to think.

"It was centuries ago. I think it was Ecuadorian Cuy." She looked bewildered. "Cuy is a cooked hamster. I must say, I burped that stench for decades." He smiled and turned to vapor.

On her appearance through The Truck Stop floor, she instructed the Zonks of this meeting and Zipper was taken much more seriously. At least they were thankful for Roger and Martha to have a heads up. But even with that, the dark horizons would not clear up any time soon.

The Submerged Carcass of Donner Appears

"Ah, come on. It is a passionate tale of life and death. Bear with me.
Here we go." — Chester to the V girls.

Snuggling under a blanket made from thick goose down, Velda and Vanora waited patiently for their story. Chester, distinguished with a pipe in his mouth, a gift from Cloise, leaned back in a chair. His golden eyes flared in the flame of a nearby lamp. "I can't get used to this damn pipe. I can't keep it lit and it will not stay in my mouth when I talk so I have to constantly hold it. Does it look okay?" His brow bristled.

"No. You look like a goat attempting to be smarter than he is," said Vanora.

"Damn. You are right." And he pitched the pipe across the room. "Better?"

"Better," they nodded in unison.

"A long time ago, perhaps in 1846, the Donner family and the Reed family got together in Springfield, Illinois. They were an adventurous lot but basically dumber than a sack of potatoes."

"Would that be Yukon Gold, Kennebec, Russet, Gunda, Red...?" Velda interjected.

"What?"

"The sack of potatoes?"

"Just a fucking sack of dumb fuck potatoes! No more interruptions! Shit." Perturbed, Chester carried on. "They made their trip slowly in oxen-drawn wagons."

"Was it anything like your mushroom trips?" said Vanora.

"What? No! Now just listen!"

"The Oregon Trail was famous, and the Donners and the Reeds took months just to get to the foot of the Sierra Nevada mountains. They wanted to go west to the gold fields of California."

"Greed will get you every time," said Velda.

Not hesitating, Chester continued. "They ran out of water crossing the great desert in the Salt Lake Basin. The oxen, mad with thirst, ran off."

"Smart oxen," said Vanora.

His bulging glaring orbs proceeded without pause. "They finally made it up in the mountains and a huge snowstorm broke from the skies. Days and days God's dandruff fell."

"Seriously unlikely," snorted Velda.

"The Donner and Reed families were stuck. No search party came since most of the men from down below were off fighting the Mexican-American War."

"You see, war is not tragic enough; it spawns tragic consequences," muttered Vanora.

"They sat there on this mountain pass and starved. No rescue was coming. The Donners most all died because they had empathy for their fellow humans. The Reeds mostly lived because they only had empathy for their own family. The Donners gave out their provisions to any needy individual. The Reeds looked after their own."

"In dire circumstances, family always comes first!" said the girls.

"Indeed," said Chester, smiling that they got the point.

"Now, do you wish for me to read The Giving Tree?" he suggested.

"Ah, nah. We get it. If you don't look after your family tree, you are destined to be a lifeless stump," they harmonized.

"Very good," he stated.

"Now, we don't mean to be rude," said the girls. "But can you please go? We need to masturbate and we don't like being watched."

"Excuse my shit." And up and off Chester went.